A Young Lady in Threadneedle Street

How not to r

CW00494162

Synopsis

When several high ranking demons decide to refurbish Hell as a nice surprise for their absent boss Lucifer, the apprentice demon Sophia is appalled. As Jehova's goddaughter, she simply cannot stand idly by while her fellow demons defraud the financial community of the City of London to pay for their improvements.

So while Agrat, the manager of the project, and her team fleece wealthy individuals for start-up capital, and their unscrupulous pet-banker Gingrich Fleabrunckle organises a syndicated loan from the financial community, Sophia accepts a position as management trainee in one of the more venerable institutions of the City. Although her unorthodox business methods almost blow her cover, she manages to remain incognito and is soon joined by the 300-year old mythical Lady of Threadneedle Street, the mighty rodent-catcher Mr Mouser, and the self-appointed priest of Mithras and plant psychologist Mithradates Devadorje, in her efforts to sabotage her fellow demons' designs.

As the action moves from London to Greenland and Mongolia, we encounter Arnapak, an octogenarian shaman who is searching for the lost soul of her great-granddaughter and confronts the evil sorcerer and Fleabrunckle-friend Florimonde, the Emerald Maiden who traps unwary humans in her Dream-Stone realm and vacillates in her loyalty between Agrat and Sophia's employer Governor Pinchbeck, and the ancient Inuit Goddess Takanakapsaluk, who lives on the bottom of the sea and hates humanity.

After many hectic adventures and innumerable unexpected plot-twists, the story reaches its finale when both sides invest all their power in two mighty musicians, who battle for the final victory in the icy waste of Greenland.

Dedication

For many years I laboured on my loom
To weave a coloured web of hope and doom.
All that remains is that I thank all those
Whose words and actions fructified my prose.

I thank my Parents who warped up the loom for me,
Karl May, who taught the basics of dream-weavery,
I thank Philosophers in Oregon at Portland State
Who made me spin tough fibres by the crate
Just like their colleagues who taught Anthropology
and mixed the dies that stained my growing tapestry.

I thank all those whose words and deeds and smiles
Provided skeins of wool to knot my piles.
All those whose lessons loving or malign
I took to heart to ponder and make mine
And turned into those little tufts of wool
Which, spun and stored upon my memory's spool
I used, when needed for a very special spot
to colour in some detail of the plot.

And lastly I thank those, who, eager to protect the vain
Had sought to cross my web with crimson wefts of pain.

A YOUNG LADY IN THREADNEEDLE STREET

A glimpse of catastrophe

Oswald Pinchback hurled his keys across the room, hit and chipped an expensive Chinese vase, and yelled, 'Peterson, go fetch Sophia!'

'Yes Sir, very good Sir,' replied the unflappable Arthur Peterson, and went to summon Sophia bint Lilith, trainee manager and recent confidante of the Governor of The Institution.

Governor Pinchback was a very worried man. Never in all his long working life in the City had he encountered a crisis of such magnitude. He was one of the most powerful men in the financial community, and had done everything possible to save it from the threatening disaster, but knew he had failed. Storm clouds were gathering to engulf many of the great old City firms, but despite all his experience, all his connections, and all his powers under the law, he had proved to be completely helpless against the demons who rode in the eye of the storm.

'You OK Gov?' Sophia asked as she entered the room; she was getting less and less deferential as her apprenticeship was drawing to a close.

'No, I am not 'OK', I am worried sick! Isn't there anything else we can do before the great opening ceremony?'

'You know very well there isn't, so stop griping and trust Devadorje!'

'How can I possibly trust a plant psychologist who worships Mithras! This will be the end of the City, I just know it!'

'Would Sir like one of his pills?' Peterson interjected.

'No I would not! Oh God what am I going to do?'

'There is no need to blaspheme', Sophia said sternly. 'Why are you so bothered all of a sudden about the fate of the City anyway? Not so long ago I practically had to drag you back to your duties here!'

Pinchback sighed. He looked out of the window of his office on the top floor of The Institution, and watched the setting sun transform the stony barren wasteland of the City into a magic wonderland of red and golden light and blue and purple shadows.

'Just look at that view,' he said to Sophia who stood beside him. 'I still remember when I joined The Institution as a young lad almost fifty years ago; I thought mystery and adventure lurked in every dark back-alley, and expected to perform daring deeds each morning after coffee. It is true that I have grown tired of the place these last few hectic years, and come to regard it more and more as prosaic, selfish, and degenerate. There have been so many scandals, so much greed-fuelled dishonesty, so much callous disregard for decency – but now that the City is threatened, I feel differently.'

'You've got to trust Devadorje,' said Sophia.

'You should take one of your pills, Sir,' said Peterson.

Governor Pinchback dropped heavily into an armchair, nodded to Sophia, took the pill proffered by Peterson, and asked to be left alone. One more week until the opening! One more week until many of the great institutions of the City would face financial ruin, and there was absolutely nothing he or anyone else could do about it, except trust Devadorje – and Devadorje was mad!

Prologue in Limbo

The whole trouble started when Socrates died. After his death (which was as dignified and exemplary as his life, if we can trust Platon's account of it), Jehovah and Lucifer could not agree whether Socrates ought to go to Heaven or Hell.

'I really think he deserves to go to Heaven, on account of his life-long efforts to further the cause of truth and self -knowledge, his heroism in battle, and his praiseworthy death,' said Lucifer.

Jehovah disagreed. 'Socrates has wilfully chosen death, despite the fact that he leaves behind a young wife and numerous children that are unprovided for. As to his supposedly exemplary life, you know very well that Socrates spent it provoking and annoying innocent up-standing members of the Athenian community, until they got so exasperated they had to sentence him to death – hardly behaviour that warrants eternal lodgings in Heaven. Moreover, Socrates, while spending an inordinate amount of time arguing about virtue, frequently neglected to care for his own family, who had to rely on the charity of relatives and friends to supply their basic needs. Obviously the man is a hypocrite of the first order, and only interested in his own pleasure,' Jehovah concluded. 'Hell is his deserved abode.'

Although Lucifer and Jehovah usually managed to come to some sort of compromise about the placement of souls, they simply could not agree in the case of Socrates. They argued for hours, and eventually even raised their voices, as can easily happen when one gets exasperated, and managed to wake up a little blond baby-demon who had been napping peacefully in Lucifer's lap. Sensing discord in her immediate vicinity, she started to bawl at the top of her voice, and would not be comforted by Lucifer, who was her father and had been pressed into baby-sitting duty by his bride, Lilith.

[It should perhaps be noted that Lucifer doubted his paternity; Lilith was not the most faithful of brides, and passed off several other children as his who had been obviously sired by others. He did not really mind this, since he was broad-minded and loved children, and happy whenever any of Lilith's offspring survived their mother's fickle attentions.]

To calm down the howling infant, Lucifer cooed and tickled it, made funny faces and growling sounds, and even swished his tails and wriggled the horns he wore back then to scare the heathens, but all to no avail. The urchin kept on screaming.

'Give her to me,' said Jehovah, and took the child from Lucifer. 'I am good with children.' Sure enough, the little demon had barely settled in his arms, when she ceased her bawling and smiled a toothless smile.

'How do you do,' she said politely, 'haven't we met somewhere before?' She was well brought up, despite her dissolute mother.

'Most unlikely,' replied Jehovah, 'and more's the pity.' He had taken an instant liking to the little girl, perhaps because he sensed immediately that there was something very special about her – or perhaps because he took an instant liking to all children he met.

'Say, what have you been arguing about with my Daddy,' she asked Jehovah, who explained to her the thorny problem of where to send Socrates.

'What do you suggest we do,' he asked her, trying to test the intelligence of the diminutive demon.

'I should ask Socrates himself,' she answered, 'after all, he is the one who will have to live with the decision.'

'He won't be the only one,' muttered her Dad, who had a shrewd idea where this would lead. But Jehovah ignored him, summoned Socrates, and apprised him of the situation.

'This little one thinks that you should be allowed to decide whether to go to Heaven or Hell.' And then he explained exactly what Heaven and Hell were, thinking that Socrates might not know, not being a Christian (no one was back then). But Socrates was not paying attention, observing the little demon instead. What a charming child, he thought, and so wise already.

'What is your name, little girl?' he asked.

'I am not a little girl, I am a demon, and demons don't get names until they have done something noteworthy that merits a name. Until then people call me by all sorts of names. Daddy calls me 'Sweetie', and Mummy 'Little Wretch!', and my nurse 'Thingy'; but I like 'Sweetie' best.'

'And so do I', said Socrates emphatically. 'Nevertheless, I think your sterling advice to Jehovah concerning my fate definitely merits a proper name. I propose that you be called Sophia, to commemorate the wisdom you have shown today.'

'An excellent idea,' Jehovah agreed. 'Yes, henceforth your name shall be Sophia, and I will be your Godfather!'

'Don't be ridiculous,' said Lucifer, who did not think the name appropriate for a demon, and was moreover worried that too much contact between Jehovah and his little girl - and surely there would be contact between a goddaughter and her godfather? - would corrupt her. 'How could you possibly be her godfather? Have you considered the theological implications of such an arrangement?'

Jehovah had in fact not considered this at all, but nevertheless waved the objection airily aside. 'I am sure there won't be a problem,' he said, 'I shall think of something later on.'

[Of course, he never did, and there was a huge scandal, which took several hundred years to die down, but that is not part of this story.]

Lucifer had heard that sort of talk before. 'What do you mean, you will think of something later on?' he asked suspiciously. 'That's what you said about Adam and Eve being punished for their sins, and then after they died you just quietly slipped them into Heaven and forgot all about punishing them. I could mention any number of similar instances …..'

'Are you presuming to lecture me on moral theology, when I am the one who invented the whole thing?' retorted Jehovah.

'Yes I bloody well am,' Lucifer shouted, determined not to give way this time.

At this stage Sophia - as she shall be referred to henceforth - started to cry again. 'I want to be called Sophia, I want Jehovah as godfather, I want my Mummy!' She peered discreetly at her father, to see whether he was growing weak. Not yet, apparently. So she continued. 'Everybody hates me, nobody loves me! I never get anything! I am just a poor abused little baby demon!' Lucifer tried in vain to calm her down.

'Now look here,' said Socrates, 'this really won't do. I have just had a difficult death, and a long journey, and all, and need some rest. So could you please postpone your theological discussions until we have sorted out my fate?'

'Oh dear, do forgive me,' said Jehovah, and 'terribly sorry,' intoned Lucifer, and then they asked him again whether he wanted to go to Heaven or Hell.

'Well,' said Socrates and scratched his head, 'I have spent all my life trying to help people see the truth, and can think of no reason why I should stop now, just because I am dead.'

Jehovah and Lucifer both sighed; they had suspected as much, which is why they were both so keen not to have the old gadfly settle in their neck of the spiritual realm.

'If I understand the respective functions of Heaven and Hell correctly, the lost souls in Hell have a lot more need of my services than the saintly inhabitants of Heaven. Therefore it seems more appropriate for me to move to Hell – I can do much more good there!'

Jehovah was delighted. 'Well, that's all settled then. I'll make sure you won't get too lonely, and send down all other philosophers to keep you company, as soon as they arrive in Limbo. I bet you will save lots of souls in no time at all.'

Lucifer muttered something unprintable.

'As for you,' Jehovah said to the little baby demon, 'I look forward to seeing you as often as possible in Heaven.'

'Ha, we'll see about that,' thought Lucifer, 'I'll make sure that she gets to see him no more than once a decade.'

But Jehovah had not yet finished. 'Why don't you come and see me every Sunday afternoon at three for tea and biscuits? We'll make it a regular occasion, so we won't forget about it.' He smiled at Lucifer, who looked morose.

'Foiled again,' he thought. 'No good will come of it.'

Lucifer had been quite right to be apprehensive. The name 'Sophia' stuck like glue to the little demon, and every Sunday she went to see Jehovah, whose wise counsels considerably mellowed her essential demonic nature. In time she became a great favourite in Heaven and Hell alike, and everyone predicted her a great future. Partly due to her influence, Hell became less and less terrifying with every passing year. However, as yet she had caused her father only minor headaches.

The philosophers had taken a much greater toll on Lucifer's nerves. Instead of sticking to the improvement of human souls, they often turned their attention not only to the administration of Hell, which was none of their business as far as he was concerned, but rivalled with each other in their attempts to improve his own soul and character!

The increasing influx of Christian philosophers, who had the temerity to try to convert him to their faith, further poisoned his existence, and he repeatedly asked Jehovah to take them off his hands. But Jehovah always referred him to Yeshua, claiming that it would be unfair for him to interfere, now that his son was running the place[1].

Talking to Yeshua was of course of no use whatsoever, because his sole purpose seemed to be to empty Hell of its inhabitants as swiftly as possible. Since Yeshua knew that the philosophers motivated an ever increasing number of souls to improve themselves and leave Hell, he was keen to keep them there for the time being. The philosophers claimed that they opened people's hearts and minds to the Good, and thereby enabled them to improve their souls until they were pure enough to graduate into Heaven, but Lucifer, from bitter personal experience, knew better, and complained to Yeshua.

'They nag, they pester, they give one no rest, until one does what they want. People improve their souls around here because they know that getting out of Hell is the only way to escape the philosophers. Love of virtue has nothing to do with it! Have you noticed how many people choose re-incarnation these days? They don't really care where they go, as long as they get away from the philosophers! I warn you, I am not going to put up with this much longer!'

But unfortunately he had no choice in the matter, and things went from bad to worse. The Enlightenment further contributed to Lucifer's problems. Some clever chap from Venice reasoned that souls, being immaterial, could not really feel pain, and convinced everyone that all the assorted tortures that Lucifer had been so proud of were only in the mind, with the result that it became almost impossible to torment anyone anymore. *[Excepting the intellectual tortures inflicted by the philosophers, of course.]*

The invention of Psychoanalysis gave Lucifer a short respite; he arranged to have Freud & Co sent to Hell, ostensibly to aid the improvement of souls, in fact to have psychological tortures inflicted on the poor souls in Hell. For a while this worked quite well, and Lucifer thought his troubles were over. But alas, the shrinks, too, could not resist applying their skills to his own personage, instead of the damned souls they were

---

[1]   Yeshua had assumed most administrative duties after his sojourn in Palestine.

supposed to concentrate on. From the middle of the 20th century Lucifer sank deeper and deeper into depression, and after a particularly nasty confrontation with a junkie, who claimed he had seen worse nightmares in his Heroin dreams than here in Hell, he was ready to quit.

'I have done this job for five-thousand years now, and never got any gratitude,' he said to Lilith, who surprised him as he was packing his suitcase. 'I am getting out of here, see how they get on without me. And don't think I am ever coming back, 'cause I won't. I am sick and tired of it all. What is the point anyway? Jehovah is completely unworldly, and Yeshua does as he pleases. Between the two of them they will let everyone into Heaven and close down Hell, and what a pretty mess that will create! But I don't care anymore! You hear me, Boss,' he yelled, 'I am getting out of here, damn it, find yourself another bogeyman!'

Jehovah was having tea with Sophia when they heard Lucifer's outburst.

'Oh dear, it sounds like he means it this time! We had better go and see what can be done,' he said to his goddaughter, and together they went to see Lucifer.

'Oh Daddy,' cried Sophia when she saw her father, who was in a high state of fury and self-pity, 'we are all so sorry that you are upset,' and gave him a big hug.

'Indeed yes,' said Jehovah, stroking his beard and looking visibly moved. 'My dear chap, I do apologize, I really should have been more considerate. Now, why don't we have a nice cup of tea, and see what we can do about the situation? Things obviously can't go on as they have.'

'Well, I hope you aren't expecting me to make the tea,' said Lilith, ever ready to do her bit for female emancipation, and rather disappointed that there was not going to be a big scene after all.

'Oh hush Mummy,' said Sophia, 'can't you see Daddy is upset? I'll make the tea!' She added some shortbread as well, for good measure, and left Lucifer and her godfather alone to discuss their affairs.

Apparently it was quite a three-cup-problem, for it took a considerable amount of tea and shortbread to smooth Lucifer's ruffled temper and produce a satisfactory solution. However, eventually they agreed that Lucifer would go on a long recuperative holiday, while Beelzebub, his deputy, would keep an eye on all things hellish until he returned.

'And when you come back we will completely re-think the entire Heaven / Hell set-up,' said Jehovah in conclusion of their discussion. 'After all, humanity has changed since we first built the place, and it is about time we made adjustments. But there is no hurry, no hurry at all; first you get some rest, and when you come back, you will have a really exciting project to look forward to.'

A few days later Lucifer bade farewell to all and sundry, and told them to mind their p's and q's and not to get into mischief while he was away, and left for an unknown destination. He was much comforted by his talk with Jehovah, and the assurances of Beelzebub that he would keep Hell shipshape until Lucifer returned. Little did he know what mayhem would be wreaked during his absence!

2　Beelzebub decides to re-furbish Hell

As soon as Lucifer was safely gone, Beelzebub called a General Assembly of the Denizens of Hell. He explained that the boss had suffered a nervous breakdown, and that he, Beelzebub, intended to make sure this would not happen again.

'I don't blame the Chief at all for having finally flipped a lid – why Hell is in terrible shape! Numbers are falling; anyone with the least bit of drive either gets out to Heaven, or signs up for re-incarnation, and Hell is left with the dregs! The bums, the deadbeats, the dimwits, and the occasional mass-murderer are all we can retain. And why is that? I tell you why! This place is a tip! Chains have gone rusty, fires have died down, and the instruments of torture are dull from disuse. Buildings don't get repaired, dungeons are no longer damp and fungus-covered, and even the Pit-of-Despair is overgrown with weeds. Then there is the attitude some of you have! Instead of doing your best to counteract the disastrous effects of the Philosophers and Psychologists, you seem to have given up the fight and are just taking life easy. I know for a fact that some of you are even playing with the idea of quitting your jobs and applying for positions in the Other Place! If we don't stop the rot now, there won't be a Hell left when the Boss returns! So I appeal to you all, as loyal Denizens of Hell, to pull together and make Hell once more a place we can be proud of! Now, shall we have a vote on this? Anyone suicidal enough to be against my plans raise your hands now!'

Apparently everyone thought his idea was a splendid one. Except Lilith.

'While I totally agree that we need to stop falling enrolment numbers, I really don't think reinstating all our old ways of making the afterlife miserable for the lost souls is going to result in an increase in their numbers! That was all very well when people were forced to remain here for eternity, but in the current climate of upward mobility and second and third chances, a horrible Hell is an empty Hell! If we don't make the place more attractive, we will continue to lose custom and eventually go out of business. No, we are simply going to have to become more competitive, and to do that we need to modernize and make Hell more comfortable! Therefore I propose that we do indeed re-furbish the place – but not by going back to the old Fire & Brimstone days, but by turning it into an up-to-date, high class, customer-focussed entertainment centre that offers diversion and satisfaction to all our clients.'

The word 'stunned' would fail to accurately describe the reaction that followed Lilith's words. Over the centuries everyone had become used to her radical ideas, but this was more than most of the decidedly conservative denizens of Hell were prepared to contemplate.

'No No and No again,' Beelzebub roared. 'Have you taken leave of your senses? Our brief is to punish people for wrong-doing, and to make their life generally miserable;

what you propose amounts to a total abrogation of our responsibilities! I am not even going to discuss this, it is simply too ludicrous. Why, it is not even legal; we would first have to re-negotiate our Terms & Conditions with the Great Bearded One, and there is no chance he would go for that!'

But Lilith was not impressed by his blustering. 'Show a bit more spirit, will you? How big is the chance that the Other Place will find out about our activities until it is a done deal and they can't do anything about it? Once the new system is in place, they will simply have to grin and bear it – or do you think they would go to war over this? Besides, you may remember that Jehovah has never really been comfortable with the concept of Hell, because he believes that people are basically good and all wickedness is the result of ignorance or bad up-bringing, and in either case he thinks it would be unfair to punish them for their deeds. Although I personally think this is just another example of Jehovah being soft in the brain, I really don't see why we should not exploit his weakness for our purposes. Therefore I propose that we go ahead and refurbish Hell as I have suggested. Furthermore, to cover our backs I suggest we commission a study to show that (a) it is unethical to punish people for their sins, and (b) it is ineffective. I recently read a report about the effect of imprisonment on re-offending, and am in no doubt that we can make a good case for abandoning our current punitive regime.'

Although Beelzebub continued to be doubtful, Agrat bat Mahalat spoke up in support of her sister's proposal.

'Lilith is right, you know. The whole set-up of Heaven and Hell has been terribly unfair from the very start. Jehovah didn't have the stomach to punish evil-doers himself, and simply delegated the job to Lucifer and the rest of us. For thousands of years we have done the dirty work for him, got the bad press and no thanks from anyone. The result? We will all be made redundant if we don't take action. Let the consultants put *that* into the report! No, I don't think we need to worry too much about Jehovah! I say let's go with Lilith's plan. Let's put it to the vote.'[2]

After much discussion, [*which I omit at the request of my publisher who felt that it would be of little interest to the general reader and a waste of paper*], Lilith's proposal was accepted by the General Assembly, and an Executive Committee was elected and authorised to evolve detailed proposals, as well as commission the aforementioned study.

Shortly afterwards the Executive Committee assembled in the Rusty Cauldron Cocktail Lounge to make plans; they agreed that the two major constraints were the lack of a suitable workforce and insufficient funding. Given the generally low moral calibre of the humans in Hell, they were unlikely to voluntarily contribute much to the re-structuring. Ashtaroth's suggestion that they might become willing labourers if they were told of the purpose of the refurbishment was not taken up. The Committee felt it would be too risky, since some of them were certain to blabber about it to their acquaintances in Heaven; besides, they wouldn't believe it anyway. Since the Committee therefore could not rely on the local workforce, they would have to recruit amongst living humans, which might turn out to be decidedly difficult. After all, who would want to

---

[2]   Although Lucifer was just as autocratically inclined as Jehovah, Hell (unlike Heaven) was organised along democratic principles, and all major decisions had to be discussed and agreed by the entire adult demonic population (ie everyone over the age of three-thousand).

work in Hell, given its reputation and notoriously sub-standard working conditions? Cash, too, was likely to be a problem – as everyone knows, Hell has no cash-flow. A complete refurbishment of Hell would cost a large fortune, and Hell did not even have a small one. In general, Hell had no need of money – if they needed something from The World, they just stole it. But stealing enough money to buy whatever materials would be needed for the refurbishment, as well as paying for the necessary labour, was a tall order even for a group of determined demons.

As usual, Agrat was ahead of everyone else. She had discussed the matter with Casanova, and he had already come up with a plan. Beelzebub was not impressed.

'You told Casanova about this? Are you mad? He is one of the few humans left in Hell who has intelligence as well as drive and ambition. I never understood why he is still here; probably spying for the Other Place, wouldn't be the first time! If he spills the beans, he could ruin our plans!'

'Quite so,' Agrat replied, 'but why should he? He has come up with a truly wonderful plan, which will solve all our difficulties. For his reward he only wants to be allowed to help with the implementation. He is desperate to get back to The World for a spell.'

'So why doesn't he reincarnate?'

'Because he would have to leave all his memories behind, and since he loves himself just as he is, and revels in the memories of his last incarnation, he is not prepared to do that. That's why he is still in Hell. Anyway, do you want to hear what his plan is or not?'

When Agrat had finished, Beelzebub jumped up and roared with laughter.

'Just wait 'till we put this to the General Assembly,' he cried. 'The guy's a genius, you are quite right. Terribly sorry I criticized you just now. Wow, what a concept! And in Greenland, of all places! Awesome.'

Beelzebub was not alone in his enthusiasm. When The Plan was put before the General Assembly they voted for it unanimously, appointed Agrat to be the project leader of the great refurbishment, and promised to reward Casanova with an honorary demonship as soon as The Plan had been successfully implemented.

'Imagine getting the City to lend us the cash for doing-up the place,' said a minor demon to his lady companion, 'and then to defraud them of the lot! This should put us firmly back on the map. The boss is going to be so pleased when he gets back!' Or would he?

3   The Plan

The General Assembly had given Agrat a free hand to pick her project team, and in addition to Casanova, who was appointed as financial advisor, she chose Cesare Borgia as her business manager, because he was intelligent, energetic, unscrupulous, and determined to do whatever it took to rise up in the hierarchy of Hell. At the first meeting of the project team, which took place in Agrat's apartment, The Plan was explained to Cesare. In a nutshell, it went as follows.

They would approach the financial community of the City of London for a massive loan to finance the development of a huge amusement park in Greenland, and promise to repay the loan with the entrance fees paid by the visitors to the park. After the park was completed, it would be transmogrified to Hell, and re-assembled there. Since there would thus be no amusement park left to visit in Greenland, it could generate no income to repay the City. And since Hell had no cash-flow, or assets of any kind to repay the loans in some other way, several dozen banks would probably go bankrupt as a result. This did not unduly disconcert the denizens of Hell; they were after all demons, and their value-systems differed from those of human beings. Moreover, demons in general have a very low opinion of financiers, having had ample opportunity to study their characters (most of them end up in Hell).

Cesare summed up their attitude nicely. 'That'll teach them to lend huge sums of unsecured money to shady characters!'

Casanova suggested that one of the first issues to focus on was getting some start-up capital together, since the financial community would be more likely to invest in the project if they had some capital of their own.

'It would be quickest if we simply persuaded a few billionaires to part with their fortunes,' he suggested. Secondly, they would need to develop detailed plans of the amusement centre; Agrat promised to discuss the matter with a few architects. Thirdly, they would need to figure out how to transmogrify the amusement centre and re-assemble it in Hell.

'Any suggestions?'

No one had any, except Damon, one of Agrat's demon spawn who were playing on the floor and listening to the debate with great interest. Damon was always overflowing with ideas, which, however, were rarely appreciated by his mother.

'I have just met this guy, Acid Icepick, who plays this cruel synthetic music,' he began.

'Put a sock in it rug-rat,' Agrat interrupted him.

But Casanova rather liked the lad, who was a bit like he had been at that age[3], and intervened in his favour. Thus encouraged, Damon continued.

'Acid has this thing about shattering glass and stuff with his music. He says he could shatter any material object, not just glass, and he could control the shattering process, provided he had the right instrument and played just the right music.'

Agrat was not impressed. 'Total rubbish; how could that possibly work?'

Damon looked at her helplessly. 'I really don't know, but I have this feeling that he could help us.'

---

[3]   Demon children, though precocious, take a long time to grow up; roughly speaking, one demonic year is equivalent to 100 human years. Damon had been born about one-thousand years ago, and thus was ten years old in human terms.

Agrat looked at him sharply. 'Where exactly do you have this feeling?'

'Eh? I don't really know, sort of between my eyebrows, I think; does it matter?'

Agrat nodded. 'That is exactly where it should be; I am glad you are developing your thirteenth sense so early on. OK, I'll go and talk to this Acid.'

Cesare suggested that someone ought to go to Greenland and study the local conditions, in case there was opposition to their plans. Casanova agreed. There were so many busybodies and environmentalists about these days, it was more than likely that a bit of palm-greasing and arm-twisting would be required.

'I am good at that sort of thing,' Cesare volunteered.

'Alright, but remember what I told you about modern business methods,' Agrat said. 'I catch you murdering anyone, or even just threatening someone a little with a knife, and you go straight back to Hell!'

'I am a reformed character, Agrat, six centuries in Hell are enough to convince anyone of the futility of violence! But what about being friendly with the natives? Am I at least allowed to have some fun with women?'

'Well that's pretty much part of the course for modern businessmen, so go ahead. But remember my views regarding female-male relationships' – Agrat was rudely interrupted by a chorus of her demon spawn, who chanted in unison:

'Treat them like ladies

Give them a good time

Don't hurt their feelings

Don't get them pregnant

Respect their husbands

And always pay up in hard cash!'

'Quite right quite right! Now get back to the nursery, you little monsters!' Agrat shouted and shooed them out of the room.

On the evening of this eventful day, Cesare Borgia checked into the ritziest hotel in Greenland, and experienced the first happy night for centuries, while Agrat discussed harmonics with Acid Icepick and concluded that her son had inherited her brains. Casanova studied Forbes' list of the wealthiest men[4] of the world and narrowed down a short-list of possible contributors to the project's capital.

And Mithradates Devadorje poured libations before the shrine of his god in the City of London, beseeching him to answer his prayers, as was his wont on the 16th of every month.

---

[4]   Like her sister Lilith, Agrat was a feminist and insisted that no woman tycoon be victimised.

Although Sophia was too young to be a member of the General Assembly, and therefore not supposed to know of The Plan, she soon enough found out about it. Her first impulse was to rush off to Jehovah and spill all the beans. However, upon reflection she decided that this would amount to snitching, which she had been taught was unforgivable and against all demonic principles. All the same, she had spent too much time in Heaven, and absorbed too many of the precepts that ruled there, to feel comfortable with the project. She was certain it would cause untold damage and grief not only to the financial community, but also to the general economy which depended on the banking sector.

How could entrepreneurs start new businesses, if the banks lost all their money in Agrat's nefarious scheme and were unable to make loans? How could young couples eager to purchase their first home get a mortgage? What would happen to people in remote areas, if the banks had to reduce their branch and cash-machine networks to cut costs? What of the pensions and life insurances of the people whose savings had been invested and lost in the scheme? What would happen to all those customers who had entrusted the banks with their savings, if the banks went bankrupt? And how would the Greenlanders cope with having their amusement park stolen over night, an amusement park which they would no doubt be led to believe would create new jobs and benefit their country? Worst of all, how could the theft of an entire amusement park be hushed up? Wouldn't it convince humanity that there were superhuman forces at work in the world after all, and didn't that violate the CAM?[5]

No, Sophia simply could not sit idly by and watch her auntie ruin the economy of an entire nation; her mother's attitude to human grief - 'it's good for their souls!' - had always remained anathema to her. After much pondering and soul-searching she decided to discuss the matter with her father. To be sure, he was difficult to get on with, and had shown little interest in her hitherto, but she felt certain that he would advise her. After all, his beloved City was threatened!

[At this point the reader will be excused for being just a little confused. Wasn't Lucifer her father? And had not Lucifer just disappeared for an unknown destination? So what's all this about him advising Sophia?

Honoured reader! Lucifer's suspicions about Sophia's paternity had been well founded. A few hundred years after she received her name, it came to light that Lilith had somehow managed to seduce the virtuous and reclusive Mithras, Persian god of light and erstwhile rival of the Christ. When confronted with the evidence, Lilith was

---

[5]   The CAM (Convention Against Miracles) was signed in the Year of Our Lord 1000 by most of the gods, saints, demons, nature spirits, etc who were still capable of producing miracles, in the wake of the Conference on Manipulating Mankind. The Conference concluded that humanity was in dire need of growing up, and any obvious manifestations of superhuman powers would retard their spiritual and emotional growth. Although the CAM was occasionally broken, most of its signatories adhered to it most of the time.

completely unrepentant. 'Now don't take it personal, Lucy,' she had told Lucifer. 'I only did it as a challenge, Mithras always being so holier than thou, and never mixing with us ordinary folk. Besides, did not Sophia turn out to be as sweet and charming a little demon as you could hope for? It's no use crying over spilt sperm, so give us a kiss and let's say no more about it.' So Lucifer accepted Sophia as he had accepted so many other illegitimate offspring of Lilith, and she continued to think of him as her Daddy. Of course she was thrilled to find out she had an additional father, particularly one who appeared to have no other children. Although he was not the most affectionate of fathers, she had managed to build up a reasonably good relationship with him over the years.]

When Sophia finally managed to arrange a meeting with Mithras, he agreed with her assessment of the damage Agrat and her team would inflict on the hapless financial community in London and the wider economy. Although he had been exiled from the City for more than fifteen-hundred years, he still maintained a few connections, and advised Sophia to get in touch with an old woman who lived under the eaves of one of the most magnificent buildings in the City, in the very heart of the financial community. This woman was considered to be the guardian of all that was good and decent in the City, a sort of self-proclaimed protectress of its institutions and conduct. Mithras felt certain she would listen to Sophia and take the necessary steps to avert the impending disaster.

'She is commonly called The Old Lady,' he told her, 'and has been known to me for over three-hundred years. Do give her my regards when you see her; she lives just a few yards from my old shrine.' Then he smiled benevolently, closed his eyes, and sank into deep meditation. Obviously the audience was over.

On her way home Sophia considered the situation. It was all very well for Mithras to tell her to seek the advice of some old biddy near his temple in the City, but how was she supposed to meet her? She was still under-aged, and demons were not allowed to spend time alone amongst humanity until they had served out their apprenticeship[6]. Bother bother bother! Oh well, it was time she got the apprenticeship out of the way - perhaps she could serve it in the City? That way she could warn the old woman, and keep an eye on Agrat et al.

Her mother Lilith, who still regarded her fondly as a tiny demon barely out of swaddling clothes, was completely unsuspecting and raised no objections to Sophia's proposal to spend her apprenticeship in the City, especially when Sophia intimated that her father was in favour of it. Her only condition was that Sophia would not attempt to find a position with a commercial bank.

'There is something afoot, and I don't want you to get mixed up in it,' she said.

'Oh sure, Mommy,' Sophia replied. 'Perhaps I could work as an intern in that large building next to the chap on the plinth near Father's old temple.' The building she

---

[6]   The apprenticeship usually lasted three human years, and had to be served somewhere amongst humans. If a young demon was able to complete her/his apprenticeship without anyone noticing that s/he was not human, s/he was elevated to the rank of Journeywo/man demon.

referred to was none other than the head-office of The Institution in Threadneedle Street, and home of The Old Lady.

5   Raising the start-up capital: Judas Monkfish III

    While Sophia was trying to worm her way into the City, Agrat was out there fundraising. After much debate she agreed with Casanova on three billionaires to fleece for the good cause. The first was Judas Monkfish III, a well-known business tycoon and arms dealer from the east coast of the United States. Less well known were his involvement with the drugs trade, insider dealing, habit of eliminating too successful competitors, and degenerate orgies where he degraded and tormented nubile young women. It was this latter vice that decided Agrat to pick him.

    'Let's see how he squirms when the shoe is on the other foot,' she observed to Casanova when they stood in front of the door of Judas' luxury flat in Manhattan.

    Judas Monkfish III was not an aesthetically pleasing man. He was of medium stature and grotesquely fat, with a comb-over, bad breath even when inhaling, plenty of pimples, and little bits of toilet paper stuck all over his face where he had cut himself shaving. His personal hygiene levels left much to be desired, and his conversation was liberally dosed with swear words and sexual innuendo – he was as good an argument for celibacy as ever walked the planks of life. However, his repulsiveness was of no concern to him. On the contrary, he rather liked the idea that the women he bedded had to endure his physical grossness as well as his assorted other abuses.

    But to Agrat he was politeness incorporated. 'My most dear Madam Mahalat,' he crooned when his PA showed in Agrat and Casanova, 'I cannot tell you how enchanted I am to finally make your acquaintance. A woman of your looks and intelligence is very rare indeed in the business world. And if your secretary is to be believed, a woman with a penchant for daring ventures as well! I must confess I had no idea that the English Channel Tunnel had been your idea! And I always thought the pyramids of Egypt were built thousands of years ago! Oh well, that's American education for you! Anyway, I am really most impressed, and delighted to meet you.'

    Agrat shot Casanova an uneasy glance; she had told him to lay it on thick when he arranged her meeting with Monkfish, and of course she knew that he had the ability to convince anyone of anything, but all the same …..

    He just grinned, and handed her a screwdriver from the butler's tray. 'Cocktail?'

    After a bit of polite social chit chat, Casanova outlined The Plan for the project they had decided to call 'Greenlandia'. Monkfish listened attentively, asked a few questions, and regretfully informed them that he was not interested in backing their venture.

    'With all due respect for your talents, Madam, I don't think even you could pull this off. You would need at least a million visitors a year just to pay the interest on the loans you will have to raise. This is clearly impossible in an amusement park located at the end of the world, where the average temperature in July is +10°C and in January -20°C. You are trying to do the impossible. Count me out.'

Agrat looked questioningly at Casanova, who had not told her about those details. He just shrugged his shoulders.

'I have defeated greater odds when I escaped from the Leads.' Then, turning to Monkfish, he said: 'You don't seem to realise that we are prepared to go to any length to have you with us on this project.'

Monkfish leered at Agrat. 'To any length, really?'

'We may be prepared to go to any length, but we are certainly not prepared to sink to any depth!' Agrat retorted angrily. She did not like the way the conversation was going; whatever had Casanova been thinking when he asked her to come here?

Monkfish sighed. He would have enjoyed a night with the raven haired, voluptuous Agrat, subjecting her to those delicious little rituals his sadistic imagination came up with so easily. Of course he still would not have invested in her venture; he would not have been one of the richest men in the world if he indulged in that sort of foolishness. Still, it was a pity. He permitted himself to sink into a little daydream, in which Agrat and he engaged in his favourite sex game, the 'Washing Machine and Toaster Ritual'.

He should not have done that. Agrat – like most demons – was adept at reading people's minds, and outraged by what she saw in Monkfish's. She delved a little deeper, and discovered in the innermost secrecy of his heart the sacred shrine he had erected there to Laura, the only woman he ever loved chastely. She had been killed in an accident before he was able to declare his love to her, and on that fateful day when he read of her death in the papers, he decided to punish the world for his loss. Ah and how he had punished, and enjoyed the punishing, for over forty years now – but the pain of Laura's death never abated. Had Yeshua looked into the heart of Judas, he would have understood and pitied him. But it was Agrat who looked into his heart, and found the shrine, and she resolved to teach him a lesson, and to defile forever the shrine and the memory of Laura.

Agrat concentrated for a second, and then pulled from her attaché case a disc that had not previously been there.

'This may interest you,' she said to Monkfish in a low, vicious voice.

Monkfish doubted it. Besides, he was getting bored.

'This is a recording of you and one of your victims, engaging in activities unlawful in the state of New York.'

Monkfish was surprised, but not terribly concerned. He was used to these little attempts at blackmail. But he would have liked to know where the video camera had been hidden; all rooms were regularly checked for recording devices since the last attempt to blackmail him with explicit photos, and he wondered which of his security men had screwed up. He eyed Agrat questioningly, but decided that it would be pointless to ask her where the secret camera was. Oh well, he would just have to ask Stojko to get the tape and eliminate anyone who had been involved in its production; no great problem, but a confounded nuisance all the same.

Turning to Agrat he said in a bored sort of voice, 'I guess you'll insist on showing it to me. The player is over there.' In a way he rather looked forward to seeing the recording; he always enjoyed himself on screen, and Agrat's reaction to the lurid scenes that would undoubtedly feature on the six foot wide display unit would no doubt heighten his pleasure. He wondered quite how deep a shade of red she would blush.

Agrat put the disk into the appropriate slot, and pushed the Play button; the film started at once. The setting was familiar to Monkfish. The purple tiled kitchen, the over-dimensional, custom-built washing machine, the bright yellow toaster awaiting its turn in the corner, the mountain of freshly sliced bread on the table, the peanut butter, the mustard, the Tabasco sauce – he had seen it all before; the film was real alright. And there he was himself wearing his chain-mail – carefully crocheted from jelly loops – fingering a woman, whose front half was hidden inside the washing machine, from behind with his pink begloved chubby fingers.

'Ho hum, is that all? Any blue movie is more explicit.' Nevertheless he continued to watch the woman whose bound legs and buttocks were slowly joined by her upper torso as she emerged from the washing machine. As the Monkfish on the screen applied the Tabasco sauce and reached for the peanut butter in preparation for the toaster ritual, and the woman let out a shrill cry of agony, the Monkfish who watched smiled contentedly; he loved to watch the pain he inflicted. He revelled in the knowledge that the women who participated in his games truly suffered under the tortures he inflicted. Ambitious business women, who wanted his support in their ventures, or career girls eager to climb up the corporate ladder, were his favourite victims. He always took care to recruit only women with normal sexual preferences for his games, never those who were interested in sado-masochism. Nor did he hire professionals, since much of his pleasure derived from knowing that he degraded decent women whose friends and relatives would be appalled if they knew what they endured for the sake of their careers.

He looked forward to the next part of the ritual, which inflicted a pain so exquisitely agonising that the victims had nightmares about it for the rest of their lives (that's what he hoped, anyway). He moved closer to the screen, anxious not to miss the slightest nuance of the screams and mad thrashings of the female animal that was just about to be subjected to the Toaster ritual, when the woman on the screen turned her head around. Suddenly her face completely filled the screen, and as Monkfish looked into her tortured agonised features he recognised that it was Laura!

His scream was louder and more agonised than those of all the many women he had victimised, and was soon matched by Agrat's wild abandoned triumphant laughter. Monkfish's barely human howls and Agrat's mad infernal laughter combined to an ever louder cacophony, which Casanova found almost impossible to endure. He crouched down behind his chair and pressed his hand to his ears to shut it out, but to no avail. Slowly his mind slipped from his grasp, and wailed and whirled in the madness of Agrat's demonic laughter and Judas' agonised screams.

Suddenly a great calm fell upon the room. Casanova raised his head, and saw both Monkfish and Agrat staring at a tiny golden flickering light that hovered above the screen. For a moment it seemed as though the light showed a woman's face, who smiled sadly and faded away; and then the flame, too, was gone.

Monkfish sat in his chair as though petrified. Agrat regarded him patiently, her fury spent. Casanova crouched on the carpet, completely exhausted.

Hour passed after hour. Monkfish had a diary full of appointments, but Agrat had woven a spell of solitude about them, and they were not disturbed. Hour after hour they sat silently, motionless, each pondering their own thoughts. Darkness fell, and still they sat in silence. All night they kept their vigil.

When the first tentative streaks of morning appeared on the horizon, Monkfish's thoughts once again assumed coherence, falling into place along the lines his cathartic experience had drawn for him. Shocked to his core he fully comprehended the extent to which his life had offended human and divine law, and accepted without reservation his duty to atone. Strangely enough, he felt neither self-hatred nor revulsion for his past life, despite his understanding that it had been evil. Instead he felt uplifted, cleansed, and ready to lead a life as purely good as it had hitherto been evil. He watched the sun rise slowly over the skyline, and saw it as he never did before, his eyes rejoicing in the colours and shapes that rushed to meet them eagerly like long lost friends. Monkfish positively radiated goodwill and happiness as he addressed Agrat in his direct businesslike fashion.

'You have obviously been sent to me by God to show me the error of my ways. I accept the loss of my fortune as part of the penance I shall have to perform to atone for my past misdeeds. I have no problems with this. However, I don't quite understand the Greenland angle; why didn't you just arrange for me to lose my fortune in a stock market crash, or something similar?'

Agrat was a little annoyed; why was it always Jehova who got the credit whenever she managed to accidentally guide a human back to the straight and narrow path of virtue? However, she reflected that Monkfish was a shrewd and clever man – if he were told the truth he might come up with some useful advice for pulling off The Plan. She was beginning to distrust Casanova a little; Monkfish's objections to The Plan last night had sounded very sensible to her.

'Alright Jack, tell him The Plan,' she said to Casanova. 'After all, he will be one of us soon enough anyway.'

Monkfish winced, but Agrat's comment made him all the more determined to atone for his sins and avoid Hell if at all possible.

When Casanova had finished, Judas shook his head and told them that The Plan was unworkable. The business community would never be convinced of the scheme, not in that location. What was so special about Greenland anyway? Why couldn't they build the amusement park where the climate was a bit more congenial? Casanova sighed, and explained that it had to do with the location of Hell.

'The transmission of the park from The World to Hell is only possible from a few points of the globe, and Greenland is the only one that is not covered by water.'

Monkfish nodded; he could see the problem. 'All the same, the project as you have described it will never work. You must think of something else.'

Agrat carefully probed his mind, and decided that he was speaking the truth. She was furious with Casanova! However, before she was able to unleash her legendary fury upon him, he explained.

'Look, I haven't live in The World for over two hundred years, and never been to Greenland. I am a little out of touch, that is all. Give me a week to get acquainted with the mentality of the mankind of today, and I'll give you an amended plan. Come on, just give me a week – what is the hurry anyway?'

Agrat considered his proposal, and thought it reasonable. Besides, Casanova was the cleverest thing on two legs she had ever encountered, and if he could not come up with a solution to the problem no one else would, either.

'Alright,' she said. 'But Jehova help you if you fail.'

He smiled suavely. 'And when have I ever failed? See you in a week's time!' With that he left, before Agrat could change her mind.

Turning to Monkfish she said, 'The wonderful thing about Jack is his optimism, with him on the team we can't possibly fail!'

Monkfish smiled dubiously; in his opinion that crazy secretary of hers was incapable of coming up with a workable business proposal, no matter how many weeks she gave him to think about it. But he was in for a surprise!

6   Sophia gets a job in the City

Getting a job in The Institution was easier than Sophia had expected. A couple of forged references, faked exam results from Oxford, a few undemanding little interviews, and she got what she wanted – a position as trainee manager. Of course, she did have the advantage of being able to employ what little magic she had picked up over the last few millennia; non-demonic applicants might perhaps have had a harder time. However that may be, less than a month after she conceived of her plan she found herself installed as an analyst at The Institution, with a desk, a telephone, a PC, and a dozen institutions to supervise.

The Head of Personnel, Winston C. Flabbergast, entrusted Sophia into the care of the assistant manager of Section 13 of the Supervision Department. Flossy Pembrokeshire was blond, svelte, and decidedly sloaney. She did not believe in overburdening her charge with excessive knowledge. Dealing with the financial institutions of the City - which is what the department was all about – was in her opinion a matter of gut-level feeling and intuition, rather than of training and experience. If you couldn't do it immediately and without much guidance, you would probably never learn, no matter how much time and money was spent on training you, so Flossy saw no reason to attempt the impossible. She told Sophia to 'just use common sense', and swanned off to see the in-house dentist.

Thus left to her own devices, Sophia looked at her colleagues; perhaps they could offer a bit of advice? But no, they were all engrossed in their respective activities, from watering the plants, to getting coffee for everyone, to reading the Financial Times. Oh well, she thought. Might as well jump in at the deep end. That's when the telephone rang.

'Greetings & Salutations! Sophia bint Lilith speaking. What? No, you don't have the wrong number. I have just been transferred to this department. No, no, been in this business these last few centuries.' The one thing Flossy had impressed upon her was to act professionally, and never to admit that she was new to this game. 'So, what can I do you for? You want to strengthen your relationship with one of your customers? Which customer might that be? What, Judas Monkfish Inc? Certainly not; an enterprise with a name like that is bound to be fishy, and "Judas" is probably a nickname. What do you mean, this is one of your most valued customers? Are you insane? I strongly advise you to sever all business connection with this company, it will almost certainly come to a sticky end. No you may not! What do you mean, you want to talk to my manager?'

At this point Flossy, who returned from the dentist earlier than expected (she had mixed up her appointments again), snatched the receiver from Sophia's hand and said, 'Hi there this is Prizzy's Pizza Parlour, you wanna place an order? Sorry about that, you were just talking to my little kid, yeah she's such a joker! You thought you were talking to an analyst at The Institution? Get Real! Bye! Have a nice Day!' Then she turned to Sophia and snarled: 'Are you out of your tiny mind? What did I tell you about not trying to run their business for them? Next time a bank calls, you answer the 'phone like everyone else in the office, and grant whatever request they have!'

Sophia was astonished. 'But if I say "yes" to whatever they ask, why do they need to ask in the first place?'

Flossy reminded herself to be patient. After all, it was Sophia's first day on the job. 'By requiring them to ask first, we motivate them to think about the matter more carefully than they might otherwise do! Just use your head, girl!'

Sophia nodded dubiously; surely the banks had figured out by now that The Institution's analysts always said yes, and treated these calls as purely a formality? She still thought that Judas was a name of evil omen, and later that day when she was asked to participate in the 'Next Bankruptcy Sweepstake' she entered Judas Monkfish Inc as her choice. Flossy smiled indulgently, and set Sophia to interpret the annual accounts of one her banks. 'Just look out for anything unusual or worrying,' she said.

Unusual or worrying! Sophia bent over the accounts of the Little Green Moose Bank, intent on finding something wrong with them. She had never seen annual accounts before, but what the heck, it couldn't be that difficult! The first unusual thing she noticed was that the name of the chairman was Habakkuk Huckleberry. His salary divided by the square root of his birth-year was one of the four unlucky numbers in the House of Ariel! Well well. She went on to examine the Profit & Loss accounts for the last five years. If one took the sum of the pre-tax profits of all five years, divided it by Huckleberry's unlucky number, multiplied it by the number of years the firm had been in business, and then applied the inverted logarithm – Sophia shuddered, and murmured to herself, 'Massive losses ahead, mainly due to Huckleberry's skilful siphoning off of funds into his private venture capital firm, I suspect. Let's see what the cards say.' Unaware of the incredulous stares of her colleagues, Sophia mixed her tarot cards, and laid out a twice-flipped five-way special crisis sequence of her own invention. The cards confirmed her worst suspicions. She went to Flossy and told her that immediate action was imperative.

'My research proves conclusively that this bank will go out of business within three years, with complete loss of capital base and massive losses to depositors and shareholders. Unless we eliminate Huckleberry, this bank has no future.' She showed her calculations to Flossy, and even offered to double-check with the Cabbala. 'But I don't think it will add anything; the cards never lie. Now who will exterminate Huckleberry; do we do it ourselves, or is there a special department for that?'

Flossy staggered to the Personnel Department and unburdened herself to Flabbergast.

'You have got to get rid of her,' she exclaimed, 'she is obviously completely unsuited for the job. Besides, she is driving me nuts! And what if she kills someone? I refuse to be responsible!'

'Now now, my dear, you really must not excite yourself in this way. You are overworked, that is all, and lost the proper perspective. It is not as though Huckleberry is not expendable. As I always say, you can't make an omelette without bereaving a few chickens, ha ha ha, and we must expect a few casualties when we train our new recruits. Anyway, Sophia has been commended to the Governor's care by the highest possible authority, so we must be as helpful as possible and ensure that she learns the ropes. The Governor would not like to hear that his young protégé was fired on her first day here, would he? You want to make sure that you are not going to be amongst the afore-mentioned casualties, my dear. Just keep an eye on Sophia, and make sure she enjoys herself. Soon her training courses will start, and then she will be off your hands for a while. Now do run along dear, I have a lunch appointment to keep.'

Flossy, although far from satisfied, had no choice but to leave. She was quite shocked that this sort of nepotism was still going on at The Institution. But who was she to question the wisdom of her Elders & Betters? If they wanted her to humour Sophia and let her run riot amongst the banks in the City, fine. Who knows, it might net her that long overdue promotion at last! But she would have to make sure that no one could hold her responsible for whatever criminalities Sophia committed while she was in her care. It was probably safest to ensure that she would not get any opportunities! To keep her out of harm's way, Flossy told Sophia to get acquainted with the various departments of The Institution and the geography of the City. 'Just walk around and get a feel for the place,' she told Sophia. 'Try not to get lost,' she added, unconvincingly.

[Dear Reader! Ten years with The Institution had grievously dented Flossy's faith in humankind; like most staff who survived that long she sought refuge in the desperate cynicism of the wounded idealist. Like so many of her compatriots, she tended to exaggerate the depth of depravity of her species. Far from being the refuge of nepotism that she suspected, The Institution had abandoned such practices some time ago. While it was true that a posh accent, good family background, and privileged education could enormously help to advance the career of a young recruit, this never went so far as to provide jobs for the obviously incompetent – certainly it did not include

the shielding of misfits like Sophia from the fallout of her misdemeanors! So why had Flabbergast refused to countenance Flossy's suggestion that Sophia be removed from her position?

Because Lilith, anxious to ensure that her daughter succeeded at her first posting, had paid the Prime Minister a little visit, and implanted a hypnotic command in his mind, to the effect that her cherished darling was a royal princess in one of the major oil producing countries of the Middle East and had better be treated with kid gloves, on pain of a major diplomatic rift, that's why! As a result of this visitation the Prime Minister telephoned the Governor, who briefed all the heads of department and told them to overlook and hush up whatever inane, insane, or otherwise foreign attitudes and actions Sophia indulged in. Flossy unfortunately was too low in the pecking order to be in on the secret, and was left to wallow in her once again confirmed cynicism.]

Sophia spent a few enjoyable days playing tourist in and around The Institution, getting to know the lay of the land and meeting interesting people. Unfortunately she was unable to track down The Old Lady; all her enquiries were met with either shrugs or incredulous stares, and Flossy had even laughed in her face[7]. However, she did manage to strike up an acquaintance with the head of The Institution's Rodent Reduction Force, Mr Mouser, and The Institution's unofficial self-appointed environmental activist and arboreal freedom fighter, Fridthjof Thorsteinson. Her acquaintance with Mr Mouser remained fleeting for the moment, since he was currently very busy dealing with an outbreak of hamsters. He did promise to drop by for a long chat once the hamster hordes had been subdued.

Sophia had more luck with Fridthjof. She came across him while he was alone in his office, talking animatedly on the telephone.

'Yes, yes, I quite understand, the roots are undermining the building, but surely that is no reason to cut down those trees? It seems to me that there is ample opportunity for a skilled negotiator to come up with a mutually beneficial compromise. I know just the man for the job; don't do anything until I have discussed the matter with Devadorje!' Then he turned to Sophia and smiled. 'You must be the new girl on Flossy's group. Charmed to meet you! What are you doing for lunch today?'

It was the beginning of a fruitful friendship.

7   Preparing the ground in Greenland

Cesare was hanging out in the Laughing Seal, surveying the female clientele, drinking Walrus Chasers, and waiting for his new friend, Jorgen Jorgenson, to show up. He met Jorgenson the night before, while the latter was throwing up near Kleinschmidt's lamppost, and struck up a conversation with the man while helping him home. Once

---

[7]   Mithras had omitted to mention – or perhaps did not know - that The Old Lady had been relegated to the realm of legend by the inhabitants of the City long ago, and was now thought of more as a vague concept than a real person, rather like John Bull or Uncle Sam.

there Jorgenson, who claimed to have excellent connections to the Greenland business community, offered to help Cesare with his project.

'I am an important man, with loads of friends in high places, even in the Landsting,' he boasted drunkenly just before he collapsed into his bed.

Cesare had scribbled down his name and hotel on a notepad, adding that he expected Jorgenson at the hotel bar the next evening at 20:00 hours, and taped the note onto the bathroom mirror. He did not really believe that his new acquaintance was as important as he claimed; still, he might come in useful all the same if he showed up.

Cesare was not unduly concerned. He was enjoying himself hugely, and savoured the experience of having a material body once more. Especially at night – one of the natives had been most accommodating yesterday. He would not really mind staying for a while until the right contact came along. But there was Jorgenson already, waving at him from the bar while ordering a drink.

After an exchange of the usual polite remarks, Jorgenson asked Cesare whether he had been serious the previous night.

'I would not blame you if you had spun me a yarn, it was such a good story and most entertaining.'

Cesare assured him that he had meant every word he said. 'In three years this place will be more popular than Disneyland, you mark my words. And whoever helps the enterprise off to a good start will be in breadsville.'

Jorgenson looked him over carefully. Cesare was good looking and self confident, with the slightly menacing air of a ruthless adventurer, and the demeanour of a successful businessman - just the sort of man who could pull off a mad venture like Greenlandia. Jorgenson decided to play along for the time being.

'I should be very interested in being involved with your venture,' he said. 'Unfortunately, I am not a wealthy man, and would be unable to help much without adequate remuneration …..'

Cesare smiled. He had immediately recognised the man for the corrupt wheeler dealer that he was, and respected him for it. 'We would not dream of taking advantage of your good nature,' he said, and took a heavy golden bracelet, delicately inlaid with precious stones, from his wrist. 'Permit me to present you with this small token of my esteem. Rest assured that your reward will be as awesome as the project that has brought me here. In the meantime, please accept this purse – I don't want you to be out of pocket on our behalf.' The purse contained $50,000 in large denominations; Cesare believed in large gestures. His business practices were perhaps unusual (well, he *had* learned them in Hell) but Jorgenson for one was suitably impressed. He had never met anyone who was prepared to throw around his money on such a scale. This was his big chance, and he was determined not to blow it.

'Look,' he said to Cesare, 'why don't you come to my office tomorrow morning, and I'll introduce you to a few of my business associates who might be of use to you. If you'll excuse me now, I've got to contact them and make sure they can be there tomorrow.'

Cesare smiled and nodded. Things were going well. Perhaps Agrat was right, and bribery and corruption really did work just as well as murder and intrigue. Having nothing better to do for the time being, he took out his tourist guide with enclosed bilingual dictionary and attempted to chat up a gorgeous brunette who was propping up the bar.

'Inuugujoq! Qanoq ateqarpit[8]?'

'Your pronunciation is atrocious, stranger boy', she answered in English. 'My name is Cheryl and I like men - are you available?' Cesare assured her that he was extremely available, and plunged headfirst into his usual routine.

In this he was observed by a fur-clad woman in her sixties. He perfectly fitted the description she had received from Judas, and his conversation with Jorgenson, which she had overheard, confirmed the preposterous story Judas told her a few days ago. His call had interrupted an immensely interesting conversation with Fridthjof about the plant psychologist who recently surfaced in London, and she had been impatient to get back to it. But Judas had beseeched her to listen to him, and to put aside their differences.

'You were Laura's best friend, you simply have to help me.' Then he told her that mad story about Laura in a sex movie, and his recruitment by the forces of evil. He told her that he simply did not dare to oppose them openly, since he could not risk that they publicly screened that movie and besmirched Laura's memory. No one would believe that the movie was a fake.

'Ragna you don't know these people! They are completely ruthless and possess unimaginable powers. They must be stopped! You know lots of people in Greenland, surely you can organise some opposition to their plans?' After promising to keep her informed of any new developments he had finally gotten off the telephone.

Now that Judas' story had been corroborated by Cesare, Ragna began to get deeply worried. She loved her country dearly, and the last thing it needed was an amusement park, with millions of visitors disturbing the countryside. But she knew that a large section of the business community would jump at this opportunity to make money. She would have to give this very careful consideration.

Ragna 'the Rational' Sturlusdottir was the last in a long line of Viking philosophers who came from Iceland to Greenland when things got too hectic in the old country. They settled in the Vesterbygd in western Greenland near modern Nuuk, and when most of their fellow settlers succumbed to disease and decadence, they joined a tribe of Inuit and were assimilated. However, they continued to pursue their scientific and philosophical interests, and there were always members of the family who went to Europe – climatic conditions permitting - to study and supply the community at home with books on the newest developments in these fields. Ragna's mother studied Analytical Philosophy and Psychoanalysis in Cambridge and Vienna, and Ragna herself had been to Oxford and Portland State, Oregon. Her famous study on Existentialism rocked the world of Philosophy, and after she published her work on the Inuit concept of Good and Evil, Princeton offered her a professorship. However, she decided to turn her back on the world of Academia to devote herself to environmentalism. Her current

---

[8]   Hello! What is your name?

project was the creation of an arctic hybrid tree[9], which she wanted to plant all over Greenland to combat global warming. Recently Fridthjof Thorsteinson visited her on her small farm near Nuuk, and tried to convince her that genetic engineering was the answer to her problem. She objected to this on ethical grounds, and argued that it was an invasion of the trees' privacy, but Fridthjof maintained that trees had no concept of privacy and that it was therefore impossible to invade it. Being enmeshed in these discussions, Ragna obviously was not in the mood for distractions – but if Judas was right, and she feared he was, swift action was paramount. She decided to enlist the help of several of her friends, who could keep an eye on the Borgia, while she decided what to do about the trees. But it was a confounded nuisance it was all the same!

8   Casanova's Dome-World

Casanova greatly enjoyed his period of freedom roaming the World. After a day in Las Vegas, where he won enough to pay for the rest of his – excessively extravagant – week, he went to Nuuk, London, Paris, and Venice, where he spent his last days in a quiet little Bed & Breakfast to digest his experiences and work out a new plan. Exactly one week after he took leave of Agrat and Judas, he was back in Judas' Manhattan flat, as previously agreed. Agrat could barely contain her excitement; her eyes shone and her expression was eager. 'Well, what have you come up with?' Judas could hardly bear watching it; such touching faith, he thought, what a pity that it will be disappointed.

Meanwhile Casanova set up his laptop, and the first slide of his presentation appeared on screen. It was the title page, and read, 'The Greenlandia Dome-World, a Tranquil Haven for the Stressed and Haunted'. Underneath, there were several subheadings, such as 'Sleeper-Dome', 'Dream-Dome', 'Meditation Refuge', 'Mind Healing', and 'Solitude Crystal'. Agrat looked at him blankly; but he had already passed on to the next screen. 'Dome-World's Basic Concept', it read.

'After my week of mingling with the humans of the current age, I have come to the conclusion that there are mainly two things they are interested in; distraction from their dreary existence, and deliverance from it. My amusement park idea had addressed the first want; a good concept, but perhaps a shade overused of late. And I do admit that our chosen location is not an ideal setting. However, my new idea addresses itself to the second great want of humanity; namely, to escape from the hectic world of work and entertainment to find some genuine peace of mind. I believe this want has never been commercially addressed on a large scale; there are of course plenty of small scale, religiously motivated retreats and meditation centres, but there is nothing on the scale that I propose. Certainly nothing quite so value-free as what I am proposing.

Most such retreats pander to a particular ideological system of thought, eg Buddhism or Catholicism, and are run by people who are committed to that ideology. Consequently people who go to such retreats have to submit to an ideology-soaked

---

[9]   It is extremely difficult to grow trees of any size in the arctic; the so called woods that are mentioned in the Icelandic sagas were composed of trees only a few feet tall. Even these small trees (alder, birch, juniper, and willow) only grow in a few sheltered areas in Greenland.

atmosphere for the duration of their visit. Many do so only because they are desperate for some peace of mind; I believe there are millions more who will come to the sort of retreat that I am proposing, a retreat that sells serenity without ideology, and does not seek to convert visitors to a set of beliefs they would reject if they were less desperate.

Now, let me explain a few details. I propose we erect several huge domes on the permanent ice of Greenland. Each dome will be built on a platform of wood; the platform itself will rest on stilts, rather like buildings do in Venice. There will be some space between the surface of the ice and the platform to ensure that the ice will not melt underneath it. The domes themselves will be made of special, crystal like glass in the style of an igloo. For each activity – eg sleeping, meditating, eating, etc – there will be a separate dome; all domes will be connected by glass-covered walkways. The setting of these domes will be an expanse of ice, surrounded by a circle of mountains, if possible. We will ask Cesare to look out for a suitable location. Greenlandia will be completely isolated from all other life, and connected to the outside world only via a small train to Nuuk. I have made a rough sketch of what it will look like.' Casanova produced the next screen, which depicted a flat white area, surrounded by rugged mountains. Several large, and a number of smaller domes, were set at the centre of the scene. The sky was black, with lots of bright stars, and a full moon was rising across the mountain range.

'Can you imagine laying in one of these domes, in total silence, completely alone, with the stars above you, watching the moon slowly move across the sky?' Casanova sounded almost lyrical, so caught up was he in his vision. 'Can you imagine a better setting for cleansing your soul of evil, for removing from your mind all the info debris that clutters up your mind? Where better to go if your heart seeks solace from the ever increasing clamour of the world? We shall build a haven for career-cripples who are not prepared to drop out of the rat-race completely, and need to re-load their batteries for yet another year of strenuous struggle. While the larger domes will be used for communal activities, the smaller ones will be reserved for the sleepers and dreamers, so that they may find peace beneath the starry sky.'

Judas was getting interested in the scheme against his better judgement. He caught himself longing for just such a place as Casanova was describing, and discovered in his heart a deep desire to lie in one of the small domes and dream of Laura, dream of a time when his soul was unsullied and he still had everything to look forward to.

While Judas was thus daydreaming, Casanova moved on to describe the purposes of the individual domes of Greenlandia. 'Each Sleeper-Dome will contain a central high-based bed, on which the sleeper rests. The base contains technical equipment that monitors the vital life functions of the sleeper, and ensures he is undisturbed by dreams. The Dreamer-Domes are similar, except that the equipment is programmed to ensure positive dreams.'

'How can you possibly ensure that a person only has positive dreams,' asked Judas, struggling to escape from the spell that Casanova's words had woven around him.

'We will prepare each dreamer in a session preceding the dream-time; this may be achieved with the aid of music, poetry, and perfumes; a sort of brainwashing, you might say. If the dreamer consents, we will inject him with drugs to ensure that the effect will continue throughout a long session; otherwise we will have to periodically awake the dreamer for re-conditioning. Lastly, we will monitor the dreamers' brainwave patterns, and awake them immediately at the onset of a bad dream. There will be special aromatic oils diffused in the domes, and piped music may be employed if the dream threatens to turn bad. Of course we cannot absolutely guarantee that the dreamer will enjoy a specified period of good dreams; but we can guarantee that we provide a better chance of this than anybody else. Moreover,' Casanova added, 'remember that Greenlandia will never actually have to function. We shall transmogrify it to Hell before it will ever be used. All we need to do is convince the financial community that the retreat will be viable.'

Judas nodded; he had almost forgotten the whole project was a sham, so caught up had he become in the plan. However, he did have another objection.

'I can understand that you would want an amusement park in Hell to attract customers, but a dome-world? Who would want that in Hell?'

Agrat explained that transmogrification would take care of that. 'We never envisaged to transfer the entire retreat as it will exist in Greenland to Hell; rather, we plan to transmogrify the entire complex to Hell, where it will be re-assembled according to a building plan my colleagues are currently working on. The important thing is that we got the material particles to work with.'

'So why don't you just go somewhere like New York and steal a few already existing buildings? Oh yes, the location; you said it had to be in Greenland. If you transmogrified the buildings that currently exist from Greenland -'

'Exactly, there would not be a single igloo left on the whole island! I am glad to see you are finally catching on,' Agrat completed his sentence. Then she turned to Casanova, and told him that she, at least, was convinced that his new plan would work, and that he could cut short his presentation. 'I am sure you have thought everything out very carefully, there is no need for me to double-check it all.'

Casanova nodded, somewhat disappointed, since he had rather looked forward to waxing lyrically about the other domes as well, but since Agrat was not noted for her patience he knew better than to insist.

The next item on their action plan was to recruit a banker with some clout and prestige who would entice the banking community to support the project financially. They also needed to find a location for Greenlandia and start to build some of the domes, since the banking community was certain to be much more likely to lend support to the project if something tangible had already been achieved. And, of course, they needed to continue building up their start-up capital. It was agreed that Agrat would focus on the fleecing of billionaires for capital, Casanova would find a suitable banker and manage the finance angle of the project, and Cesare would remain in Greenland and deal with all matters that pertained to the building of Greenlandia. Judas was told to remain on stand-by in case he was needed, and to otherwise get on with his own affairs as usual.

9   Stress Lucozade, Rodent Economist extraordinaire

Had it not been for Stress Lucozade, Sophia would have made friends with the Mouser much earlier than she did, and met The Old Lady before Casanova found a banker to put together a syndicated loan consortium, thus giving The Old Lady some time to warn the banking community off the Greenlandia project; but alas, the Mouser was occupied with a plague of hamsters that was mysteriously overrunning The Institution.

The problem began when Stress Lucozade, a whiskey-swilling, sandy-haired lover of rodents, was given employment in the Information Department of The Institution. Having been expelled for acute alcoholism by his alma mater Cambridge three weeks before his final exams, Stress had been obliged to forge his degree papers and applied for jobs with all the major financial institutions. Perhaps surprisingly - for people who innocently associate the City with business acumen and robust common sense - he received several offers. He chose to accept the one from The Institution because of its central location and spacious vaults.

Stress studied Economics and the Environment and was forever trying to improve the human condition and his own financial position by pioneering research work in the field of rodent economics. He considered the rodent to be one of the last under-utilised resources on earth, and felt it his duty to convince the world of the potential benefits of human-rodent co-operation. While still at university he distinguished himself with the introduction of the 'Student Pet-Rat', a rat specifically bred and trained for life as a pet for students and other people unable to keep larger animals. In addition to providing the warmth and companionship that the modern city dweller had come to expect from a pet, the rats ate all leftover food found on floors and furniture, including the bits of mouldy biscuits under the bed. As though this was not enough, they also held spiders and cockroaches at bay, and guarded the premises against intruders when their owners were out. Given these considerable advantages of the pet rat, no one was surprised that Stress managed to sell enough of them to put himself through graduate school (only a one-year course, but still!).

Buoyed up by this success, he immediately started on another project, which involved training gerbils to detect bombs in packages and letters. Usually dogs performed this service, but Stress figured that gerbils needed less food than dogs, and were therefore a low-cost alternative. Moreover, due to their small body weight gerbils were less likely to set off bombs if they accidentally stepped on a letter. However, unfortunately he was unable to duplicate the success he had had with his Pet-Rats; the time of the Sniffer-Gerbil had not yet come. He only managed to sell a single specimen, to the Chairman of the Board of Bog Bank, Sir Wilbur Wellbeloved, who purchased Freddy, the most intelligent of the Sniffer-Gerbils, who was now doing sterling duty at the bank's head office in the City.

Stress had barely started his job at The Institution when he put in place the arrangements for stage 1 of his current project in one of the sub-vaults, namely a share-cropping scheme involving Homing Hamsters. Being acutely aware of the prejudices that employees can encounter from their employers when they set up such projects, Stress decided to keep the venture secret for the time being. Deep within the bowels of The Institution, away from prying eyes, he built his research laboratory.

Hamster are noble little beasties. They spend their time roaming the countryside, searching for nuts and seeds which they carry home in their cheeks, and place in storage pits for usage in the winter. Although it is true that they occasionally stray into fields and co-harvests together with the farmer, they usually restrict themselves to the collection of grass seeds and grain kernels near country roads and amidst the brambles that line our railway tracks. Stress calculated that ten properly trained hamsters could collect each summer enough seeds that would otherwise go to waste to supply a child of eight with bread or porridge for an entire year, in addition to the food they needed for their own survival. Thus he conceived Project Homing Hamsters.

The objective of the Homing Hamster Project was to teach the rodents to collect food faster and more efficiently, and to motivate them to return the collected food to a central collection point, where they would be rewarded for their efforts. Using Pavlovian motivation techniques, Stress soon trained the hamsters to return to the research vault whenever he blew the special homing whistle he kept for that purpose. Every evening before he left work he opened their cages in the sub-vault, so they could roam freely through the premises of The Institution to search for sandwich crumbs and stale crisps, and each morning he blew the whistle and locked them into their cages again after they returned.

The project was successful – and remained undetected – in every respect, and the hamsters multiplied quickly; soon Stress would be able to move on to stage 2 of the project, which consisted of re-locating the hamsters to the countryside, and placing them in the care of a full-time hamster-handler who could continue the project on a commercial scale. Then disaster struck.

10   While Thérèse goes shopping, Fleabrunckle spins intrigues

Thérèse Thermidor was in a great mood. She had just received her annual bonus, and she was rich rich rich!!!! Of course, this would have been a good time to balance her chequebook and pay off all those debts - she actually toyed with the idea for a moment or two – but then she decided to fly to Paris for a long weekend of shopping instead.

Life had been good to her, she reflected as she scrutinised her appearance in the large mirror of her hotel suite the following day. She had lots of lustrous black hair, green eyes, classic features, a perfect complexion, and a body with all the right curves – oh yes, she was beautiful! Only yesterday Alessandro had told her so, Alessandro who headed Customer Services at Bog Bank and was so very boring, and so very devoted to her. And she was not only beautiful, she was also very talented! Fleabrunckle had not given her that fat bonus for being beautiful, but because she was the best damn derivatives[10] dealer in the world, and had made huge sums of money for the bank ever since she started to work there. She was good at making money, and she loved to spend it, and after all, why not? There was plenty more where it came from! She would have a

---

[10]   Derivatives are financial products that 'derive' from primary products like stocks and shares; for example, a 'future' may consist of a number of shares that are traded with the understanding that the purchase will take place at a specified date in the future.

simply wonderful weekend with her friend Claudette, shopping and dining and going to the theatre and, last but not least, bewitching every man she encountered. Because she was Thérèse Thermidor, and the world was where it always had been and where it belonged, at her feet! Throwing a hand-kiss at her reflection, she grabbed her purse and went to meet Claudette at the reception.

Thérèse was born 26 years ago in Paris. Bored with school, she drifted into an apprenticeship with one of the major French banks (her family had pulled a few strings), and graduated into the dealing room by the time she was twenty. When Gingrich Fleabrunckle recruited her for Bog Bank Bros two years ago she was considered to be one of the best derivatives dealers in Paris. She was also known as the most spendthrift dealer in Paris, which – unbeknown to her - had played a not inconsiderable part in Fleabrunckle's decision to recruit her.

She quickly rose to become the star among Bog Bank's dealers, and when Fleabrunckle moved on to the Syndicated Loans Department she was offered his job, and soon assembled a team of equally bright traders under her auspices. Fleabrunckle continued to keep an eye on the team and occasionally interfered; but she always had the final word, and when she rejected several of his choices for the derivatives team he accepted her decision without demur. Her team of dealers was the best in the City, if not in Europe – and they were all paid accordingly.

This suited Thérèse excellently, because she always needed money. She loved shopping, and always bought at least two of everything. She also had a habit of paying for the purchases of her impecunious friends, who had to subsist on measly £50,000 a year or so and would have starved to death if Thérèse had not helped them out – that's what they claimed, anyway. Outside of the dealing room Thérèse was incredibly gullible and good natured, and plenty of people took advantage of it. So with one thing and another, no matter how much she earned, she was always in debt. Luckily for her, she always managed to find a man who offered to pay her debts; her father, her mother's current husband, an ex-boyfriend, and once even an old man she met at a funeral – someone always rescued her from destitution.

When Gingrich Fleabrunckle hired her he bought her spendthrift habits as much as her talents as a dealer. No sooner had she arrived at Bog Bank's impressive head office in Threadneedle Street, than he began to deepen and reinforce her proclivity for wasting money. He gave her introductions to various exclusive stores and encouraged them to grant her large store card limits, suggested to various exclusive charities to ask her for large donations (she always gave generously), and took her to the races and casinos, and other venues that specialised in separating people from their cash. After two years of this Thérèse's habits were like those of royalty and film stars rolled into one; she had a huge salary, and an even greater annual bonus, but remained deeply in debt. Just like the rest of Bog Bank's trading team. Just like Fleabrunckle had intended. Unlike Thérèse and her colleagues, he was playing a very long game.

While Thérèse was shopping in Paris, Fleabrunckle had lunch with John de Bourg, the Treasurer of the Bank of Libraria. The two men were old friends, and de Bourg – being an honest simple man – had more than once benefited from Fleabrunckle financial advice, which helped his career immeasurably. Such selfless friendship was rare in the City, and de Bourg was very grateful to Fleabrunckle. On this occasion Fleabrunckle was trying to convince him to set up a derivatives trading team at Libraria.

'It's easy money, with the right team you could triple the bank's profits within a few years!'

But de Bourg was hesitant. 'As you know, Bank of Libraria was founded during the Great Depression as a bank for librarians, and to this day the board is entirely composed of retired librarians and archivists. The bank's conservatism and risk aversion are simply unbelievable; they never take an avoidable risk. It would be almost impossible to convince the board to build up a derivatives trading team; besides, good dealers are hard to come by – and I don't even have enough experience to distinguish between good and bad ones!'

But Fleabrunckle dismissed these difficulties as mere excuses. Hey, aren't I your friend, and can't I help you pick a good team?'

'My dear Gingrich, how could I possibly take advantage of you like that! If a good dealer becomes available, you may need him for Bog Bank! You can't possibly jeopardise your own career just to help Bank of Libraria make some easy money.'

'I may not be as disinterested as you think. I am considering to move to another bank in the medium term, and exchange my current hectic job at Bog Bank with a more leisurely one at another bank – perhaps even the Bank of Libraria? Anyway, there is no great need to hurry. All you have to do is suggest to your board at regular intervals that the bank could do with a successful team of derivatives traders, and I'll do the rest.'

This was not the first lunch Fleabrunckle and de Bourg had, nor the last. The subject of a derivatives trading team was regularly brought up by Fleabrunckle, and slowly but surely de Bourg, and through him the board of the Bank of Libraria, began to warm to the idea. Fleabrunckle was biding his time.

11   The Entrapment of Gilligan Wang

Gilligan Wang was the rich – the excessively rich – son of a Chinese warlord who made millions in the drug trade in the seventies; Gilligan turned them into billions by dint of prudent investment. At the time of this story he spent most of his days socialising and throwing parties; especially his murder mystery parties – complete with real murders – were justly famous. He was also destined to be the next victim of Agrat's capital accumulation spree. A bit of research informed her that Gilligan was an avid collector of dream-stones, and she decided to use this obsession to relieve him of his fortune.

Now dream-stones, as everybody knows, are stones whose surface naturally exhibits a pattern which could be said to resemble a picture, a portrait perhaps, or even a landscape. There are special dream-stone hunters, who search for them in wild and rocky regions, and when they find one, sign it with their name and give it a title. Some Chinese connoisseurs pay large sums of money for stones that depict a particularly realistic face, or an especially beautiful landscape. When such connoisseurs manage to acquire a really fine dream-stone specimen, they not infrequently change their name, for example from

'Charley Jia' to 'Owner of the Translucent Waterfall at Sunset Dream-Stone, formerly known as Charley Jia'. There are numerous ballads and stories connected with the finding and coveting of special dream-stones, which are full of deceit and theft and even murder. But none has more stories attached to it than the Exalted Heavenly Dream-Stone, and it was this dream-stone Gilligan Wang had set his heart on to acquire.

The Exalted Heavenly Dream-Stone is ancient, and had allegedly been stolen thousands of years ago from the Jade Emperor by the Great Sage Monkey-God. Since then it has been sighted about once every century, and dream-stone connoisseurs all over China have hunted for it through the ages. Innumerable murders and lesser crimes have been committed for its possession, and Gilligan coveted it with an unquenchable desire. Once she decided to defraud Gilligan by exploiting his desire for the Exalted Heavenly Dream-Stone, Agrat set about to locate it, and found it in the San Antonio mansion of Ernie T Dinckleschwartz VII, the famous Texan collector of oriental antiques. Since Ernie's grandfather had acquired the Exalted Heavenly Dream-Stone on the black market in Yokohama, from a Japanese moneylender who sold it illegally as an unredeemed pledge before the redemption period was up, having accepted it as security from a soldier who stole it during the rape of Nanking, Agrat felt no compunction at stealing it forthwith, and depositing it in a bank vault in Hong Kong for safekeeping.

Gilligan Wang immediately granted Agrat an audience when he received a short note from her, intimating that she had the Exalted Heavenly Dream-Stone in her keeping and was willing to trade for it. During their meeting, which was stormy and full of insults, Gilligan absolutely refused to pay the price Agrat was demanding, namely, half his fortune, including his extensive gold reserves hidden in Taiwan, which she worryingly knew about. Since he proved so intractable, Agrat made him another offer.

She knew that Gilligan, in addition to his love for dream-stones and parties, had another great weakness. He loved dares and bets of all sorts, and was never able to resist a challenge. She was certain he would accept her offer, and was proved right. After they visited her bank, and obtained proof that she indeed owned the Exalted Heavenly Dream-Stone, and to his bank, to instruct them to pay Agrat half of Gilligan's fortune (inclusive of the gold reserves) if Agrat were to present a cheque from him for that amount, they flew off to Scandinavia where the challenge was to take place. After landing they bought some supplies, rented a jeep, and drove to a region near the centre of Scandinavia[11]. There, atop a tall wooded mountain, grew the giant ash tree that Agrat had chosen as the site of Gilligan's challenge.

The deal she proposed to Gilligan was simple. She had hidden the Exalted Heavenly Dream-Stone at the roots of the ash; if Gilligan could find it within three days without help from outside of the area, he would be allowed to keep it. If he did not succeed in finding the Exalted Heavenly Dream-Stone, he would pay Agrat half his fortune for it. Gilligan liked the deal, because he would end up as the owner of the Exalted Heavenly Dream-Stone, no matter who won the bet. Besides, he was quietly confident that he would find the Exalted Heavenly Dream-Stone. Although the tree was big, the Exalted Heavenly Dream-Stone, too, was large, a foot tall and almost half as

---

[11]   I can't reveal the precise location, because Kalle, the Master Met Gnome, threatened to hang me up by my entrails onto one of the higher branches of Yggdrasill if I did. He values his privacy.

wide! How hard could it be to find the Exalted Heavenly Dream-Stone amidst the ash's roots? If Agrat could hide it there, he could find it!

As soon as Agrat left, Gilligan set up his campsite and considered how best to tackle the job. He thought it would be easiest to fell the tree, and then to rummage about its roots for the stone. But as soon as the little axe he had taken along to chop firewood landed the first stroke, the ash screamed as if in great pain, and lashed out at him with many branches; to his horror, green blood oozed from the wound. Gilligan sat down at a safe distance from the tree and considered his options. Since he could not cut the tree down, could he perhaps dig it up? But would the tree stand for it? Moreover, it would take a lot longer than three days. He began to look amidst the tree's roots half-heartedly, conscious that he was not welcome.

In this he was observed by a small gnome, about a foot high, who finally accosted him and introduced himself as Kalle, the Master Met Gnome of the area.

'Hello there! You look troubled. Would you care for a taste of my latest batch of met? It is bound to cheer you up!'

Gilligan thanked him, but declined. He had other things on his mind. 'I have only three days to find the Exalted Heavenly Dream-Stone at the roots of this ash tree, and have no idea of how to go about it.'

'Oh, is that why you were attacking the ash with your little axe just now?' Kalle replied. 'You need chainsaws for a big tree like that, and several lumberjacks, you know. However, there is an easier way to come by the stone, and I can help you - provided you are prepared to return the favour, of course.'

Gilligan was all ears, and promised to repay him with any favour he might ask for.

'Good good. Now listen carefully. The stone is not outside of, but within, one of the roots of this tree. You can only find it by going inside of the tree. I shall give you a special potion, which will reduce you in size, and allow you to go inside of the ash. In return, you must promise to help me brew my next batch of midsummer-night met.'

Gilligan promised with alacrity, but was a little taken aback when the gnome asked what forfeit he suggested. Gilligan had not thought of giving any sort of forfeit, indeed, reneging on promises had always been one of his specialties. However, the gnome explained that forfeits were designed to stop people from getting out of bargains they had struck, and no one in Great Ash Country would dream of ever concluding a deal without a forfeit. He suggested Gilligan's right hand as an appropriate forfeit, considering the importance of their agreement. Gilligan stared at Kalle incredulously.

'You demand my right hand?'

'Well, only if you don't keep to your side of the bargain,' the gnome replied. 'If you try to run off with the Exalted Heavenly Dream-Stone without helping me with my next batch of midsummer-night met, your right hand will shrivel up and die.'

Superstitious mumbo-jumbo, Gilligan thought. But if that's what it took …. Accordingly he promised Kalle his right hand as a forfeit if he failed to keep his side of the bargain. Thus satisfied, Kalle gave him a small thimble made of an acorn, which contained a few drops of brown liquid, and advised him that the potion would shrink his size, and transport him from and to a little chamber inside the ash tree for exactly twenty-four hours upon drinking it.

'During these twenty-four hours you can roam all over the ash tree and look for the stone, but you must return to the chamber before your time is up. If you are not in the chamber and return to your original size while inside the tree you will die a horrible death.'

Gilligan had no sooner drunk the potion than he fell fast asleep. When he awoke he found himself inside a small wooden chamber. There was a dim greenish-brown light about him, and almost complete silence, except for a faint gushing noise, like a creek at the far bottom of the garden. He did not doubt that he was inside the ash tree, and walked down one of a number of wooden passages that led from the chamber, intent on exploration.

Unfortunately the tree remembered him well, and, not having forgiven his axe stroke, was determined to trap Gilligan inside and never let him out again. Gilligan spent hours exploring passages, but never got anywhere. Sooner or later every passage he followed led to a dead-end, so that he had to retrace his steps back to the chamber he had awoken in. Having finally explored every passage that led from the chamber, he sat down on the floor to take stock of his situation. Since there was obviously no passage to lead him to the stone, he decided to cut his losses and return to the chamber to quietly wait until his twenty-four hours were up. That's when he realised that he could no more leave the tree than find the stone, because suddenly *all* passages were blocked up, including the one that led to the chamber. Upon this realisation Gilligan began to weep, bitterly regretting his folly that led him into the tree.

'Woe is me for having trusted Kalle the Met Gnome,' he wailed, 'double woe to have made a bargain with Agrat, and triple woe for having developed an interest in dream-stones!'

He continued in this vein for some considerable time[12], but just before he had reached his penultimate woe, a bark beetle happened to meander by, and when he saw Gilligan's pitiable state stopped by for a little chat. Predictably, Gilligan had no compunction to pour his heart out to the beetle, and ask for help and advice. The beetle considered the matter for a while, all the while grooming himself to aid his cognitive powers (which, it must be said, were but slight), and finally offered up a plan.

'I shall lead you to the stone, as it happens I know exactly where Agrat has hidden it. After that I will help you return to the exit chamber, and, if necessary, gnaw a way into it.' However, he demanded a stiff price for his services. 'Once the Ash finds out that I have helped you escape from your doom, and enabled you to make off with the stone, she will be furious, and I shall no longer be able to live here. Therefore I want you to take me with you when you leave. Before I help you, you must promise to make me your companion in all things. I will eat off your plate, drink from your cup, sleep in your

---

[12]   Ever anxious to appease my publisher who can be most eloquent on the subject of costly paper and expensive printing processes, I cut short these Gilliganesque wailings, in the interest of keeping this narrative as short as is practically possible.

bed, and watch television from your favourite armchair. We shall be best friends and never part again. As to the forfeit …….'

Gilligan sighed; why did folk around here have to be so terribly suspicious?

'The forfeit,' concluded the beetle, 'shall be your left hand, seeing as the right one is already taken.'

Although Gilligan was not exactly happy about the prospect of having to share the rest of his life with a bark beetle, he consoled himself that beetles, after all, had very short life spans, and that living with one had to be preferable to dieing inside of the vindictive ash tree before the day was out. He therefore agreed to both deal and forfeit, and followed Anastasius (as the beetle liked to be addressed) down the passage whence he had emerged. The passage had been stopped-up by the tree, of course, but Anastasius chewed through the blockage and on they went. After two hours of walking down passages, intermittently interrupted by the beetle's mandibular activities, they finally came to the chamber which contained the Exalted Heavenly Dream-Stone.

The chamber was quite small, barely able to contain both Gilligan and Anastasius and the Exalted Heavenly Dream-Stone, which rested on a green velvet pillow on a carved wooden pedestal. Overcome with reverence and awe, Gilligan gazed at the object of his lifelong devotion. The Exalted Heavenly Dream-Stone was about twice the size of his head[13], and depicted a landscape of craggy pine trees on a rocky mountain range overlooking a deep gorge in the background, and meadows and forests and a lake in the foreground, all topped off with a cloud-filled sky. Its colours were white and grey and blue and green. It bore the signature of the Emerald Maiden, a famous and fabulous divine artist who was closely associated with the Jade Emperor.

Gilligan reverently approached the Exalted Heavenly Dream-Stone, wrapped it in his duffle coat, and put it into the rucksack he brought along for the purpose. In doing so he sealed his fate, for he omitted the three precautions necessary when taking a dream-stone without inciting the wrath of its guardian. He should have firstly, before even touching the Exalted Heavenly Dream-Stone, knelt down before it and ask its forgiveness for removing it from its esteemed abode; secondly, he should have wrapped the Exalted Heavenly Dream-Stone in ancient cream-coloured funeral silk from the tomb of an emperor of the T'ang dynasty; and thirdly, he should have placed it reverently on a lacquered tray made from acacia wood to carry away. But Gilligan had violated all these conditions, and the Dream-Stone Guardian officially in charge of the Exalted Heavenly Dream-Stone, one Adamantina, was livid with rage at this lack of decorum, and vowed eternal vengeance. However, Gilligan was blissfully unaware of his many transgressions. Happy in his possession of the Exalted Heavenly Dream-Stone, he followed Anastasius back up through the passages that led to the exit chamber. Exactly twenty-four hours after he entered the tree, Gilligan awoke at his campsite again, in the company of Anastasius and clutching the dream-stone.

Gilligan thought he had done rather well; Agrat had given him three days to finish the job, and he found the Exalted Heavenly Dream-Stone in less than twenty-four hours.

---

[13]   While inside the tree, the stone was shrunk, just like Gilligan; it returned to its original size once it left the tree.

With his arms wrapped around the Exalted Heavenly Dream-Stone, fondly rehearsing the proud and boastful words he would address to Agrat upon her return, he fell asleep that night.

The following morning after breakfast – where Anastasius disgusted Gilligan by eating off his plate and drinking from his mug, at one point falling into it and having to be rescued - Gilligan decided to have another look at his prize. He placed it on his folded duffle coat, and gazed into its depths, entranced by the intricate landscape it depicted. He suddenly remembered an old story he once read, which claimed that given the right conditions a person could enter a dream-stone and explore its hidden secrets. Unfortunately the story had not specified what the right conditions for entering a dream-stone were; he sighed; he would have dearly loved to enter into the world of the beautiful Exalted Heavenly Dream-Stone.

[Wise reader! Are you pained and surprised to read that Gilligan Wang, having only just escaped from the ash tree, dreamed about entering yet another alien realm, where he might get lost and trapped forever? Alas, he simply displayed that curious human tendency to forget immediately whatever lesson a kindly fate cares to bestow. Moreover, having managed to extricate himself from one predicament, he innocently assumed that he could do so again should the occasion arise. Therefore his entrapment and miraculous deliverance from the ash tree, far from serving as a warning to the hapless Wang, only reinforced his already inflated self-regard, and convinced him of his special status as Fortuna's favourite child!]

While Gilligan thus pondered ancient dream-stone lore, a beauteous maiden was ascending up the mountain. Upon reaching the summit and ash tree, and Gilligan who was camping at a safe distance from it, she offered him her greeting, and sat next to him to admire the Exalted Heavenly Dream-Stone. Commenting on its beauty, she asked Gilligan whether he had been inside yet.

'Oh, that is just a silly fairy tale,' he replied.

'You mean to say you are in possession of the most famous and mysterious dream-stone in the entire Middle Kingdom, and do not know this basic concept of dream-stone lore? Of course you can enter into a dream-stone - how do you think they got their name? If this was my dream-stone, I would enter immediately to explore its mysteries.'

Gilligan, hapless fool that he was, took the bait, and implored her to impart to him her dream-stone knowledge. At first she pretended to be most unwilling, and asserted that a boor like himself, who dared to touch a dream-stone in such an appalling state of ignorance, did not deserve such knowledge. However, as he continued to plead most eloquently, and promised her ever increasing treasure if only she would impart to him her secrets, she finally relented and agreed to tell him about the Exalted Heavenly Dream-Stone, provided he did her a favour in return.

When he heard the word 'favour', Gilligan hesitated. He preferred to settle his debts in cold hard cash. But the maiden would not hear of it.

'If you want me to tell you how to get into the Exalted Heavenly Dream-Stone, you will have to promise to help me plant ash seeds for the next pria[14].' This sounded pretty bizarre to him, but in the ash tree country weirdness seemed quite normal, so after some hesitation he promised the maiden to help her plant the seeds. 'Regarding the forfeit,' the maiden continued – Gilligan groaned. Not again! – 'I think your head would be fitting.'

That was too much for him. 'My head? Who do you think you are? What about a nice mink coat, or a Cadillac?'

The maiden regarded him scornfully. 'If you value your head at the prize of a coat or a Cadillac, then that is your affair. I insist on the head. A forfeit is intended to stop you from reneging on the bargain. If you intend to keep to the agreement, then you should not mind any forfeit, since you will not have to pay it. The secret you ask me to impart is of the greatest importance, and much exceeds your head in value! Do not expect to obtain it cheaply.'

What was Gilligan to do? The maiden was clearly highly strung and arrogant, and unlikely to tell him anything unless he agreed to her stipulations. Trusting once more to his good luck, he assented to both seed planting and forfeit.

Satisfied with his compliance, the maiden proceeded to enlighten him. 'The procedure for entering a dream-stone is as follows. Eat three tablespoons of honey, bow low three times before the Exalted Heavenly Dream-Stone, and intone in a loud voice 'Mutabor, mutabor, mutabor!' Then you will find that you can step into the Exalted Heavenly Dream-Stone without further ado. When you wish to leave, repeat the procedure.'

Gilligan was surprised by the simplicity of the procedure, but, being a bit of a fool when it came to dream-stones, did not hesitate to put it into practice. He distinctly remembered that his food supply included some honey - clearly his luck was with him. He followed the procedure carefully, tried to step into the Exalted Heavenly Dream-Stone – and found that he was able to enter it without difficulty.

12   Cesare meets Nuliajuq

Cesare was waiting in front of the Skraelingshaven Mutual Branch in Kolonihaven for Cheryl, his new friend, who was a bank manager. She turned up half an hour late, explaining that she had to evict a drunken customer who refused to understand that cheques bounced if they were written against an overdrawn bank account.

'This is such a dump,' she said to Cesare as they went for dinner. 'I'd leave like a shot, but it is so difficult to get a job abroad, I think I am stuck here. My only hope is to escape as a visa-bride; are you, by any chance, still unmarried?'

---

[14]   A pria is a period lasting three years; the maiden loved to use obscure and recondite term (rather like me, actually), and hoped that Gilligan did not know for how long he was committing himself. However, she did not really intend to take him up on the favour – she intended to trap him in the Dream-Stone for all eternity!

Cesare wondered whether his marriage to Charlotte was still valid after all these years, and concluded that it was not. But before he could answer, Cheryl had already moved on to the next subject.

She wanted to know where he was going to take her for the evening, and before he could think of an answer suggested the Laughing Seal, which held a dance night every Wednesday – or couldn't he dance? Currently the Jacuzzi was all the rage. Cesare was not familiar with that particular dance, but did not let that bother him. Cheryl was sure to teach him.

At eight o'clock it was already dark, and the Laughing Seal was filling up quickly. The music sounded unfamiliar to Cesare, but it had a good beat to it, and he looked forward to having a try at dancing to it. The couples already dancing certainly looked as though they were enjoying themselves; the dance was fast, sensual, and allowed plenty of physical contact between the partners. His kind of dance! To Cheryl's surprise and delight he picked up the basics very quickly, and was soon gyrating with the best of them. When they took a short break for drinks he told her that he used to be quite a dancer in his youth, discretely omitting that this was six centuries ago.

While downing their Walrus Chasers Cesare noticed a young woman dancing all alone at the back of the room, where the light was dimmest. He had never seen such grace, such passion, such energy, in a dancer. Upon enquiry Cheryl told him that he was watching Nuliajuq, the best dancer in Nuuk, if not in Greenland.

'Poor thing, dancing is all she's got.'

'Anyone who can dance like that is not a 'poor thing' in my book!'

'You speak from ignorance. No one who knows her fails to pity Nuliajuq. All day long she hides behind the curtains of her room, watching people walk by, crying and cursing her fate and wishing she was dead. Only at night she comes alive, going to dark places to dance, where people can't see her face. All the locals know her and respect her need for privacy, but sometimes a tourist or foreign business man becomes enamoured with her dancing, and approaches her in the darkness, and dances with her. Sometimes they insist on taking Nuliajuq out to a restaurant or even their hotel room, not knowing any better, and are mortified when they see her face – one ran screaming from a café! Even her grandfather, who dotes on her, can scarcely bear to look at her. Do not allow yourself to become bewitched by her dancing, my dear stranger; you will only get hurt, unless indeed you are a stronger man than anyone in Greenland. Don't think I say this out of jealousy; there are many men I can have if I desire them, but Nuliajuq can have no one. I would not begrudge her a man who could bear her looks, but I doubt that you have such strength.'

Cesare was intrigued; only consideration for Cheryl, who he after all had a date with, kept him from approaching the mysterious girl. But Cheryl had seen the signs before; she sighed, and told him to go to Nuliajuq if he so wished, but warned him to deal kindly with the girl, and conceal his revulsion as best he could when the time came, if he valued the goodwill of anyone in town.

'She may be ugly, but she is our very special pet, and much loved, although she does not believe it.' She sadly watched him make his way towards the girl; he was so handsome, and so charming, and so rich! Ah well, he probably would not have married her anyway! Weaving her way between the customers waiting to be served at the bar she caught the eye of a young American and smiled. 'Hello, I am Cheryl, and I like men! Would you care to dance?'

Meanwhile Cesare reached Nuliajuq, who was dancing alone in the dark, entirely self-absorbed. He tried to take her hand, but she turned from him, and danced further away into a darker corner. Undeterred, he followed, dancing all the while, and began to dance around her, mixing his newly acquired Jacuzzi steps with the movements he had learned in his youth. Persistently he wooed her with his dance, which was rapidly turning into an elegant and erotic courtship ritual, until she finally relented and let him take her hand.

'Your dance is most strange,' she told him after a while. 'Where did you learn it?'

'A long time ago in Italy; but truly, my dance is nothing compared to yours; your whole life seems contained in it.'

'You don't know how right you are, my dance is my whole life.' They spent all evening dancing, but shortly before midnight she excused herself to go to the toilet, and then the lights turned on because it was closing time and she had vanished.

The following morning Cesare went to see Jorgenson in his office. In addition to Jorgenson three men were waiting for him. Thorvald Karsfeldt owned a construction company, Inger Christiansen was a shipping magnate, and Hans Schulze owned a supermarket chain. Jorgenson had already briefed them about the venture, and they were very excited about it.

'This is the hottest thing since the Americans set up their base,' Thorvald enthused. 'You will probably want to bring in your experts from Europe, but there should be plenty the locals can do for you.'

'Cesare assured him that he had the highest regard for the native talent, and would use local expertise and labour whenever possible. First of all he had to find a suitable site – could any of them suggest something? Although no one knew of a site off-hand, they all promised to think of something suitable and meet again soon.

Before parting Cesare enquired whether they could recommend anyone else who he might cultivate to ensure a smooth run for the project, and was advised that he could do no better than befriend old Walgren. He was a retired businessman but still had his fingers in every pie in Greenland. Originally from Sweden, he arrived in Greenland fifty years before, married an Inuit woman, and built up a business empire that included anything from a small airline to reindeer breeding. However, finding an excuse to approach him was not easy.

'You could present yourself as a suitor for his granddaughter, haha, just a joke,' suggested Jorgenson. 'He collects fifteenth century devotional pendants, so offering him an unusual piece for sale might break the ice.' They parted the best of friends, and were determined to ensure every possible success for the venture.

Later that day Cesare reported to Agrat, and mentioned the devotional pendant idea.

'As it happens I just got a hold of a Prayer Nut,' she told him, 'it would make quite a decent bribe for this Walgren chap.' Then she yet again impressed upon Cesare the need for speed; she was worried that he would try to make the project last as long as possible, so as to maximise his time away from Hell. 'Spare no expense, brook no resistance, and get started now, no matter what the difficulties are. Casanova will brief you about his new plan shortly; as soon as you have picked the site, start building. I am sending Imhotep, Anthemius, and Andrea on the same plane as Casanova. They have drawn up the plans, and are ready to adjust them to the site as soon as you have found one. We have negotiated construction deals with Lakehurst in New York and Hodgepodge & Drymble in London, they are ready to begin construction within the month, so we need a site asap. Keep up the good work, and don't seduce too many women – I am told they've all got syphilis!'

'Well, they did not get it from me, I cured mine ages ago!' Cesare retorted angrily.

'That's not what I meant, you fool! Never mind, but try and seduce someone who will be of help with the project, OK? Someone important.'

Twenty-four hours later the Prayer Nut arrived, Cesare placed a telephone call with Mr Walgren, and when he mentioned the nut was immediately invited to tea that afternoon.

Mr Walgren lived in a beautiful old house in Kolonihavnen. The doorbell was answered by the Inuit housekeeper, who silently took his coat and showed him into the drawing room. Mr Walgren, a tall, white-haired gentleman in his late sixties, welcomed him warmly.

'My dear Mr Borgia, you cannot imagine what a pleasure it is for me to welcome a man of your learning,' he told Cesare (who had boned up on fifteenth century devotional pendants overnight and had waxed knowledgeably during their telephone conversation). 'Unfortunately my granddaughter is indisposed and will not be able to join us.'

The round mahogany tea table was already set with sandwiches and cakes, and after the housekeeper brought in the tea Mr Walgren poured it himself.

For the next half hour the discussion centred solely on the subject of prayer nuts, which bored Cesare exceedingly, but he somehow managed to fake an interest for the sake of business. At the appropriate moment he took a small heavily carved wooden box from his pocket, which he opened and passed on to his host.

'This is the item I mentioned on the telephone,' he said. 'I thought you might care to look at it.'

Since he had invited his guest for that express purpose, Mr Walgren needed no prompting to examine the prayer nut. After several minutes of careful examination, aided by a large magnifying glass, he finally exclaimed,

'Upon my honour, Mr Borgia, I have never beheld such a fine specimen, not even in a museum. How ever did you come by this treasure?'

His excitement had attracted attention; Cesare noticed a slight movement behind the curtain that cordoned off what appeared to be an alcove. Ever suspicious of assassins and spies, Cesare jumped up, drew his dagger, and pulled aside the curtain. So swift and silent were his movements, that neither his host nor the lurker behind the curtain were able to prevent him. Thus he found himself face to face with Nuliajuq, in the bright light of the afternoon sun, softened only by lace curtains. Nuliajuq froze and stared at him in terror; Walgren bowed his head in resignation, patiently waiting for the inevitable horrified reaction of his guest – but Cesare smiled.

'So we meet again, my dear,' he said.

13   Further adventures of Sophia in the City

It was the Friday morning before a bank holiday weekend, and Sophia was busy attending introductory courses in her chosen profession. She had already finished a course on the Banking Act, where she learned, inter alia, that two one-eyed people could not set up a bank because of the 'four-eyes principle', that the contract she had signed upon joining The Institution required her absolute secrecy regarding anything at all about her work place, including the quality of the toilet paper, and that anybody suspected of illegal deposit-taking could be dragged out of bed before – but not after - midnight without a warrant and incarcerated in the famous dungeon in the Tower of London without further ado. She should have been worried about her future, having already spilled every available bean about The Institution when she discussed her new job with Mithras – demons are very careless when it comes to keeping secrets – but as usual she assumed that these rules did not apply to her.

Today's series of lectures were conducted by Flossy Pembrokeshire, who was concluding her talk on 'Decorous Banking – the Pythian Approach to Finance' which Sophia understood quite well, given her numerous discussions with her old friend Socrates. Flossy had been emphatic on the need for non-committal phraseology ('never put anything down on paper that can be interpreted in only one way'), and was finishing with an exposé on the advantages of the 'We're all Gentlemen Here' approach to business.

'Style, ladies and gentlemen, is everything in finance. Any idiot can give unsound financial advice, but giving it such that the recipient feels honoured to have obtained it even after it has turned out to be worthless, that boys and girls, requires class! Remember, an incompetent gentleman will still command respect; but a cad, no matter how sound his financial advice might be, will always be despised. That's all for now; after lunch we will turn our attention to the regulators' need for secrecy, and the role of the public in maintaining a competitive banking sector.'

Sophia looked forward to that talk. Flossy had explained all this to her before, but somehow she could not get her mind around it. How could the public chose to deposit their money with a prudent well-run bank rather than an irresponsible basket case, if the regulators refused to give them any information about these banks? All the regulators were prepared to say was that a bank was licensed under the Banking Act, but that was no quality guarantee – plenty of such banks had gone bankrupt. Of course there were several agencies that provided information about financial institutions, but they charged dearly for their services and most people didn't even know they existed. Sophia sighed; banking supervision was much more difficult than she had imagined, so full of concepts too complicated for her to grasp.

Before going to lunch, she nipped into her office to check whether there were any letters or messages. While rooting through her in-box, she overheard a most peculiar conversation of Flossy's on the telephone.

'Listen Stan, I am worried about one of your banks. I have the feeling that it is going down fast, and I am talking Vault-level here! It is imperative that you watch the seven o'clock news tonight. Yes, tonight, absolutely! Goodbye!'

Behind Flossy's back several of her colleagues were grinning knowingly; her longstanding attempts to meet her would-be stud, Stanley Hunzucker, on The Institution's premises, had not escaped their attentions. As one of them explained to Sophia over lunch,

'Rumours have it those two have never yet managed to consummate their affair, something always crops up to intervene. It's good fun listening to Flossy trying to arrange her secret assignations 'in code', so we don't smell a rat. Talking of rats, have you noticed the recent sudden increase in mousetraps in the Feederia ? I wonder if we've got a rodent invasion?'

Sophia was happy to be able to contribute something to the conversation. 'Apparently there has been a mysterious influx of hamsters recently; Mr Mouser is working flat out to get them under control.'

'Who on earth is Mr Mouser?'

'You know, the charming tabby who comes by the office every day. He is the Head of The Institution's Rodent Reduction Force; it even says so on his collar.'

'To tell you the truth, I don't much like cats, and have never looked that closely. By the way, I hear you have got a date with Fridthjof Thorsteinson tonight?'

'Oh, it's not a date really, we are just going to a wine bar for a drink.'

'You want to be careful with that guy, he has got a funny reputation. Is heavily into saving the environment, and hangs out a lot with Devadorje. You met Devadorje yet? A complete nutter! My aunt once asked for his help, when she found out about my cousin's suicide pact with her aspidistra, and Devadorje spent three days talking them out of it. Half a year later my cousin passed her A-levels and the aspidistra burst into bloom. So have a care; you don't want Fridthjof introduce you to the office plant, do you?'

Sophia shook her head, but privately resolved to ask for just such an introduction - that plant probably knew a lot of secrets!

Evening had finally arrived at The Institution. Flossy, having received a mysterious telephone call, impatiently cleared her desk of confidential papers.

Indiscriminately shoving the 'Second Banking Directive Regarding the Theft of Stationary', 'When Banks go Bankrupt – a Guide for Regulators', and the Annual Accounts of the Little Green Moose Bank into her desk, she bid her colleagues good night and vanished from sight.

Deep within the bowels of The Institution, where the ill-lit caverns of the Vault hide much that flees the neon-flooded upper halls, there lurked behind a pillar in the shade Ms Pembrokeshire's paramour, a tall blond dishy man with sinful intentions. 'Darling,' she cried, and 'Honeybunch', he sighed, as he gathered her up in his strong arms. Undoubtedly they would have continued in this vein, and undertaken numerous unchaste manoeuvres, for lust was on their minds - but alas, they were rudely interrupted.

Fridthjof Thorsteinson was already waiting at the Toad's Crusade, a small but well known wine bar in the heart of the City, when Sophia arrived. After the usual enquiries regarding each others health, work, home-owner status, and sexual predilections, she asked him about the fabled Devadorje.

'The concept of communicating with plants has always fascinated me; is it something anyone can learn, or does one need inborn talent?' she asked.

Fridthjof confessed that he fervently wished it could be learned, but alas, talent was all important in this matter. He himself, for example, had no aptitude in this regard at all, and had to confine himself to catering to the needs of his green friends as best he could, without any guidance from them on how they wished to be treated.

'Still,' he said, making an effort to pull free from the despondent mood Sophia's question had plunged him into, 'even those of us who lack talent can be of use to the plant community. My methods are crude when compared to those of Devadorje, but far from ineffective. As founder and chief operative of the Bonsai Liberation Front I have achieved much, even Devadorje grants me that.'

Then he realised that he had just revealed an important secret to Sophia in his attempt to impress her, and was mortified. 'Look, you must keep this absolutely secret; what we are doing is highly illegal, and I could get into serious trouble if anyone found out.'

Sophia assured him of her absolute discretion, and asked for further details.

'The Bonsai Liberation Front is an organisation dedicated to the protection and furtherance of the interest of bonsai trees, said Fridthjof. 'Bonsais are poor, maltreated, twisted, deliberately retarded little trees, who are suffering agonies in their unnaturally tiny pots. Their suffering is like that of Chinese girl children who used to have their feet bound to keep them artificially small. Foot-binding is illegal now, but the suffering of the Bonsais continues unabated. It just shows the relative importance society places on little children and trees. When I first encountered one of those poor helpless pot-bound cripples I was barely seven years old, but so shaken by the experience that I resolved on the spot to dedicate my life to the eradication of the custom. I spent the next few years arguing with garden centre managers, writing irate letters to the International Club of Bonsai Fanciers, and trying to convince individual Bonsai keepers to grant their slaves a bigger pot. When I was fourteen I decided to set up the Bonsai Liberation Front. Over time I have perfected the art of liberating bonsais from garden centres and flower shops, planting them in an appropriate location somewhere in the woods, and slowly guiding them towards living an existence more appropriate for their kind.' He almost wept as he went on to tell Sophia the efforts that some of those Bonsais had to make to overcome their pot-addiction.

When Fridthjof finally re-gained his composure, he proceeded to entertain her with his tales of high adventure and daring-dos amidst the horticultural outlets of the capital. He bragged of his innumerable sorties into Bonsai-selling shopping arcades, and how he often managed to replace the Bonsais with realistic looking silk and plastic imitations, which were occasionally not unmasked as frauds for weeks. He told her about the secret plot in the Chilterns, where, amidst majestic beeches and evergreen firs the Bonsais had found a new home. He even told her of the cheap, sticky bonbons he put into the empty bonsai pots after each successful replanting, and the hurtful, cutting poems he composed and returned to the erstwhile owner of the Bonsai together with the bonbon-filled pot.

Sophia was most impressed with the information Fridthjof had imparted to her, and listened with a rapt attention that was most gratifying to him. It was therefore with considerable regret that Fridthjof took his leave from her; but he planned an important raid in the Plant Plaza later that night, and had to make preparations. They both agreed to meet again as soon possible, since they were obviously of a similar ilk.

Before Sophia returned to her digs in Islington, she went for a quick visit to her father's old abode at Victoria Street. It was a beautiful balmy night, with a full moon above the City, which bathed the ruins in a pale eerie light. As she approached, she noticed a tall slim figure near the centre of the temple, where a makeshift altar with a stele of Mithras had been erected. The figure wore a long, heavily embroidered garment, and held aloft a Persian looking vessel. Whispering an incantation in a male sounding voice, the figure poured the contents of the vessel out before the altar, whispered a few more incantations, carefully packed up the vessel, stele, and altar, and melted into the night. Thus Sophia first caught sight of Mithradates Devadorje, but she did not know it was him.

14   The seduction of Gilligan Wang

We left Gilligan at the entrance of the Exalted Heavenly Dream-Stone, exulting in his good fortune. Poor deluded fool! If he had spent a few moments considering the peculiar conditions set by the mysterious maiden, he would surely have grown suspicious. None were related even remotely to Chinese dream-stone lore. Instead they were obviously a hodgepodge of unrelated ideas, randomly thrown together by someone anxious to come up with something vaguely creditable at short notice. The mysterious maiden was in fact none other than Adamantina, the Dream-Stone Guardian officially in charge of the Exalted Heavenly Dream-Stone, who had sworn to wreak vengeance upon Gilligan for treating it with disrespect. The planting of ash seeds had suggested itself by the presence of the ash tree, and the honey by its inclusion in Gilligan's supplies, which Adamantina had noticed. 'Mutabor' was simply a term she picked up from reading an old fairy tale. Incoherent as her story was, it had been enough to convince Gilligan, and that was all she cared for. Making herself comfortable under the ash tree, she settled down to watch Gilligan's adventures in the realm of the Exalted Heavenly Dream-Stone.

Gilligan looked about himself in wonderment. He seemed to be inside a fairy tale. The light in the Exalted Heavenly Dream-Stone world was a pale lilac, and hazy like fog. He stood on the shore of a lake that was beautifully framed by large pines in the background, and grass of a bluish hue in front. At one side of the lake he saw a small, low, white-washed house, surrounded by a garden filled with chrysanthemums. He slowly walked towards the house. There was an eerie calm; no insects or birds seemed to inhabit the Exalted Heavenly Dream-Stone. Only a slight breeze, which gently rustled the pines and raised slight waves on the lake, disturbed the silence.

As he approached the house he noticed a young woman in the garden who was tending the chrysanthemums. Coming nearer, he was able to observe her more closely. Thick black tresses, like raven's feathers, were piled upon her head, contrasting sharply with the snowy whiteness of her temples. Blue-black eyebrows were curved like the sickle of the new moon, and almond shaped eyes met his look with a cool, clear gaze. The cherry mouth exhaled a fragrant breath; the small nose was like rose-coloured jasper. Her full, round cheeks were delicately pink, her figure slender and pliant like a flower's stem. Her fingers were like tender onion shoots, her small waist supple as an osier.[15] Gilligan found himself in the presence of a seductive beauty.

'I am Goldlotus, and held position of the fifth concubine of a high ranking official before curiosity led me into this dream-stone. The mistress of the Exalted Heavenly Dream-Stone, the Emerald Maiden, who discovered it and has chosen it as her everlasting abode, has assigned to me the task of welcoming and entertaining male visitors to her realm. Since you are the first male visitor for a long while, and comely into the bargain, I greatly look forward to teaching you several variations of the wind-and-moon game that you may still be unacquainted with.'

Gilligan was, of course, enchanted. Her beauty, so suggestive of spiritual purity, contrasted in a strangely alluring fashion with her lascivious words. Fleetingly he remembered the warning in an ancient manuscript on dream-stone lore that it was perilous to linger too long within a dream-stone, but he quickly dismissed this thought; after all, he had only just arrived. So he accepted her invitation to enter the house, where a meal composed of a few but select dishes was set upon the table, together with a number of choice wines. They took their seats opposite one another, and while partaking of the meal engaged in that intimate, exploratory conversation that couples have before retiring to the seclusion of the bedchamber, to discover yet more personal details about one another. At last, when the meal was over and they had rinsed their mouths with jasmine scented tea, Gilligan lifted Goldlotus from her seat and carried her to an enormous red lacquered bed in the adjoining chamber. He then closed the door firmly from the inside, and no reports of their lovemaking ever reached this author.

After several hours of their phoenix play, Gilligan enquired of his ladylove exactly how long he would be able to remain in the Exalted Heavenly Dream-Stone

---

[15]   I could go on, but am loathe to bore the reader.

world before having to leave. Goldlotus replied that the Emerald Maiden had specified one hour as the correct period. However, this need not concern him any longer, since his hour had elapsed before they had even finished their meal.

Gilligan was frantic. He snatched up his clothing, dressed hastily, and ran towards the entrance portal whence he had come. But alas, it was no longer visible. Goldlotus, who followed him, attempted to reconcile him to his lot.

'We who live in the Exalted Heavenly Dream-Stone world never grow old, nor does sickness assail us. Provided you don't upset the Mistress, your life will be pleasant enough. So why upset yourself? Come back with me to the house, so that we may continue what we have barely started.'

But Gilligan, all thought of debauchery driven from his mind, would not be reconciled to this fate. Like others who possessed the Exalted Heavenly Dream-Stone before him, his love for the precious artefact was not so great that he desired to remain inside of it indefinitely.

'Where is this emerald hussy,' he wildly cried, 'I shall seek her out immediately! How dare she try to imprison me, Gilligan Wang, inside her stony realm?'

Goldlotus sighed; he was not the first lover who left her bed prematurely to seek out her mistress. However, there was nothing she could do. She told him to follow the path that lead to the highest of the mountains, where at its feet the Emerald Maiden dwelled, and advised him not to take quite so high-handed a tone with her if he valued his comfort. But Gilligan scarcely listened, and went off to meet his doom.

The Emerald Maiden was sitting at the mouth of a cave practicing her calligraphy, when Gilligan arrived in high dudgeon. She looked most displeased when she noticed his approach and attitude, and, laying her brush aside, addressed him thus.

'Well Gilligan Wang, have you finally deigned to pay a visit to your new mistress? What have you to say for yourself, defiler of the Exalted Heavenly Dream-Stone, seducer of my serving wench, possessor of an uncouth tongue?'

Gilligan listened to her open-mouthed, unable to immediately comprehend all the insults and half-truths she addressed to him. But she was far from finished.

'Worthless Wang,' she cried, 'when will you recover your manners? Onto your knees, I say, and pay me homage!'

Gilligan was too taken aback to reply, nor did he make any attempt to kneel down. Exasperated by his boorish manner, the Emerald Maiden raised her hand, and several brutish looking men, each equipped with a bundle of hazel switches, came forth from the back of the cave where they had been waiting. They grabbed the hapless Gilligan, threw him upon his belly, removed his shoes, and applied their hazel switches with grim earnestness. After they had applied twenty strokes, their mistress bade them halt, and once again addressed her newest subject.

'Hearken to my words, worm-like Wang. You are my subject now, for good or ill, and there is nothing you can say or do to persuade me to let you go. I advise you to accept your fate with equanimity, for if you don't you shall receive one stroke for every word you utter. Now quick be gone, lest I imprison you within my deepest dungeon!'

With that she picked up her calligraphy brush, and continued the labour that Gilligan's arrival had interrupted.

Gilligan was thunderstruck; no one had ever spoken to him like that, nor dared to lay hands upon him, much less accost his feet with hazel switches. What little spirit remained to him flew off to the four far corners of the world, and he miserably shuffled as fast as his insulted feet would carry him back to where the entrance portal had once been. There he sat down and meditated upon his manifold transgressions, and sobbed his heart out as quietly as he could contrive, so as not to disturb his new mistress.

15   Casanova meets a Techno-Queen

Once Casanova had completed his discussions with the three resident architects in Hell, Imhotep, Anthemius, and Andrea Palladio, he went to London to find a banker suitable to put together a consortium of lenders for the Greenlandia project. Instead of approaching a reputable merchant bank, as any sensible person would have done, he went to Chippy's, a casino cum rave club notorious for attracting criminals and sociopaths of every description. He spent several nights gambling, rapidly amassing a fortune, while keeping his eyes peeled for delinquent bankers and businessmen, without much luck so far.

Suddenly the heavy velvet curtains that separated the casino from the dance floor were dramatically flung apart, and a woman of unusual appearance entered the casino and stepped up to one of the gaming tables. She was swathed from head to toe in a black, lacy, see-through mantilla. Under the mantilla she wore a purple, lacy brassiere, chemise and knickers of the same material, and suspenders with black fishnet tights. Her pumps were velvet black and dangerously high, her purple hair piled high upon her head, and her face was half painted purple, and half left unadorned. Her black eyes were heavily lined with kohl and dripped red tears, her mouth was a blotch of carmine, and her inch long fingernails gleamed red and dangerously in the neon light. Casanova was smitten to the core.

Unfortunately her skill at gambling did not match her decorative talents. She lost heavily, and soon there were no chips left in front of her. Apparently unperturbed, she rose as dramatically as she had appeared, and vanished from the casino into the dark night. However, Casanova, being an expert poker player himself, was not taken in by her performance, and followed her after a decent interval had elapsed (and he had cashed in his chips).

He finally tracked her down to a bench in a nearby park, weeping disconsolately. However, when she saw him approach her crying stopped immediately, and she drew herself up to her full six feet and two inches, prepared to deliver a haughty little speech intended to send him scurrying back to his hole (her opinion of men was low, and Casanova was obviously a rat). Unfortunately this display was cut short by a sudden attack of nausea, which forced her to bend over to allow the partly digested constituents of a hastily devoured hamburger meal and a litre of champagne issue forth from between her carmine lips. Casanova waited patiently until this ritual was completed, handed her a spotlessly clean white pocket handkerchief and proceeded to address her in paternal tones.

'There is no need for pretence with me my dear; I have been cleared out at the gaming tables more often than you number years. You obviously can ill afford to loose your money, and must allow me to help. It is a pity about your beautiful make-up, though.'

Her facial decoration had indeed been ravaged by her tears and sickness, and Casanova hoped that this ungallant remark would re-kindle her vanity and lead her to repair the damage, and thus distract her – she was obviously still suspicious of him.

To his surprise she completely disregarded his comment about her face, and accused him instead of attempting to 'purchase her virtue with gold'. Casanova could not completely repress his amusement.

'My dear girl, however much I adore and admire your appearance and attitude, I can assure you I would not dream of approaching a woman in your condition with amorous intentions; I fear it might disturb the child. No, rest assured that my interest in you is purely platonic, at least until after your confinement.'

The girl was ill inclined to believe him, but truth be told, she had no money left and few options, so she allowed him to escort her to her bed & breakfast to pay her overdue bill, help her pack her suitcase, and install her in his own hotel in a comfortable room two floors below his own. Since he made no attempt to 'get fresh with her', she gradually lost her suspicions, and finally told him her recent adventures over a belated but much needed dinner.

Despite his own considerable experiences, Casanova had to admit that her story was remarkable even by his standards, and resolved on the spot to take care of her and the child when it was born (since clearly no one else was going to do it). He enquired whether she had any plans regarding her future, and although she had none, and simply relied on playing it by ear, she confessed after much prodding that she had always dreamed of living in a little cottage in the Cotswolds, with climbing roses and honeysuckle and a thatched roof. Casanova rather fancied himself in the role of fairy godfather, and promised to look for a cottage with her the following day. 'Incidentally, where are the Cotswolds?'

At first she would not hear of it, and said that she had some distant relatives in Lyme Regis who would take her in, but several Sherries later she admitted that she hated them, and would be miserable there.

'Well, that's all settled then,' Casanova smiled at her. 'There is no need to worry about taking my money, you know, I won it all gambling, and there are plenty of fools left for me to fleece if I need more!'

Finding a cottage proved easier than expected, and three days later Casanova had settled his ward in a charming little house, that answered in every particular to her specifications, in Willowmere-upon-Stout, just fifteen miles from Oxford and its excellent facilities for patients with babyosis. Casanova loved the cottage as much as the girl, and was especially taken with the great open fireplace and large rambling garden, which even contained a small pond with assorted amphibians. He arranged for everything, including a gardener and daily help, and was just wondering whether to lay the foundation for a sensible wine cellar with the help of several catalogues from London wine merchants while lounging in an easy chair in front of the fire, when the idyll was cruelly shattered by a shrill voice.

Agrat was standing in the doorway, consumed with wrath and determined to give her financial advisor a tongue-lashing of truly epic proportions.

'You miserable Venetian scamp, have you forgotten why you have been allowed to return to The World? You were supposed to meet Cesare in Nuuk three days ago! Instead I find you here, gallivanting with one of your hussies – how did even you manage to get her so pregnant so fast?'

The hussy in question felt compelled to intervene. 'You must be Agrat, the manager of the project Jack has told me so much about,' she gushed. 'I am so honoured to meet you, I have heard so much about you and your incredible business ventures.'

Agrat was somewhat becalmed; she had a soft spot for pregnant members of her sex, and this girl obviously admired her. Casanova, sensing her changing mood, intimated that the time he spent with the girl had not been completely dominated by passion. It was true, he continued, that he had been carried away in his attempts to comfort her in her predicament, for which he apologised profusely, but it had all been done in a good cause.

And Agrat, reading his mind, discovered both the chaste nature of her lieutenant's attentions to the girl, and the service she had rendered to the project. Although Casanova did not wish the girl to know this, he had decided which banker would lead the consortium to finance the project on the basis of information she had given him when she told him her life story.

Agrat admitted that she had been hasty in her wholesale condemnation of her financial advisor, and asked the girl whether she would mind telling her life story to her as well, seeing that it had been important enough to distract Casanova from a multi-billion business venture? Sensing the opportunity to repair whatever damage she had unwittingly done to Casanova's standing with his employeress, the girl readily agreed. They made themselves comfortable around the fireplace, after Agrat stoked the fire, telling the girl that she must take things easy so close to her time, and Casanova got the tea things ready, and the girl told her tale again.

16   The Hamsters are coming!

While Casanova was playing homemaker, the rodentification of The Institution had completely gotten out of hand. Stanley Hunzucker and Flossy Pembrokeshire, last seen embracing intimately in a dark recess of the Vault, could tell a sad tale about it, if only they weren't so discreet. Just when their hearts began to beat in perfect harmony, and their hands groped to mutual satisfaction, a small furry creature rubbed against Flossy's leg. At first she thought that it was Stanley - she had not yet been able to ascertain the exact degree of hairiness his legs possessed – but when she felt a tiny but cold nose at the centre of the hairiness she recognised the loathsome beast for what it was (well, almost; she actually thought it was a rat) and took swift action. A mighty kick from her well-muscled leg sent the hamster into orbit, and her swirling handbag made light work of several other rodents who lurked improvidently in the vicinity. Having thus successfully routed the invaders, she remembered that she was just a wee weak lassie in the presence of a strong male, collapsed onto the manly chest of the astonished Hunzucker and sobbed: 'Stanley, save me!'

Mr Hunzucker cautiously eyed the shady corners just beyond their meeting place, and after some reflection suggested that they draw short their assignation, since the rodents were certain to renew their attack. However, upon seeing her disappointment, he added, 'don't worry love, we'll try again next week. I already have a foolproof plan.'

When Winston C. Flabbergast, Head of Personnel and eminent employee of The Institution, returned to his office after the long bank holiday weekend he experienced a nasty shock. Several hamsters were sitting on his desk, eying him sternly. They evidently did not approve of his spotlessly clean office, which had sentenced them to a very meagre diet over the three-day weekend. No sooner had he dropped his briefcase on the floor – easily done when one experiences shock – than two rodents hastened forward to investigate its contents for food. Before he could voice his protest, they had chewed through the outer leather, and when they discovered that a metal casing prevented them from gaining access – Flabbergast's briefcase was well armoured and designed to protect confidential papers from riffraff – they turned on him. Flabbergast fled in terror, leaving his case behind.

Flabbergast was not the only one at The Institution who encountered hamsters in places that ought to have been hamster-free. The reckless rodents were discovered in the kitchens, office filing-cabinets, wastepaper baskets, and even in the bullion vaults. By lunchtime the entire Institution was at panic station. Hamsters were sitting on people's desks fighting them for their sandwiches, and climbed up their legs in the Feederia to get onto the tables to eat from their plates. Although some animal lovers welcomed the hamster invasion, the majority of the harassed employees did not. Several hundred staff members were having a sit-in strike in front of the Governor's office, and the union was making urgent representations. Swift action was imperative, so senior management convened a meeting.

Speedwell Klimpft, Head of the Fraud Division, chaired the meeting and opened the discussion. 'I found a dead hamster in my office slippers this morning!'

'Obviously the rodent was overcome by fumes and passed away,' said Isabella Kaputnik, who was in charge of the Economics Division and had a sense of humour.

Klimpft took this as a personal insult. 'I have you know that I wash my feet daily!' However, the episode did suggest a solution to the problem; 'why don't we call in a rat catcher and gas the lot!'

Isabella Kaputnik disagreed, and warned that this could easily alienate the Royal Rodent Lovers Society. 'The last thing we need is bad publicity! Caroline, you are the Pest & Accident expert, what do you think we should do?'

Unfortunately Caroline Green was mortally afraid of rodents. 'I don't think hamsters are part of my remit. I blame the Mouser and his dozen 'indolent, overfed, good-for-nothing cats for the problem, and suggest that we replace the entire Rodent Reduction Force with younger specimens - the current ones are obviously not up to the job anymore!'

This raised the heckles of Flabbergast. 'The Institution is a caring employer and does not fire employees just because they are 'fat cats'. The Mouser and his team have always done a splendid job, and it is unfair to blame them for what is obviously a one-off freak invasion. Besides, the entire feline contingent is unionised, and the last thing we need right now is a strike.'

'He is quite right, you know,' said Ms Kaputnik. 'The rodent invasion is highly unusual, in that it involves hamsters. We have often been plagued by mice, and occasionally by rats, even the odd mole – but hamsters are completely unheard of. It is unfair to blame this all on Mr Mouser.'

Everyone admitted that she had a point; moreover, they were inclined to listen to the voice of experience – Ms Kaputnik had routed plenty of rodents in her days – and readily agreed when she advised to ask Fridthjof Thorsteinson to investigate the problem.

'He is not only interested in environmental matters, and therefore unlikely to antagonise the Royal Rodent Lovers, but, in the two years he has worked for me has shown himself to be decisive, speedy, and common sensical in his approach to problems.'

'I have to admit Fridthjof is a thoroughly good egg,' Klimpft agreed. 'Didn't he get the century against Pinkkipaccy Bank last year at the Governor's Garden Party Match?' That clinched the matter, and everyone agreed that Thorsteinson should be put on the case.

Fridthjof was happy and eager to accept the assignment. His raid on the previous Friday night had been very successful (five trees rescued, one given a mercy-injection and buried with full military honours), and he was ready for a new challenge. He had been pondering the hamster invasion recently, and wondered for some time whether the alcoholic and eccentric Stress Lucozade, might have a hand in this. After all, Stress had long evidenced signs of being obsessed with rodents of all sorts. Fridthjof's first port of call was therefore Stress' office, were he was informed that Stress unfortunately had suddenly been taken ill on Friday afternoon and not yet returned to work. 'How very interesting; Friday afternoon Stress takes ill, Friday evening first sightings of out of control hamsters in the vaults are reported.'

The Security Force, who received most of the reports on the rioting rodents over the weekend, confirmed that the majority of the early sightings occurred below ground-level. Consequently Fridthjof began his investigation in the basement, and worked his way down to the vaults and sub-vaults. The evidence of a heavy rodent presence was everywhere. Droppings, fur-balls, and miscellaneous chewed-up matter littered the floor, and the lower he got the more literate it became. The stench, too, was increasingly pungent, until he approached Sub-Vault No. 432D, where both the litter and the stench were overwhelming. Surely this was the nest whence the invasion had originated; he quickly went to fetch the keys from the Security Force and unlocked the door with trembling hands, while the guard who had accompanied him – not trusting him with the key – watched him suspiciously.

A single light bulb cast a dim and melancholy glow over the hamster-dominated scene that presented itself to the astonished Fridthjof. The room was simply awash with hamsters! Hamsters on the floor, up the walls, on the tables and filing cabinets, in and on top of the numerous cages – there was not a single inch of space to be seen that was not occupied by one of the creatures. Lesser natures would have fled, but Fridthjof was made of stern stuff. Let there be light! he cried, and sent the guard off to get a few portable floodlights. These were scarcely installed when the majority of the rodents broke into a confused mass panic and scampered from the room, while a minority sought refuge in their cages. Fridthjof used this breathing space to investigate the nature of the operation he had stumbled upon. Three walls were taken up with cages from floor to ceiling, and one by a long table and shelves. A case of whiskey stood beneath the table, and a laboratory notebook filled with Stress' inimitable scrawl lay upon it, both proofs – if any were needed – that it was indeed Lucozade who was responsible for the hamster plague. A quick glance at the contents of the lab book - Fridthjof was one of the finest analysts of The Institution - revealed the basic set-up of Stress' 'Project Homing Hamster', and soon Fridthjof knew enough to bring the hamster hordes under control. A detailed analysis would have to wait until afterwards.

Fridthjof opened all the little cage doors, put a portion of Hamster-Nip into each feeding bowl, and blew the special homing whistle he found hanging on a nail next to the door. The whistle barely left his lips when the hamsters came flooding back to the room and rushed into their cages; even a few mice, who had developed an addiction to Hamster-Nip, were among the crowd. When all the hamsters had returned, and every cage been closed, he carefully locked the door to Sub-Vault No 432D, and went to report to the authorities. His request to deal with the hamsters as he saw fit was granted, on condition that they were all removed from the premises as soon as possible. Thus law and order was restored to The Institution, and the Mouser was finally able to take a bit of well earned rest.

17   Trish Trash in Trouble

It is perhaps time to reveal the name of the young lady who put Casanova to so much trouble with his employer. She shrouded her real name, which she did not approve of, in thick layers of secrecy, and was called by all and sundry Trish Trash. We left her ensconced in a comfortable armchair near the fire in her little Cotswold cottage, preparing to tell her story to Agrat bat Mahalat.

'My troubles started when I met Gingrich Fleabrunckle at the Love Parade in Berlin,' she began. The Love Parade was an annual gathering of techno fans that Trish had attended these last few years. She had just broken up with her boyfriend, Snortface (a nickname which referred to his cocaine habit), and was looking for a steady, dependable kind of guy to take his place. When she met Fleabrunckle she thought she had won the lottery. He was handsome, urbane, witty, in secure employment, and talking babies and family – just the sort of man she needed after the hectic, spaced out, hand-to-mouth existence she had experienced with Snortface. Moreover, he seemed very much in love with her, attentive, indulgent, and ready to laugh at her feeblest jokes! Of course, had she known that he was into devil worship and had chatted her up with the sole purpose of offering her as a sacrificial victim to a High Priest of Evil in central Asia, she would have been less keen.

At this stage of her narrative Agrat looked at her quizzically; just how much did this girl know? But Trish did not notice, and continued undeterred.

After she and Fleabrunckle returned to London, he asked her to move into his luxury flat in the Barbican with him, and she readily consented. His flat was one of those high tech minimalist affairs, and totally impersonal, except for a small Japanese-style alcove in the bedroom. This alcove consisted of a raised platform with a beautiful simple ancient Chinese drawing for a backdrop, depicting a group of craggy pine trees on a rocky mountain overlooking a deep gorge. The alcove was dominated by an intricate Ikebana arrangement which Gingrich changed every Saturday afternoon. They spent many a happy Saturday morning scouring the markets and parks for materials for these arrangements, and Trishy loved to watch him compose them afterwards. First he spread out all the materials they had collected in the morning on one side of the bedroom floor, and then he arranged the dozens of vases and other receptacles he used for his flower arrangements on the other side. Then he bowed low in the direction of the alcove, and sat down in the lotus position. He sat quite still, in a state of utmost concentration, and spent hours meditating upon the various blossoms and twigs and climbers they had collected. Finally he would pick one of the vases, and arrange within it the ingredients he had chosen for his current composition. At last he added water, and placed the vase on a wooden stand in the alcove. He bowed again before the alcove, sighed deeply, shook himself like a dog come out from the rain, and snapped out of his meditative mood. He returned all the unused vases to their cupboard, swept up the remainder of the plant material they had gathered that morning, and threw it into the rubbish bin. Somehow that last bit had always jarred on her; wouldn't it have been more suitable if he disposed of the material more reverently? But he just laughed, and called her a sentimental little fool. Trishy often wondered about this ceremony afterwards, because it seemed so out of character for Fleabrunckle. In all other respects he was thoroughly unsentimental, matter of fact, and practical. Was the Ikebana ceremony the one outlet he allowed his finer instincts, the last remnant of an otherwise suppressed part of his personality?

After they had co-habited for a few months, he suggested a hiking holiday in the Altai Mountains in Mongolia. A friend of his lived there in a very isolated chalet, and always welcomed company. Trish had only very vague notions of the location of Mongolia, but as always was ready to have a go. They flew into Ulaanbaatar, rented a Jeep, camping equipment and supplies for a few days, and headed for Dalandzadgad. Their drive was most memorable, especially the mountains, which were very beautiful and reminded her of Switzerland. In Dalandzadgad they were met by a couple of nomadic guides sent by Fleabrunckle's friend, who insisted that they exchanged the jeep for horses, and led them into the mountains. Trish had never sat on a horse before, so they made slow progress. Indeed, after a few days Trish got the distinct impression that the guides were purposefully travelling as slowly as possible, and employed numerous delaying tactics. She figured they were probably paid by the day, and trying to extend the journey to increase their payment, so thought no more about it.

Trish was apparently a great hit with the native guides, although none of them spoke English. One evening while they were sitting around the fire, and Fleabrunckle had to answer a call of nature, one of them went so far as to urge her - with many unmistakeable gestures - to sneak off that night and return with him to Dalandzadgad. She could barely suppress a giggle, and refused as politely as she could, but the guides continued to treat her with special consideration, and often, when they thought themselves unobserved, looked at her pityingly. Of course she did not mention this to Fleabrunckle – it was just too silly.

After five days on horseback, they finally arrived at their destination. Perched halfway up a mountain was the 'chalet', although it looked more like the medieval castles she had seen while on holiday in France. It was certainly most impressive, several stories high and twice as wide, with a moat and a great wall around it, and battlements; it even had a keep. A small dusty path wound its way up the mountain and to the chalet. Apparently this was as far as their guides were contracted to go. They refused all payment, but while they took their leave, one of them slipped a note into Trish's pocket when Fleabrunckle was momentarily distracted, and put his finger before his mouth to advise her to be silent. Before she could react they all turned their horses around and galloped off. Fleabrunckle commented that this was very unusual behaviour, since they usually hung around for a tip, and that he would never understand these barbarians. They led their horses up the path, and prepared for a dusty climb.

Although the 'chalet' looked like a medieval castle to Trish, Fleabrunckle's friend told her that it was in fact an old Buddhist temple which he had bought cheaply while Mongolia was under communist rule, and temples were derelict and not much in demand. He had fixed it up and rebuilt to suit his taste and needs, and it made an admirable head office for his worldwide business empire. Fleabrunckle's friend had come to the lowered drawbridge to welcome them, and seemed very friendly - he even kissed her hand when Fleabrunckle introduced her. Trish found it hard to describe him; he was tall and thin, with very black hair and very white skin, and eyes like black ink. But what she could not describe what the vague aura of evil that seemed to emanate from him; she could sense it, though she knew not with what sense. His name was Florimonde.

Upon hearing this name Agrat jumped up from her chair as though stung by a needle. 'What was that name? Are you quite sure?'

Trish was certain. She heard other people use it a number of times while she stayed at the castle; did Agrat know him?

'Do I know him?' Agrat shouted. 'Do I know him, the adept, the imposter, the oath-breaker, the sorcerer, the quack, the warlock, the charlatan, the dwimmerlaijk! Florimonde Florimonde, so that is where you are hiding now! He was in the Rockys when I saw him last; I should have done away with him then, like the vermin he is, orders to the contrary be damned! Florimonde Florimonde Florimonde – the very name makes me rage!' Shouting these last words, Agrat paced the small room with angry strides. Her fists beat the air, her eyes blazed with fury, and her hair seemed to have developed a life of its own; several strands rose up like snakes above her head, and almost seemed to hiss. Casanova recognised the signs; Agrat was working herself into one of her famous rages.

'What was Florimonde doing in the Altai Mountains,' he asked Trish, hoping that Agrat's curiosity would overcome her rage.

'I don't know exactly,' Trish replied, 'but he seemed to be involved in some strange satanic rituals.'

'Don't you dare call them satanic,' Agrat yelled, 'Jehovah is my witness that Hell has no truck with the doings of Florimonde!'

Trish looked at her uneasily, clearly shaken by Agrat's impressive display of anger. 'I am sorry if I have offended you, I am trying to describe what I saw as best I can.'

Casanova reassured her. 'Florimonde is an old enemy of Agrat, but you must not distress yourself; please go on with your story.'

Agrat calmed down, and Trish continued. Florimonde had given her a large room with adjoining bathroom in the castle, furnished and supplied with every luxury she could desire. Her initial uneasiness quickly disappeared, and she spent a few wonderful days with Fleabrunckle exploring the countryside. Each evening after dinner (which was always excellent) they sat around a huge fire in the library, and Florimonde entertained them with tales from his youth.

'All lies, no doubt', Agrat commented.

However, this idyllic life was not to last. About a week after they arrived at the castle, Trish went to bed one evening early after dinner, feeling unusually sleepy. She awoke from the cold a few hours later, and when she tried to turn around and dive deeper under her bedclothes, realised to her surprise that she was unable to move. Slowly opening her eyes, she noticed that she lay spread-eagled upon a large stone table in the courtyard of the castle, covered with only a thin black sheet. There was a full moon, and several figures in black hooded robes that hid their faces surrounded the table. She felt very sluggish and unable to see or think clearly; she probably had been drugged. They were chanting strange songs in an unknown language, and she saw them dancing slowly around the table. Then she fell asleep again. She awoke with a start when someone tore the sheet off her body. A tall figure with a silver moon on his hood came towards her, with a long, slim, glinting knife in one hand, and a silver goblet in the other. When he reached the table he raised both hands, and the chanting stopped; everyone stood still, and watched him expectantly. He cut his index finger with the knife, and when the blood began to ooze from the wound he used it to trace a strange design upon her naked belly. She desperately tried to collect her wits and think of a way to escape, or at least to scream – but she was unable to make even the slightest effort. She even tried to pray, but could only think of snatches of a silly little bedtime prayer a maiden aunt had taught her long ago, which seemed wholly inadequate for the desperate situation she found herself in. She truly thought that her last hour had come.

At this point Trish was overcome with emotion, and took refuge in a cup of tea and a toasted crumpet. Agrat and Casanova waited patiently for her to regain her composure, and presently she was able to continue her story. When the figure with the knife had finished his bloody drawing on her body, he lifted the knife high above his head and prepared to strike. But then he hesitated, and looked closely at her belly. He laid aside the knife and goblet, and held his ear to her stomach, and touched it with his hands. Then he threw up his hands and turned around so suddenly that he lost his hood and yelled at another figure,

'Are you completely mad, bringing me a pregnant woman for the supreme sacrifice? Do you want to get us all killed?'

Trish would have recognised him by his voice then as Florimonde, even if he had not lost his hood. He rushed towards the other figure and kicked and beat him, until the other cowered on the ground and grovellingly begged for mercy – that voice, too, she recognised - it belonged to Fleabrunckle. Finally Florimonde gave Fleabrunckle one last kick, and came back to Trish, laid his hand upon her head, and lulled her with many words she could not comprehend, until she fell asleep.

She remembered little of the days that followed; apparently having slept most of the time. But there were odd snatches of memory; Fleabrunckle carrying her down a long flight of stairs; Florimonde forcing her to look at a flame again and again; her crawling along an endless dark cold passage; the smell of a camp fire and shouting in a strange tongue; and sitting on a horse in front of someone who was holding her. When she finally came to she was in a little tent in the Gobi desert, surrounded by the native guides who had escorted her and Fleabrunckle to Florimonde's castle. With the torturous help of a little bilingual dictionary they explained to her what had happened.

Apparently Florimonde was feared and loathed among the natives of the Altai region where he dwelled. Ugly rumours about visitors who never returned from the castle abounded, and people were convinced that he was a powerful magician who could destroy anyone who opposed him. No one was therefore prepared to cross him openly, but in secret many people tried to foil his plans. The note the guides had slipped Trish before they left was an example of this. They spent several evenings, with the aid of their little dictionary, to write a note of warning to Trish, and it had been a sour piece of work, given their limited knowledge of the Latin script. But they did not begrudge the labour, since it had obviously saved her life![16] After leaving Fleabrunckle and her at the foot of the castle, they roamed the area in the hope of being able to come to her aid if necessary. Two weeks later they stumbled upon Trish, crawling on hands and knees, wild eyed, bleeding, and incoherent. One of them quickly scooped her up, threw her across his saddle, and rode back to their camp. They decamped immediately, and headed for the most inaccessible part of the Gobi, hoping that Florimonde would not follow them.

They spent about a month in the desert, all told. After that they decided it would be safer for Trish not to go home via Altai and Ulaanbaator. Instead they took her across the border into Sinkiang, where they commended her to the hospitality of a band of Turkoman nomads, who escorted her to Tibet. In Tibet she was befriended by an underground Buddhist monk, who helped her get to Kathmandu, where she worked in the kitchen of a hotel catering to foreign tourists until she saved enough to pay her way to

---

[16]   As a matter of fact, Trish had completely forgotten the note and never read it – but she thought it better not to let her guides know this.

Bihar. In this fashion, always working for a few weeks to pay for the fare to the next big town, Trish made her way across India, Pakistan, Iran, Iraq, and Turkey.

In Istanbul she came across an old, starving beggar, with whom she shared her last food and to whom she poured out her story, since he miraculously spoke English. Actually, this was not miraculous at all, as she found out when she accepted his invitation to stay with him that night. He was a high ranking government official, who had been raised by his grandmother on stories about Harun-al-Rashid and considered begging in disguise an excellent way of keeping himself informed of the public mood. Touched by her misfortunes, and by her sharing her last morsels of food with who she thought to be a poor old beggar, he not only made her stay in his house for a few days, but also paid for her ticket to London and even gave her some money as a farewell gift with typical Turkish generosity when she insisted that she had to return home. Her trip across Asia had taken almost six months, and when she arrived in London two weeks ago she was eight months pregnant and almost at the end of her tether. For a week she unsuccessfully tried to find a job, and finally decided to force her luck at the gambling table with her last fifty pounds. 'If I had not met Jack I really don't know what I would have done,' she ended her narrative. 'My luck had well and truly run out.'

Agrat laughed. 'Any woman who meets Jack when she is in your kind of trouble is not unlucky,' she said. 'But Jack was quite right, your story is easily worth a missed business meeting and a cottage. So Florimonde did not dare to lay hands on a pregnant woman! The warning hit home after all. Still, he needs attending to, but it shall have to wait until the Greenland business is over.'

Then she asked about Gingrich Fleabrunckle, and what he was up to now. Trish did not know, but Casanova had made enquiries; he was still in the banking business, doing his old job as though nothing had happened. Trish was seething about it, but felt there was nothing she could do. He was a respected and trusted senior executive of a large merchant bank, and she a spaced-out techno-queen from Hackney; no one was going to believe *her* story! Indeed, probably no one would believe her story no matter who she was! Agrat suggested that there were other ways of getting even with the likes of Fleabrunckle; how would Trish feel about helping them to utterly destroy the reputation, livelihood, and sanity of her ex-lover?

Trish beamed an angelic smile. 'I should absolutely adore it,' she said.

After a few more hours of plotting and lingering over the teacups, Agrat regretfully took her leave of Casanova and Trish Trash. She had to attend to Gilligan Wang, who was still trapped in the Exalted Heavenly Dream-Stone, and devise a plan of how to relieve Hajji Kurt of his excessive wealth. Casanova, too, would have to be off soon, but Agrat gave him leave to stay for a few more days, until he found a companion for Trish, who would help her with the preparation for her confinement. She also promised to send her a special amulet that would protect her during childbirth; her sister Lilith was a specialist in their preparation.

After Agrat had gone, Trish tried to pump Casanova for information about her, but heard little that she could understand. She liked Agrat enormously, but was a bit worried about her great knowledge about Florimonde – was Agrat, too, in touch with the forces of evil? Casanova burst out laughing and said jokingly that Agrat *was* a force of evil – 'you should see her during a shareholder's meeting!' He also told Trish that Agrat felt very protective towards pregnant women, and that she was a bit of a feminist; if she had to step on someone's toes they tended to be male. To distract her from this dangerous subject, Casanova raised the issue of who might stay with her until her impending confinement. The only one she could think of was her old friend Varus Vampyrus, who was a busker in Oxford and probably had nothing better to do.

Varus turned out to be a 'gothic ' looking individual in his late twenties, dressed in a tatty black silk ball gown and a bowler hat, with a spider web tattooed onto his face, who played the violin in front of the Clarendon Building in Oxford. Despite his eccentric appearance he was a gentle, caring soul who seemed genuinely concerned for Trish, and readily accepted the charge Casanova laid upon him. Having supplied them with a sum of money, and countless reams of good advice, Casanova took his leave of Trish, but not before promising that he would drop in on her as often as he could. He left with some reluctance, for he was in many ways domestically inclined and would have liked to stay with Trish in the little cottage for a while, at least until the baby was born and she had settled into a new life. Instead it was likely that Varus would reap the rewards of his labours, and remain in the cottage as adoptive father of the child and resident protector.

'Oh well, some things never change,' he thought as he looked out of the window of the plane to Greenland.

18   The Rescue of Gilligan Wang

Meanwhile Agrat returned to Great Ash Tree Country in search of Gilligan Wang. She had rather counted on the gnomes, beetles, and assorted spirits who lived in the area, and were famous for their mischief and cunning, to ensnare Gilligan in the course of his quest. She was anxious to keep him busy for a few years, so that he could not make a pest of himself trying to regain his lost fortune while she was busy with the Greenland project, and the Great Ash Country denizens usually dreamed up innumerable traps that delayed their victims for some considerable time. Indeed, that was the reason she had chosen this area for the Exalted Heavenly Dream-Stone quest in the first place!

She was therefore not surprised when she found the haughty Dream-Stone Guardian Adamantina sitting underneath the ash while gazing serenely at the Exalted Heavenly Dream-Stone reposing on a pillow made of ancient cream-coloured silk from the tomb of Ch'öng T'ang, with the master met gnome and the bark beetle nearby. Agrat bowed low before Adamantina and addressed her thus:

'Allow the most unworthy of your insignificant servants to introduce herself. I am the little known and least important of all demons, called Agrat by the one or two of my fellow demons who can remember my name. It is my entirely undeserved pleasure to finally meet the noble and virtuous guardian of the Exalted Heavenly Dream-Stone.' Then she bowed again thrice.

Adamantina beamed with pleasure when she heard this courteous greeting, and replied in a similar vein. 'Most honourable and esteemed Lady Agrat, do not make my face red with shame by praising your worthless slave. It is only your incomparable kindness that can possibly have induced you to address me at all. I am only a simple-minded servant, who cannot find the proper words for this occasion; allow me therefore to express my humble admiration in silence.' Then she took her turn to bow repeatedly.

Agrat sighed inwardly; she hated the self-abasement that was part of the ritual the Jade Emperor[17] imposed on his subjects and those who dealt with them.

'May I enquire whether the Honourable Emerald Maiden is well and content inside the Exalted Heavenly Dream-Stone world?' she asked when Adamantina finally ceased her bowing.

'My mistress is as well as can be expected,' replied Adamantina, 'considering that her repose was recently disturbed by a scoundrel from the southern provinces, a worthless dog who defiled the Exalted Heavenly Dream-Stone in his ignorance and greed. I asked the mistress to hand him over to the Thundergod Lei Kung for punishment, but the ever merciful and compassionate Emerald Maiden chose to imprison him indefinitely inside the Exalted Heavenly Dream-Stone world instead. I lured him there myself; if you look carefully, you can observe him sitting at the entrance gate, next to the peach tree.'

Agrat bent down, and sure enough, there was Gilligan, his sorrow unabated, although his tears ran dry after a long week of mourning and self pity. Judging him ripe for any deal she might offer, Agrat told Adamantina that she was minded to visit her old friend, the Emerald Maiden, once again. Moreover she had business with the hapless Wang, and might have to remove him from the Exalted Heavenly Dream-Stone world to achieve her purpose.

Adamantina was none too pleased with the prospect of losing Wang, for she was spiteful and cruel and enjoyed to watch him suffer. However, she did not dare to give voice to her thoughts. Despite Agrat's humble words during their meeting, she knew very well that Agrat's power was to hers as a thunderstorm to a raindrop, and that even the Emerald Maiden could not hope to win against Agrat if there was a fight. Resigning herself to the inevitable, she once more bowed to Agrat, and with a welcoming wave of her hand opened the portal to the Exalted Heavenly Dream-Stone world.

'Pray enter, honoured guest, and forgive the miserable welcome I am offering you. Being the guardian, I am alas unable to accompany you, begging your pardon.'

Agrat smiled graciously, and stepped across the threshold.

After having adjusted to the ethereal quality of the Dream-Stone-World, she directed her steps towards Gilligan Wang, who was sitting nearby thinking uncharitable thoughts about all and sundry. Upon seeing Agrat his face became contorted with anger, fear, and hope all fighting for supremacy, and he rushed to meet her eagerly.

'So you have come at last!' he cried. 'As you can see, I found the Exalted Heavenly Dream-Stone, but met with an accident and was trapped inside it. Dearest, most noble Madame Agrat, I beseech you to rescue me from the fierce mistress who rules this realm! Please save me, for the sake of our business connection and my poor ailing

---

[17]   The Jade Emperor is the greatest of the ancient Chinese Gods, and supreme ruler of the hierarchy of heaven.

mother!' He fell upon his knees, and began to kowtow repeatedly, until the blood rushed to his head and he was overcome with dizziness and could not continue.

Agrat could barely stop herself from laughing, but managed somehow to address Gilligan in her severest tones. 'You miserable cur! Don't you know that the honourable Emerald Maiden is an old friend of mine?'

Wang paled and let out a shrill cry, and immediately took up his kowtowing again. 'I meant no offence ….'

But Agrat interrupted him. 'Silence, worthless scum! You think I don't know that you have defiled the Exalted Heavenly Dream-Stone, and only obtained it in the first place with the aid of that scoundrel, Anasthasius the bark beetle? As for mentioning your old mother, that is really the limit! You think I do not know how you have neglected her ever since you left for university? Even if you had committed no other crime, this neglect alone would be enough for the Emerald Maiden to have you slowly tortured to death in the Dungeon of Ten Thousand Sighs deep beneath her palace. It is only for the sake of your distant ancestor Wang Xi Feng, who is well regarded by the Emerald Maiden and lives in a similar dream-stone, that you were spared such a fate.'

Gilligan was astonished; he had no idea that he was related to that notorious female[18].

Agrat continued. 'My advice is to bend your knees to your new mistress, beg her forgiveness for your many transgressions, and humbly ask how you might be of service!'

By now the news of Agrat's arrival in the Dream-Stone-World had spread throughout the realm, and the Emerald Maiden herself came to the entrance gate to welcome her exalted guest and offer the traditional cup of welcome. Gilligan, mindful of Agrat's advice, threw himself on the ground again, and, while kowtowing, offered his worthless services to the Emerald Maiden, only to be quite ignored. The two women, having completed the customary ritual greeting *(which is here omitted for the sake of brevity),* repaired into the wooded hills, submerged in deep discussion.

The Emerald Maiden was worried about the future, and confided in Agrat that she knew of several dastardly plots to steal the Exalted Heavenly Dream-Stone and abduct Adamantina. 'I heard rumours that a strange man living in Mongolia has offered a reward of 10,000 taels in gold – imagine that! – for Adamantina; apparently he wants to use her in some ritual or other. His power must be great indeed if he aspires to use my guardian thus – have you heard of him?'

Agrat thought she had, but did not deem it necessary to share her knowledge with her hostess.

The Emerald Maiden continued. 'I also heard that a secret criminal organisation in the western lands is trying to obtain the Exalted Heavenly Dream-Stone, though for what purpose I cannot imagine. They lived in a country called Ire-land, presumably because the natives are easily moved to anger' – she shuddered at the thought of the Exalted Heavenly Dream-Stone falling into such barbarian hands.

---

[18]   He had every right to be astonished; Agrat just made this up to embellish her tirade; incidentally all demons are rather fond of doing this, which is why the wise never quite trust what they say.

Again Agrat did not think it necessary to educate her hostess. On the contrary, she rather hoped that she could turn the appalling ignorance of the Emerald Maiden to her advantage – that would teach her to hide for centuries in a dream-stone while everybody else had to live in the real world!

When the Emerald Maiden finally finished her lamentations, Agrat assumed the role of commiserating friend and world-wise counsellor.

'I am very sorry to hear the Exalted Heavenly Dream-Stone and Adamantina face so many threats; is there no one you can ask for assistance and protection?'

'I had rather hoped you would provide both, now the Exalted Heavenly Dream-Stone is in your possession,' replied the Emerald Maiden.

'Alas, no, I won't own the Exalted Heavenly Dream-Stone for long. I only acquired it in the first place to barter to Wang for half his fortune, which I need rather badly.'

'But that witless Wang is now safely trapped inside my realm; why can't you keep his fortune and leave him to moulder forever in my care?'

'Because modern financiers are crafty; I will only get the money if Gilligan himself writes out the cheque – and unfortunately he did not bring his chequebook into the Exalted Heavenly Dream-Stone!'

'Surely Wang can be persuaded to part with his fortune as well as the Exalted Heavenly Dream-Stone in return for his freedom? I would be more than happy to exert my influence!'

Agrat knew what kind of 'influence' the Emerald Maiden had in mind, but felt that Gilligan did not deserve to be tortured just for being an unpleasant gullible dream-stone fancier. 'I am certain you could persuade Gilligan to part with both the Exalted Heavenly Dream-Stone and half his fortune, but I really don't think it's right to deprive you of your prisoner; I know the rules that govern dream-stones.'

'I beg you not to waste a thought on this. In the interest of the security of the Exalted Heavenly Dream-Stone, I am more than glad to sacrifice Wang; he is a worthless, useless subject anyway.'

Having concluded their deal, to wit, that the Emerald Maiden would release Wang, while Agrat promised to take the Exalted Heavenly Dream-Stone under her protection, they returned to the entrance portal were Gilligan was still busy kowtowing in their general direction. This pleased them both exceedingly.

'He seems to have learned a bit of humility in your realm,' Agrat remarked to her hostess, 'I should like to send my son Damon to stay with you for a while, he needs discipline badly.'

The Emerald Maiden smiled weakly; she hated children, and the prospect of having to contend with one of Agrat's unruly demon spawn who had probably inherited many of her powers was a loathsome one. But Agrat had already turned her attention to Gilligan Wang.

'Gilligan, you worm,' she thundered when they reached him.

Gilligan continued kowtowing.

'Your gracious and merciful mistress has indicated that she might perhaps be prepared to release you if you accept certain conditions.'

Gilligan looked at her expectantly, but did not cease kowtowing.

'Firstly, you must promise to atone for your irreverent treatment of the Exalted Heavenly Dream-Stone by making a pilgrimage to the Lung-hu mountain in Kiang-si.'

Gilligan promised this solemnly between two kowtows.

'Secondly you must write with your own hand ninety-nine copies of the Tao Te Ching and distribute them amongst the poor.'

Gilligan, though bemused, promised this as well, kowtowing all the while.

'Lastly, you must hand over half of your fortune to me, as well as let me keep the Exalted Heavenly Dream-Stone, so that I may protect it from further defilement by the likes of you.'

Gilligan assented eagerly; he was more than glad to be rid of the wretched stone, although he would have liked to keep his fortune intact; still, if that's what it took ….. He was so happy to be released from the Dream-Stone-World that he thanked both ladies for their mercy, which was entirely undeserved, and expressed his gratitude in many flowery and poetic words, and did not omit the kowtows, just to be on the safe side.

At last Agrat took leave of the Emerald Maiden, and crossed the threshold of the Dream-Stone-World in the company of Gilligan Wang. Adamantina was still sitting beneath the ash, chatting with Kalle the met gnome and trying his special thrice-enchanted Mid-Winter brew. Anastasius was nowhere to be seen; apparently the uncouth bark beetle had not been invited to try the met.

Adamantina was ill pleased when she saw Gilligan emerge from the Dream-Stone, but since there was nothing she could do about it she kept her counsel. Agrat informed her of the deal she struck with the Emerald Maiden, and said that she would appoint Azazel as co-guardian of the Exalted Heavenly Dream-Stone, to help Adamantina take care of it, since she herself was obviously too busy.

This incensed Adamantina even more than the liberation of Gilligan Wang; Azazel was a goat demon, ill-spoken and worse looking, without any respect for his elders and betters, and without regard for any of the finer things in life.

Agrat noticed Adamantina's displeasure with great amusement, and said that she rather counted on her civilising influence on the unkempt demon. But Adamantina just tossed back her head, and sniffed disdainfully.

Hoping to salvage at least something from the unmitigated disaster that this day had been for her, Adamantina returned to the subject of Gilligan Wang, and informed Agrat that he had promised her to collect and plant ash seeds for the next three years. Surely Agrat would not let him off that obligation, too? Gilligan rather hoped she would, but he was not to be so lucky.

'Obviously the seeds need to be planted[19], and since Adamantina has to accompany the Exalted Heavenly Dream-Stone to other realms, you will have to do the entire planting yourself. Make sure you follow the sacred procedure laid down for this activity to the letter, and do not rest until you have planted all 568,358 seeds!'

Agrat turned to Adamantina. 'I assume you asked for a forfeit?'

'The forfeit is Gilligan's head,' replied Adamantina.

'Excellent, I am sure that will do the trick. Now Gilligan, let's see what your schedule looks like for the next few years. First you will spend at least three years collecting and planting ash seeds – full-time, mind! Then you go on the pilgrimage to the Taoist shrine of Lung-Hu, and after that you copy Lao-Tse's book ninety-nine times. Does that sound right to you?'

Actually, it sounded horribly wrong to Gilligan, but he dared not voice this opinion. This was just as well, since things were getting even worse.

Kalle the Master Met Gnome piped up. 'Gilligan has promised to help me brew my Yuletide Met, which I reckon will take nine months, nine weeks, and nine days.'

'Well, he'll have to do that first, of course, even before he plants the ash seeds,' Agrat decided. 'We can't let your met go sour from lack of attention; I know how everyone always looks forward to your brews at Yuletide!' Kalle was most gratified and bowed, while Agrat turned to once more address the downtrodden Wang.

'Gilligan, you heard what I just said to Kalle. Before you do anything else, you help him with the met. After nine months, nine weeks, and ten days you will start to plant the seeds. You will observe that I allow you a day's rest after the met brewing, and will acknowledge that this is generous.'

Gilligan bowed again, not trusting himself to talk; he was already forgetting his humility and felt hard done by. It would take him at least five years to complete all the tasks Agrat had laid upon him! He was a busy man! He had a business empire to run! But perhaps he would not have to do all the chores after all; they probably would not keep watch over him for all the time.

Agrat was well aware of what he was thinking, but did not comment; after all, she knew he had given a forfeit. Having asked for and received a cheque for half his fortune, she told Gilligan sternly to perform all his tasks meticulously, and as a parting shot added, 'by the way, the forfeit you gave Adamantina applies to all the tasks you have to complete, not just the seed planting.' Then she took her leave of Adamantina, assured her that Azazel would arrive shortly, said goodbye to Kalle, and drove off.

Kalle was a very good-natured gnome at heart, and felt sorry for Gilligan and Adamantina. Not daring to approach the latter, who was obviously nursing an almighty sulk, he attempted to at least cheer up Gilligan.

---

[19]   This is altogether laughable, there is no need whatsoever to plant ash seeds, since their seedlings spring up all over the place without any help. That's why Adamantina had chosen this task for Gilligan Wang; she wanted to waste his time without giving him the satisfaction of doing worthwhile work.

'Don't look so glum,' he told him; 'consider yourself lucky to have escaped from that Dream-Stone alive! Few people who have dealings with the mistress of that Stone can say as much. And the Lady Agrat has shown you mercy beyond anything I ever expected! Believe me, if it had been one of the local demons, Fenris say or Loki, you would have come off much worse.'

The gnome was obviously right, but Gilligan remained discontent.

He cheered up somewhat when Azazel arrived in a four wheel pick-up truck, which he referred to as the 'Shit Mobil' and into which he immediately bundled Adamantina and the Exalted Heavenly Dream-Stone, completely ignoring all the sacred rituals involving ancient silks and lacquer trays one was supposed to follow, and heedless of Adamantina's protestations. He drove off almost as soon as he arrived, laughing as he went at break-neck-speed whence he came from. Adamantina sat in the back on a bed of straw, clutching the Exalted Heavenly Dream-Stone and looking terrified. This was rather gratifying to Gilligan, of course, and his mood improved considerably.

But at dinner all his irritation and discontent returned when Anastasius the bark beetle re-appeared. He shambled up his trouser-leg, climbed onto his plate, and proceeded to gorge himself. Gilligan watched this with increasing disgust, and when the shameless beetle defecated onto the plate after having eaten his fill, Gilligan cried out:

'You disgusting horrid little beetle, have you no manners at all?'

'Nope,' said Anastasius, and burped as if to reinforce the point. 'What about some met now? Just pour a little onto the plate, there's a good chap, I can't drink it well when it's in the mug.'

'You wretched ill-bred beetle,' cried Gilligan, 'how much longer will I have to suffer your company?'

'For the rest of my life, of course! Remember, you promised!'

But Gilligan was not in the mood to honour any promises. 'Take that, and that, and that,' he cried as he threw the plate to the ground and repeatedly stomped onto the beetle, 'you nasty loathsome pest!'

The beetle looked quite crushed, but whether it was the insults or the boots that caused most damage was hard to ascertain.

'You should not have done that,' said Kalle quietly while watching Gilligan's left hand. 'Don't you remember you gave him a forfeit?'

But Gilligan paid him no heed; he was staring incredulously at his left hand, which was rapidly turning a grey, sickly colour. The kindly gnome attempted to comfort him.

'Don't upset yourself, after all you still have the right hand, and getting rid of that pestiferous beetle was a virtuous act. Anastasius had many enemies who will be eternally grateful to you.'

But Gilligan was not in a receptive state of mind; he was still watching his hand, which had begun to shrivel up, and increasingly resembled that of an ancient mummified corpse. When the change was at last complete, his hand looked brittle as an autumn leaf and was the size of a child's. He took it gently into his other hand, to hold there tenderly – when a terrible scream issued forth from his throat! His left hand had come off his arm, and was crumbling into dust. Dazed and numb, he looked up and met the eyes of the gnome, who said:

'I hope you are not planning to go back on any of your other promises.'

19   The sad tale of Nuliajuq

It is high time that we returned to Greenland, where Cesare had come face to face again with the memorably ugly dancer Nuliajuq. She stood in the alcove, resigned to the inevitable reaction of disgust and loathing that her face always provoked, but also defiant – after all, he had no right to expose her in her own home like that!

But Cesare was made of sterner stuff than the other men Nuliajuq met in the ill-lit bars of Nuuk. While still alive he encountered plenty of faces horribly ravaged by smallpox, partly eaten away by leprosy, or disfigured by syphilis, as indeed his own was before death restored him to his original handsome self. And what he saw after his death in Hell simply beggared description! No, it cost him little effort to smile at the girl, and take her hand to draw her to the tea table.

'I bless the day I took up collecting devotional carvings,' he told her gallantly as she sat down, not quite believing her good fortune. 'Otherwise I might never have seen you again, after you ran off.'

Mr Walgren, overcome with gratitude and surprise at his guest's gracious manner towards his granddaughter, tried hard to make conversation.

'So you two have already met while dancing, you say?' Cesare nodded, not taking his eyes off the girl, and smiling all the while.

'With your permission, sir, I should like to take her out sometime.' Mr Walgren could hardly believe his ears, nor could his granddaughter.

'Of course, certainly, you must, Mr Borgia, I should be delighted if you two went dancing again. Are you going to stay in Nuuk long?'

'For a few years, I hope,' replied Cesare. 'I am involved in a large business venture here.'

Mr Walgren was a shrewd man, and it occurred to him that the dashing Italian only pretended to be interested in his granddaughter because he thought that Walgren could further his business interests. Indeed, how could it be otherwise? No man had ever been even remotely interested in Nuliajuq for her own sake! He looked at her, sitting transfixed with happiness in her chair, and privately resolved to do whatever he could to keep her that way; why, she looked almost pretty, smiling like that! For a moment he wondered whether it might not be worse for her in the long run to go out with a man who did not seem to mind her ugliness, only to be left again later on, than never to go out at all, but he brushed that thought aside. After all, he considered, this was something that happened to everyone, even those who were beautiful. Nuliajuq had become so quiet and withdrawn these last few years, that he feared daily she might do away with herself – no, he decided, it was worth taking the risk. But all the same he felt he needed to know Cesare's motives, so after a decent interval of small talk had elapsed he asked her to leave, because he had some business to discuss with Mr Borgia. When the girl had left, he turned to Cesare.

'Mr Borgia, I cannot tell you how grateful I am to you for being so kind to my granddaughter. She never had anything but loathing from people, even I myself can scarcely bring myself to look at her. Please forgive me for what I have to say to you now, but life taught me to be suspicious of the motives of others. I am a greatly respected businessman, and often approached by people who want me to use my influence in their favour. No one has ever tried to gain my help by being friendly with Nuliajuq, maybe people thought that a price too high to pay. If your motive for courting my granddaughter is to obtain my aid for your venture, I will not hold it against you. I would be more than willing to help you in any way I can in return for you going out with Nuliajuq and giving her some happiness. But I do want to know exactly where I stand.'

Cesare smiled. 'My dear Mr Walgren, I understand your concern exactly, and shall be completely open with you. I met Nuliajuq in the Laughing Seal and was attracted by her dancing; I had no idea that she was related to someone influential. I have to confess that I had come to your house solely to obtain your aid for my venture; the prayer nut was intended as a bribe for you. I do hope you will accept it, as a token of my appreciation of your good will?'

Mr Walgren was uncertain whether he should believe this man. Cesare continued.

'To be honest, I am not really a fit companion for your granddaughter. I have done much evil in my day, and am not, moreover, in a position to offer her any long-term relationship. However, I really do want to dance with her, and perhaps give her dinner, and take her to parties, and show people that not everyone finds her repulsive. Perhaps after a while people will get used to her, and she will meet someone more appropriate, someone nice, who will fall in love with her. I would not offer myself as her escort if there was someone else, someone less unsuitable, than myself.'

Mr Walgren was most astonished; he had not expected such candour, such self-effacement, from his guest.

'Believe me, Mr Walgren, I am not a modest man!' continued Cesare, observing his host's disbelieve. 'I know my faults, that's all. But I am not a complete cad, and believe me, I would never do anything to hurt Nuliajuq; not after all the other trouble she must have had.'

Mr Walgren believed him; he could scarcely credit it, but there it was, he trusted this stranger he had only just met. Cesare was not yet finished. To Mr Walgren's greatest surprise he said:

'There is something odd about the ugliness of Nuliajuq. I don't know why, but I could almost swear that it is something that does not belong to her, as though someone has painted a terrible mask onto her face. As though if one only knew how, that mask could be removed. Have you ever tried?'

Mr Walgren sighed, and told Cesare that he had tried everything the doctors recommended, and lots of other things as well, but nothing had worked.

'But you are an unusually perceptive man, Mr Borgia, and you are right, Nuliajuq's ugliness has a strange cause, and might perhaps be removed if one knew how. If you are indeed resolved to become her friend and companion for a while' – here he paused to allow Cesare to withdraw gracefully, but Cesare nodded, and he continued – 'I will tell you the story of her life. I have never told it before, and must ask you to keep it confidential.'

Cesare nodded again, and Mr Walgren proceeded to tell him one of the strangest tales he had ever heard.

About twenty years ago, Mr Walgren's son Niels and his daughter-in-law Elisabee, an Inuit from Baffin Island, became obsessed with witchcraft and black magic. Neither of them had any interest in business or the outdoors or in learning a profession, and found life in Nuuk too boring for their taste. At some stage they thought of going abroad, but Mr Walgren had been dead against it, since Niels was his only child. They agreed to stay, but in their boredom began to dabble in the occult. Mr Walgren's mother-in-law was a shaman, or Angakkoq, and his wife, though outwardly Christian, continued to follow some of the old pagan traditions. Niels grew up in this atmosphere, and developed an early interest in all things supernatural. But Mr Walgren's mother-in-law refused to teach Niels to be a shaman, claiming he had 'no horns in his guts', which apparently meant that he had not the aptitude for being a shaman. So Niels sought other ways, and taught his wife to follow in his steps.

They were both in their twenties when they went away to seek a 'mighty magician who lives in the Rocky Mountains in America and will teach us all the secrets of the universe', as their leaving note read. Several years later Elisabee returned, without Niels, but with a baby girl who was terrible to look upon. The little girl never smiled, or cried, or showed any sign of emotion; she looked as though she had been scared to death before she ever came to live, and aged a century before she was even born. According to Elisabee his own son had done this to the girl! Mr Walgren could barely contain his grief as he said this. Cesare watched him compassionately; he had a good idea of what had happened to the little girl, indeed he witnessed such scenes himself, but in this day and age? Presently Walgren continued.

Elisabee told him what had happened. She would not go into details, but apparently the great magician in the Rocky Mountains conducted a satanic mass - Cesare flinched a little – during the course of which Elisabee was to be sacrificed. She was over eight months pregnant then, and somehow that seemed to be an important part of the ritual. Towards the end of the ceremony the young woman realised that the ritual was not just the usual orgy, but in dead earnest, and when she understood what was happening she had panicked, and gone into labour. Her little girl was born at the exact instant the magician's dagger plunged into her mother's throat! The poor woman had shown the scar to Mr Walgren; it was a marvel that she managed to survive, and she only did so because the ceremony was interrupted. Elisabee never divulged all the details, but the ones she did tell were so fanciful Mr Walgren suspected that she was hallucinating at the time, which was only to be expected.

Elisabee claimed that a blazing figure like a comet came rushing out of the sky, and landed before the altar where she was being sacrificed. It was a tall, fiercely beautiful woman, with hair that seemed to be alive, each strand moving and striking out like a snake, and she was crowned with flames so bright that the hilltop on which Elisabee was being sacrificed was bathed in the flickering light. The woman threw back her head, and screamed as though all the powers of hell had broken loose, her scream rising to an ever higher crescendo until even the magician cowered before her wrath, hiding his face in his cloak and covering his ears with his hands. As she screamed her halo of flames rose ever higher, until the mountains all around were red with their light. When she finally stopped, there was no one to be seen, the trees and bushes had lost their leaves, and the grass on the ground was scorched.

The woman stepped close to Elisabee lying on the stone altar, and touched her neck gently. The wound closed upon her touch, but the woman shook her head and sighed and said: 'Poor girl, you will not survive this. But you have enough life in you to take your baby home, and to die there peacefully.'

Despite extensive enquiries, Mr Walgren had not been able to find out what became of the magician and his dark sect, nor of his son, nor did he know how his daughter-in-law got back to Greenland. But one morning she stood at the door with her baby Sara in a body sling, just as he was going out to buy a newspaper, and almost collapsed into his arms.

In the evening of Elisabee's arrival Mr Walgren's mother-in-law Arnapak, whom he had immediately notified of Elisabee return, arrived from her home in east Greenland and had a long talk with her grand daughter-in-law, asking many detailed questions about her ordeal. She also asked for her permission to help baby Sara, if she might, using the old ways of the shamans, and although Mr Walgren felt very dubious about this Elisabee readily gave her consent.

That night Mr Walgren was awoken by someone hammering on the door and calling his name. Mr Walgren rushed to the door, certain he recognised his son's voice, and was about to open the door when his mother-in-law pulled him back, and said, 'You must never open that door to Niels again. He is now a dead man who can't find the way to the land of the dead and haunts the living instead.' But the pounding on the door grew louder, and Niels begged to be let in with a most pitiful voice, until at last Mr Walgren could bear it no longer, shook off the shaman, and opened the door.

'What can I tell you, Mr Borgia, he looked so terrible, I nearly fainted. When I saw him I knew in my heart that he was indeed dead, and I had been a fool to open that door. But as Niels slowly walked across the threshold, Elisabee called out and asked who it was, and when I answered it was her dead husband, she rose from the sofa where she was resting, and exhausted as she was staggered to the door. There she pulled herself up, and with a loud voice, her right arm thrust out with the hand pointing to the door, cried out, 'Leave this house immediately, and bother us no more, Tupilaq[20]!' My hapless dead son, dazed and bewildered, left the house and walked into the dark night, and was not seen again.'

---

[20]   Some Inuit believe the Tupilaq are souls of the dead who dwell for one year with the Takanakapsaluk in Adlivun, before they go to a land of the dead.

However, the old Angakkoq continued to be very worried, and the next morning told Mr Walgren she would have to go on a long quest, both to guide Niels to Adlivun, and to find out what could be done for the little girl. Arnapak was also most concerned about the so-called Magician in the Rockies. She felt it her duty to bring this man to justice, partly for what he had done to her family, partly because she was one of the last great angakkut[21] alive and therefore felt it her duty to protect the people from evil magic. But while she was away the girl would need a new, more powerful name to protect her, and the shaman proposed to call her Nuliajuq. She explained that every name contained some of the power and wisdom of its previous bearers, and that the name of a powerful person gave powerful protection. This was the reason why she had so strenuously argued against the use of European names for her own, the Inuit people.

'What possible use can a name like Elisabee or Sara have for a girl who lives in the arctic', she said, 'such names have too short a history in these parts to be of use! Most previous bearers of these names knew nothing about survival in Greenland, their names will be of no use in a snowstorm or during a famine! Our children need good old-fashioned Inuit names, to succour and protect them from evil.'

She told Walgren and Elisabee that Nuliajuq was the most powerful name one could give to the little girl; she would not have dared to suggest it if she had not been told to do so in a dream last night by the Takanakapsaluk herself. Nuliajuq was one of the many names of the Takanakapsaluk, and by bearing her name the girl would be under the greatest possible protection. So the little girl was duly re-named, and shortly thereafter the old Angakkoq took her leave and disappeared, and had not returned to this very day.

Elisabee died several weeks later, leaving Mr Walgren in sole charge of her little girl. Although Nuliajuq thrived physically, and never knew a day's illness, she apparently had never overcome the shock of her terrible birth, and her face remained the mask of fright it was when he first saw her.

After Mr Walgren finished his story they both sat quietly for a while, not knowing what to say. There was much Cesare could have told his stricken host, but nothing that would have given him comfort. Mr Walgren already wondered whether he should have told the strange tale to his guest, who might now re-consider any proposed connection with him. But of course he need not have worried on that account.

As though divining what his host was thinking, Cesare told him that he was very grateful for his confidence, and promised to take every care of Nuliajuq, and do everything he could to make her happy and, if possible, help remove the burden that had disfigured her for so long. 'This I swear by the power of Agrat bat Mahalat, who saved your daughter-in-law.' At these last words he stood up and raised his hand in oath.

Mr Walgren did not know what to say. Although he could not know that Cesare Borgia, overcome by his finer emotions, had just bound himself by an oath that could not be broken to take care of Nuliajuq, knowing full well that this could land him into considerable trouble with his employer, he sensed that something deeply significant had taken place, and looked at his guest almost with awe.

---

[21]   Plural of Angakkoq (shaman)

But Cesare, as if ashamed of his lapse into sentimentality, reverted to the business that had brought him here, and told Mr Walgren of his plans, which surprised the old man even more than Cesare's interest in Nuliajuq.

Subsequently a deep friendship was to spring up between Mr Walgren and Cesare, and the old man turned out to be most helpful to the Greenlandia project. This was just as well, since Agrat might otherwise have objected strenuously to the amount of time Cesare spent with Mr Walgren and his granddaughter. Eventually Mr Walgren had to abandon his secret hope that Cesare would marry Nuliajuq after all, and came to realise that the strange Italian was somehow 'not of this world'. But in the meantime Cesare often went out with Nuliajuq, and after a while her grandfather noticed a change taking place in her. She slowly seemed to grow less ugly in Cesare's company, and people, perhaps ashamed of being unable to overcome their revulsion when a stranger so obviously could, began to stare less at her and were less uneasy in her presence. For the first time in her life Nuliajuq was happy.

20   Starting the building work in Greenland

Courting Nuliajuq was not Cesare's only activity in Greenland. After numerous discussions with his Greenland contacts, he chose a site for Greenlandia, within easy reach of the capital, but not too close to be a nuisance. Imhotep, Anthemius, and Andrea drew up architectural plans for the whole venture, and Cesare was busily putting the final touches on his negotiations for the site, when Jorgenson put a spanner in the works. When he saw the draft plans, and especially when he was informed that the magnificent domes would be build on stilts on wooden platforms, he began to worry about his commission, which would certainly not be paid if the venture ran aground. On the other hand he was loathe to discourage Cesare, lest he decide to build his retreat somewhere else altogether. It was therefore with extreme reluctance that he requested a meeting with Cesare and the architects.

He carefully explained to Cesare and the architects that the wooden platforms idea would not work. Although it was true that the ice underneath the platforms would not melt, given the construction of the platforms on stilts, the nature of ice made it a highly unworkable proposition. Ice moved and shifted about, and eventually it would break the stilts and the platforms would collapse. Cesare had to admit there might be something to this, and asked the architects for their opinion, but since they all came from hot climates none of them had any experience with ice. Of course, Cesare knew that the domes did not have to last long enough to be destroyed by the ice, since they were going to be transmogrified to Hell, but the banking consortium that Casanova was hopefully putting together in London was sure to make a few enquiries before parting with their cash - what if they discovered this fatal flaw?

Imhotep decided to accept Jorgenson's objections as valid, and asked why the domes had to be build on ice at all. Surely there was a sufficiently large ice-free site somewhere which they could appropriate for their plans? Jorgenson replied that there was indeed such a site, of a similar distance to the capital as the original site, equally secluded and encircled by a ring of mountains, called Qooroqsuaq. The surroundings were very beautiful, too, and Jorgenson thought the site could be adapted without too much trouble, provided the government would allow them to lease it. Christiansen and Schulze agreed it would be perfect for Greenlandia, but Karsfeldt disagreed. 'Qooroqsuaq is perfect all right, but have you forgotten that Simone the Stylite has moved there with twelve of her disciples?'

None of the others had even heard of Simone, and Schulze thought that they could surely buy her out. He doubted Qooroqsuaq was a good place for hairdressers anyway, and expected her to jump at the chance to leave with enough capital to open a salon in Nuuk – provided Cesare's company was prepared to split with the necessary cash. Not for the first time Karsfeldt felt he was in with the wrong crowd. 'Stylites, Mr Schulze, not stylists!' he admonished his bemused companions, and proceeded to inform them wearily that Simone and her disciples were pillar hermits, who had erected thirteen stone pillars near the edge of the site, each twenty feet high and surmounted by a small platform, where they lived a life of holiness and quiet reflection.

This was news indeed to Cesare, who had thought stylites went out of fashion sometime in the Middle Ages. He was curious to see how far these modern day followers of Simeon Stylites carried their fervour, and suggested the party went to Qooroqsuaq to investigate both its usefulness as a site for Greenlandia and its curious inhabitants. Everyone agreed, but Karsfeldt, the knowledgeable one, gloomily predicted utter failure with regard to the pillar hermits, since they had taken a vow of perpetual silence and therefore did not negotiate.

Qooroqsuaq was within an hour's flight of Nuuk, and the weather was freezing when they landed on a large open space was almost completely enclosed by mountains. Near the extreme far edge they discerned the thirteen columns, each topped with an igloo-like structure. There was an eerie silence, only interrupted by the wind and an occasional hacking cough from one of the columns.

After an hour or so of exploring the site the three architects declared themselves satisfied that it would do, mainly, Cesare suspected, to get out of the cold. While they and his Greenland business associates went to back to huddle in the warm plane, Cesare visited the hermits.

He walked up to the first pillar and yelled: 'Ahoy! Anybody at home?' There was no response whatsoever. He looked around. Twelve of the columns formed an orderly circle, while the thirteenth stood in its centre. A rope hung down from one of the pillars, but was hastily drawn up when he approached. Aha, so someone was at home! But how could one get them to communicate?

After a bit more useless shouting, Cesare went back to the plane to fetch a long supple rope he always carried with him. He attached a spanner to one end, and threw it across the platform of the centre column, hoping it would catch, which it did after a few attempts. But he had scarcely begun his ascent up the rope, when he was assailed by a shower of snowballs. He climbed down again, and examined his opponent. An unkempt creature in heavy furs was kneeling on the pillar's platform, preparing to hurl a few more missiles.

'What's this, in a bad mood,' he yelled. 'Missed your period, or something?'

The hermit answered by hurling a frozen cube at him, cutting him on the left cheek. He was getting annoyed. 'Two can play this game,' he cried, 'and I bet you'll run out of ammunition before I do!' With this he hurled snowball after snowball at the platform, and scored several direct hits. The hermit indeed ran out of snow very soon, but when she began to dismantle her igloo Cesare decided that things had gone far enough - he did not want her to freeze to death up there without her igloo - and retreated.

He was in an excellent mood when he re-joined his compatriots in the plane, feeling he had acquitted himself rather well in his first ever snowball fight, and resolved not to worry about the hermits. If they could not be budged, they would be fitted into the operations somewhere; who knows, they might prove an excellent addition to the Meditation Refuge Dome!

Gaining possession of Qooroqsuaq was not as difficult as he had feared. Thanks to his generous bribes and Mr Walgren's good connections the home rule government, who owned the site, was quickly persuaded to grant a 99-year lease to Cesare's company. Indeed, most of its members were genuinely pleased such a major project was coming to Greenland, and did not need much persuasion. The only real opposition came from the environmentalists, who were worried about the impact such a major development would have on the country's wildlife, but they were neither consulted nor heeded when they gave unsolicited advice. Within a month of their visit to what we shall henceforth call Greenlandia the building works began, and when Casanova finally arrived, things were well under control.

However, there was a great deal of strife among the architects. They bickered over every detail of the project, both between themselves and with Cesare. Imhotep especially was intent on trouble. He had never approved of the dome structure of the buildings, and continued to argue that they should be replaced with pyramid shapes, which were so much more durable. In vain did Cesare tell him that durability was of no importance with this project; Imhotep argued that it was the principle of the thing that mattered. Imhotep had to be handled carefully, because he considered himself infallible ever since the Egyptians deified him a few thousand years ago. Cesare had tried to keep him out of the project altogether, but was overruled by Agrat, since there were so few decent architects in Hell. They all either went to Heaven for having built churches, or languished in Tartaros[22] for having designed ugly municipal buildings; either way they could not be used for the project. And Imhotep was undoubtedly a genius, one of the very best architects that ever lived! So Cesare had to humour him, and got increasingly short tempered about it. When Casanova arrived, he appealed to him for help.

Casanova rose to the occasion, and persuaded Imhotep to re-assess his priorities for the project. After all, the really important part was the re-assembly of the parts of Greenlandia once they were transmogrified to Hell. The only purpose of the design of Greenlandia was to impress potential investors; but the reassembled parts in Hell, which would form what had been dubbed Hellysium by some joker, would last through the ages! 'Just think what a monument to your genius the new development will be! Eternal

---

[22]   Tartaros is an annex to Hell, reserved for the most evil of its human inhabitants.

glory, when even the pyramids have crumbled into dust!' Eventually Imhotep allowed himself to be convinced by this line of reasoning, and spent most of his time in Hell, badgering Beelzebub who was in charge of planning Hellysium, much to the relief of Cesare.

In the meantime Agrat cashed Gilligan's cheque, and Judas, too, had deposited his billions, so there was plenty of money available to finance the early stages of the project. Given the rapid progress made, Casanova had no doubt he could persuade the financial community to lend them the funds necessary to complete the project. It was time he had attended to Gingrich Fleabrunckle.

21   Adamantina and the Exalted Heavenly Dream-Stone are kidnapped by terrorists

After Agrat appointed Azazel, the uncivilised and disrespectful goat demon, as joint guardian of the Exalted Heavenly Dream-Stone with Adamantina, he had loaded the Exalted Heavenly Dream-Stone and its guardian onto a pick-up truck and hurled towards the next major airport. There he bought three tickets - Adamantina refused to put the Exalted Heavenly Dream-Stone into a suitcase and send it as luggage - and took Adamantina to the local burger restaurant while they waited for their plane to arrive. This was a new, and most distasteful, experience for the Dream-Stone Guardian. She watched with increasing horror as Azazel devoured a dozen hamburgers, ten large portions of fries, three milkshakes, and seven large cokes. The primitive table manners of the demon did not improve her temper, either. By the time they boarded the plane to London, she was physically sick with loathing.

But Azazel was in high spirits, commented on everything and talked incessantly of the Exalted Heavenly Dream-Stone and its attributes. Adamantina tried to shush him in vain. He chattered on and on, much to the delight of the terrorists who sat in the row behind them, and quickly realised the Dream-Stone's potential use for their trade. When the plane touched down, they were determined to follow Azazel and Adamantina until they had a chance to steal the Dream-Stone. Given Adamantina's idiosyncratic character, which they had amply witnessed during the flight, they considered her an easy victim. Azazel they judged to be more formidable, but luck was on their side.

Once in London, Azazel rented a cheap room in a shabby hotel, dumped Adamantina and the Exalted Heavenly Dream-Stone there, and announced that he had business to attend to. 'Don't move, I'll be back in a jiffy,' he told Adamantina and left.

Alas and alack! The shiftless demon had hardly gone when there was a knock on the door. Adamantina, thinking Azazel had returned, opened the door, was immediately chloroformed with a very filthy rag, and knew no more. She was folded up expertly into a large suitcase, and taken along with the Exalted Heavenly Dream-Stone to a small van waiting outside the hotel. The entire operation was over in five minutes.

She recovered her consciousness in a small dark cold uncomfortable cellar room, sitting in a badly sprung armchair with fraying dingy slipcovers, firmly tied up with a bright pink clothesline. She shuddered at her surroundings; had not her sufferings at the hands of Azazel been enough to atone for any of her past sins, real or imagined by whoever vengeful deity was persecuting her? But her tribulations had only just begun. Two young men, who had been lounging in armchairs similar to hers, approached her, evil intent writ large upon their coarse unshaven features.

'Luk Love, you'd better pour-out real right quick-like, 'course if you don't I'll biff you 'till you've snuffed it', one of the men said.

Adamantina evinced incomprehension, so the second man clarified his companion's utterance.

'If you don't tell us how to make use of the Dream-Stone, we will torture you until you either tell us or die.'

Adamantina drew herself up haughtily, and told her abductors that she feared no pain, no matter how excruciating, and would not divulge the secrets of the Exalted Heavenly Dream-Stone under any circumstances.

'I'll get me tools Paddy,' said the man who had spoken first.

'I don't think that will be necessary Connor,' replied Paddy. 'Remember what we overheard in the airplane while sitting behind her and her friend? This is a high-born lady, who has been protected and cherished all her life. Crude physical torture would be clearly inappropriate.'

Adamantina was not displeased to hear herself described in such terms. However, she became dismayed when Paddy continued.

'Little Lady, do you see what I have in this mug? It is good strong Irish Breakfast Tea, made with *ordinary tab* water. Connor here is going to make you a mug just like this – unless you talk!'

Adamantina looked at the mug; it was thick and chipped, and filled with an evil looking brew. She shuddered, and replied haughtily, 'I only drink Tranquil Joy Tea of Imperial Grade 2, from the upper slopes of the sacred fog-shrouded Eternity Peak in the Blue Mountains, made with water from the purest snow of the loftiest heights of the Himalayas. Anything else would kill me.'

Connor burst out laughing, but at a wink from Paddy went to the little adjoining kitchen and proceeded to make a strong sweet milky tea in the dirtiest, most chipped mug he could find. He handed it to Paddy, who approached Adamantina with a cold smile, and put the mug to her lips. Adamantina fainted.

'Do you have your snuff handy,' Paddy asked Connor, and was obliged with a small tin. He took a good pinch, stuffed it up Adamantina's nostrils, and massaged her nose until he was rewarded with an almighty, most unladylike, sneeze.

'Barbarians, what have you done to me!' Adamantina exclaimed when she recovered from her sneezing fit.

'Nothing compared to what we still have in store for you,' replied Paddy cruelly. 'Connor, hand me the mug for our lady friend!'

Adamantina tried to faint, but the snuff that remained in her nose defeated her efforts, and she merely sneezed again.

'Connor, hand me the funnel,' Paddy said, much to Adamantina's horror.

'You wouldn't dare!'

But Paddy did; he pushed back her head, shoved the funnel into her mouth, and poured the entire mug of the by now lukewarm tea into it. She involuntarily swallowed, and almost choked, but could not stop herself from drinking down the revolting liquid to the last drop. Then she fell back into her chair, and sobbed,

'You fiends, you have defiled me!'

Connor roared with laughter, which brought her back to her senses. Would they dare to repeat the experience, or construe even worse tortures for her? But what would the Emerald Maiden say if she shared the secrets of the Exalted Heavenly Dream-Stone with her abusers? While she was pondering this, Connor busied himself in the kitchen, and presently returned with a pudding basin full of a glutinous greyish mess.

'Real Oyrish porridge,' he said smacking his lips,' with cream and everything – we can't let the little lady starve, Paddy.'

'Or perhaps she would prefer a proper fry-up, with a bit of blood-pudding and fried bread!' Paddy wondered aloud.

That was too much for Adamantina. She shuddered yet again, and declared herself willing to explain the secrets of the Exalted Heavenly Dream-Stone to her abductors, provided they promised to treat her with all due respect and made no further attempts to force their barbarous food and drinks upon her. Both men assured her they would torture her no more once she had told them about the Dream-Stone, and Adamantina believed them, because she had no choice.

Having been apprised of the relevant details of Dream-Stone lore that Adamantina was willing to divulge, the two terrorists packed up the Exalted Heavenly Dream-Stone, bade goodbye to their captive, and left for their headquarters in high spirits.

'What a precious little madam,' said Tony as they left the building.

'Amen to that,' Rupert agreed. 'What luck we overheard so much of her conversation with her friend in the airplane!'

While Tony and Rupert, the Islington terrorists, took the Exalted Heavenly Dream-Stone to their current hide-out in Miss Minnie Moochmerry's spacious Georgian pile, Azazel returned to the hotel to pick up Adamantina. He opened the door, smelled the chloroform, saw the over-turned furniture, and deduced that Adamantina had been abducted. Now what? He decided to first complete his business in London, and then search for the Dream-Stone Guardian. After all, what harm could possibly befall her? At worst some hare-brained collector of ancient Chinese artefacts would shut her up in his mansion with the Exalted Heavenly Dream-Stone, and she would be mollycoddled as usual. No, Adamantina could wait.

Meanwhile Adamantina did just that for three days and nights, but her co-guardian of the Exalted Heavenly Dream-Stone failed to materialise to set her free. At last she concluded that he had either gone straight after the Exalted Heavenly Dream-

Stone, or, and she considered this the likelier alternative, had abandoned the Exalted Heavenly Dream-Stone as well as herself. Since she therefore had no one to look to for her liberation, she resolved to take action herself. She managed to wriggle out of the clothing line that tied her limbs, and braided it into a noose, which she tied onto the light fixture above her head. Having said her last prayers, she commanded her soul to make full speed towards K'un Lun Mountain and seek an audience with Queen Mother Wang,[23] to ask her to interfere on her behalf with the Incarnation Tribunal. Then she climbed onto a chair she had dragged under the light fixture, put the noose around her neck, and prepared to jump. She had failed in her duty to guard the Exalted Heavenly Dream-Stone, and had to pay the price.

However, fate had other plans. Just opposite the suicidal dream-stone guardian was an old, full-length mirror, and as Adamantina prepared to jump she caught a look of herself in the cracked glass. Her appearance was as always impeccable, even after her deprivations these last few days. Her hair was long and silken and black, her face a smooth mask of disdainful superiority, her clothes in perfect order, her shoes impeccably clean. But then she saw the rope! A rope the colour of shocking pink, a pink which clashed furiously with both her garments and her complexion. In fact, it made her skin look sallow! It was not to be endured.

Adamantina pulled her head from the noose, got off the chair, and readied herself to escape from the cellar. Escape was laughably easy, and she managed to crack the door open with a knife she found in the kitchen within a few minutes. She climbed up a flight of stairs, and emerged from the house into the bright sunlight without further obstacles. She had no idea where she was, and had neither money nor friends who might lend a hand, but this did not deter her. Full of courage and steely determination Adamantina set out to find a rope that matched her complexion.

22   Sophia meets The Old Lady

Stress Lucozade was not a happy man. He had been in bed with a nasty bout of flu for a few days, and was worried about his hamsters. Usually he went to work early in the morning, blew the homing-whistle, and locked his charges back into their cages before anyone would notice them. But since he had been unable to do this, the rodents had probably run around The Institution for more than four days now. It was therefore with dread and gloomy foreboding that he returned to work on Wednesday morning, not fully recovered but intent on minimising the mischief his hamsters might have caused. He tried to sneak in by the back entrance, but was waylaid by the head of the security force just as he entered the building. 'Sir, I should appreciate if you would follow me as quietly and unobtrusively as possible. I have been instructed to escort you to Mr Flabbergast, who wishes to speak to you on the subject of rodents!' Rodents! Stress broke out into a cold sweat. Obviously his absence had resulted in the uncovering of his

---

[23]   Queen Mother Wang is married to the Jade Emperor, and rules the abode of the Immortals in K'un Lun.

sharecropping scheme with the hamsters; he entered the presence of the Head of Personnel trembling with trepidation.

Rightly so! Mr Flabbergast minced no words, and came straight to the point.

'My dear boy, have you quite recovered from your illness yet? I was told you were unwell.'

Stress admitted that he was still not quite back to normal.

'Nothing a little whiskey and soda can't cure, I trust.' Mr Flabbergast poured them each a glass of this tried and trusted magic cure. 'Now, with regard to those rodents of yours.' He leaned back in his chair and eyed Stress with concern; he hoped his necessary tirade on the subject of hamsters would not throw the young man back onto his sickbed. Well, it could not be helped; Mr Flabbergast plunged in head first.

'Your hamsters have turned us into the laughing stock of the City! They ate almost a third of our dollar reserves, and the Treasury expressed doubts over our ability to handle a currency crisis. The New York Fed sent a condolence fax, the Tannu Tuva Central Bank assured us they once had similar problems and offered help, and the Frankfurters have made snide comments. Yet worse, your rodents chewed through some cables in the Feederia and caused a power failure – there will be no hot lunches for at least a week! Have you anything to say in your defence?'

Mr Flabbergast was a fair man, and perfectly prepared to forgive Stress his transgressions and give him another chance, provided he came up with a good excuse. After all, he had been to Oxbridge, had a degree in Economics, and played cricket – there was a very important match coming up! He therefore listened patiently to Stress's long explanation, and was pleasantly surprised by the enterprise and ingenuity of the young man – so unlike the general run of youngsters these days! When Stress finally finished his tale, Mr Flabbergast shook him warmly by the hand, and said that men like him were a rarity in the City.

'I really must commend your efforts to improve the economy with your unusual project, and wish you the best of luck with it in future. However, you do understand that your labours have caused some considerable damage to your employer's reputation and purse, and that I must therefore be seen to punish you in some way?'

Stress acknowledged that his enthusiasm had carried him too far on this occasion, and declared himself prepared for whatever sanctions Mr Flabbergast saw fit to impose.

The deep regard Mr Flabbergast felt for Stress increased even further. He poured them each another inch or two of whiskey, and suggested a few possible 'punishments'.

'What do you think of being transferred to another division, for example, and having your bonus docked for a year?'

'Sir, I hardly think that is sufficient! What about a reduction in rank and pay?'

But Mr Flabbergast considered this excessive; 'after all, we don't want trouble with the union now, do we?'

Reluctantly Stress allowed himself to be convinced; after all the Head of Personnel knew more about these matters than he did. They finished their drinks and parted on the best of terms, but not before Stress had been invited to lunch by his kindly superior.

Having taken leave of Mr Flabbergast, Stress went to see Fridthjof, who was currently in charge of the hamsters. Fridthjof welcomed him with open arms, and immediately raised the subject of what to do with the imprisoned rodents. Stress said the indoor training stage of the hamsters was almost complete, and they were ready for relocation to Barton-under-Water[24], where his uncle had agreed to take on the hamster project and develop it commercially. Fridthjof was tempted to ask whether this was the uncle who was responsible for people referring to his hometown as Bourbon-without-Water, but refrained; he was too happy to get rid of the hamsters.

If anyone was even more relieved to be rid of the hamster plague it was the Mouser. His entire workforce of twelve cats and one ferret (an unpaid volunteer) had been run ragged for weeks, and needed a break badly. Moreover, his social life was considerably curtailed by the invasion; he had not seen his many friends throughout the City for months. Hunting, sleeping, and eating were his sole occupations, and he had begun to resent it. However, now that the hamsters had been disposed off he was able to take an interest in other matters again, and one of the first things he did was have a long chat with that interesting new girl, Sophia. Being a cat of many talents and long experience, he recognised immediately that she was no ordinary employee, and therefore not surprised when she told him why she had taken a position with The Institution. But when she informed him of her desire to speak to The Old Lady, he shook his head doubtfully. The Old Lady, he told Sophia, lived in a mansard directly underneath the roof, at the end of a secret passage that was only known to the Governor and himself. She had been hiding there for over three hundred years now, watching over the City, observing transactions, eyeing business practices, judging the characters of the main players. She was ever alert for fraud and crime, but only roused herself to action when she felt that the City itself was in danger; all lesser problems she left increasingly to the regulatory authorities. The older she got she less inclined she was to interact with anyone, and the Mouser doubted that she would be prepared to talk directly to Sophia. But at least he could let her know what Sophia had just told him; it was certainly important enough for her attention! Mithras had been quite right when he suggested to Sophia to contact her, because it sounded as though the Greenlandia Project could seriously undermine the financial strength of the City. The Mouser promised to talk to The Old Lady that very evening, and report to Sophia the following morning.

The Old Lady was very interested indeed in the story the Mouser related to her, and much to his surprise immediately agreed to grant Sophia an interview when he mentioned that she was related to Mithras. Consequently the following evening, when most of The Institution's employees had left for the day, the Mouser led Sophia to the top floor, through innumerable doors, and down a multitude of corridors, until he paused before an innocent looking, very narrow closet door. After he impressed upon Sophia the need for utmost secrecy, he pushed against a panel near the floor, and a door opened to reveal a dark, narrow, seemingly endless passage. He pushed her inside the passage,

---

[24]   Please note that Barton-under-Water reverts to Barton-just-above-Water from March 21st, and to Barton-upon-Water after May 12th. It will become Barton-under-Water again on November 16th.

pressed another panel to close the door, and proceeded to guide her through the rabbit-warren of corridors and passages that had to be negotiated by visitors of The Old Lady.

At long last they stopped in front of an apparently solid wall that blocked off the passage they had followed. The Mouser lightly scratched at the wall, and a deep voice growled: 'Well, come in already'. The wall moved sideways, and revealed a small but cosy chamber, with several dormer windows, a desk with computer consoles, and several shabby, though comfortable looking, armchairs. The walls were lined with books, and next to the fire – it was still rather chilly in the evenings – sat a weighty old dame reading the Financial Times. Her white hair was piled carelessly on top of her head, black mustachios and equally black eyebrows beetled across her face, and steely blue eyes looked keenly out from amidst her deeply wrinkled countenance. She was smoking a big cigar, and a whisky tumbler at her elbow proved how wrong her detractors, who so often accused The Old Lady of excessive sobriety, were.

'Well, take a chair and have a little something,' she boomed. 'You are not one of those modern girls who like mixed drinks and crave gin-and-tonics, I trust?'

Sophia replied that she was more of a rum kind of girl[25], and was supplied with a pint sized pewter mug of a 200-year-old Haitian spirit The Old Lady had excavated from The Institution's cellars.

'Not much call for it these days, it's all white wine and orange juice, no wonder things are going from bad to worse. What about you, Mr Mouser, still on the wagon?'

The Mouser nodded, and coughed discretely; the atmosphere in The Old Lady's chambers was, as always, rather concentrated, and did not agree with his lungs.

When they were all comfortably settled around the fire, The Old Lady quizzed Sophia about 'that disgraceful fraudulent loan business' she had been told about. Was there anything to it, or had the Mouser been telling 'tails' again?

The Mouser sniffed indignantly, and his tail began to twitch. 'Really, Madam, since when have I ever' –

'There there Mr Mouser, I meant no offence, just having my little joke. Now, Sophia – may I call you Sophia, you are such a young little thing, it seems silly to address you as Miss?'

Sophia nodded, although she thought privately that 'young' was hardly the appropriate word for someone who had lived for almost three-thousand years, and told The Old Lady as many details about the demonic plot to defraud the City as she saw fit, starting with Beelzebub's decision to refurbish Hell, and concluding with a description of the building works in Greenland.

The Old Lady sat quietly staring into the fire after Sophia finished her narrative, poked around in the coals, took a big gulp from her whiskey, and twirled her mustachios. Finally she turned to Sophia.

'So the project leader hasn't found a lead bank yet, to help her form a consortium to raise the loan, you say?'

---

[25]   Most demons prefer rum to all other spirits; rum from sunken ships is the greatest favourite.

'Yes M'am, but I have reason to believe that they are close to finding one.'

'It is a pity that I was not told about this two weeks ago,' The Old Lady bellowed at the Mouser, who immediately went into a sulk. He pointed to his heavy workload, occasioned by the influx of hamsters, and why did it matter anyway whether The Old Lady knew it a bit earlier or not? No loan had been raised yet! The Old Lady sighed.

'Oh well, it can't be helped now. But you see, two weeks ago I attended the annual meeting of the Maisonettes, the highly secretive female Masonic Lodge that was founded by me and several other City ladies to counteract the predominance of the male element in the City. Our influence is secret but extensive; had I known about the plot to defraud the City before the annual meeting, I could have warned my fellow Maisonettes to be aware of anyone approaching them with a loan proposal involving a large project in Greenland; they would have taken my word for it, and not asked for any explanations. When we meet next, the loans are likely to have gone ahead.'

'But surely,' Sophia said, 'you can contact them somehow before the next meeting? This is the age of telecommunications!'

The Mouser sighed; he had had similar discussions with The Old Lady in the past, and knew how she loathed revealing herself in any way to anyone. He explained to Sophia that The Old Lady did not trust modern methods of communication, since other people were liable to eavesdrop in on them. And of course, being old and set in her ways, she was highly averse to leave her hide-away.

'What about the Governor', Sophia asked. 'Surely he could be informed, and warn the City?'

The Old Lady snorted. 'Ha, that guy doesn't even believe in my existence! Few of them do these days, why the last one I summoned into my presence was ......' she stopped in mid sentence. 'Anyway, it was a long time ago. Even if I were to talk to young Oswald, he would hardly be likely to believe me. Like most people, he will not be convinced until damage has been done. No, we can't count on the Governor in this matter. What is to be done?' She lit another cigar and stared morosely into the flames.

Sophia was greatly disappointed; she had expected a bit more vim from The Old Lady. Why did famous legendary heroic fidures always prove such a let-down upon acquaintance, and failed to live up to their admirers' expectations? It looked as though she would have to rescue the City all by herself.

'Don't look so gloomy,' said the Mouser. 'I am sure we will come up with something; just give it a bit of time.'

'Quite so', The Old Lady agreed. 'For now we must keep an eye on things, and try to find out exactly what their plans are. We will enlist the help of others as and when required. In the meantime, we should have meetings at regular intervals.'

Sophia was not exactly satisfied with this; 'keep an eye on things and have meetings' - what sort of an action plan was that? Moreover, she was wondering whether the Rat-god had been roped in by Agrat to further her cause – that sudden hamster invasion seemed mighty suspicious to her. That would be grievous news indeed!

Gingrich Fleabrunckle worked for one of the more illustrious of the City's merchant banks, Bog Bank Bros. The bank had been founded by several survivors of the Knights Templars, and continued to owe much of their success to their Masonic connections. Bog Bank were justly famous for their skill in arranging capital flotations, and in arranging syndicated loans. They had extensive international connections, particularly in obscure third world countries where no one else seemed to be able to do business.

Gingrich Fleabrunckle was one of the stars at Bog Bank. He had successfully managed several large syndicated loans, and been given a seat on the board as a result. He was also a genius at bringing in capital from rich but shy foreign investors – his Masonic connections were of great help there. Fleabrunckle was involved in those parts of the bank that few of its employees and customers even knew existed; he invested capital from drug barons, dictators, and tax evader. In doing so he continued a long and dishonourable tradition at 'The Bog', as insiders called the bank; they had been involved in shady business from the very beginning, partly necessitated by their obviously secretive nature as survivors of a disgraced order. Recently, as other merchant banks also ditched their scruples and competed in the shadows, things had become more difficult for The Bog. On the advice of Fleabrunckle, The Bog entered the derivatives market and managed to resurrect their profits; their team of dealers were the most successful in the City. Sir Wilbur Wellbeloved, the bank's chairman, knew nothing of the shady activities of Fleabrunckle. He was, moreover, uncomfortable with the trading team, and rarely set foot into the dealing room. Nor did he like Fleabrunckle, although he himself had hired the man a few years ago, at the insistence of Monsieur Florin Mondé, the bank's most valued customer.

Florin Mondé dealt in miracle drugs. One day at a sherry party for his important customer Sir Wilbur mentioned his increasing infirmity - 'but what can you expect at my age!' - and Florin Mondé had presented him with a sample flacon of 'Aqua Benedetta', a veritable water of life that was guaranteed to restore and preserve vitality indefinitely – provided it was taken regularly. After a month of taking the wonder-drug, Sir Wilbur's health improved markedly, and when he tried to purchase another flacon he was informed that the price was the employment of Fleabrunckle. Usually Sir Wilbur would not have agreed to such an arrangement, but the Aqua Benedetta had become quite necessary to him, what with his wife on hormone replacement therapy and Pips having to be walked twice a day (oh how he hated that energetic mutt!). So he gave in, and The Bog did not have to regret employing Fleabrunckle, who was an excellent worker, attracted lots of new business, and rapidly rose through the ranks. Sir Wilbur's continuing dislike of Fleabrunckle was increasingly dismissed by his colleagues, who considered him irrelevant and probably senile, and only allowed him to continue as chairman because some of the older customers seemed to like him. Also he owned a controlling share in the bank.

Casanova was well aware of the internal politics at The Bog, having been briefed by Trishy. Since Fleabrunckle was an intimate of Florimonde, who was likely to warn him against any dealings with an associate of Agrat, Casanova decided to discuss his plans with Sir Wilbur in the first instance. After all, once the old man was committed to what looked like an excellent business opportunity for Bog Bank, Fleabrunckle would have little choice but to go along with it. However, given the position of Sir Wilbur as semi-senile figurehead, he thought it prudent to include the Head of Treasury at Bog Bank in their first meeting.

Both men were impressed with the magnitude of the plans for Greenlandia, and when they heard that Judas Monkfish III was a major backer any and all doubt as to the feasibility and lucrativity of the project departed from their excited minds. It was obvious Casanova had no need to mention that Gilligan Wang was also a backer of the project, but did so anyway to further inflame them. This was just the sort of venture they both liked, rather than that new-fangled gambling in the derivatives market! They were a little taken aback when Casanova informed them that Fleabrunckle, and no one else, was to be in charge of putting together the consortium, and that the deal had to be signed within three days.

'Mr Seingalt, you do understand of course that we will need to get approval from the Board first for such a major commitment, and this might take a little time,' the Head of Treasury of Bog Bank exclaimed.

Casanova nodded pleasantly. 'Of course, of course, I completely understand your position. Bog Bank Bros is a conservative and risk aversive institution, and insists on doing its research before committing itself. I must commend your prudence, and shall not seek to dissuade you. However, I have been instructed to complete the financial side of the project immediately – we are most anxious to press on, and my employer is not noted for her patience. To ensure maximum speed, I shall have to contact the Little Green Moose Bank as well, and see if they might be able to come to an agreement within the time frame I have suggested. I had chosen your bank because of your reputation and Mr Fleabrunckle's well known expertise in such matters; however, since speed is of the utmost necessity, I shall have no choice but to negotiate with LGMB as well. Personally I should regret if Bog Bank Bros were to lose the contract, but what can I do? Madame Mahalat will not be gainsaid.' He threw up his hands, and prepared to leave the room.

Sir Wilbur was appalled. 'My dear Mr Seingalt, you have completely misunderstood my colleague. He only meant that the proposal has to be processed internally, but this is nothing, a mere formality; I give you my personal guarantee as chairman and majority share holder that Bog Bank Bros will accept your proposal, on the terms you suggest. Indeed, I am personally most interested in your project, and would like to invest in it myself. I cannot wait to spend a relaxing few days in one of the sleeper-domes, and agree with you that the project must go ahead at full speed!'

Casanova's hand remained on the door handle, and he continued to look doubtful. But before he could voice his doubts, Sir Wilbur continued.

'Mr Seingalt, surely you will not deprive an old man of the pleasure of being able to boast to his great grandchildren that he had a major role in creating the most exciting new resort in the world?'

Casanova relented, and went back to the table. 'Well, Sir Wilbur, if you put it like that - alright, let's shake on it, and sign the contract in three days' time.' From that day onwards he had a great liking for the old man, and resolved to protect him from the negative fall-out that would inevitably result from the venture. We'll pin all the blame on The Flea [26], he thought. Trishy would approve.

Gingrich Fleabrunckle was just as excited as Sir Wilbur when he heard about the deal; he lived for his career, and treasured every opportunity to advance it. However, his enthusiasm vanished when he read through the draft contract that covered Bog Bank's involvement with the Greenlandia project, and discovered that Agrat Bat Mahalat was the project leader. Florimonde had warned him against having any dealings with her and anyone associated with her, after the disastrous failed sacrifice of that trashy little tramp Trish Trash in the Altai mountains. He often wondered what had become of Trish, and why on earth Florimonde had let her go. But Florimonde rarely told him anything, and Gingrich, who was dependent on his good will, was not in a position to insist on an explanation. As soon as he spotted Agrat's name in the contract, he e-mailed Florimonde and asked for guidance.

He was told in no uncertain terms to get out of that deal, at whatever cost. 'Tell old Wilbur I will cut off his supply of elixir if he refuses to pull out,' Florimonde wrote. But Fleabrunckle was never to use this threat; before he had a chance to discuss the matter with Sir Wilbur, Casanova paid him a visit.

24   Hajji Kurt is bored

Hajji Kurt Nemsi ben Hajji Sadek abu en Nassr ibn Hajji Kara el Mott ben Hajji Halef Omar ben Hajji Abul Abbas ibn Hajji Dawudh al Gossarah [27] was lolling beside his pool in Jeddah, bored out of his mind. It was late afternoon, but still hot, and he spent most of the day wondering how he could avoid the amorous attentions of Amsha, his third wife, whose turn it was to be visited that night. Hajji Kurt did not exactly dislike Amsha; he would have divorced her a long time ago if he did. Rather he was simply tired of the same old ritual, 'Hey, it's Wednesday night, time to romance wife number three!' He was sincerely grateful to the Prophet for having allowed only four wives to a man; that way he managed to get three days off each week. But even four nights a week of conjugal duties were usually too much for the multi-henpecked Hajji.

Life would have been so very much nicer, so very much more leisurely and comfortable, if his mother, the beautiful and romantic Gisela Kiesewetter, had married the shy - but very infatuated - clerk from the post office just around the corner from her parents' house in a sleepy little town near Dresden. Her parents had been all in favour of the match, and sung the praises of the worthy post office clerk, who had a regular income, would get a nice little state pension in forty years' time, had saved up enough for a deposit on a small house, and – last but not least – had a steady, dependable character; in fact, just what a flighty, unstable girl like their Gisela needed. But Gisela had spent

---

[26]   Trish Trash's nickname for Gingrich Fleabrunckle, which Casanova adopted.
[27]   Henceforth simply referred to as Hajji Kurt, to save paper.

her youth reading books by Karl May, who, as is well known, wrote eloquently and excitingly about life in the desert amidst noble nomads. She refused to be persuaded, and ran away from home, to make her way into Arabia with many adventures along the way. Once there she managed to get a position as German teacher and babysitter to Fatima, one of the many princesses of the desert kingdom, and in this capacity caught the eye of Hajji Kurt's father Sadek, one of Fatima's innumerable grandsons. As in any good love story, the two young people fell violently in love with each other on first sight, and married shortly after their first meeting. The groom's family absolutely approved of the match; they had some connection with the above mentioned author whose stories had set Gisela on her path to Arabia. The founding father of the clan, Hajji Halef Omar ben Hajji Abul Abbas ibn Hajji Dawudh al Gossarah, travelled widely with said German author in the 1870s and always retained fond memories of him; in fact his son Kara was named after May. The family continued to treasure the connection even after Hajji Halef died, and encouraged its members to learn German and keep the memory of the author green by reading his many novels. A woman who had been inspired by Karl May to run away from home and have adventures in Arabia was more than welcome to join their family.

After her marriage Gisela quickly settled into nomadic life. In between collecting camel dung for the fire, making coffee, and cooking for the family, she spent her time translating May into Arabic. In this latter activity she was encouraged by her husband's family, partly because they approved of her translations, and partly because they disapproved of her cooking. Having adopted Arabia as her new homeland, she was determined to be a model Arab wife, and her cooking was along strictly traditional lines, consisting of questionable delicacies long since abandoned by the sensible Bedouin family she married into. The meals she prepared were soon legendary, and she was discouraged from cooking for anyone except ill-regarded relatives. Whenever she tried to grind some coffee, or pick up a cooking pot, one of her female in-laws firmly disengaged her hands and led her back to the library tent. 'You work on your translations, dear,' they would say, 'that is so much more important than housework; just leave that to us.' Exactly nine months after the wedding Kurt was born in a hospital in Riyadh.

Unfortunately the birth was attended by many complications, and an emergency hysterectomy put paid to Gisela's plans to start a whole new Arab tribe of Germanic extraction with Sadek. To make up for her sudden deficiency, Gisela tried to persuade her husband to take on a few subsidiary wives – she was singularly lacking in jealousy – but Sadek firmly refused, for a variety of excellent reasons. Firstly, he liked his peace and quiet, and had no intention of burdening his life with a gaggle of bickering females. Secondly, he did not really like sex. Thirdly, he was devoted to Gisela, the only person whose presence rarely annoyed him, probably because she was too practical to try to change him, and just got on with life and worked around his little peculiarities.

Much could be told about the loving, harmonious life that Sadek and Gisela led for many years, and about the battles Sadek fought against his family's frequent attempts to breach the barriers of his chastity and marry him off to a few more fertile females, but alas, that is not the purpose of this narrative. Indeed, I only touch upon these matters to explain why Hajji Kurt was suffering beside his pool.

Having fractured most of their teeth (metaphorically speaking) on the bedrock of Sadek's stubborn chastity, his family – led, it must be noted, by Gisela– focused their efforts to increase the tribe on Hajji Kurt. Although that youth took after his passive and peace-loving father, spent his time reading cheap romantic novels about the love life of medieval German peasant girls, and sophisticated aristocratic Russian gamblers in Monte Carlo, and showed no inclination whatsoever to wed, he was hitched by the offspring-hungry clan to a desirable virgin before he even hit eighteen. Hajji Kurt's first wife, who dutifully produced a child or two every other year, was soon joined by several other, equally fertile, maidens. By the age of thirty-five he was the father of several dozen children and on the verge of becoming a grandfather.

After the arrival of Hajji Kurt's fifth child Sadek could cope no longer with the demands of grandfatherhood, and decamped to an unknown destination, with very scant resources. When Gisela discovered this, she swore she would go after the fugitive and hunt him down, either to re-unite him with the family, or to share his exile, whichever came cheaper. However, Fatima, who was quite ancient by now, urged her grand-daughter-in-law to disregard the financial angle of the situation, and bring him back 'Dead or Alive!' She meant to have a few harsh words with him upon his return on the subjects of duty, family, honour, and so on and so forth ad infinitum, and she was still talking when Gisela set off several days later. At the time of this narrative nothing had been heard of either Sadek or Gisela for a great many years, and it was commonly assumed that they had perished. However, their son Kurt never gave up hope that they would resurface one day, and relieve him of the burden of running the clan that had fallen – like a ton of bricks! – onto his unwilling shoulders after their departure, since he was the oldest surviving capable male descendant of Fatima.

Hajji Kurt was not enthusiastic about his responsibilities. Since he had little interest in business, he delegated most of the day-to-day work to a distant cousin, Abdullah, who managed to increase the family fortune modestly but steadily, and rarely bothered him by discussing financial matters. The running of the clan, however, was not so easily disposed of. The family had settled in Jeddah and abandoned their nomadic life style after Sadek and Gisela left, which made it difficult to avoid his relatives. Anyone with a problem in the family came to Hajji Kurt, and expected him to do something about it. Whether it was a distant cousin who needed a dowry, a child who refused to go to the dentist, a reckless youth whose driving licence had finally been revoked after one too many accidents, or even what name to bestow on a new racing camel, he was supposed to come up with an answer. It was not only members of his own clan who sought his advice; members of the families of his four wives also flocked to his side and demanded attention, and all hell broke lose if he refused to help any of them! The wife whose family he had supposedly 'snubbed!' infallibly came raging at him with raised fists and a shrill voice, demanding to know what she had done to deserve this humiliation, how her family would lose face, why he could help the families of all the other wives but not hers, etc etc etc. By the time of this story, when he was pushing fifty, he was thoroughly sick of the whole business, and spent a lot of time next to his pool, daydreaming of living a simple life in a little German village, with just one wife and maybe two children in a small cottage with a Volkswagen Beetle in the garage. Though not a man given to strong emotions, he often cursed his mother at such moments.

Today his musings were interrupted by his daughter Suleika, who was running towards him with an air of excitement, wildly waving a report card.

'Look Daddy, I got four A's!' she yelled loudly. Apparently she expected some sort of response.

'Well done, my dove,' he mumbled. 'You certainly deserve a reward; next time I go out, I will bring you back a large box of liquorice candy.'

Suleika pouted. 'Liquorice is for infants, Daddy! I am a young woman, and I demand a real reward! How about a shopping trip to Paris?'

He was astonished; he could have sworn that Suleika was no older than eight. However, now that he looked at her more closely, he had to admit that she was indeed no longer a little girl. 'Do forgive me, Suleika, I am so sorry. But I could have sworn that we only just celebrated your eighth' birthday last week.'

Suleika grew purple with outrage. 'Oh Daddy, when are you ever going to learn my name? Suleika *is* eight years old, and her birthday *was* last week! I am Hanneh, and seventeen years old! Oh, you are hopeless, just hopeless; I wish you would give me up for adoption, so I could have a real Dad!' Tossing back her hair, she stomped off, wearing a very disagreeable expression, to talk to her mother.

Hajji Kurt remained in his deckchair, filled with remorse and apprehension. He acknowledged that, given the trouble his wives went through to give birth to their children, he could at least make the effort to remember their names. Actually, he did remember their names; he just occasionally forgot just what child went with which name. On the other hand, he defended himself, fifty-eight children was a lot of offspring, and he had already overloaded his memory banks trying to remember all the names of the innumerable brothers, sisters, uncles, aunts, parents, etc of his four wives. On balance, he felt, he was not doing badly. All the same, Suleika – no Hanneh! – would have to be propitiated somehow. Perhaps a trip to Paris would not be such a bad thing after all; he certainly could do with a holiday. But then he suddenly remembered the last trip abroad. He had gone to London with two wives, twenty-four children, a dozen nannies, two dozen servants, and innumerable bodyguards – just organising it had been one long, exhausting, horrific, nightmare. He seemed to have spent most of his time extracting his older sons from undesirable locations - strip joints, low boozers, and garden-centres [28]- and in buying presents for everyone. Presents for the wives, the children, the uncles and aunts, the nieces and nephews, and cousins and other relatives several times removed, not to mention all the in-laws! Of course, one could not just give them any old present, but it had to be just right in terms of their relative rank in the family and importance in the social hierarchy, and once when he had given the youngest brother of his third wife's second stepmother a more expensive present than one of the older brothers of his first wife by sheer accident, there was a huge – and ultimately very expensive - row when

---

[28]   Visiting English garden centres is a soul-destroying activity for Arabs, since few of the plants on sale there can be grown at home in Arabia. Nevertheless, they continue to buy plants by the truckload, and take them back to their gardens, only to see them suffer and die within weeks if not days. Hajji Kurt's sons were particularly addicted to this habit, and once one of them almost committed suicide after a particularly choice collection of ferns succumbed to the fiery climate of Jeddah.

they got back. Hajji Kurt shuddered at the memory of the London holiday; a trip to Paris was definitely out of the question.

He was distracted from his morbid recollections by a loud voice wafting across the courtyard, a voice which hurled insults and he identified as belonging to Amsha, who was to be his companion of the night and also happened to be the mother of the girl who had just left in a huff – now what was her name again? Emmeh? Maryam? Amsha's arrival beside his deckchair left him no time to jog his memory banks.

'You should not father children if you can't remember their names,' was her opening shot in the battle she intended to wage on behalf of her daughter. According to her plan, Hajji Kurt would hotly deny he had forgotten her daughter's name, thus giving her the opportunity to accuse him of lying, to which he would retort that he doubted his paternity, etc etc, and to cut a long story short, the upshot would be that they all went to Paris for a nice long vacation, courtesy of a guilt-tripped Kurt.

But Hajji Kurt was not in the mood. 'You are absolutely right,' he agreed with Amsha. 'As you well know, I never intended to have all these children, and if you and your fellow wives had taken the pills I gave you, you would now have no cause for complaint. But have it your own way; from now on I shall sleep alone, to ensure that none of you will ever have another child by me. And if I hear any more complaints, I'll divorce the lot of you and move to Switzerland!'

After which violent outburst the despot sank utterly exhausted back into his chair, and unfolded a several weeks old copy of the Berliner Bosheitsblättchen, his favourite German newspaper, to indicate to Amsha that her audience was at an end.

Realising that she had chosen a bad moment for her campaign to holiday in Paris, Amsha duly retreated. Kurt was not usually so unaccommodating, but she had noticed of late an increasing unwillingness to assume his family responsibilities; perhaps it was better to leave him alone for a while. She warned the rest of the household to keep away from him, and consequently he remained at peace in his deckchair until after evening prayer, when Abdullah arrived for his customary business chat. Having been briefed by Amsha, he decided to keep it short.

'All I need is a few signatures from you,' he told Hajji Kurt without even bothering to sit down first, 'just sign here and here and here for me', he continued while pointing to several dotted lines on the documents he placed on to the table next to Kurt.

But the Hajji was still in a truculent mood. He refused to be rushed or cajoled, and informed Abdullah with a scowl that he did not feel like signing anything for him; not now and perhaps never again.

This alarmed Abdullah considerably; did his cousin intend to take an interest in the business, perhaps even run it himself? His conscience was not entirely clear, and he knew full well that his accounts would not withstand close scrutiny. So he hurriedly took his leave, mincing obsequiously and promising to come back the following week.

Hajji Kurt, gratified by the ease with which he had slipped into the role of family tyrant, once more settled into his chair, hoping he had scared off his relatives for a while.

Although he recovered some of his good spirits after a restful night unencumbered by female company, he reflected that his personal situation was becoming unsupportable; unless he made some significant changes, he was headed for a nervous breakdown or worse. Unfortunately he had no idea what to do; running away to Germany and living there incognito was obviously not an option – or was it? Thinking that it might be easier to clear his mind and get new ideas away from home, he told the family that he was off on a holiday, and would not return for some time. Then he flew to Cairo, to visit his old friend Hammad Emin.

Hammad Emin was an ancient scholar who spent a lifetime translating accounts of arctic exploration into Arabic. Hajji Kurt was greatly fascinated by the arctic regions, and keen to find out whether his friend had finished another volume of translations. He was not disappointed; Hammad had just completed his translation of Snorri Rasmusson's famous work on Inuit funerary practices when Kurt arrived. Even more excitingly, he had fascinating news for his friend. Only the previous week he met a most remarkable woman, he told Hajji Kurt over coffee and pipes. But Hajji Kurt just groaned.

'Don't even mention women in my presence! All I want is peace and quiet in an all male environment.'

Hammad shook his head disapprovingly. 'You are so impatient, my young friend. Why do you always interrupt before I have told even the smallest part of my stories? This woman is connected to an epic arctic adventure! I thought you would give your eye teeth to hear the tale she has entrusted to me. Instead you make me break off after the first sentence. How can you hope to prosper with such an impatient temper?'

Upon hearing the words 'arctic adventure' Hajji Kurt pricked up his ears, and begged Hammad Emin to tell him more.

However, that worthy octogenarian seemed no longer eager to tell his tale. Shaking his head again sadly, he sucked his pipe in a meditative fashion, ruminated about the hastiness of youth and their lack of respect for their elders, and slowly drank three cups of sweet strong coffee, while Hajji Kurt beseeched him to hurry up and tell his tale. But Hammad Emin would not be hurried.

'You have put me off my stride, you have,' he said. 'Perhaps it would be better if you came back tomorrow to hear my story.'

Hajji Kurt was beside himself. Surely Hammad would not send him away and make him wait until tomorrow? But apparently Hammad did. After another ten cups of coffee and three pipes – liberally interspersed with Kurt's beseechments to continue his tale – the ancient scholar escorted Hajji Kurt to the door of his little house, and bid him goodbye.

The Hajji was shattered; how could his good friend do this to him? But he had barely walked ten paces away from Hammad Emin's house, when he heard his friend laugh out loud behind him.

'Hahaha, I got you good this time! Really had you convinced I wouldn't tell you, didn't I? You should have seen your face just now when I told you you'd have to wait until tomorrow! My word, I have not laughed this much since I tied firecrackers to the mayor's car and made him think terrorists booby trapped it! Get back into the house you fool, so I can tell you about Madame Mahalat.'

Uncertain whether to strangle his lunatic friend or embrace him gratefully because he was going to tell his story after all, Kurt decided to excuse him on grounds of senility and followed him back into the house.

Having settled back into the cushions, and refused yet another cup of coffee, Hajji Kurt finally heard the story of Madame Mahalat's Arctic Endeavour. Hammad Emin told Hajji Kurt that Agrat was creating a haven of peace & tranquillity in the middle of the eternal ice of Greenland, designed for stressed executives and family men in need of rest. It seemed too good to be true, and Kurt was keen and eager to meet Agrat bat Mahalat, the Chief Executive of the Greenlandia project. Since Agrat was no less keen to meet Kurt, there was no difficulty in arranging a meeting for the following day.

Agrat had come to Cairo with the sole intention of ensnaring Hajji Kurt and getting him to contribute some money to the Greenlandia project. She struck up an acquaintance with Hammad Emin because she knew that he could introduce her to Hajji Kurt, whom it would have been difficult to meet in Jeddah.

After she drank several cups of coffee and had enquired after his health, Agrat asked Hajji Kurt why he was interested in the arctic; it seemed a strange passion in a desert dweller.

But Kurt disagreed. The snowy wastes of the arctic and the sandy ones of the desert had much in common, he said. Both were sparsely inhabited by animal and plant life, both possessed extreme temperatures and striking landscapes, and most importantly, both were largely unsullied by the presence of human beings. He then enquired whether visitors to Greenlandia would be protected from intruding relatives, and was assured by Agrat that there would be a special security force dedicated to excluding undesirables (however defined) from the retreat. 'We will be nothing if not exclusive,' she said.

Predictably Hajji Kurt was fire and flames for the Greenlandia project. 'Do you take early bookings?'

Agrat shook her head. 'Alas the project is a little low on initial funds, and needs an injection of another billion or so before serious building work can commence.'

'But that is terrible! You must press on and build Greenlandia immediately! How much money do you need? Use my entire fortune if you have to! But start building those sleeper domes!'

Though gratified by his enthusiasm, Agrat counselled caution. 'Are you certain you can afford such a large investment? I hear your finances took a downturn recently.'

This was news to Hajji Kurt – what had Abdullah been up to recently? Agrat was not slow to enlighten him.

'Apparently – but that's just rumours, you understand - your business manager has accepted huge bribes in exchange for involving you in some very risky enterprises.'

Hajji Kurt was appalled. 'I wonder how much money I've got left, is it enough do you think to invest in Greenlandia?'

'Oh yes, you are still worth a goodish amount, and can invest one or two billion without too much trouble. However, Abdullah needs watching; I can lend you one of my own financial advisers to straighten out your finances, if you wish.'

Hajji Kurt was delighted to accept, and after he signed away much of his remaining fortune to the Greenlandia project he returned to Jeddah with Mifleh, a minor demon with considerable experience in creating accountancy irregularities, who would prove to be the bane of Abdullah.

25   On the subtle psychology of plants

Frederick Hornblower stopped before a small dark passage that led off a quiet side street near the Embankment, and paused to reconsider. Was he right to have succumbed to the entreaties of his wife and daughter to consult a plant psychologist on the matter of the giant elm that had made his life a misery for these last twenty years? He had a very poor opinion of psychologists, even where humans were concerned; consulting a psychologist for plants went against every grain of his being. But since he had tried everything else to no avail, he neatly folded up his principles, put them into the inner pocket of his raincoat, and entered Coromandel Corner, sighing deeply.

The narrow passage led to a tiny courtyard overgrown with all sorts of vegetation not usually associated with downtown London. Mr Hornblower saw a bougainvillea, several bilberry bushes, a coconut palm, and a rubber plant, which all grew companionably around a small pond filled with papyrus, sacred lotus, and irises. Towering over the jungle was a giant sequoia, which was even higher than the many-storied houses that surrounded it. At a height of six feet the sequoia bore a polished brass plaque reading 'Mithradates Devadorje, Plant Psychologist'; please ring bell for service'. Looking up, Mr Hornblower discovered an old toilet chain-pull, and pulled it, half expecting to hear a flushing sound. But all he heard was a slight rustle. A rope ladder was lowered to the ground, and a tall, slim, handsome young man descended from the tree. He had shoulder-length, curly, dark hair, and friendly brown eyes. His attire was made up of faded denims, a chequered flannel shirt, and very tired looking trainers. The young man jumped off the ladder while still five feet off the ground, bowed low before the speechless Mr Hornblower, and welcomed his guest.

'Pleased and honoured to meet you, Sir; how are your wife and daughter?'

Mr Hornblower was somewhat taken aback by this greeting; had his relatives spoken to Devadorje behind his back? But Devadorje, who seemed to have the ability to read minds, assured him that this was not the case.

'You have the look of a family man about you, that's all,' he explained. 'Now, what can I do for you?'

But Mr Hornblower was not yet ready to explain the purpose of his visit; he needed a few moments to adjust to the situation, and stalled by making small-talk.

'An interesting collection of plants you have here,' he observed, 'and all of them seem to thrive.'

Devadorje beamed at him. 'All strays, you might say, I found most of them abandoned in rubbish bins, and took them here to nurse back to health. Most of my strays go on to good homes, but some can't bear to leave, so I give them a home here.' Devadorje led Mr Hornblower to a small garden bench, and invited him to sit down and explain the purpose of his visit.

The story Mr Hornblower related was a good example of how bad relations between humans and plants can poison the existence of both.

'Shortly after we moved to a detached house in the suburbs some twenty years ago, an elm tree that dominates the back garden opened hostilities against me,' Mr Hornblower began. 'No matter where I tried to catch a bit of sun, whether indoors or out, the wretched tree somehow managed to arrange its branches such that I was cast into deep shade. At first I didn't realise that the tree singled me out for this treatment, but I soon noticed that my wife and daughter did not like me to be around when they sunbathed in the garden, but that they welcomed my company on those baking hot days when a bit of shade is a relief. When autumn came things got even worse; large numbers of birds came to roost in the elm, and after having spent an hour or two in its boughs they flew low over my car and defecated onto it in mid-flight. It badly affected the paint, and I had to have the car re-sprayed. I can't explain it, but I swear those birds are in league with the elm,' he said, feeling very ridiculous.

But Devadorje just nodded, as though the allegation did not surprise him in the least.

Mr Hornblower continued his narrative. 'The tree seems to have the power to drop its leaves at will, and several times I was enveloped in a veritable shower of them. This happened usually at night, and frightened me considerably before I realised that the attacker was just a heap of leaves. After a while the tree increased its hostility, and began to drop small branches on me. Finally things came to a head during the summer, while I was taking a nap in my wife's hammock, which was strung between the elm and the garden shed wall. I had hardly gone to sleep, when the branch to which the hammock was tied broke, and I nearly injured my spine when I fell on the paving stones underneath. After this nasty experience I decided to have the elm cut down, but found to my horror that this was impossible, since the tree was protected by a preservation order. We live in sad times indeed, if ill-intentioned trees are allowed to terrorise upstanding householders and there is no recourse to the law,' he finished his narrative.

'This does appear to be a serious problem,' Devadorje said, 'is there anything else you can tell me?'

'Well, there is little left to tell. The wretched elm must have found out that I am not allowed to harm it, and has started to undermine the foundations of the house, just to spite me. I am at my wit's end, and if you can't help me, I shall have to move house.'

'Worry no more, good Sir, I am sure you can come to some sort of understanding with the elm. With your kind permission, we shall set out and discuss the matter with her forthwith.'

And off went Devadorje with confident measured strides, while Mr Hornblower followed dubiously in his wake.

The Hornblowers lived in a large semi-detached house in one of the leafier suburbs of London. The elm that caused them so much trouble was huge, a magnificent specimen of its kind, which completely dominated the neighbourhood. Mr Hornblower, noticing Devadorje's admiring look, agreed that it would be a pity to cut it down.

'But what can a man do who has been tried beyond endurance?' he cried out. 'It's either me or it!'

'Her, actually,' replied Devadorje, walking up to the tree, 'Ermengarde Elmentree is her name.' He put his front head against her bark, and thus stood for a good twenty minutes communing, while Mr Hornblower watched anxiously. However, when Devadorje began to giggle, and even burst out laughing, he became suspicious, and demanded to know what was going on, and whose side Devadorje was on anyway.

Reluctantly Devadorje let go of Ermengarde, and faced his irate client. 'We were not laughing about you,' he informed Mr Hornblower, 'Ermengarde just told me a very funny joke about two squirrels and a hedgehog. I am sorry we got to chatting, I know you are anxious to find out why Ermengarde is so hostile towards you.'

Mr Hornblower nodded; so the confounded tree was called Ermengarde and was a female. He had been taught to treat all females chivalrously, and fleetingly wondered whether trees had to be included in this. These musings were interrupted by a stern question from Devadorje.

'Is it true that twenty-four elms died shortly after you moved away from Bristlegrove-on-the-Twee? Ermengarde tells me that they died of Dutch Elm Disease, which you introduced when you planted a young sapling you bought from a dodgy tree-dealer in a car boot sale. What have you to say in your defence?'

Mr Hornblower admitted that he had bought the sapling at a car boot sale, but claimed there had been no reason to assume that it was suspect. He had no idea the twenty-four elms had been infected and died.

He turned to Ermengarde and asked her, 'Is that the reason why you are persecuting me?'

The elm slightly swayed her lower bows, as though to nod.

'That means yes, I know it does,' cried Mr Hornblower excitedly, 'my dear Ermengarde I am truly sorry about those trees, really I am – eh, is it OK that I call you Ermengarde, or would you prefer Mrs Elmentree – Oh no, what am I doing, I am talking to a tree, have I gone mad?'

He turned to Devadorje. 'I am going mad, aren't I? Of course one can't talk to trees! Only it would be so very wonderful if one could! When I was just a little boy I used to talk to an elm almost as large as Ermengarde Elmentree here, and I thought it understood every word I said. I had forgotten all about it until now. It was in Holly-cum-Lightly, where I grew up, standing near the village pond, on the green.' Mr Hornblower sighed nostalgically.

Devadorje had another exchange with Ermengarde, and told his customer that Ermengarde knew the tree he had just mentioned; he was called Mirrormere Elmentree and was one of her cousins twice removed. If the tree confirmed Mr Hornblower's claim of having shown friendship to him when he was a child, she was prepared to forgive him for having unwittingly caused the death of her twenty-four relatives. However, it would take a few days to contact Mirrormere.

Mr Hornblower grew terribly agitated again. 'Dear me, I do hope Mirrormere will remember me, such an apt name, I remember how beautiful his reflection looked in that village pond! I have not been back for forty years! How could he possibly remember one small boy for all those years? There must have been dozens of children who played under his bows.'

On and on he went, agonising, until Devadorje felt moved to assure him that large trees like elms have incredibly long memories, especially for confidences entrusted to them, which, incidentally, they never betray. He also informed Mr Hornblower that Ermengarde had proposed a truce until word came from Mirrormere. In the meantime Devadorje advised him to spend as much time as possible with Ermengarde, so that they would get to know one another. 'I'll drop in again in a few days to see how you are getting on,' he promised before he took his leave of them.

Several days later a crow confirmed Mr Hornblower's story[29]. That good man was so overjoyed with Ermengarde's forgiveness that he resolved to never err again against any plant, great or small. He organised a fabulous reconciliation party, to which every plant in the garden, as well as Devadorje and all the pot-plants of the neighbourhood were invited. Anxious to establish a good reputation in the floral kingdom, he neglected not a single flower, and even the lowliest weeds were included in his benevolent attentions.

The party was a huge success. Eternal declarations of friendship were exchanged with the aid of Devadorje, who acted as interpreter. At the highpoint of the party a solemn compact was agreed between the Hornblowers and the plants in their garden, to the effect that the plants promised not to overstep their allotted space, and the Hornblowers swore not to disturb or damage them without prior warning and agreement.

Devadorje left the party laden with plant-food for those denizens of Coromandel Corner who were not mobile enough to attend the party. He refused to charge for his services. 'We are all friends now, I would not dream to take any money off you. Besides, I live very cheaply anyway, and don't really need much cash.' Promising to return for visits as often as he could, he returned to Coromandel Corner well past midnight.

In time Mr Hornblower and Ermengarde became great friends, and learned to communicate most effectively. Indeed, after many years of diligent application Mr Hornblower learned the language of many other plants, and there never was a garden with plants more thriving and luscious than his. Eventually Mr Hornblower became a plant doctor himself, and almost as famous as Devadorje. But that lies outside the scope of this narrative, and the Hornblowers are now out of the story.

26   Sophia falls in love

---

[29]   Crows are the messengers between trees and also keep them up to date with non-arboreal gossip.

Sophia had recently completed what little training was available to prepare her for her position in the Supervision Department. Although privately resolved to use her own methods, which she regarded as superior to anything she had learned during her training, she accepted that life would be easier if she acted as though she was like everyone else. During her last visit in Hell, her mother's advice was along similar lines. 'Once they get suspicious, it becomes much more difficult to take advantage of them.'

Jehova, too, agreed, although for different reasons. He warned her not to disturb the current belief of humankind that magic, and supernatural forces in general, did not exist. Until she had more experience, anything she said or did could shake someone's religious convictions, and although it was true they often needed shaking-up badly, it would be better if this was done in a controlled way, not by accident. For now Sophia ought to focus on her apprenticeship, and after she had passed all examinations her godfather and Lucifer would consider in what capacity Sophia could best develop her potential. Therefore Sophia tried her utmost to remain inconspicuous.

This was not always easy, and many evenings she left The Institution completely exhausted from having to suspend her judgment and acting completely irrationally. One such evening, just before cycling to her flat in Islington, she noticed a strangely familiar figure sitting on the steps of the Royal Exchange, apparently talking to a pigeon in his lap. She went up to him, but found herself completely ignored. After a few minutes the conversation seemed to come to an end, and the pigeon hopped from the lap onto the ground, bowed decorously, and flew away. The young man gazed after it, until Sophia, unused to prolonged ignoration, accosted him.

'You must be Devadorje!'

'What if I am? It's hardly an offence! Why ambush me like this?' The young man clearly did not wish for her company, and prepared to walk off.

'No wait, that's not what I meant at all, it's just that it has been so hard to track you down!'

'My dear young lady, I am in the telephone directory, and live less than fifteen minutes walk from here – if you wanted to meet me, why didn't you make an appointment?'

'Well I did not know that, did I!' Sophia was getting exasperated. 'I had so looked forward to meeting you properly, but if you must behave like an ass, suit yourself; I'm off.'

'Feel free,' said Devadorje, 'you don't look like a customer anyway.' They fairly glared at each other.

'Next time I meet Fridthjof I'll tell him to get stuffed with all his flaky friends,' Sophia said and turned away.

'You know Fridthjof? Why didn't you say so at once?'

'Why, are you only civilised to customers and people who are known to your cronies?' Once again the atmosphere between them deteriorated.

Just then a scruffy looking sparrow, who observed the ongoing exchange between the two young people with interest, let out a high pitched double trill. Devadorje blushed. The sparrow produced a triple trill, and jumped onto Devadorje' shoulder. Devadorje shook his head emphatically, and trilled what seemed to be a reply. Sophia was intrigued.

'Oh do tell me, what is he saying?'

'Something completely ludicrous. He says we are exhibiting all the usual symptoms of having fallen in love, and are going through the first stages of the human courtship ritual – that is why we are behaving so ridiculously. I ask you, was I behaving ridiculously just now?'

'Well,' said Sophia, 'seeing as you ask, yes you were, and upon further reflection I must admit so was I.'

The sparrow was hopping up and down excitedly, and trilling like a police whistle.

'Alright, alright, alright,' Devadorje admitted grumpily, 'perhaps we did act a little ridiculously – but that does not mean we are in love!'

'Absolutely not,' Sophia agreed, 'my place or yours?' She held out a hand to Devadorje, who took it in his. But suddenly he dropped it, and looked at her strangely.

'You are not human,' he said.

27   Casanova has a chat with Fleabrunckle

Casanova was well aware that Fleabrunckle would have objections to Bog Bank's involvement with the Greenlandia project, so before he approached him he spent a few hours with Camilla, the best informed gossip in Hell. He left fortified with several juicy bits of information, mainly about Florimonde, which, according to Camilla, where unknown even to Agrat.

Thus prepared, Casanova went to see Gingrich Fleabrunckle. He patiently listened to all objections raised by the Flea, demolished them one by one, and eventually, when Fleabrunckle paused for breath, told him not to worry about displeasing Florimonde by falling in with the Consortium. Fleabrunckle visibly paled when he heard Casanova mention the name of Florimonde. Smiling coldly at the discomfort of the other, Casanova suggested Fleabrunckle should call his boss for permission.

'His is your boss, isn't he? Your real boss, I mean?' After a slight pause, to maximise the impact of his words, Casanova added, 'you may want to mention Shefaka to Florimonde; tell him it has been a good year for spiders!'

Although this was only so much nonsense to Fleabrunckle, he thought it better to call Florimonde for advice.

A furious dressing down from Florimonde regarding this telephone call - Florimonde guarded his privacy like a newspaper tycoon - was cut short by Fleabrunckle who just said 'Shefaka'. Florimonde stopped in mid-sentence abuse, and asked where Fleabrunckle had heard about her. Fleabrunckle explained, and Florimonde demanded to speak to Casanova. But the Venetian refused.

'I might, possibly, consider discussing Shefaka after we have completed the Greenlandia project, but only if we finish on time and within budget.'

To the utter astonishment of Fleabrunckle, Florimonde, instead of trying to argue with Casanova, yelled at him, 'Make damn sure that the project is a total success, you are responsible to me for it with your head!' Both Florimonde and Casanova refused to give any explanation whatsoever to the confused and angry Fleabrunckle, who was in for some very difficult years ahead, and knew it.

While Fleabrunckle began to beguile four score and ten banks to invest in the Greenlandia project, Casanova went to visit Trishy. Thanks to the numerous protective amulets supplied by Lilith, and possibly the excellent facilities provided by the maternity ward of the Oxford hospital where she gave birth, Trish had survived childbirth without any lasting damage, and was happily nursing her baby when Casanova arrived in her cottage. Varus was sitting on a little stool at her feet, looking at the baby as though she was his own. A heart-warming scene, which touched even Casanova, who had financed it, and consoled him somewhat to the loss of Trishy, whom he had originally marked out as a possible future mistress after she recovered from the birth. Positively biblical, he muttered to himself, seeking refuge in sarcasm before he was overwhelmed by sentimentality.

After having admired the child, and half-heartedly praised its many amazing precociousities, he told Trish about the Greenlandia project's progress so far. Then he asked her whether she was still prepared to go ahead with their plan when the time came; perhaps she felt, now she had the baby and – Casanova slightly hesitated – a man friend, she would rather not be involved any more? She just smiled.

'If that bastard had had his way, this little baby would have lost her Mom and died an awful death while still womb-bound; you just name the time and place, and I will be there!'

Casanova warned her that things could get very nasty, but she laughed and said, 'Have you forgotten already what I told you about getting from the Altai to England? How can you possibly think that I am afraid of a little nastiness, especially when it is in aid of ridding the world of such monsters? I'll be there, never you fear! Varus and I have already discussed it, he will watch the child while I am away; he has already learned how to change nappies and bottle-feed and stuff, so no worries there, either.'

Casanova bent over her hand and kissed it, apologising that he had forgotten her gallant spirit, and presumed to think that childbirth might have changed her. However, her contribution would probably not be needed for a few more years yet, so until then she could devote herself to the child and rebuild her life.

Which is exactly what she did. In the years until the project was completed, Trish and Varus and her child settled into a peaceful useful life in their little village, and were blissfully happy.

The same cannot be said for Florimonde. After he hung up the telephone he remained deeply shaken. He pondered his long gone past, and how fate snatched away the only true happiness he ever had. It took him quite some time to subdue his long-forgotten memories once more, and for some time his nights were haunted with nightmares of a large, cold, filthy stone sarcophagus, populated by woodlice and spiders. The dream always ended with the lid being lifted, and the beautiful face of Shefaka coming into view. And he always woke up screaming.

28   Sir Wilbur gets his way, and Libraria acquires a team of dealers

Sir Wilbur Wellbeloved was a happy and contented man. Ever since he had agreed that Bog Bank Bros would lead the consortium of banks that financed Greenlandia, and browbeat the board into accepting it, his prestige and influence had increased immeasurably. Suddenly people who had written him off as a mere figurehead decades ago showed him respect and sought his advice and goodwill. Once again he was a power in the City.

While in this expansive mood he yet again pondered Bog Bank's supposed need for a derivative dealing room. Surely now that the bank had pulled the most lucrative contract in the City, and established itself as a major player in the syndicated loans business, he could get rid of the dealing room, and Bog Bank could return to the solid, honest sort of banking business which lay at its roots and which Sir Wilbur could understand! He recently dropped a few hints in that direction to his fellow board members, and felt that he might soon be able to put it to a vote successfully. Moreover, his great benefactor and major customer Monsieur Florin Mondé had advised him some time ago that the stars were not favourable to Bog Bank – their success in the syndicated loans business had aroused astral enmity! He told Sir Wilbur to reduce his own commitments on the speculative side of the business, and even hinted that he might move his fortune to another bank altogether, lest Bog Bank overextended themselves and experienced severe financial difficulties. 'I don't want you to go bankrupt, old chap,' he told Sir Wilbur over canapés and cocktails during the annual reception of the City's Ironmongers' Guild, 'so do take care.'

As luck would have it, later that week Fleabrunckle informed Sir Wilbur that the dealing room had just incurred a major loss connected with the Verdigris'[30] Futures scandal, and was set to loose several million more if their portfolio in Artificial Christmas Trees[31] further deteriorated. All Sir Wilbur's suspicions and antagonism towards a business he neither understood nor cared for came to the fore, and he insisted that the future of the dealing room was put on the agenda of the next board meeting.

---

[30]   A green substance often found on copper, which was much in demand to colour pickles, and to poison rats. Unfortunately a lot of people died from eating the lovely bright green coloured pickles, and the market for verdigris dropped like a stone over night.

[31]   Trees made of green plastic and dressed up as Christmas trees. Fleabrunckle believed people were sick of dropping pine needles at Christmas, and invested heavily in this product. Unfortunately for him people instead switched from cut to potted-up real trees, so the Artificial Christmas Tree market withered and died.

During the meeting Sir Wilbur performed a dizzying feat of elegant loquacity, and since the main defender of the team, Gingrich Fleabrunckle, was unable to attend because he was in Greenland on urgent business, the motion to dismantle the dealing room was carried without a single dissenting vote. Sir Wilbur had won at last.

When Fleabrunckle returned from Greenland he affected to be both outraged and appalled. 'Is this how you repay your faithful dealers, who have made millions for the bank these past few years?' he shouted at Sir Wilbur when he heard the news. 'What am I supposed to tell them now? I do believe you have gone senile at last!'

Sir Wilbur turned pale, and curtly advised Fleabrunckle to watch his language in future if he valued his employment with Bog Bank. Fleabrunckle murmured something that could be construed as an apology, and left to go to the dealing room to bring his faithful employees the awful news.

But the news had already been leaked to them, and they were in an angry aggressive mood. Almost all of them were deeply in debt, and could ill afford to lose their well-paid jobs. They made it abundantly clear to poor Fleabrunckle that he owed them firstly a major redundancy cheque, and secondly a really brilliant reference so they could impress their next employer. Fleabrunckle assured them that he was just as upset about the loss of The Bog's dealing room as they were, promised to secure them both the redundancy money and good references, and concluded by saying that the Bank of Libraria had long been interested in setting up a dealing room, and he would do his utmost to convince them to hire the entire Bog Bank team. At this the dealer calmed down, and returned to their desks to attend to their outstanding positions, while Fleabrunckle went to see his good friend John de Bourg.

'I've built the greatest team in the world,' he complained to his friend, 'I just know that Sir Wilbur is only closing down the dealing room to spite me. The derivatives business had been one of the backbones of my power at The Bog, and Sir Wilbur has been waiting for a long time to clip my wings. Now that the Greenlandia business has strengthened his position, he takes advantage of my absence in Greenland to axe my team. If my work in the Greenlandia project wasn't so crucial, I would quit myself immediately!'

John de Bourg was very sorry for his friend, and suggested that he might try for a position with Bank of Libraria when the Greenlandia project was completed in a year's time. 'I can't guarantee anything, of course, but I will do my utmost to convince the board to offer you a job.'

Fleabrunckle smiled gratefully, and warmly pressed his friend's hand. 'Thank you so much John, you can't imagine how much your friendship means to me! But just now I am more worried about my faithful team; I do hope they will all be able to find new jobs soon.'

'I hesitate to mention this,' said de Bourg, 'but you know I have finally convinced the board that Bank of Libraria should set up a dealing room, and they have authorised me to hire the best dealers money can buy – no point in paying peanuts and getting comic book characters, as the saying goes.'

Fleabrunckle felt obliged to chuckle at this feeble joke.

'However, I feel it is really not quite right if I were to hire your team, I feel I am taking advantage of your predicament ....' De Bourg hesitated and then stopped.

But Fleabrunckle was overjoyed, took his old friend's hand, and pumped it vigorously. 'My dear chap, my bestest buddy, it would be such a load of my mind if you hired my team! I have been worried sick for them ever since Sir Wilbur told me he was closing the dealing room. Why to work for Bank of Libraria would be like a dream come true for them! And if I were to come and work for you after the Greenlandia project it would be like being reunited with my family! Thank you, thank you, thank you!!!'

John de Bourg was quite overwhelmed by Fleabrunckle's gratitude, and felt that he hardly deserved it. 'My dear Fleabrunckle, after all you have done for me in the past, it is the least I can do. Besides, it is no hardship to employ the best team of derivatives dealers in town! I am the one who should be grateful, really.'

They parted on the best of terms, and rushed to their respective banks to disseminate the good news. Within a few months the entire dealing room of Bog Bank had moved to Bank of Libraria, and Thérèse and her tem fell once more into their money-making routine. The only difference to Bog Bank was that they were dealing in stocks and shares as well as derivatives, but since they were all experienced dealers this did not concern them. Sir Wilbur was happy because he didn't have to feel guilty for having made a dozen employees unemployed, de Bourg was happy because the banking community was full of admiration that he had acquired the greatest set of dealers in town, and Fleabrunckle was happy because he had protected his beloved dealers from financial disaster. His e-mail to Florimonde after the trading team had left The Bog read, 'Everything went according to plan, I await your instructions in due course.'

29   Adamantina finds her feet in London

After Adamantina had been abandoned by the terrorists and her faithless fellow Dream-Stone Guardian Azazel, she spent several months wandering the streets of London in search of a suitable rope with which to hang herself. However, although she came across numerous ropes which appeared on the outset suitable for her purpose, her fastidious mind always found a reason to reject them. Some were too short, others too rough, many had colours that clashed with her complexion, and others were malodorous. What was a Dream-Stone Guardian to do?

During her wanderings she met many interesting individuals, and even struck up an acquaintance with some of them. Among these was a kindly old priest who ran a soup kitchen on Cheapside where Adamantina sometimes helped out. Father Gottlieb was quite fond of the beautiful girl, and one day when he saw her peeling potatoes with a particularly mournful expression, he took his courage into both hands and dared to ask her point-blank what the problem was. Adamantina felt rather dejected just then, and had almost given up hope of ever finding a suitable rope, which explains why she did the hitherto unthinkable, and confided in a mere mortal. She told him of her human past, and how she had entered the service of the Emerald Maiden, how the Exalted Heavenly Dream-Stone was stolen from her, and of her fruitless search for a perfect rope.

Father Gottlieb listened to her with open-mouthed astonishment. He was a simple man, but steadfast in faith and trustful of God. When Adamantina completed her tale by bewailing the lack of suitable ropes, he asked her whether she was certain she wanted to die. Had she considered that perhaps she rejected all ropes as unsuitable because deep down she really wanted to live? This was a new idea to Adamantina – could Father Gottlieb be right? Surely, the priest continued, she would be better employed in trying to recover the Dream-Stone – had it occurred to her that the Dream-Stone might be in danger, and that her mistress had need of her? Did she think it right to abandon the Dream-Stone to its fate, just so she could indulge her morbid desire for suitable ropes? Having thus set off a new train of thought in Adamantina, the priest left her to her peelings, and when he returned two hours later she had not only peeled every last potato from the larder – a week's supply at least – but also come to a conclusion.

'You are quite right,' she told the priest across a small mountain of potato peelings, 'I have been self indulgent. I must find the Exalted Heavenly Dream-Stone and rescue the Emerald Maiden; I can always commit suicide afterwards.'

Father Gottlieb wholeheartedly approved of this new goal, and since Adamantina had already taken him into her confidence, he thought it admissible to ask her a few more personal questions, to wit, how she earned her keep and where she lived. Adamantina replied that she made a living by utilising certain hitherto unknown talents, and had become an accomplished pick-pocket. She generally stayed in cheap hotel rooms, using the passports she had stolen as identification. Father Gottlieb was horrified. 'My dear child, surely you can do better than that? I shall have to give you a hand.'

So the next time Oswald Pinchback, the Governor of The Institution, came to the soup kitchen with a basket of spare vegetable from his allotment – he currently had a glut of carrots – Father Gottlieb asked him whether there might not be a job going at The Institution for Adamantina. Since Pinchback was always willing to help those less fortunate than himself, he arranged a job for her in his office as a secretary, although she could neither type nor take shorthand. But since she made a mean cup of tea, had impeccable manners, and knew how to fold lovely origami birds from internal briefing papers, nobody really minded. Kind Father Gottlieb even found her lodgings with an old parishioner who lived nearby and felt the need for a bit of youthful company.

Adamantina settled quickly into her new life, and after a while almost forgot that she was an immortal Dream-Stone Guardian and not a human being. She attended adult learning courses and learned typing and taking minutes, and even acquired the Computer Driving License. After her first year in The Institution she was promoted from third undersecretary to second uppersecretary, and Mr Flabbergast shook her warmly by the hand and prophesied a great future for her. 'Why you may even become chief secretary to the Governor one day,' he beamed at her over lunch. And Adamantina, the once haughty disdainful guardian of the Exalted Heavenly Dream-Stone who despised all mortal men, blushed at the compliment like a schoolgirl.

When Devadorje told Sophia that she was not human, she smiled and replied that was as may be, and suggested they go to his place, since it was closer than hers, to exchange secrets.

Sophia's story astonished Devadorje, but not as much as she had expected, and the only bit that impressed him was that Mithras was her father. However, it also outraged him, since Mithras was supposed to be a chaste and sacred god who did not commit adultery.

'As his High Priest, who follows all his strictures, I am entitled to demand a similar purity from my God,' he pronounced.

Sophia burst out laughing; her new love sure had some strange ideas about the relations between gods and their followers! 'They do as they please, and if their human believers don't like it, tough shit! Incidentally, does my honoured padre know that you are his High Priest – and only priest, I should think! – or are you self-appointed?'

Devadorje admitted Mithras had so far not honoured him with an indication that his sacrifices were benevolently regarded, but no doubt this would come in the fullness of time. Now that he had met the god's daughter, Mithras' epiphany was certain to be imminent. Sophia declined to voice an opinion on the matter, and instead asked Devadorje to tell her his life story.

Apparently his childhood and early youth were entirely unremarkable, but when Devadorje turned fifteen he happened upon the name of Mithras in a book on ancient religions. As soon as he read the name, before he had any idea who the god was and what he stood for, Devadorje was convinced he had been Mithras' priest in a previous existence, and resolved to become his priest again. The local public library yielded only meagre scraps of ancient gossip – much of it libellous - on the subject, so Devadorje enlisted the aid of his form teacher to obtain the information he needed. He told his teacher he wanted to write his literature / history project on Mithras, and since this worthy scholar rarely had the opportunity to help a student with such an obscure topic, he was more than willing to assist this hitherto unimpressive pupil to gain access to the necessary books and treatises in the British Library.

Rarely had a student put such effort into a school project, and the A+ Devadorje received for it was certainly richly deserved. Little did his teacher and parents - who already envisaged him as going to university and becoming an anthropologist or similar exalted being - realise that Devadorje was not so much preparing a school essay, as studying for the priesthood. Upon completion of the project he also completed his studies, and deemed himself fit to take up his duties. He often went to the remnants of the Mithras temple in the City of London, to pray and pour libations and commune with the god. On his eighteenth birthday he changed his name by deed poll, severed all relations with his unsympathetic family, and devoted himself entirely to the service of his god. Since he was as yet the only follower, and could therefore not collect any tithes to pay for his up-keep, he decided to go into business as a plant psychologist; he had always been a sensitive lad, and was adept at communing with both animals and plants. 'Of course I could have become an animal psychologist, but you need a formal qualification for that,' he completed his story.

Sophia realised that she had stumbled across a rare lunatic, but this did not dissuade her from entangling him in an amorous affair - she was a demon, after all. Her first priority was to lead him away from his obsession with chastity, so she told him his research had misled him a little on this subject.

'Mithraism was a major competitor to Christianity,' she told him, 'and most of the information about it available to modern scholars was distorted by Christian priests who wanted to discredit their rival. Take, for example, chastity. The priests of Mithras were not supposed to be chaste in the sense that they had to avoid women altogether, but in the sense that they had to remain faithful to one woman at a time!' She knew very well that she was somewhat twisting the teachings of Mithraism, but did not let that trouble her. She was determined to experience at least one intense physical relationship with a human being as part of her apprenticeship, and did not scruple to tell a little white lie to achieve her end.

Although Devadorje was only partly convinced, he found it increasingly difficult to fight off Sophia's amorous attentions. The sun set just in time to miss the spectacle of Sophia divesting Devadorje of his trousers, the moon felt compelled to hide behind an accommodating cloud several times in order not to witness the young man's attempts to escape from his demonic lover, and the innumerable stars did their best not to peek through the foliage that hid the couple from view. However, when rose-fingered Eos at last ushered in the dawn, she found Devadorje reconciled to, and even secretly delighted with, his fate at the hands of Sophia. At breakfast the newly minted couple received the congratulations of several birds that roosted amidst the branches of the sequoia; they had always considered the abstinence of their beloved and revered friend disturbing and peculiar. Devadorje, although still a little huffy about Sophia's intrusion of his private sphere, reluctantly agreed that his entrance into the realm of physical affection was not wholly without merit.

Alas, Sophia's father, the honoured and esteemed Mithras, took a dim view of this development, and peremptorily summoned his daughter into his presence, as soon as he was made aware of the unchaste nature of the relationship between Sophia and Devadorje. He was displeased with the liaison for two main reasons. Firstly, he completely disapproved of Devadorje. 'That young fool is no more my priest than the rogue Fleabrunckle! I did all I could to discourage his attentions, to no avail. The idiot prays to me using all the wrong incantations, thus disturbing my meditations, and pours libations at my old temple, making me honour-bound to lend him an occasional hand in his endeavours. What is more, he is completely mad. Escaped from one of those nut-houses; and just look at his so-called profession! I will not have you run around with him and that is final!' Mithras' second reason to forbid the relationship was that Sophia had managed to seduce his one and only priest, a priest whose commitment, virtue, and chastity were unrivalled in this lax and selfish millennium.

'How dare you lead one of my own priests astray!' he yelled.

However, Sophia was not impressed, but pointed out that his two objections to her liaison with Devadorje were inconsistent (she had been trained well in logic during the long hours spent with Socrates).

'First you claim that Devadorje is not your priest, and then you complain that I am corrupting your priest. You can't have it both ways, you know,' she told her genitor. 'Besides, even if he was your officially acknowledged priest, I would have still seduced him; that'll teach you to demand the impossible from your followers! What's so wrong with me sleeping with the man I love, anyway? Perhaps I should remind you that I am the result of a similar union myself!'

Mithras knew he was beaten, but refused to be nice about it. Pulling himself up to his entire – not inconsiderable – height, he thundered,

'I don't want to see either you or your paramour again until you have regularised your union in holy matrimony!' Sophia's laughter pained his ears and wounded his soul.

'Father dear, I am a demon! How could I possibly marry a mortal? Get real!'

But Mithras, who spent the last two thousand years becoming increasingly unreal, refused to listen to the voice of reason, and retreated sulkily into his cave. Sophia blew him a kiss and promised to come to dinner the following Saturday; but he just grunted and retreated further into his cave.

Being not insensitive to the sufferings, real or imagined, of her biological father, Sophia went to see Yeshua for a little chat.

'Now be honest,' she asked him, 'am I doing anything wrong? Is it really true that Devadorje is a complete nutcase?'

Yeshua assured her that she was behaving impeccably, for a demon, and much better than most demons during their apprenticeship.

'The Honourable Mithras tends to forget that you are a demon, not one of his priests, or even an angel. Besides, moral standards amongst humans are changing, and as long as you sincerely love this youth, I see no harm in your relationship. Regarding Devadorje's mental state' he paused, and sighed, and told her not to worry about it.

And since they were both in the mood for a little gossip, and Sophia promised to keep stumm, and anyway Yeshua thought she ought to know, because she might do Devadorje some good and he certainly would not mind, and as she was a demon it wasn't really breaking confidences, etc etc, Yeshua told her the story of Devadorje.

Devadorje came to Yeshua's office some thirty years before, weak as a newborn lamb, exhausted into death by drug taking, excessive sexual experimentation, lack of sleep, and a generally wild and undisciplined existence - 'Bless him!' and insistent on being re-born immediately. Of course this was out of the question; Yeshua put him into a recovery chamber, where he slept soundly for several years. When the young man finally woke up, Yeshua had a long chat about his past and future lives with him, and warned him not to repeat the mistakes made in his past life in the next one. It was all very well to seek after the true nature of things, and try to gain an understanding of the essence of creation, but drugs and physical ecstasy, though valuable, could only get one so far. 'Why not stay here for a while, and absorb some wisdom from Aquinas, Kant, and Wittgenstein?'[32] But the impetuous youth would not listen, and insisted on incarnating

---

32   The only Philosophers who had slipped through the net and ended up in Heaven rather than Hell.

again without delay. Yeshua was not too surprised; this sort of thing often happened with people who died while still young, and had not managed to experience an entire human life time, from childhood to old age.

Eventually they agreed that Devadorje could incarnate again later that year, on condition that he would abstain from all drugs and irresponsible living whatsoever. To make up for the loss of insight this would occasion, Yeshua bestowed upon Devadorje the ability to know and understand all beings by simply watching and touching them.

This was a most perilous ability, and rarely granted for fear of exposing recipients to such a wealth of emotional experiences that it would almost certainly overburden them. Few people indeed are able to know and understand all living creatures, and not despair, but rather grow and mature. For who but the emotionally most stable and strong, or conversely the most callous and brutalised, are able to observe daily the tooth and claw spectacle Nature puts on stage, and not be adversely affected? Those desperate struggles to survive just long enough to pass the flame of life on to the next generation, those harrowing attempts to wrest an existence that is more than just survival from an unforgiving world, and yes, the folly, the laziness, the cowardice, the wanton disregard for the future! Could anyone, even the most compassionate and mentally strong, intimately witness this every day and not despair of Nature and all it contained? Indeed, was it not likely that such a person, unable to endure any longer this world with a sickened and pain-stricken heart, would hide away and avoid all contact with those who could not or would not be helped? Or, yet worse, become hard and uncaring and join the world which seemed, in the end, to be all there could ever be?

Yet Yeshua did grant this talent to Devadorje, knowing this youth, who had squandered his previous life for want of cares and purpose, needed a heavy burden to anchor him to existence, and hard tack to chew slowly and carefully, if he was to succeed at his next life. There was no fear that Devadorje would falter under his burden, for there was great strength and enthusiasm for living in him. 'He has a great soul, but needs a hard and meaningful life to recognise his worth and calling,' Yeshua finished his talk with Sophia, and admonished her to deal kindly with the young man. 'This is an important incarnation for him, and its success will have a bearing on the future of this world.'

Sophia marvelled greatly at all Yeshua told her, and locked it in her heart in secrecy. For despite his easy manner, commonplace appearance, and humble demeanour, Yeshua was considered by the demons to be the kingpin of the universe. He was deep in the counsels of Jehovah, profound in his knowledge of all creation, and the mediator between the three worlds. And it was rumoured amongst the demons that one day, at the end of time, Yeshua would forge an alliance between Heaven and Hell and The World, and create a new universe where all beings, be they demon or angel or creature from earth, would live together in harmony and everlasting blessedness under his benign rule. But when this would come about, and what the roles of Jehovah and Lucifer would be, no rumour told.

31   Devadorje joins the Foilers

At the next meeting of the Foilers - as Sophia had nicknamed them - in the rooms of The Old Lady, Sophia proposed that Devadorje be accepted into the group. She had discussed the Greenlandia project with him, and he immediately offered his help. Sophia thought his excellent relations with the plant and animal kingdoms would enable him to obtain invaluable information about their opponents, and might help defeat them. Moreover, as a plant psychologist and generally accepted harmless fool he made friends quickly, and easily gained access to every building in the City.

The Old Lady and the Mouser raised no objections, and Sophia went to fetch him from the Library in the basement, where he was loitering with the excuse that Alfie, the ten foot dracaena marginata, was pining for his homeland.

This was, of course, an outrageous lie. The librarians took excellent care of Alfie, and Howard, who was in charge of parliamentary papers and legal abstracts, even read him those articles from the Manchester Telegraph which he considered suitable for a potted plant.[33] Alfie told as much to Devadorje during his sojourn, and indeed suggested that the entire staff of the Library should be asked to join the Foilers, to ensure that something worthwhile would be achieved. Alfie's opinion of analysts and bureaucrats was as low as his esteem of librarians and security guards was high.

After Devadorje had been introduced to The Old Lady – he obviously already knew the Mouser – that venerable guardian of the City's interests had to admit she had no idea how to stop the dastardly plot of the denizens of Hell. She proposed they should wait until they knew how the transmogrification of Greenlandia to Hell was to be accomplished, before they took action. Devadorje was visibly unimpressed, and Sophia, too, voiced her discontent. The Assertiveness Training and Personality Improvement courses The Institution sent her on were bearing fruit.

'We have to be more pro-active,' she exclaimed. 'Firstly, we need to keep a close eye on the community of the City, and especially on all banks who are signing up to the Greenlandia Consortium. Secondly, we need to spy out Agrat's office at Bog Bank, and find information pertaining to the transmogrification procedure. Thirdly, we need someone in Greenland to keep an eye on developments there, and build up a network of supporters that will help to torpedo the transmogrification plan once we know details.'

Devadorje agreed with all these suggestions, and volunteered to go to Greenland for the group. However, before committing himself, he wanted to know why they seemed content to allow the building of Greenlandia to go ahead, and only wanted to foil its transmogrification to Hell.

'Why don't we stop the Consortium from getting off the ground by persuading the banking community not to finance the project?' he asked.

The Old Lady sagely shook her head. 'Surely you know that it is impossible to dissuade a banker from investing in a project that promises a huge financial return? Agrat and Casanova have promised them fantastic financial rewards, and even the

---

[33]   Mainly the gossip (including politics) and the Royal Engagement section, but no sex or crime or sports.

Governor, if he could be persuaded to join our cause, which is unlikely, could not stop them from investing in such a profitable venture. No, the solution to the problem is not to prevent the Greenlandia venture, but to ensure that it will remain un-transmogrified in Greenland, and become indeed a success! That way we will both foil Agrat's project and benefit the community of the City!'

Sophia was somewhat stunned by this little speech; she had been concerned only with preventing the City from committing financial suicide, not with enabling it to bag one of the greatest financial windfalls in its history. Was this the real reason why The Old Lady had refused to warn the banking community until it was too late? She realised how little she still understood The Old Lady and the financial community she guarded.

Keeping an eye on the City, and especially on Bog Bank, was not considered a problem, but watching over the project in Greenland and recruiting a group of helpers to foil the plot was more difficult. The Old Lady could not go, because she had to watch over the City and anyway never left the house. Sophia was in the middle of her apprenticeship and had to stay in London. The Mouser did volunteer somewhat half-heartedly, but it was well known that he abhorred ice and snow and was at his best in moderate climes.

After discussing and dismissing several obviously unworkable schemes, they agreed to accept Devadorje's offer to go to Greenland, ostensibly to set up a new Mithras temple in Nuuk, but in fact to spy out the progress of the Consortium, and help evolve a plan to foil Greenlandia's transmogrification. Of course he would miss his newly found love Sophia, but he consoled himself with the thought that he would finally meet that great defender of the rights of all living things, and friend of Fridthjof, the Viking Philosopher Ragna Sturlusdottir. He was a little concerned regarding his visa. He had escaped from a mental hospital his parents committed him to several years ago, and wondered whether the Greenland authorities be willing to let him set up a new religion in their country.

But The Old Lady was able to reassure him on that front. 'Greenland has so few significant buildings that a roman-style Mithras temple will be welcomed with open arms as a tourist attraction. Moreover, I know a Maisonette who works in the visa section of the Danish embassy in London, and is sure to oblige if I put in a good word.'

Finance for the venture was provided by several successful stock market speculations which were engineered by Sophia, who was able to look into the future to some extent and therefore had little trouble in picking stocks and shares that unexpectedly increased in value, and within the month Devadorje was on his way to Nuuk, well provisioned with funds and good advice.

When Sophia next visited Mithras he played the happy and supportive father figure, who doted on his beloved daughter and was proud of her achievements. Not only was she now separated by an ocean from that young lunatic Devadorje, but she was also helping Mithradates set up a new temple to him, a brand new place of worship, with all modern comforts and necessities for pilgrims - nothing like those sad ruins that remained of his once mighty temples in the rest of the world. Mithras intended this new temple to be a resounding success, and planned to visit it often once it was complete, and smile upon his worshippers. And if a few small – or even large – miracles would help to attract followers to the temple, he was not averse to producing a few, even if it meant flouting the CAM (Convention Against Miracles).

32 Devadorje meets Ragna, and Mithras Looks Favourably Upon his New Temple

Once he arrived in Nuuk, Devadorje wasted no time and immediately went to see Ragna Sturlusdottir, the old Viking Philosopher and friend of Fridthjof, on her tree farm. That worthy woman had done little more than keep an eye on things in the year or so since Judas had tipped her off about Greenlandia. In fact, she had pretty much given up the fight before it began. Everyone was so thrilled about Greenland becoming a major tourist attraction, that she thought there was little to be done to stop the Greenlandia project. Besides, since the whole structure would be transmogrified anyway, and presumably leave nothing behind except a few disappointed businessmen, she really did not see why she ought to do anything about it, busy as she was with her tree farm As for the City of London being financially ruined, she thought it served them right for being so greedy.

She was busy mulching a few dozen fir trees when Devadorje arrived at her farm.

'Tsk tsk,' he muttered disapprovingly when he saw the mulch she was using, 'you will kill them using that rubbish. Mulch with their own needles, and cover with old carpet.'

He bend down to the trees, and greeted them one by one, completely ignoring Ragna, who felt a little put out by his way of greeting her with an admonition. But since she had read extensively about him in the letters from Fridthjof Thorsteinson, she waited patiently for him to complete his conversation with the trees. At long last he was finished, and turned towards her.

'You are feeding them wrong, too,' he said, and proceeded to tell her in great detail how to treat her furry friends. Half way through his lecture he looked up at her and said sternly, 'you are not writing this down!'

'I don't have any paper and pencil out here,' Ragna excused herself, 'why don't we go into the house and I write down your instructions there.'

They duly went to the house. But if Ragna had thought Devadorje could be sidetracked with tea and biscuits, she was mistaken, for he refused all nourishment until she had taken down his dictation regarding the welfare of the fir trees in minute detail. Finally, after two hours of speedy scribbling, he relented and told her they could go into the nitty-gritty's in a few days' time. 'You've got the basics,' he assured her, 'and enough to be getting on with.' Only then did he accept her hospitality, and was prepared to discuss his plans.

Although Ragna was thoroughly annoyed at being treated like a greenhorn by a young man who had barely outgrown his short trousers and was moreover just a foreigner, she nevertheless had to admit that he knew his stuff. She had been most unlucky with her arctic hybrid tree project, and was really very grateful for his help. So she pulled herself together, swallowed her pride, prepared to be gracious, and asked him why he had come to Greenland. Despite all injunctions for secrecy from The Old Lady, Devadorje, who instinctively realised that Ragna already knew the truth about the Greenlandia project, told her both parts of his business, about the Mithras Temple, and about the Foilers' plans to stop the Consortium from transmogrifying Greenlandia into Hell once it was completed.

Well, that was a bag of news and no mistake! Ragna was quite appalled at the Foilers' plan to keep Greenlandia from being transmogrified. 'It will be an absolute disaster for the environment,' she told Devadorje. 'Just think of all those tourists arriving by plane, polluting the atmosphere! We will have to import food for them, and fuel to keep them warm, and so on and so forth! How can you possibly lend your hand to such a venture?'

'These are all problems that can be managed,' Devadorje replied. 'Surely there are building regulations that will make Greenlandia energy efficient? With regard to food, it is possible to grow special arctic varieties of most food crops in Greenland; this can be incorporated into the basic layout. Obviously tourists will not arrive in planes, but in Zeppelins! They will take advantage of air currents part of the way, and if the improved type of Zeppelin that is being developed by Zuper-Zeps is employed, will be both fuel-efficient and non-polluting.' When he noticed the look of incredulity on Ragna's face, he exclaimed, 'you mean to tell me that you and your fellow environmentalists have not insisted on these few simple measures? What have you been doing all this time?'

At this point Ragna was rescued by the entrance of her friend Lars, who returned from Nuuk with some fertilizer. After he had been apprised of the facts, Lars admitted they and their fellow environmentalists lacked enterprise and had been too idle. All the same he agreed with Ragna that Greenland would be better off without the retreat. 'Even if Greenlandia incorporates all the measures you suggest, it will still be a disaster, both environmentally and socially. Greenland would never be the same again!'

'Greenland is going to change anyway, regardless of the presence of Greenlandia! The icecap is melting, temperatures are increasing, and hunting and fishing will change for the worse. The old ways are changing, and the Inuit will have to find new ways to earn a livelihood. Greenlandia will give you a breathing space, and tide you over until you have decided Greenland's future. It will only be viable for ten or twenty years anyway, after that the geography and climate of Greenland will have changed too much to retain the main attraction of Greenlandia, which is its icy seclusion.'

Lars and Ragna were far from convinced, but promised to think about Devadorje's argument. In the meantime they would make up for their past inactivity and try to persuade the Greenlandia consortium to at least implement Devadorje's suggestions for making the retreat more environmentally friendly.

'We have several good friends in the Landsting[34], I will get onto them immediately. But before I go, can you guarantee that it would indeed be possible to grow all necessary food in Greenland?'

---

[34]   The Greenlandic parliament

'Of course I can, and I will prove it! Let's see now, I need five square meters for every crop you want grown ....'

It turned out to be a very long day, and night, and week, and month. But eventually everything was set up, and Devadorje was able to turn his attention to the temple.

The Old Lady had been as good as her word, and used her contacts with the Nuuk chapter of the Maisonettes to purchase a large property at the edge of town. There was no trouble with obtaining a building permit, either, especially when Devadorje submitted his plans which showed a building entirely energy self-sufficient, with a horticultural annex for growing fruit and vegetables for the pilgrims that were expected to flock to the new temple. Devadorje intended his temple to be an example of how human habitations can be incorporated into the environment without causing damage or disturbance, and hoped it would stimulate the debate about Greenlandia which Lars and Ragna had kick-started in the Landsting. 'If I can do it with my limited resources, then so can the Consortium with their bottomless purses,' he told Ragna who had come to inspect the new the temple.

Progress had been swift and impressive! Being by nature impatient and energetic, Devadorje implored and harangued, pleaded and cajoled, bribed and flattered, and had his temple completed for its great opening three months after he arrived in Greenland.

The occasion was as great as the temple that occasioned it. Sophia and Fridthjof attended the inauguration ceremony, as well as Ragna and Lars, and practically every Greenlander who managed to make their way to Nuuk. There was food and drink for everyone, and the temple thronged with admiring visitors.

At the height of the celebrations were great fireworks, which culminated in a huge image of Mithras himself, who lifted his arms in benediction and blessed his new temple, saying: 'I am well pleased with my new abode, and shall look with favour upon it and my servant Mithradates Devadorje, and will bless all my new worshippers.' Then he vanished.

Everyone was most impressed by this spectacle, and none more than Devadorje and the pyro-technicians who built and set off the fireworks, and knew that the appearance of Mithras had not been part of their preparations.

'Finally I have been accepted by my god,' Devadorje told Sophia afterwards. 'At last my life has meaning.'

Sophia, though severely tempted to make a few extremely cutting sarcastic comments, refrained and congratulated her first human lover on his good fortune. I wonder what Daddy is up to, she wondered when she returned to London after the ceremony. Surely he wasn't going to re-enter the human stage and break the CAM?

That was exactly what Mithras had in mind. If Beelzebub and Agrat could do it, so could he, he reflected after the opening ceremony of his new temple. Of course eventually he would have to toe the line again, but until then he would perform as many miracles as possible, and revitalise Mithraism for centuries to come!

When Arnapak, the old Angakkoq, knocked on the door of Mr Walgren's house one sunny afternoon a few years after the building works on the Greenlandia Project began, she had been gone for almost twenty years, and her son-in-law had almost given up hope she would ever return. The old shaman seemed to have hardly aged, and was full of her accustomed vigour. After several cups of sugary tea and a special meal of frozen raw caribou meat to celebrate the occasion, she settled herself near the fire and told Walgren the tale of her adventures, suitably abridged, since she was in a hurry and suspected that her son-in-law was unlikely to believe most of it anyway.

After the return of Elisabee and the visitation of the dead Niels, Arnapak had gone to stay with her great friend Ragna Sturlusdottir, who did not scoff at her shamanising like most other Greenlanders, and agreed to tie her up and watch over her while she went on her long spirit journeys. Thus her great adventure, which was to bring her not only to various spiritual lands and the realm of the Takanakapsaluk, but also to North America, the Middle East, and Siberia, began.

After Ragna tied her up as instructed, to prevent her body from flying away and injuring herself on the journey, Arnapak began to breathe deeply and regularly to put herself into a trance. One by one she summoned her spirit helpers, starting with the first one, a small spider, and continuing with seals and dogs and bears and long dead angakkut, until she had summoned all 23 of them. When they were all assembled, she began to chant rhythmically, and fell deeper into trance, until at last she was ready to leave her body and enter the spirit world.

Her first endeavour was to consult Tornarsuk[35], and enlist his help in finding Adlivun at the bottom of the sea, both to guide Niels there if necessary, and to talk to the Takanakapsaluk who lived there. But although she stayed in trance as long as she dared, and continued to repeat the experience as soon as she recovered from a spirit journey, for three long months, and searched the whole world for him, both under-world and over-world, and was even carried by her spirit helpers to the moon and beyond, she was unable to find Tornarsuk. 'I also looked out for any soul your granddaughter might have lost,' she told Walgren. 'I suspected that her disfigurement was the result of one of her souls having fled in shock during her birth, but again, I could not find anything.' At last Arnapak resolved to visit the Takanakapsaluk by herself, with only the aid of her spirit helpers.

The Takanakapsaluk, whom Arnapak was so determined to visit, is the most powerful of the spirits who affect the lives of the Inuit. She is known by many names; Sedna, Nuliajuq, Takanakapsaluk, Arnaquashaq, Immapukua, and Nerrivik are some of the names given to her by the Inuit; she is also known as the Mother of the Seals. She is particularly concerned with the way arctic animals are treated by the Inuit, and how their souls are treated after and during death. If the soul of a slain animal is treated with disrespect, it may not be able to reincarnate again, and then there will be a shortage of animals, as well as an abundance of evil spirits, for animals turn into evil spirits just like

---

[35]   A sort of primordial shaman-god, who helps shamans in their quests.

humans when treated disrespectful. There may also be a shortage of animals because sometimes the Takanakapsaluk deliberately shuts them up and refuses to let them go to where humans can hunt them, to punish humankind for having broken too many taboos too often. She also controls the weather, and can cause great suffering to the Inuit, again to punish them for evil deeds. In the past it was the task of the Angakkut to visit the Takanakapsaluk and propitiate her, often by combing her hair, which was the surest path to her heart. After they entered into her good graces, the Angakkut would beg her to forgive humankind their digressions, and set the animals free so that the Inuit may hunt them again and avoid famine. But the Angakkut have almost vanished from amongst the Inuit, and few now know how to visit the Takanakapsaluk. Of those who do know few would dare to visit her, for it is exceedingly dangerous, since the Takanakapsaluk strongly dislikes humankind.

It is said that at the beginning the Takanakapsaluk was an orphan girl who lived among the Inuit. However, since she had no protectors or family she was treated badly, and eventually, when the tribe was moving in boats to a new settlement, they threw her overboard. But she struggled, and with one of her hands clutched the rim of the boat. Then someone cut off her fingers, so she had to let go of the boat and sank to the bottom of the sea, where she turned into a powerful spirit. But her cut-off fingers turned into seals, and because of this she is often called the Mother of the Seals. Since she received such cruel treatment from humankind, she has little liking for them, and punishes them harshly for any breaches of taboo. Many Angakkut believe that she will rejoice when the last human has finally died, and that is why she has not arisen in wrath to punish the destruction of the animals, and the damage to land and sea that humankind have unleashed upon them in recent times.

Although Arnapak knew all this better than anybody, she decided to brave the Takanakapsaluk for the sake of Niels and Nuliajuq, and because she wanted to save the world from the evil magician. She hoped for a good reception, since the Takanakapsaluk had honoured her with a dream about the naming of Nuliajuq, and therefore seemed favourably disposed towards her.

Having once again assembled her 23 spirit helpers, Arnapak fell into deep trance and descended to the bottom of the sea. She looked about herself, and observed the languid movements of the sea creatures in the pale green light that filtered down from the surface of the sea which was still covered with ice. But her spirits urged her on, and hurried her through the first of the obstacles on the way to the Takanakapsaluk, which consisted of three large rocks that were in continuous motion and crushed all unwary visitors. Having successfully negotiated them, she came upon an incredibly deep crack, slippery with ice, which she managed to pass only with the aid of her spirit helpers who lifted her up in their arms and carried her across while flying with wings they did not possess. She then encountered a huge iron cauldron full of boiling blubber, which was populated by a group of irate seals who demanded at least one of her souls, in return for the hundreds of seals she had hunted and skinned and eaten during her long life. However, she had foreseen this contingency and was well supplied with herring-flavoured boiled sweets and candied caribou entrails which she fed to the seals, who calmed down considerably after this and allowed her to pass, and even directed her to the path that led to the house of the Takanakapsaluk. While following this path several large sea creatures subjected her to sustained attacks and one shark even tried to bite her left leg off, but she managed to deflect them all with the aid of her 23 spirit helpers.

The house of the Takanakapsaluk was made of stone and stood on a foundation of rock. It had a narrow entrance, which was guarded by a dog with bared sharp teeth, who was supposed to savage all visitors; but when he saw Arnapak he wagged his tail and said, 'manifold greetings to you Arnapak, what are the tidings of Kanajoq and the family?'

Arnapak recognised the dog as Aua, one of her husband's sledge-team dogs who died many years ago and had always been one of her favourites. 'Both my husband and my children died long ago, but I still have a great-granddaughter who lost her soul, and a grandson who died and seems to have lost his way. I am hoping the Takanakapsaluk might advise me on how to help them.'

'It would be most unusual if she did, but one never knows. There have been no visitors at all for almost fifty years, and her hair has grown very tangled, so perhaps she will welcome you and ask you to comb her hair'.

Arnapak thanked Aua, and went inside the house to see the Takanakapsaluk, 22 spirits trailing in behind (one stayed outside to chat to Aua, whom he knew well when still was alive).

The Takanakapsaluk sat on a far corner of the sleeping platform that took up half of the house, and she looked filthy and unkempt (as was the house). Since she only had fingers on one hand, she always had trouble keeping herself tidy, and rather relied on visiting Angakut to comb her hair for her. Decades of neglect had taken their toll, and she now looked quite like a hag. She was playing cards with several seals, and pointedly ignored the shaman. Undeterred, Arnapak repeatedly cleared her throat loudly, and when the Takanakapsaluk at last looked in her direction, she approached and introduced herself.

'I am Arnapak, whom you advised in a dream to name her great-granddaughter after you,' she told the Takanakapsaluk, 'and I have come in great need.'

The Takanakapsaluk shot Arnapak a nasty glance. 'I sent no dream to you, Angakkoq; I take no interest any more in the foolish doings of the Inuit. What are you and your petty troubles to me? Do I look as though I care? Be gone, before I muster enough strength to cut your throat!' With that she returned to her card play.

Arnapak's heart sank when she saw and heard the Takanakapsaluk speak these harsh words, and she cried out, 'Is it true then what the white men say, that all our gods are dead and gone or have ceased to care about us, and that we have no choice but to believe in their Christ, who is the only god left with any power, or perish utterly? Tornarsuk I could not find, and you, the Mother of the Seals, have forsaken us – what should an old shaman do, who wouldst but help her people?' With that she sat down on the threshold of the house, and cried and wailed bitterly.

'Oih, move yourself,' she heard a sudden cry from the doorstep, which turned out to be yet another seal who had been resting there. 'Get off me, you landlubber, and let's see what we can do to rouse the little woman. I am Nuliktoq, one of the original fingers of the Mother. You must forgive her for being a bit unaccommodating, but it has been a long time since the last visit from a shaman, and you will agree that mankind has not improved since then.' He went to the Takanakapsaluk, and said, 'Bestir yourself, Mother Dear, your days of slumber have come to an end, for great changes are afoot in the world. Remember what The Bright One said when he last came by? Why not let this shaman comb your hair, you know I can't do it with these flippers. And while she combs, let her tell her tale, and then perhaps we shall see whether we can help her, and think how to shape a place for ourselves in the new world that is to come!'

The Takanakapsaluk looked at Arnapak and asked, 'Nuliktoq, did you sent the dream to the Angakkoq?'

'I did indeed, and proud of it I am! Someone has to take a hand, since you do nought but sleep and play cards.'

'Well, in that case I suppose we ought to at least listen to her,' the Takanakapsaluk said, 'and she might as well comb me a little while she is doing so.'

Greatly encouraged by this upturn in her fortune, Arnapak took a large unbreakable steel comb from her pocket, and began to comb the Takanakapsaluk's matted hair, which was full of dirt and vermin, while telling her tale. The longer she combed the softer grew the Takanakapsaluk's hair, and along with it her temper, and when Arnapak requested, towards the end of her story, whether she might not wash her face as well, to 'reveal its natural beauty', the Takanakapsaluk smiled almost graciously and consented.

'I do declare that was a powerful yarn, and no mistake,' exclaimed Nuliktoq after the Angakkoq finished her tale. 'There is much afoot on the surface world that has scarcely penetrated even into our dreams. We must take heed now Mother, and gather information, and consider our future.'

The Takanakapsaluk, now once again fully alert and fair of face, and strengthened somewhat from having eaten all the lice Arnapak had combed from her hair, agreed with the seal. 'Indeed Nuliktoq, we must do as you say. But in the meantime, how might we help this worthy shaman? She cannot stay here for long, but long enough perhaps to hear the tidings of our people. Send out messengers to all corners of the ocean, and ask for news about the world in general, and about any evil magicians in particular.'

Arnapak stayed in the house of the Takanakapsaluk for three days and nights, and heard much from the messengers as they returned with tidings from all over the realm of the Takanakapsaluk. Also while staying there her heart was set at rest about her grandson Niels, who had found Adlivun at last and greeted her when he came to the Takanakapsaluk's house. He told her about the great magician, who had caused his and Elisabees' death, and was known as the Cosmocrator among the magic-minded of the world. Niels was certain the Cosmocrator had stolen and hidden one of his little daughter's souls, and that her face would be restored to its normal state if her stolen soul returned to her. Although he did not know of the current whereabouts of the magician, he did have a crumb of comfort for Arnapak; namely, that the magician had an enemy, a woman of great power who had sworn to destroy him – the very woman indeed who saved Elisabee. 'She is a spirit or god of some sort,' he said, 'but a foreign one and alien to our people.'

Most of the tidings that reached the house of the Takanakapsaluk were very grave indeed. The temperature of the sea was increasing, the seals and whales and herrings and other sea creatures reported, and the coastlines were changing, some because land became flooded, others because the land was rising. There was more ice floating on the sea, and less remaining on the land. Fish were forced to change their ancient spawning grounds and migration routes, and the animals that followed them, too, had to change their age-old journey patterns. Much of the water was getting increasingly polluted, and illness and infertility were spreading; some areas had become uninhabitable altogether. The messengers who reported this to the Takanakapsaluk gave no tidings of the cause of all these changes, but there were rumours that a great new magician had arisen somewhere on the dry land, so powerful that he could change the weather and cause new lands to rise from the oceans by chanting his incantations. But since they lived in the sea, and the magician dwelled on land, they knew little definite about him and where he lived.

The Takanakapsaluk was not inclined to believe that a single human, no matter how powerful, could be responsible for all the changes that were being reported to her. She knew only too well how limited the abilities of even great spirits like herself were to effect significant changes in the world. Instead she remembered the words of The Bright One, who continued to visit her occasionally ever since he first came and introduced himself two millennia ago.

'Humankind are shaking off the constraints that have bound them since they first came into being. Arrogant, selfish, and supremely self confident, they are intent on making themselves masters of the world, little heeding the rights and concerns of other living creatures. They will cause untold damage, and enslave and destroy much that was free and beautiful, and may well destroy themselves in the process. But much as it grieves me to sit idly by while they indulge their follies, they have grown too mighty to be constrained by us anymore. Like children who have outgrown their parents' rod and counsel, they are no longer our responsibility. For good or ill, humankind must make their own life and shape their own future, and the rest of creation must endure them until they have either fully matured and become valuable members of the community, or caused their own extinction, or, and that seems the most likely outcome, have caused such a reduction in their numbers by their reckless selfishness that they cease to be a threat to others. The next hundred years or so will determine the future of humankind, and there is little we can do to influence events. However, we must not remain entirely idle during this time. Whatever the outcome of the human experiment, it will be at great cost to all creation, and we must labour and prepare as best we can for the changed world that will result. Hitherto there has been little contact between you, the Takanakapsaluk, and the other powers that labour secretly and unceasingly to protect and preserve the world, and if it is your choice this need not change. But I would have you be comforted in your times of grief over the state of your realm and the well-being of your people, so remember that you are not alone, and in times of need I will be ever ready to aid you. Just send a message, by any bird that traverses the oceans, to Yeshua ben Maryam.'

The Takanakapsaluk had long pondered these words, but as the years grew longer and lonelier and no one paid her any heed or helped her with her hair, she ceased to think of The Bright One and retreated into herself, and allowed herself to become despondent and uncaring and weak. But now that she was fully alert she thought again of Yeshua, and resolved to contact him. 'For I am alive and strong, and the Mother of the Sea, and must not abandon my people to their fate, so that I may laze about and grow filthy and play the victim.'

Although she did not believe that the self styled Cosmocrator was causing all the changes to her world, she felt all the same that he needed watching and investigating, and she discussed this with the Angakkoq.

'It will be a big task, but not too big for you,' she told her. 'There is not much I can do to help you, since your task is on land and I am the Mother of the Sea. However, you are welcome to come and visit me as often as you like, to hear new tidings and consult with me. I shall give you a special amulet, which will obtain you the aid of any animal in the sea and many on land as well. I will also entrust to you an amulet given to me by Yeshua ben Maryam, who I believe is mighty in some of the lands where you will travel, and has assured me that he will come to the aid of anyone who will invoke him with it.' Speaking these words, she hung around Arnapak's neck an amulet made of sealskin, which contained tooth of whale, hair of caribou, feather of ptarmigan, and a fish head, as well as several dried plant fragments.

But the amulet from Yeshua consisted of nothing but a little golden cross, and Arnapak hesitated to accept it. 'Surely you know that this is a talisman much used by the Christians, who have abandoned you in favour of a dead man from Palestine called Christ?' she asked her.

The Takanakapsaluk had never heard of anyone called Christ. 'The Christians have probably stolen and copied the amulet from someone who received it from Yeshua. Or do you know of any instances where a bearer of the Christian talisman called upon the help of their Christ and actually received aid?'

The shaman had to admit that she was not aware of any such instance, and the Takanakapsaluk smiled. 'Well, there you are then. The Christian talismans are just fakes, whereas you have the real thing, directly from Yeshua himself. I am confident that it is the most effective amulet anyone could ask for, which is no doubt why the Christians have faked it so copiously.'

But if anyone thinks this was the extent of the gifts the Takanakapsaluk bestowed on Arnapak, they greatly underestimate her generosity and practicality, for she also gave the shaman a complete set of garments, made in the traditional way from caribou and seal skins and prepared by herself to ensure their indestructibility. Furthermore, she gave her a thermos flask cunningly made of bear hide and blubber, and filled with hot strong sweet tea that never ran dry, a small sealskin filled with an inexhaustible supply of blubber together with a soapstone lamp with an everlasting wick, a small bag with an inexhaustible supply of muktuk[36] and another with frozen caribou meat, and lastly a very light but sturdy fold-up kayak that doubled as a sledge.

'Now let me think,' said the Takanakapsaluk, as she looked at all this equipment, 'is there anything else you might need to travel across the world without delays or hindrance?' And then she laughed. 'Ah, what a fool I am! You need a dog to pull the

---

[36]   A fatty substance just beneath the skin of whales, which is a sought after delicacy among the Inuit.

sledge and keep you company in foreign parts! I will lend you Aua, who is very attached to you and keen to see the world once more.'

Thus she sent Arnapak on her way, well provided for with provisions and many admonitions and good counsel. Arnapak emerged from the spirit realm quite shattered, and had to rely on her 23 spirits and Aua to carry the gifts of the Takanakapsaluk back to the house of Ragna, where her body had lain like dead for three long nights and days.

34   One shaman and 24 spirits in search of the Cosmocrator

Ragna got used to Arnapak's long spirit journeys during the three months she was searching for Tornarsuk, and was therefore not unduly concerned about her friend's long absence from her body. However, now that she had returned Ragna refused to listen to her adventures until she had eaten her fill – she had eaten nothing in Adlivun, since that might have imprisoned her forever in the realm of the Takanakapsaluk – and slept off her exhaustion. 'It can all wait until tomorrow,' Ragna kept repeating, until at last Arnapak did as she was told, drank several large mugs of tea, ate three or four kilo of frozen raw seal meat, and sank into deep slumber.

Thirty-six hours later she felt like a new woman and was at last permitted to relate her experiences to Ragna, who was most interested in all she said, but especially in the reports from the sea animals regarding the recent changes in the sea and coastlines they had observed. Ragna had long been a prominent member of the environmental movement, and was not surprised at Arnapak's tidings.

'Have I not said the same thing for thirty years now,' she kept on grumbling during the tale. But what really surprised her was the appalling ignorance of the Takanakapsaluk. 'Imagine anyone not knowing that Christ and Yeshua are the same person, and not even having a radio in her house to hear the news!' she tut-tutted[37]. However, she admitted that the gifts the Takanakapsaluk had bestowed upon the Angakkoq would come in very useful while she was roaming the world in search of the magician, whom Ragna refused to call 'Cosmocrator'. 'Master of the Universe, indeed! He'll excite the wrath of some god or spirit, you mark my words, and come to a sticky end! I really don't see why you should have to become mixed up in this at all; it seems that he has enough powerful enemies already.'

But Arnapak would not be dissuaded. 'I am the Angakkoq of my people, and have to protect them from evil spiritual influences. Moreover, this is a matter of family honour and blood revenge, and of reclaiming Nuliajuq's stolen soul. Lastly, the Takanakapsaluk has asked me to track him down and find out as much about him as I can, and I will do as she asks.'

But Ragna knew her friend was sixty years old, and considered it unlikely that she would live much longer, Inuit life expectancy being what it was; she wished a peaceful

---

[37]   Perhaps Ragna was a little unfair. Like all great personages the Takanakapsaluk was only told what her visitors thought she wanted to hear, and certainly no visiting shaman would have been so rude as to mention a foreign deity.

old age for Arnapak, and tried to dissuade her from taking on the Cosmocrator. Arnapak listened politely to all of Ragna's objections, but when she was finished just laughed, and said that the blessing of the Takanakapsaluk was upon her, and she did not fear death, but would live as long as was necessary to complete her task.

The next morning Arnapak packed up her gear, waved at Ragna standing on her sledge, and soon disappeared from view. It was only then that Ragna realised the sledge had moved by itself, without any dogs pulling it, and that it moved across land, not ice or snow, which was impossible for any normal sledge. 'Oh well, perhaps she will make it after all, with all those magic gifts from the Takanakapsaluk,' she murmured as she went back indoors. 'What strange times we live in!'

But the Angakkoq held a steady course for Canada, and made rapid progress, for Aua pulled her sledge with supernatural strength, and her 23 spirit helpers never left her side and ensured that she did not encounter any treacherous storms or rotten ice along the way.

Arnapak did not recount to Walgren all the details of what befell her during the long search for the Cosmocrator, nor did she mention all the help she received while on her travels. She just stuck to the basics, and told her son-in-law how she found and carefully examined the site in the Rocky Mountains where Elisabee had been assaulted, and how aided by an obliging grizzly bear, several well informed crows, a group of unusually observant sharks, and a colony of very gossipy corrals, she managed to find tracks of the Cosmocrator in New Zealand, central Africa and Ethiopia, across the Red Sea in Yemen, in the valleys of the Caucasus, Mesopotamia, and finally Mongolia.

When the shaman mentioned Yemen, Mr Walgren could no longer restrain his incredulity, and exclaimed: 'Are you seriously telling me that you, an old female Inuit who has never before left Greenland, travelled alone and unaided all over the world, even into remote desert places like Yemen? No offence, but really I can't believe it!'

Arnapak laughed. 'I am not offended in the least, my dear son-in-law. It is indeed a most unusual tale I have to relate. If I had not myself experienced it, I would not believe it either! There I was, an old Inuit shaman, dressed in Caribou skins, riding a sledge pulled by an invisible dog across American prairies, the endless oceans, and Arabian sand dunes, always followed by 23 spirit helpers. Ah, what a sight it was when I raced across the desert on my sledge, pursued by a group of Bedouins intent on retrieving a certain magic amulet I had stolen from their secret temple in the Syrian mountains! Oh the shouts I heard from the black people in Congo when I turned my sledge into a kayak and shot down the great waterfall they felt sure would stop me! And the jokes I played on the priests of the underground caves in Kôr! You should have seen their faces when my spirit helpers lifted the roof of their secret sanctum and exposed the relic in their precious shrine, which was actually just a piece of dried camel dung enclosed in a cedar wood box!'

Walgren grew more and more alarmed as he listened to this catalogue of sins and petty crimes his mother-in-law had committed. 'Do you really think it is safe to insult and make fun of the gods of other people like that?' he cautiously asked the hyperactive octogenarian.

'Of course it is safe, everyone knows the gods have a sense of humour and enjoy a good joke, even at their own expense! Besides, what did you expect? For two decades I was away from home, without family or friends. I had to enjoy myself somehow!'

Walgren had to admit that this was not entirely unreasonable, though he did not share the Angakkoq's belief in the gods' sense of humour; in his experience they had none whatsoever. But of course, his experience was much more limited.

These musings were interrupted by Arnapak, who took up the thread of her story again. Although she found information and rumours about the Cosmocrator in all the different hide outs he used over the years, she had not actually met him until quite recently in Mongolia. After Arnapak had unearthed the main history of the Cosmocrator in the Caucasus (her spider spirit came in very useful there), she moved on to central Asia, roaming freely and learning the languages and practices of the various tribes that lived in the area. Most of them had a tradition of shamans, although the few that still survived were not very powerful or knowledgeable. However, they recognised her superior abilities, and welcomed her with open arms. Within a few years she was well established as one of the foremost shamans in central Asia, and people travelled far and wide to ask for her aid. She was therefore in a good position to gather information about the Cosmocrator, who was well known and feared by all the native tribes of the region.

Both during her travels and while practicing as a shaman in Mongolia, Arnapak continued to spirit-journey to the Takanakapsaluk in Adlivun once or twice a year, to bring her tidings and to learn from her wisdom. It was here that she heard about the continuing deterioration of the environment, about the building of Greenlandia, and about the renewed relations of the Takanakapsaluk with Yeshua ben Maryam. He turned out to be indeed the Christ of the Takanakapsaluk's enemies, but convinced her that he was much misunderstood by his followers and had never intended his gospel to be used to alienate people from their own gods and traditions. More important than this, however, was the advice that the Angakkoq received regarding her conduct when confronted with the Cosmocrator.

One evening, while visiting the Takanakapsaluk, she actually met Yeshua himself, and shared with him much of the information and rumours she collected since first setting out from Greenland. In return Yeshua told her that the great woman who was the Cosmocrator's enemy bore the name of Agrat, was a demon and had been strictly forbidden to interfere with the Cosmocrator for the time being. However, there was no reason why Arnapak should not try her luck with him.

'It is essential not to act before you are ready,' Yeshua impressed upon her. 'The Cosmocrator is adept at probing people's minds, and you first need to learn to cloak your mind effectively before you can dare to approach the magician. I suggest you go to the Buddhist Lamasery of Tseten-Nor, on the border between Tibet and Outer Mongolia, where a monk well versed in the secrets of the mind can teach you what you need to know to confront the Cosmocrator. Show him my talisman, the one the Takanakapsaluk gave you, and he will aid you in all things and ask no questions,' Yeshua said.

The Angakkoq glanced at the little cross she carried on a chain around her neck and asked, 'Is the Takanakapsaluk right then, that this is the real talisman and all the others that the Christians wear just ineffectual copies? Or does the monk lend his aid to any of the millions of people who carry these crosses?'

Yeshua smiled. 'You must allow me to keep just a few of my little secrets,' he replied, and would say no more about it.

But when Arnapak went to see the Buddhist monk and showed him the talisman, he indeed did what she asked of him, and trained her to cloak her mind against mental intrusions.

Eventually, less than a year ago, Arnapak felt strong enough to meet the Cosmocrator. Ever since she first arrived in the Altai region, she had disseminated misleading information about her background, motives, and intelligence, and her many customers and admirers swiftly carried the tale far and wide. The basic story line was that Mampüi, as Arnapak called herself in Asia, came from an ancient family of Mongolian shamans, and had inherited a great deal of knowledge and magical implements, but was a bit fluffy minded and childlike, and therefore unable to achieve the same successes as her ancestors; however she was quite a good shaman for all that. She claimed to have lived until recently with distant relatives in Tibet, where she learned more ancient family lore and practices, and had acquired a bit of common sense. Mampüi returned to her ancestors' tribes in the Altai mountains only because she had been told they were in dire need of a shaman, and although she felt scarcely up to the task considered it her duty to practice among them as best as she might. She affected to be a simple, trusting soul, eager to help all who were afflicted or desired to learn, utterly without guile, and full of apologies about her lack of knowledge and ability. In a nutshell, just the sort of person who could be exploited and manipulated by someone like the Cosmocrator, who was forever lusting after knowledge of magic and sorcery from the olden days. When she finally received an invitation to the Cosmocrator's castle she was ready, and spent the evening before she answered the summons recollecting all she had found out about the great magician from her manifold and obscure sources.

35   Freddy the Sniffer-Gerbil is of assistance to the Foilers

Gerbils do not have a reputation for moral rectitude. They are considered to be frivolous, fun-loving little rodents who go with the flow and rarely care for the long-term consequences of their actions. Whether this reputation is well deserved by the majority of gerbildom I cannot rightly say, but I am happy to report that it was most certainly not true of Freddy, the bomb-detecting whiz rodent at Bog Bank who had been trained by Stress Lucozade. From the start Freddy understood the importance of his work, and never once failed in his duties. During the year he had been at Bog Bank he detected a dozen letters and packages filled with explosives, including one very professionally made bomb that would have blown the entire building sky-high if Freddy had not raised the alarm. He was very highly esteemed by his employer, and at the time Devadorje left for Greenland the gerbil's fame had spread throughout the City, and Stress began to receive more and more orders for sniffer-gerbils from the banking community.

However, Freddy's head was not turned by his fame, and he continued to meet up with his friends and acquaintances all over the City. Some of his best friends were the sewer rats, who, though wily and cruel, were also highly intelligent and worldly-wise, and appreciated a fellow rodent of similar ilk. The great plan to defraud the City had been the talk of the sewers for some time, and inevitably popped up during several of Freddy's chats with the sewer rats. Freddy had gained a deep understanding of the working of the City during his time at Bog Bank, and unlike the sewer rats knew that a crisis in the banking sector could have grievous consequences for both humans and non-humans throughout the economy. If the banking sector was unwilling or unable to lend money to the business community, many firms, including agricultural ones, would go out of business or not get started up in the first place.

'And that will affect all of us,' Freddy lectured the sewer rats. 'If a firm closes down, they shut up the building and there will be no food for any of us for months. If farmers can't borrow money to expand and modernise their farms, less food will be produced and again, we will all suffer. I think us rodents should not sit idly by and watch the Consortium defraud the City. Moreover, our great friend and benefactor Mithradates Devadorje has gone to Greenland to work against the Consortium, and we all know that he is always on the side of righteousness!'

The sewer rats were impressed, especially when they heard that Devadorje supported the counterplot against the Consortium, but they did not volunteer their help, being notoriously reluctant to interfere in human affairs.

'Ever since we were afflicted by those bubonic plague-carrying fleas, and came out of hiding to approach humans and warn them about the danger of the fleas, and got blamed for spreading the disease, instead of being thanked for having warned mankind, we steer clear of them if we can.' However, they promised to keep their ears open and inform Freddy of all new developments. This way he eventually found out that The Old Lady was looking for the blueprints and business plan of Greenlandia.

The blueprints and business plan were located in Agrat's office at Bog Bank, and once Freddy knew they existed he had no difficulty in locating them. But how was he to get this information to The Old Lady? He dared not enter The Institution building, in case he ran into a member of the Mouser's Rodent Reduction Force. Luckily the sewer rats volunteered for the job of go-between. 'It'll freak out that uppity Mouser,' they cackled, as they climbed into a heating duct that lead to a false ceiling, which had a small air vent, just perfect for communicating with a cat one did not wish to be caught by.

Thus it came about that one night, as the Mouser was doing his rounds, he heard a sharp 'hist' from an air vent.

'Hey you, Micky Mouser, wanna hear some news about the Consortium?'

The Mouser could not believe his ears (which were excellent). He went to the air vent, and started to scratch it and tried to insert a paw into the vent.

The rats cackled cheerfully. 'Nothing doing, Cat-Boy, we chose this vent carefully. But listen up now. We have a message for The Old Lady from Freddy, the Sniffer-Gerbil at Bog Bank. The blueprints and business plan she is looking for are hidden in a secret drawer in Agrat's desk in her office at Bog Bank, and if you can smuggle someone into the building you can have copies made. But have a care, the place is well guarded.'

The Mouser thanked the rats for their information – though it did go against the grain – and asked how they managed to get in.

'Never you mind Cat-Boy,' they sniggered, 'that's for us to know and for you to never find out.'

They were ready to depart, when the Mouser called after them. 'I just want to warn you,' he shouted, 'be careful where you walk! This building is riddled with asbestos, and you can get some very nasty diseases if you get into contact with it. I am telling you this because I am grateful that you told me about the blueprints, 'though how I will ever live down helping rats I do not know!'

The rats were much obliged. 'Blimey, we are living in strange times, when rats pass on a gerbil's information to a cat and the cat warns rats against risking their health. Still, if Freddy is right this business will affect us all, so perhaps we should declare a cease fire until it has been sorted.'

The Mouser replied that this was not a bad idea, and they all agreed this needed to be discussed at the various committees and clubs, and voted on and authorised, as indeed in time it was. Eventually even the birds of the City joined the cease-fire, and almost the entire animal population of the area united against the Consortium, which incidentally never found out about it.

36   Sophia uses her demonic powers to burgle Bog Bank

At the next meeting of the Foilers, now minus Devadorje, the Mouser told them what he had heard from the sewer rats, and offered to sneak into the building and steal the plans for Greenlandia. The Old Lady just snorted derisorily at this suggestion.

'You are hardly in a position to pry open locked drawers, Mr Mouser, and besides the plans have to be copied, not stolen – what if Agrat gets suspicious and changes them? This is clearly a job for a human, ie Sophia.'

'Who are you calling a human? Alright alright, I agree I am much more likely to succeed at copying the plans of the Consortium than either you or the Mouser. But how can I get into the building?'

The Mouser suggested that she have a chat with Fridthjof; 'After all he breaks into all sorts of buildings in his efforts to liberate imprisoned bonsai trees.'

'But what do I tell him? You know he would never countenance breaking the law unless it was to free his precious midget trees!'

They sat morosely around the fire for a while, sipping their drinks and feeling disheartened, until the Mouser had a Eureka moment. He suggested they send a bonsai to Agrat as a present from 'a shy unknown admirer', and then ask Fridthjof for advice on liberating it. And while Sophia was busy stealing the bonsai, she could also find and copy the Greenlandia plans.

'Not bad, not bad,' Sophia murmured, 'but what if Fridthjof insists on lending a hand? He is quite the gentleman, you know.'

'Oh for goodness sake,' said The Old Lady, 'what are you a demon for? Use your powers of persuasion!' And before Sophia could explain the complicated protocol regarding the usage of their powers that apprentice demons had to obey, The Old Lady went on-line and placed an order for the biggest choicest bonsai Harrods had in stock, with the instruction to deliver it to Agrat bat Mahalat, The Greenland Consortium, Bog Bank Bros, Threadneedle Street.

The next day Sophia arranged to have lunch with Fridthjof, and asked him how to liberate a bonsai from a guarded building, using all her feminine whiles to disarm his innate suspicion, to no avail. He simply refused to let her endanger herself in such a dangerous undertaking, which was moreover the preserve of the Bonsai Liberation Front. Having no patience worth mentioning, Sophia decided to change tactics, fixed him with her steely 'I am an evil demon, so no crap from you mister' stare, and ordered him to look deep into her eyes. Then she proceeded to comb his mind for info.

The details thus gained proved most useful, *[but are not disclosed here because my publisher insists that it would amount to incitement of entering & burglaring].* Suffice it to say that it allowed Sophia to enter Bog Bank's premises without detection the following night. She quickly located Agrat's office, cast a swift opening spell, took the plans from Agrat's desk drawer, and copied them on the photocopier in the next room. That done she returned the plans to the drawer, pronounced a closing spell, and retraced her steps until she was outside of the building, where she was hit by a horrible realisation – she had forgotten to take the bonsai from Agrat's office! 'Fridthjof will kill me,' she shrieked.

'There is no need to tell him Dearie,' commented a sewer rat who had watched the whole performance with great interest. 'Now hop it, before the porter returns from his coffee break.'

Unbeknown to Sophia, two other employees of The Institution were still awake within the building, and might have observed her raid from the bathroom window on the fifth floor, had they not been completely engrossed in each other. Stanley Hunzucker's latest attempt to rendezvous with Flossy Pembrokeshire had led him to the handicapped toilet on the fifth floor. He stole a sign reading 'lavatory closed for repairs', attached it to the door, and explained to Flossy that there was simply no chance of their being discovered this time. Firstly, they were the only employees in the building except for the guards who had their own toilets in the sub vault, secondly there were currently no handicapped people employed by The Institution, and thirdly no employee of this company would ever disobey a sign. 'Oh Stan,' Flossy sighed as she sank onto his manly chest for the umpteenth time, 'at long last our desires shall be satisfied.'

But alas! Fate conspired against them yet again. The sign, attached with only a bit of beyond-its-sell-by-date sticky tape, fell off the door shortly after they entered the toilet. Consequently Fred Flynt, a security guard on night duty, saw no reason not to indulge his own secret fantasy, which consisted of entering a handicapped toilet and pretend that he was paraplegic. He turned on the light, set eyes on the entangled couple, and promptly fainted.

'Quickly,' whispered Stanley as he pulled Flossy out of the lavatory, lightly stepping over the prostrate form of the security guard, 'let's escape before he comes to.' Flossy followed, weeping bitterly.

'Oh Stan, why can't we just go to a hotel? I want you like mad, and all this cloak-and-dagger stuff is ruining my nerves.'

'If you love me you will wait,' Stanley replied. 'You know very well how I feel about hotels and such like. It would be most unsporting.' And Flossy, who fenced, shot, swam, and kept a horse in her parent's stable for cross country, had to leave it at that.

The next evening Sophia told her fellow Foilers of her successful burglary, and showed them the plans and blueprints she had copied. 'Look,' she said, 'I have all the details of the transmogrification!' She read them to The Old Lady and the Mouser, who thus found out about Acid Icepick's grand symphony, which was to transmogrify the entire Greenlandia to Hell. Since they had the musical score and exact specification of the organ that would be used to effect the transmogrification, they should have been shouting with joy. Instead they felt empty and defeated; they simply could not think of a way of stopping the transmogrification.

The Mouser was the first to recover his good humour. 'There is obviously nothing we can do for now,' he said, 'we need to wait until the last minute and sabotage their plans in Greenland. If we steal the score, or destroy the organ, just before the transmogrification during the great opening ceremony, it will be too late for them to find another copy of the score or build another organ. We shall have to put our trust in Devadorje.'

It seemed unsatisfactory, but since no one could think of anything better, they agreed with the Mouser that Devadorje would have to sort out the problem at his end. 'In the meantime we will keep an eye on things and continue with our meetings,' The Old Lady concluded the evening in her usual, utterly predictable, fashion.

37   A mystic's fall from grace

The man who now called himself Monsieur Florin Mondé, or Florimonde, and styled himself the Cosmocrator, had received the name Selim at birth. He belonged to the family of the Lords of Alamut, and started out life as an Ismailite mystic, as befitted his ancestry. Being of such exalted birth, everyone assumed he was of impeccable moral character and quite incorruptible, and no attempts were made to guide his studies or watch over his education. He read what books he pleased, and it pleased him to read many. He soon acquired a reputation for great learning in all branches of Philosophy and Religion; but of the arts, literature, law, or politics, he knew nothing. Even before Khulagu Khan destroyed Alamut, he had outgrown his home and rarely stayed there, preferring instead to travel to the important centres of learning of his time, to converse with the great Philosophers and learn what they had to teach. It was only a matter of time until he came across alchemists and black magicians, and listened to their evil whispers as eagerly as he had learned the wisdom of Philosophy. However, he still learned only for the sake of knowledge, and did not practice what was contrary to the commandments of his religion. He followed the ways of the Prophet in all things, and never strayed from the path of righteousness. In this he was greatly aided by his other great passion, retreating into lonely places, where he could contemplate the mysteries of the Qur'an, and the martyred figure of Ali, without distractions. Thus time passed, and he grew old and feeble.

Feeling that his time on earth was drawing to a close, he prepared to return to the land of his birth, to die there peacefully, and be buried amongst his forefathers. He travelled light, and without companions, so that he might use the time to prepare his soul for death. Thus he came at last to Alamut again, but it had been destroyed so thoroughly that he could not find a single hospitable house where he might rest from his long journey and find peace. Eagles and ravens circled over the ruins, foxes had built their drays in the remnants of the once mighty fortress, and wild goats climbed the walls to eat the weeds that grew upon them. Overcome with grief for his destroyed home, he hid his face in his cloak, and resolved to travel on. He spent the night in a small valley within a copse of trees, huddled against his donkey for warmth, and wondered where he should go. His dreams were filled with strange images, and he awoke deeply troubled.

A feeling of impending doom continued to haunt him all through his morning routine, and did not dissipate when he finally climbed back onto his donkey and steered the animal towards the path that lead from the valley. But before his donkey managed to get into its stride and fall into its customary trot, he found himself hailed by a cheerful voice from beyond the trees, where he now spied a small house he had not seen the night before in the darkness. A very delicate, elfin looking young woman was running towards him, waving a coffee pot and inviting him to stay a while longer. She apologised for not having noticed his presence earlier, being such a sound sleeper, and told him her name, which was Shefaka. A most cheerful and engaging creature she must have been, for Selim, who in all his long and virtuous life never once felt the urge for female company, fell deeply and immediately in love with her, and resolved to gain her hand by any means possible, and thus was lost henceforth. He stayed with her only long enough to ascertain her circumstances, and satisfy himself that her heart was still unclaimed. Then he bid her farewell, and went away to find a way of winning her.

He first rode to Harran, to obtain certain secret scriptures that had been offered to him for sale before, but which he previously refused to purchase, both on account of their high price and because of their blasphemous contents. Among them were the fabled Necronomicon by Abdul al Hazred, an original copy of the 6th & 7th Book of Moses' Magische Geisterkunst, and Tummy Ticklers from Tartary, a cookbook by the famous Mongol patissier and pillager, Tengri Khan. He also managed to purchase several glass flacons filled with multi-coloured potions, numerous evil smelling powders and ointments, guaranteed original mummy bindings from Egypt, a sack full of magical odds and ends that had no immediate usefulness but 'might come in handy' some time, a dozen pots of honey, a donkey load weight of dried fruit and nuts, and a few pounds of assorted spices. [38]

He then repaired to Baghdad, where he had a home and many acquaintances, and bent all his accumulated knowledge and expertise to resolving his problem, namely to restore himself to youth and beauty and thereby win the heart and hand of Shefaka. But he had not reckoned with the effect his long virtuous life had had upon his body; since every pore was saturated with virtue and wisdom, his body proved quite impervious to any of the potions and magical procedures he tried out. 'Your spirit may have grown weak, but the flesh shall remain strong,' was the clear message coming from his body. But his love for Shefaka burned fiercely within him, and Selim in his desperation fell ever deeper into sin. He searched the city for a comely though feeble-minded youth, enticed him under cloak of darkness into the basement of his house, and managed to effect an exchange of spirits between himself and the youth. Selim then killed the youth, whose spirit was trapped in his aged body, to prevent him from ever laying claim to his own body again. Having thus achieved his aim of being young and handsome again, Selim assumed a new identity and travelled once more to Alamut to see Shefaka. He courted her successfully, was duly married within the week[39], and set up house with his new wife in Mosul – he did not dare to return to Baghdad with his stolen body, lest relatives of the murdered youth recognised him - where they quickly settled down.

The union was extremely happy, and Shefaka proved to be not only cheerful, affectionate, and good looking, but also possessed of great intelligence and sensitivity, and was indeed the perfect partner for a man of Selim's character and inclinations. Selim returned to the life of a faithful follower of Islam, and only used his secret books for concocting the most delicious cakes and desserts and sweetmeats, much to the delight of his wife and friends. For many years all seemed well, and he had almost forgotten the means by which he had achieved his current state of happiness, when Shefaka fell grievously ill. Her body was ravaged by a mortal cancer, and although she managed to bear her fate with great stoicism, her husband was inconsolable. He knew he could enable her to survive by the same means he had used to obtain a young man's body, but realised that she would never consent to such a course of action, being scrupulously pious and morally upright in every way. As Shefaka grew ever weaker and closer to death, an evil plan grew in Selim's breast.

Since he did not think it prudent to indulge in sorcery in Mosul, and draw attention to himself, he suggested to Shefaka that they travel to the place of her childhood, so she could say goodbye to her friends and relatives before she died. Shefaka readily agreed to this, and Selim hired a maid to serve her during the journey, a lovely winsome creature with a strong body, good teeth, and healthy constitution. They set out on their journey, and got on very well, although riding became increasingly painful to Shefaka as time went on. A week's ride away from Alamut they discovered a very beautiful secluded little clearing in the woods, with the ruins of an ancient Christian church and several large, well preserved stone sarcophagi in the adjoining overgrown cemetery. So lovely was the spot, and Shefaka so weary from riding, that she readily agreed to rest there for a few days. But Selim knew this place of old, and had planned all

---

[38]   Selim was passionately addicted to sweetmeats, and even his quest for Shefaka could not entirely blunt his passion for stuffed dates, marzipan covered pistachios, figs in syrup, etc.

[39]   I omit any description of the wedding ceremony and festivities, since no account of them was passed down, and honesty prevents me from inventing them just to amuse the reader.

along to utilise it for his purposes. He knew that church and cemetery were consecrated ground, and that the dust in one of the sarcophagi contained the remnants of an ancient saint, powerful to those who dared to use it. Selim had chosen this location to save his wife from death, even before they left their home in Mosul.

That night after dinner he put a strong sleeping draught into the coffee of both women, and while they slept he prepared the transfer of spirits between his wife and the serving maid. The night was balmy and beautiful, with a full moon, and singing nightingales, which the love-struck Selim took as a good omen for the task he was about to perform. Having assured himself that both women were fast asleep, Selim took the lid off one of the sarcophagi, scooped out a large handful of dust, and poured it into an earthenware bowl. He replaced the lid on the sarcophagus, and placed the bowl on top of it.

He then proceeded to add any number of potions and powders to the dust in the bowl, tasted the resulting mix, added a few more drops of an orange liquid, tasted again, added a minuteness of an especially vile smelling powdered resin, shook his head, added a little honey, tasted again, decided it needed a little cinnamon – reminded himself rather sternly that he was not concocting a sweet, 'now do concentrate, the mixture is perfect now, never mind how it tastes, get on with the programme!' - and visibly chastised went back to his saddlebags for the mummy wrappings.

Selim then bandaged the women one after the other in the mummy wrappings, and carried them over to the sarcophagi. He took off the lid of another of the sarcophagi, and lowered the serving maid into its depths. But his wife he placed onto the closed sarcophagus of the dead saint, next to the bowl that held his magic mixture. Around his sleeping wife he placed 17 beeswax candles, kindled them, and by their light began to chant his songs of sorcery. After several hours of continuous chanting, a sudden gust blew out all candles but one, and Selim smiled contentedly – everything was going smoothly. Intoning a new, very high pitched and sibilant melody, which put great strain on his voice and nearly caused him to cough, he took the one remaining burning candle and dripped some of the wax on to the magic mixture in the bowl. A sweetly sickening smell arose from it – 'probably the honey,' he muttered. He went to the serving maid in her sarcophagus and put a teaspoonful of the mixture into her mouth, which she opened obediently. He then went to his wife, and began to spoon-feed her the rest of the mixture, which she, too, swallowed automatically without awakening from sleep, all the while chanting his melody in that throat-afflicting way. The bowl was almost empty, and he was preparing to pronounce the words that would effect the spirit exchange, when he heard a loud and piercing cry from the serving maid: 'Eek, a spider!'

A giant black spider with hairy legs and huge fangs -or so the wench claimed later on when she related her experience in the local tavern - had crawled across her face and thereby destroyed the trance Selim had so carefully cultivated in her. She jumped out of the sarcophagus, tripped over the mummy wrappings, hopped away on both legs, stopped to rip off a few of the bandages, finally managed to break into a frantic run, screaming all the while, and rapidly vanished into the distance. Meanwhile Shefaka also awoke, sat up, observed the scene before her, and understood in a flash of clairvoyant insight exactly what was taking place. Smiling sadly, she looked down at her husband who was now kneeling anguished at the foot of her sarcophagus, and addressed him thus.

'My dearly beloved husband, you have sinned grievously for my sake, and I shudder at your crimes. Whatever made you think I would accept life in the body of the unhappy maid you intended as the new habitat of my soul? Don't you know that I would have killed both you and me if your foul scheme had succeeded, mourning for my old body and your lost virtue? Now we shall both be punished for your iniquity, and I within the hour. For know this, husband, that your procedure to loosen my soul from my body was almost complete when you were interrupted, and so I must leave my body in a few moments, and enter into another. I have some choice in the matter, and to atone for my part in your crimes, unwittingly though it was, my soul shall enter the body of the spider that scared the serving maid, and for a few short years lead a life of furtive hunting in gloomy places. Although Allah may show me mercy and let me rest in Heaven, I would rather remain in this world, to be re-born time and again in humble form, until at last we meet once more and live in reunited harmony; my love for you is too strong for me to be at peace anywhere but at your side.'

With that her body shuddered, and fell back upon the top of the sarcophagus. But a small spider, with quite hairless legs, and very tiny fangs, scuttled towards the doorway of the old church, and began to spin a web across it.

The following morning, glittering with dew, the web spelled out Shefaka's last message to Selim: 'Farewell my love, be true of heart, and henceforth do no evil.' But even as Selim read the web's message, and looked longingly at the little spider at its centre, a bird came out of the church and, disregarding him, swallowed the little weaver and flew off. This was too much for Selim and his already severely strained nerves. 'Oh woe is me, now all is lost forever!' he shouted and fell to the ground, clawing the earth while moistening it with tears.

After a while his donkey meandered over and nudged him with his nose, as if trying to ask whether anything was the matter. This restored Selim to the requirements of the present, and he got up to see what he might do about breakfast. And in his great sorrow, and utter desperation, he quite forgot himself, and ate every single fruit, nut, cake, sweetmeat, and all the honey he could find, and emptied into his stomach both bottles of medicinal alcohol his donkey carried in his saddlebag for dire emergencies. Afterwards, sick and bloated and unsteady on his legs, he lifted the corpse of Shefaka from the sarcophagus and lowered it into the one from which the serving maid had so screamingly disappeared the previous night. Then he climbed onto his donkey, and made his way towards Khevsuria, both because he felt the need for solitude and because he thought the serving maid might tell her tale and rouse the population against him.

At this the Angakkoq glanced at the grandfather clock and remarked that it was too late to complete her tale that evening, but Walgren, who had become quite caught up in the story, protested and asked Arnapak to tell him at least how she managed to find out so much about the early life of the Cosmocrator, since it appeared as though there had been no witnesses for much of what the shaman told him.

'No human witnesses,' replied Arnapak. 'You forget I have 23 helping spirits, as well as Aua of course, many of whom are animal spirits and able to talk with other animals. For example, the first spirit helper I acquired is a spider, and she managed to gather much of the information about the Cosmocrator I have just told you. If people only realised how much spiders observe, and what conclusions they draw!' But she refused to say anything else that night, so Walgren had to go to bed with many questions burning on his tongue.

38   The making of an Adept

The following morning Walgren barely waited for the Angakkoq to complete her breakfast, before he ushered her back to the capacious armchair next to the fireplace, where a coal fire had already attained a steady sustained glow. Having instructed the housekeeper to accept no telephone calls and refuse entry to all visitors, Walgren settled himself in front of the fire across from his mother-in-law and urged her to continue her story.

The old Angakkoq smiled, and said, 'so at last you are beginning to believe that I have not just dreamed the contents of my tale?'

Walgren admitted that although he initially had his doubts, he was now quite convinced everything the shaman said was true. 'Come now, tell me what happened when you met the Cosmocrator in the Altai Mountains – did he realise that you were Niels' grandmother?'

But the Angakkoq refused to have a good story ruined by rushing through the details, and slowly stirred the tea in her cup, to dissolve the inordinate amounts of sugar she added to it, and remarked casually, 'Say what you will, but the tea from the thermos flask of the Takanakapsaluk is still the best I ever had; even after drinking it for twenty years I have not grown tired of it.'

'The story, will you please continue with the story,' Walgren cried. So the shaman took up the thread of her story again, lest her son-in-law completely lost all self control.

At the border of the valley of Khevsuria the would-be Cosmocrator said farewell to his faithful donkey, who could not follow him into that mysterious refuge of all fugitives who were desperate, courageous, and hardy enough to enter it, and climbed down the rope suspended from a mighty tree and reputedly the only entrance to that fabled country. It was a long and weary descent, lasting most of the day and even into the night, and the skin on Selim's hands was well nigh pulled to shreds when he finally felt solid ground beneath his feet and let go of the rope. There he was found by one of the dogs of Alleman Bey, who lived in splendid isolation in his nearby castle.

Alleman Bey fled to Khevsuria many years ago to avoid the long hand of the Inquisition, who desired to question him closely (and painfully) regarding the various unorthodox experiments he indulged in while a student at Paris. Although he studied under all the great Christian teachers of his time, including Albertus Magnus, Arnold of Villanova and Raymond Lully, he managed to altogether disregard the religious contents of their teachings and focussed exclusively on the alchemical and magical aspects. In Selim he found a kindred spirit, and the two men became devoted friends and colleagues in no time at all.

In their knowledge of the dark and esoteric arts, gathered primarily in the East by Selim, and the West by Alleman Bey, they complemented each other so completely, that together they presented the most formidable occult power extent at their time. Together they delved deep into the mysteries of the world and of life itself, so deep in fact they began to find their progress checked by unexpected barriers. This angered and frustrated them, because they had grown haughty with secret knowledge, and no longer accepted that defeat was the eventual fate of all human endeavours. When they had explored all other avenues, and found their way blocked in each one of them, they decided to choose the way of the adept, for they were desperate for new knowledge.

The term 'Adept' perhaps needs an explanation these days. Adepts seek knowledge, of all sorts and in any way. They are utterly without scruple when it comes to extending their mental horizon, and react with fury to anyone who seeks to constrain them in this endeavour. Thus adepts have been known to fight valiantly and often successfully against great odds with princes and popes, demons and spirits, and even the gods themselves, who sought to prevent them from accessing some little scrap of knowledge they set their heart on. If adepts hear of a new theory or invention or discovery, they immediately set out to investigate it, and seek to control it and make it their own. They have been known to sacrifice their dearest relatives and closest friends to this passion for knowledge, and are possibly the most dangerous beings in the world. For even the angriest of demons and most disgruntled of gods still maintain certain moral standards of behaviour they will not offend against, but adepts in search of knowledge have no conscience and accept no limitation on their behaviour whatsoever.

If adepts die for some reason, and this is exceedingly rare, their souls, instead of going to Limbo, or coming before the Incarnation Tribunal to be judged, enter into the body of some small animal that happens to be nearby, a spider or mouse or little bird, and continue to live on in this new shape just as before, having lost none of their powers and experience, and lust for new knowledge. However, living in such a small body renders them in many ways less effective, so they strive to acquire a new human body as soon as possible. To do so they have to overcome a human being and eject the soul, so they can appropriate the body, which is not easy, considering the size of a spider or mouse or bird, even if they achieve their goal by intermediate stages, and first overpower for example a squirrel, then a dog, then a goat, etc. Nevertheless most adepts accomplish this within a few years, which shows just how determined they are. Death holds very little fear for adepts, who consider it mainly a temporary nuisance they have to overcome before they can get back to their studies. Aside from this obsession with acquiring knowledge, however, adepts are the best of people, generous, polite, helpful, funny, reasonable, tidy, with simple needs, and in every way pleasant companions and model citizens.

This then was the state of being Alleman Bey and Selim aspired to, so as to overcome the barriers they encountered in their quest for new knowledge. By then Selim had been in Khevsuria for a number of years, and although his life was dominated by his lust for knowledge, he did not entirely forget Shefaka. Indeed, he managed to convince himself that he was doing it all for her, that he was seeking her soul in its current shape, and investigating ways of returning her to her human form when she was finally found. He seemed to have forgotten her last words to him, and the influence of Alleman Bey continued to weaken her memory, until she became a creature idealised and shaped entirely by his mind to suit his current occupation, and finally dwindled to a pleasant memory, relegated to a Sunday afternoon existence in his heart.

Having resolved that they would translate themselves into adepts, the two men set about preparing the various rituals and procedures required to achieve this state of being. There were seventeen stages in all, but when the Angakkoq proceeded to describe each one in tedious detail, Walgren, who was growing increasingly restless at the meandering way the shaman's story developed, begged Arnapak to confine herself to essentials.

'Oh very well,' said the shaman, who liked her stories long and full of minute detail, 'I guess that sort of knowledge is quite wasted on a pragmatist like you.' So she confined herself to the description of the last remaining ritual, the ritual that was to have completed the transformation of the two men, but went disastrously wrong.

By this time the men had already achieved the following:

(1) an indestructible, ever youthful, immortal body, that healed itself of injuries;
(2) immunity to all diseases;
(3) the flexibility of a contortionist;
(4) the lung capacity of a trumpeter;
(5) the liver of a teetotaller;
(6) the stomach of an aurochs;
(7) the eyesight of a sniper;
(8) the olfactory ability of a bloodhound;
(9) the hearing of a mother;
(10) the taste buds of a tea taster;
11) the sensitivity of an ethnographer;
(12) the ability to read the thoughts of certain men and women;
(13) the ability to direct the thoughts of certain men and women;
(14) the ability to move objects at a distance;
(15) the ability to travel short distances through the air; and
(16) the ability to destroy life by pure thought in certain circumstances.

The last remaining ritual (17) was to have given them the ability to defy the power of the gods, and break through the spiritual barriers the gods have erected around those realms they deem unfit for human observation. And in this last, most important, ritual the adepts failed. Just as the purple lightning of ultimate understanding was to have descended from the thunderbolt in the left hand of the statue of Ahriman on the pillar of pain on Mount Borbalo and strike the heart of Alleman Bey, the statue's right hand was struck by a piercing bright yellow-and-green flash from Heaven, and passed the flash on to Alleman Bey, who, emitting a loud scream, spontaneously combusted and burned brightly and completely, until only a little heap of ashes remained. Just as Selim was about to scoop them up so he could resurrect his friend in due course, a huge bear appeared and licked up all the ash before Selim could gainsay him. Having thus accomplished his aim, the bear proceeded to give Selim a long and serious lecture on the correct behaviour of a follower of Islam, and the rewards of pious living, for he was a very religious bear[40]. But Selim, though shaken, had strayed too far from the path of righteousness to take this sermon to heart. He henceforth pursued his studies on his own, and took up travelling again.

For six centuries Selim travelled the world, occasionally settling somewhere for a few decades, until his continuing youth caused suspicion among the natives and he had to move on again. During a stay in the south of France just before the Revolution he acquired the name of Florin, Marquis de Monde, and somehow got used to it, and adopted it permanently. 'Selim' seemed increasingly old fashioned to him, and he was at any rate not keen to remember his past.

Over time he perfected his knowledge and skills, until eventually he became the greatest adept of his time. Many of those who were mighty among humankind were indebted to him for his advice and potions, and his influence reached into the highest circles. Although by nature neither evil nor cruel, his great power increasingly corrupted him. No longer content with knowledge for its own sake, he began to enjoy the power over others it gave him, and by the time the 20th century dawned he had degenerated from an adept into an evil sorcerer. He indulged in bloodthirsty rituals and licentious practices of all kinds, telling himself he was simply exploring all avenues that might lead beyond the doors the gods had sealed against inquisitive humanity, and kept from him the ultimate knowledge of the universe. But in reality he no longer really cared about such knowledge. All he craved now was power, power for its own sake. As for those rituals, he frankly enjoyed them, and considered them valuable because they gave him additional power over those of his acolytes who participated. When one of them fawningly suggested that he call himself the 'Cosmocrator[41]', because of his great power and knowledge, he agreed with alacrity. Shefaka and his virtuous early life were all but forgotten.

39   Governor Pinchback restores a vegetable garden

It was now almost a year ago since Rupert and Tony had stolen the Exalted Heavenly Dream-Stone from its rightful guardian Adamantina, and secreted it in the basement of the house in Islington of their innocent and obliging friend, the spinster Miss Minnie Moochmerry. They spent days and weeks arguing how they could best utilise its unique properties, but had come to no conclusion. Finally they stored it beneath a huge pile of logs in Miss Minnie's coal cellar, and pretty much forgot about it.

One day they were sitting in Miss Minnie's kitchen drinking hot chocolate with plenty of miniature marshmallows and eating her excellent hot cross buns while watching the telly, when a news item caught their attention. The City of London, that unloved powerful neighbour of Islington, had been granted planning permission for a huge underground parking garage right underneath Paternoster Square! Rupert was incensed. Here they were, doing their darndest to save the planet by recycling their rubbish,

---

[40]   He was, in fact, a descendant of the Cave Bears, who were intimately connected with the cult of the Great Mother, and continue to be dedicated to her to this day. It was the protection of the Great Mother that enabled him to ingest the ashes of an adept without being taken over by him.

[41]   Ruler of the universe

velocipeding everywhere, and holidaying in Wales, and the fat cats in the City were building a huge parking garage to enable yet another thousand stockbrokers to drive to the City in their gas-guzzling luxury cars.

'Tone,' he said to his fellow terrorist, 'it is time for some direct action!' Tony agreed. 'Let's use that stone in the basement.' In no time at all a plot was hatched. Basically, they would trick the most illustrious of the City's luminaries, the Governor of The Institution, into the stone, and keep him there as a hostage until the City agreed to abandon their pollution-generating project.

It was well known that Governor Pinchback was a keen gardener, and always visited the annual Islington Flower & Produce Show, which was due to open in a few days. Miss Minnie Moochmerry had a stall at the show, and readily agreed when Rupert and Tony offered to watch her stall during the first few hours of the show, which were always quiet since most visitors arrived just before lunchtime. Little did she know that far from being the generous young men she thought them to be, they simply wanted her out of the way when Pinchback came for his customary early morning visit to the show.

Luck favoured the two terrorists. The morning of the Islington Flower & Produce Show dawned shrouded in cold fog, and there were very few visitors to be seen. They did not have to wait long before Governor Pinchback ambled over to Miss Minnie's table. He appeared fascinated by the Exalted Heavenly Dream-Stone, which had been granted a place of honour amongst Miss Minnie's prize parsley pots, and when he bend over to get a closer look Rupert gave him a shove while Tony whispered the secret word Adamantina had imparted to them all those months ago. Pinchback vanished into the Exalted Heavenly Dream-Stone without a trace, and no one noticed his disappearance. The two terrorists continued to man the stall as though nothing had happened, and when Minnie arrived to take over they packed up the Exalted Heavenly Dream-Stone and left with that warm inner glow that comes from a job well done. They returned to Minnie's house to hide the Exalted Heavenly Dream-Stone once more, this time in the attic amidst a profusion of discarded household items, and went off to consider how best to present their demands to the City.

Governor Pinchback meanwhile, having received a heavy push in the back that sent him tumbling into the Exalted Heavenly Dream-Stone, found himself rolling down a gentle slope. However, soon the momentum from the push exhausted itself, and Pinchback came to a halt. He got up, dusted himself off, and noticed a young woman nearby tending her chrysanthemums, none other in fact than Goldlotus, the Exalted Heavenly Dream-Stone Seductress who had delayed Gilligan Wang so disastrously.

But Pinchback was more interested in her chrysanthemums than in Goldlotus, and when she suggested a session of the wind-and-moon game he indignantly refused – 'I am a married man, I have you know!' He asked her where he was, and told her that someone had pushed him into this world and down the slope.

This seemed most strange to Goldlotus; hitherto all visitors to the Exalted Heavenly Dream-Stone had been volunteers. She therefore thought it wise to lead the new arrival directly to the Emerald Maiden without delay, and walked with the bemused Pinchback to her mistress' abode.

The Emerald Maiden immediately recognised that her new visitor was not the usual Dream-Stone addict who entered her realm with manifold romantic notions and could be abused with impunity. She ordered tea to be made and refreshments to be prepared, and invited Pinchback to sit on her right side and make himself at home. To Pinchback that seemed only right and proper, but her attendants had never before witnessed such a display of cordiality towards a mere mortal by their mistress, and stood there goggle-eyed until she told them sternly to get a move-on and obey her orders!

She listened to Pinchback's tale with great astonishment, and questioned him closely regarding any details he may have neglected to mention, especially whether he had come across the Guardian of the Exalted Heavenly Dream-Stone, one Adamantina. That name rang a bell with Pinchback, and he told his hostess that although he had no recollection of a woman being connected in any way with the Dream-Stone, he did have a young girl of that name working in his office. At the Emerald Maiden's request he described her carefully, and she concluded that the girl was indeed Adamantina. But why had she not entered the Exalted Heavenly Dream-Stone for all this time? And what was the current location of the Dream-Stone? It was really very mysterious.

Governor Pinchback was getting restless, and told the Emerald Maiden he unfortunately would have to leave the Dream-Stone now, since he was already late for a very important meeting. But the Emerald Maiden disappointed his hopes of a swift exit.

'Unfortunately it is impossible for anyone to leave the Exalted Heavenly Dream-Stone without the assistance of the Dream-Stone Guardian Adamantina. So until that irresponsible hussy –'

'Now now,' interjected the Governor who rather liked his second upper-secretary-

'- returns to her abandoned duties, you will have to remain in the Exalted Heavenly Dream-Stone. The question is, how will you make yourself useful until then?'

The Emerald Maiden refused Pinchbeck's offer of taking over her investment portfolio, because she did not have one. 'We have no need for money in my realm, and anyway I do have my hoard of silver bullion.'

'Silver bullion?' Pinchback was interested in bullion. 'Perhaps I could guard and dust the hoard?'

But the Emerald Maiden rejected this offer, too. 'The silver is deep within the mountains in an underground cave, and does not attract dust. As for guarding it, nobody can leave the Exalted Heavenly Dream-Stone without my permission and Adamantina's help, so it is quite impossible for anyone to remove the hoard from my realm without my leave.'

Meanwhile it was lunchtime, and the Emerald Maiden invited Pinchback to join her in the repast. Although all dishes were delicious, and cooked to perfection, he noticed that there were precious few fresh fruit and vegetables being served.

'Don't you like fresh fruit and vegetables?'

'Oh I love them, but ever since my gardener Liu Ming contrived his escape during the Great War, we haven't managed to produce a steady supply of fruit and vegetables. Perhaps it is the climate or maybe the soil is exhausted, but somehow we don't seem to be able to harvest anything except some puny carrots and a few miserable onions.'

'Rubbish,' snorted Pinchback, 'the weather looks perfect and the soil seems fertile – have you got any decent seeds left at least?'

His hostess directed him to an antique looking potting shed that stood amidst a thoroughly wild looking old kitchen garden.

'Ah yes, I'll take it from here,' Pinchback said after he examined the contents of the shed, and sent the Emerald Maiden back to practice her calligraphy, while he tackled the real work. The shed yielded seeds, spades, rakes, pruning shears, wooden shoes, and even an old straw hat, and he set to with real gusto.

'Nothing as satisfying as saving a neglected vegetable plot,' he told Goldlotus who had come around to enquire after him. Before she knew it, Pinchback handed her a spade and put her to work on an overgrown asparagus bed. 'You do like asparagus, I assume?'

'Not enough for this,' she muttered as she spaded the neglected bed, but did not dare to disobey him, since he exuded an air of authority and seemed moreover in high standing with the Emerald Maiden.

40   Adamantina discovers the Exalted Heavenly Dream-Stone and is reunited with Azazel

But Governor Pinchback's sojourn in the Exalted Heavenly Dream-Stone was not to last until even the first crop had matured. While he was weeding and pruning, mulching and sowing, the City was frantically searching for the lost head of The Institution. Indeed, so hectic were these efforts, and so stark the warnings issued by the police to whoever had caused the Governor's disappearance, that Rupert and Tony, who had somewhat underestimated the furore caused by the disappearance of Pinchbeck, did not dare to go public yet with their ransom demands. Instead they decided to lay low for a few weeks until the excitement had died down, little dreaming that their prisoner would have escaped by then.

Meanwhile Adamantina was helping Father Gottlieb with his great annual charitable jumble sale in aid of the homeless, and one fine Saturday afternoon she rang the bell of Miss Minnie Moochmerry's residence to help her sort out her attic and decide what to donate to the jumble sale. Miss Minnie was quite chatty but very well-intentioned, and the two women got on very well over several cups of tea and delicious home-made biscuits. At last they wended their way up the stairs, and began to sort the wheat (which was to remain in the attic) from the chaff (which was to go to the sale). A large pile was accumulating on the chaff side, mainly clothes but also a lot of bric-a-brac, when the telephone rang and Miss Minnie excused herself. 'Won't be a minute Dear, do go on without me,' she gaily told Adamantina while she rushed down the stairs. Adamantina did as she was told, and tucked into a large pile of old blankets in a corner of the room. 'Nothing here Miss Minnie would want to keep,' she murmured while going through the pile, examining the blankets one by one. Suddenly she stopped, blanket in midair, and exclaimed: 'Praise be to the Jade Emperor, I found the Exalted Heavenly Dream-Stone!'

She went to the stairs that led from the attic, and listened – Miss Minnie was still chattering on the telephone. Adamantina wrapped the Exalted Heavenly Dream-Stone in one of the better blankets, put the bundle into the reusable carrier bag she always carried in her purse, and calmly continued to sort through the blankets[42]. Presently Miss Minnie completed her telephone call and hastened up the stairs, crying as she run, 'Ada my dear, I am afraid we have to continue this some other time, my niece and her new husband have just invited themselves to dinner and there are a thousand things I need to prepare! I am really terribly sorry about this!' But Adamantina assured her that she had already done more than enough to help the homeless folk. All those blankets would keep dozens of them snug and cosy in the upcoming winter. Without giving Miss Minnie a chance to inspect the blankets she had selected, Adamantina loaded them into and onto her bicycle-basket and cycled, a little precariously, back to the City, leaving Miss Minnie to deliver the rest of her donations later.

Adamantina's first stop was the Cheapside soup kitchen, where she quite literally overwhelmed Father Gottlieb with most of the blankets, and then she cycled on to the side entrance of The Institution. Since she quite often worked on Saturday, she had no problem getting past the security guards – they did not even want to search her carrier bag.

Adamantina decided to hide the Exalted Heavenly Dream-Stone in the Governor's office, where she hoped it would at least be safe from terrorists, until she had a chance to visit the Emerald Maiden and discuss the future location of the Exalted Heavenly Dream-Stone. Once inside the building she felt quite safe, and relaxed visibly. She set the Exalted Heavenly Dream-Stone onto an empty table in a corner of the office, and breathed a sigh of relief, when she heard a sudden voice: 'So this is where you have been hiding!' Azazel, who spotted her cycling down Cheapside, had slipped invisibly behind her into the building.

Before she had the chance to rebuke him over having deserted her with the Exalted Heavenly Dream-Stone over a year ago, he immediately went on the attack. 'You have led me a merry dance, I have been looking for you all over!' He omitted to tell her that his business had detained him for a great many months, and that he only picked up the search in earnest after Agrat noticed him hanging around in Hell without the Exalted Heavenly Dream-Stone, asked a few pertinent questions, and threatened him with her considerable wroth if he did not find the wretched Dream-Stone and treat it with all honour – after all, she had given her word to the Emerald Maiden!

But Adamantina had other problems than his disappearance just now. Did Azazel think that it would be safe to keep the Exalted Heavenly Dream-Stone in the Governor's

---

[42]   The reader may have noticed that Adamantina neglected even the most rudimentary rituals proscribed in dream-stone lore when she unceremoniously bundled up the Dream-Stone in an old blanket, without a prayer or kowtow. This was the unfortunate but probably inevitable result of her recent employment in the City, which had hardened her spirit and replaced the poetry in her soul with cold calculating practicality.

office? Azazel agreed that The Institution was a safe place for the Dream-Stone, but would the Governor's office be the correct location? Had not Adamantina herself lectured him long and exhaustively on the need to keep the Exalted Heavenly Dream-Stone in a location that befitted its importance? Adamantina, who had neglected her duty towards the Exalted Heavenly Dream-Stone for so long, privately admitted the error of her ways and suggested storing it in the Treasure-Vault of The Institution. She had never actually been granted the privilege of visiting it, but knew that it contained untold riches and was very heavily guarded. Azazel agreed that a treasure-vault was the only possible place to store a Dream-Stone of the value and standing of the Exalted Heavenly Dream-Stone. He cast his invisibility cloak around himself and Adamantina, and together they entered The Institution's Gold Vaults.

But what a disappointment awaited them! Endless dusty rows of utilitarian pallets loaded with orange coloured gold bars, dimly illuminated by a few dull light-bulbs. There were no hanging lamps to illuminate the treasure, no divans to rest upon while feasting one's eyes on the riches gathered from all four corners of the world – in fact, there were no treasures or riches at all! Only rows upon rows of gold bars, completely unadorned and functional! 'This is no place for a Dream-Stone,' Adamantina declared as she viewed this dismal scene, and Azazel agreed. 'What a way to display gold! Who could possibly be impressed with a sad spectacle like this?' Even his unromantic soul was stirred to indignation. 'We must take action, and we must do it now!' they exclaimed, united at last by the uninspiring view before them. All night they laboured, and the new day awakened to observe an exciting new display in the former Stock Office which was currently used as a museum.

41   Governor Pinchback is rendered speechless and joins the Foilers

When Sophia entered The Institution the following Monday morning she immediately sensed that something was amiss. The Security Force was silent and forbidding, and searched everyone who was leaving the building, which was a reversal of their usual policy. Policemen and women could be spotted everywhere, sporting what looked like tommy-guns and equally grim of face as the Security Force. The doors to the Museum were reinforced with triple bars of bronzed steel, and museum staff had not been able to enter their work place that morning. Sophia went to the library, hoping to pick up some gossip, but no one had any idea of what had happened. However, her immediate boss, Flossy Pembrokeshire, was already in the library, and proffered one of her usual ridiculous theories. Apparently she had been attending to some business in the Museum late on Saturday night – everyone snickered and thought they knew what sort of business that was – when all of a sudden a huge number of gold bars had appeared out of nowhere. When she approached them to investigate, she received a sharp blow on the head and lost consciousness. She awoke in the presence of a male colleague who luckily happened to be in The Institution that night – more snickers could be discerned amongst her audience – and found her and took her home. 'I believe enemies have broken into the gold vault and stolen all our capital,' she finished her account. Gloomily predicting that none of them would be paid this month or any month ever again, she consoled herself with a swig from Howard's emergency flask of Sloe-gin.

Sophia had heard enough, and returned to the office to consult the oracular crystal she kept in her lower desk drawer. It confirmed her worst suspicions, and since she was obviously the only one in the building who could restore order in The Institution, she went to the Ladies Loo in the basement, powdered her nose, and blinked herself into the Museum.

She could hardly believe that she was indeed in what had only two days ago been the Museum. The former Stock Office was a large marble rotunda, a lofty hall crowned with a multi-windowed dome, and many noble columns that soared upwards to gracefully support the vaulted ceiling. Sunlight streamed through the handsome windows, and bathed in golden haze the treasure that was gathered there to comfort weary hearts and up-lift worried mortals.

The background was composed of red-gold bars of heavy bullion, the foreground dominated by low, opulent, silk-covered divans well supplied with many downy pillows. There were tables in front of the divans, laden with three-tiered silver stands that had deep plates with delicious sweetmeats, dried fruit and nuts, and marzipan and chocolates, as well as coffeepots and cups, and oriental water pipes and jars of best Djebeli tobacco. Bottles of choice wines and rare liqueurs shared table space with lead-crystal carafes of scented water, and sherbet drinks and ices, too, abounded.

Scattered about were many well-made caskets of fragrant woods, bound all around with iron bands and overflowing with precious antique coins in gold and silver. There were numerous large metal jars, inscribed with flowing arabesques and filled with precious stones and many ropes of pearls. Large hanging-lamps of pierced brass work, well decorated in Moroccan fashion, were suspended from the ceiling in profusion, and promised to gently light the treasure-vault once darkness fell. The floors were covered with exquisite oriental carpets and kelims, and great swathes of rich brocades in glowing colours were suspended from the ceiling to form a tent-like roof above several divans.

And on a delicately carved centre table, resting on a pillow of cream-coloured silk, reposed the Exalted Heavenly Dream-Stone, his two devoted guardians lolling on opulent couches nearby. Behind them stood a servant with a silver tray that bore a coffeepot and tiny cups, and another held a fan of ostrich feathers which he gently waved. Both servants were attired in ancient Turkish fashion, with red fezzes, golden-yellow silk shirts with large comfortable sleeves, wide green trousers gathered at the ankles, red open vests embroidered with golden thread, red sashes round their waists, and large upward-pointing slippers. Azazel was smoking from a hookah larger than himself, and Adamantina had just finished a cup of strong Turkish coffee, when they spotted Sophia.

'What an unexpected pleasure,' Azazel exclaimed when he saw her. 'Come, take a divan, have some coffee and try the Turkish Delight – best I ever had!'

But Sophia was not in the mood for Turkish delights, sweet or otherwise. 'I insist that you release the Governor immediately! Half the City is looking for him, and the other half is wringing their hands over the lost gold reserves! Have you no sense of responsibility whatsoever?'

'Sophia, I am a demon,' Azazel replied. 'And you have to admit that this looks much better that the musty dungeon were we found the gold. As for the Governor, I have no idea what you are talking about. He isn't here, as far as I know.'

'But haven't you been in the Dream-Stone recently?'

Adamantina had to admit that she had put off her next visit, being a little worried about the Emerald Maiden's wroth; after all, she had lost the Exalted Heavenly Dream-Stone and not been in it for a quite some time!

Sophia said that she had a point there, but nevertheless insisted on entering the Dream-Stone immediately to free the Governor. Since she was a demon of exceptional powers and could pretty much do as she pleased, she disregarded all entreaties from Adamantina, who would have preferred to first talk things over with the Emerald Maiden herself, and walked straight into the Dream-Stone-World.

Her demonic thirteenth sense led her to the Emerald Maiden, who was busy inspecting the vegetable garden Governor Pinchback had so miraculously restored to its former glory. The carrots were sprouting, the asparagus beds promised a magnificent crop, several fruit trees were in bloom, and the raspberry canes and bilberry bushes bore a profusion of tiny unripe berries. 'One month at the most,' Pinchback was saying, 'the climate is so regular and mild here, that you should be able to dine on raspberries with cream in four weeks' time.' The Emerald Maiden was clearly delighted with her newest subject. 'You think the peas will be ready in a fortnight?' Sophia heard her ask just as she walked around the potting shed and came into full view.

Governor Pinchback had no chance to reply to this question, because Sophia ran towards him and slapped him on the shoulder. 'Boss, I found you! Boy is that going to be a load off everyone's mind! Come on let's go!' The Emerald Maiden looked displeased when she heard these words, but since she recognised Sophia for what she was did not dare to gainsay her. But Pinchback himself was ill inclined to abandon his peaceful life in the Exalted Heavenly Dream-Stone. 'I can't possibly leave before the broad beans are ready,' he told Sophia, 'I am needed here.'

'Will you come out of this Stone,' cried Sophia, who was getting exasperated, 'can't you see you have fallen under the spell of the Dream-Stone-World and its wych-weaving mistress? You've got to come out and assure the authorities that you are alive and well, before things go any further! You can always come and visit afterwards, if you must!' It took some time and all Sophia's eloquence to finally convince the Governor that he had better return to his responsibilities immediately, and after taking courteous leave of the Emerald Maiden and having promised to visit as much as possible, he followed Sophia out of the Exalted Heavenly Dream-Stone, with many a yearning backward glance towards the vegetable garden.

Once outside, he looked about him with great astonishment, and asked with an unsteady voice where he was. Upon hearing the answer he sat down heavily on one of the divans, drank three cups of coffee in quick succession, looked around again in pained wonderment, asked for a glass of water, swallowed two of his pills, and turned to Sophia to demand an explanation.

'Well, you can have it but you're not gonna like it,' said his adoring employee, and proceeded to give him an account of the happenings of the last week or so.

'I am going back into the Dream-Stone,' he said when she had finished, 'I can't handle all this at my age. Let someone else sort it out.'

Sophia rolled her eyes heavenwards, and told him to pull himself together. 'Life isn't all growing raspberries and harvesting broad beans, you know. Now listen up, we need your help.' Since Azazel and Adamantina had meanwhile fled to avoid her anger, and she was therefore alone with the Governor, she told Pinchback all about the dastardly plot to defraud the City, and how the Foilers were trying to stop it.

'Of course if that's how it is I shall have to go back to my old job,' Pinchback reluctantly agreed when Sophia had completed her tale.

'But what are we going to tell everyone about the gold reserves being in the Museum?'

Sophia already had that covered. 'You say you have decided to open the gold reserves for viewing by the paying public, and had hired outside contractors to effect the necessary transformation of the Museum, so that it would be a surprise for everyone. Since you personally had to supervise the operation to ensure that everything went smoothly, you had to disappear for a few days. Tell them that you expect the refurbished Museum to generate a significant revenue stream, which will be your leaving gift to The Institution when you retire in another year or two.'

'You think they are going to believe such an obviously fabricated explanation?' Pinchback asked Sophia when she had finished.

'You are the Governor of The Institution and therefore inherently believable. Besides, you have told them far greater lies – remember that line you fed them on the Dandelion Bank fiasco? Heck, they'll believe anything!'

'I resent that! I spoke nothing but the slightly altered truth on that occasion.'

'Well, if you'd rather tell them that a bunch of demons are running riot all over the City on your watch …'

Shortly afterwards the Governor emerged from the opening doors of the Museum, and announced he would hold a press conference in an hour's time. Then he went to his office, and called for his personal butler, Arthur Peterson.

'Peterson, I have returned.'

Yes Sir, very good, Sir.'

'I think this calls for a celebration.'

'Yes Sir, certainly Sir.'

'I want you to go out there and buy a one-scoop ice cream cone for every single one of my employees, Peterson.'

'Yes Sir, very good Sir. Any particular flavour, Sir?'

The Governor considered this a little before replying. 'Better make it vanilla – after all, this is The Institution. Mustn't be seen to be doing anything too radical.'

The Press Conference went better than Pinchback had feared. Although he had to field some downright hostile question about his disappearance, he conquered all when he proclaimed his undying love for The Institution, the City, and the country as a whole.

'This last week has not been easy for me,' he told his audience, implying he had personally shifted every last one of those gold bars, and paid for each coin and pearl that had so miraculously appeared in the Museum. He rejected as ridiculous the notion that the gold would not be safe if kept so openly in the Museum; after all, no one ever stole from The Institution, and in the unlikely event that someone tried they would get a nasty electric shock, because the reserves were protected by 240 volt wire netting that went all around and over them.

'I did it all for the good of the City,' he concluded, 'and hope the Museum will generate enough income to make The Institution financially independent.' After the applause died down, he invited all those present to come and inspect the Museum under his guidance. 'It is not quite finished,' he told them as they walked down the corridor towards it, 'but should open to the general public within a few weeks.'

Everyone was suitably awed, many pictures were taken, and articles written, and miraculously everything Governor Pinchback had promised soon came to pass. Sophia helped him install the high voltage wire netting, and the Exalted Heavenly Dream-Stone was placed in a hand wrought silver filigree cage[43] and placed on a pillar towards the back of the room. Extra seats and tables were installed, serving staff were hired, trained, and kitted out in suitable costumes, and a five person strong band was retained to fill the Hall with oriental music. In time there would be special belly dancing evenings, and foreign dignitaries would be entertained in true fairytale splendour. Within six weeks of the Governor's return, the miraculously transformed Café Aladdin (also called Bullion Yard by disrespectful employees) was opened for business by a member of the Royal Family, and welcomed an astonished and delighted public.

But all that was still in the future when Governor Pinchback was dragged to the Old Lady's digs the night after he had left the Exalted Heavenly Dream-Stone. That worthy guardian of the City was not amused when she saw the Governor entering her rooms behind Sophia and the Mouser.

'You might have consulted me first before betraying my secrets,' she grumbled. 'Young Oswald isn't going to believe anything you tell him, and even if he did, would do nothing about it. Useless young whippersnapper!'

But the Mouser intervened on the Governor's behalf. He had observed the Governor for a dozen years now, and found him to be dependable and honest, occasionally decisive, always courteous, and very sound on rodent control. It was he

---

[43]   The cage prevented innocent bystanders (like the Governor) from being pushed into the Dream-Stone against their will, while a small door in the back provided access for visitors (like the Governor) who wanted to call on the Emerald Maiden.

who had authorised the installation of cat flaps in all doors within the institution, and several cat-ladders from the second floor so the Mouser and his Rodent Reduction Force could leave and enter the building at their pleasure. 'A man like that must not be easily dismissed,' he declared. 'Of course he does smoke, but then nobody is perfect.' With that closing shot at The Old Lady and her fumiferous habits, he jumped onto Sophia's lap and curled up.

Sophia agreed. 'No offence,' she told The Old Lady, 'but you are not exactly a bundle of industrious helpfulness yourself! The Mouser and Devadorje and I do all the legwork, and you just counsel caution and do nothing. We need someone active and alert on the group, someone with get-up and go, with influence and intelligence! I say let's recruit him.'

Oswald Pinchback listened to all this with slight incredulity. He was used to being courted and respected, and welcomed onto any committee he wanted to join, and this strange little assembly actually argued about admitting him to a club that held its meetings in his own building! However, the Greenlandia issue sounded very serious to him, and these people - could one call a cat a person if he spoke English? – well, anyway, they seemed to have strange powers and knowledge he could not otherwise access, so he decided to play along and do whatever was needed to gain acceptance to their club.

The Old Lady was still dithering. She felt offended by Sophia's outburst, and feared the Governor would dominate the group if he was allowed to join. On the other hand he was the Governor, and potentially very useful.

'Tell me,' she addressed Pinchback, 'if we were to allow you to join our little group, how would you be of any use to us?' She then subjected him to the most exacting interview he had ever endured, even worse than the one before being made Governor. 'I sweated through three shirts,' he told his wife that evening, 'the old crone obviously enjoyed herself immensely.'

However, they all knew that the outcome was not in doubt, and three hours later the Governor was officially allowed to join the Foilers. 'Drinks are on me,' he proclaimed as they drank to his good health, 'tomorrow night I shall bring up a case from The Institution's cellar myself.' 'Normally I just steal them,' muttered The Old Lady to herself, still a little miffed about him joining.

42   The Cosmocrator's Castle

The morning after Arnapak had reviewed all she knew about the magician, she made her preparations for the journey to his castle. Since the magician was liable to recognise the value of some of her amulets and talismans, and try to take them from her, she decided to hide them in a cave, together with the magic gifts she had received from the Takanakapsaluk. She also thought it unwise to take her spirit helpers with her – the magician was bound to be on guard against all spirits and magic. After much consideration, and consultation with her spirits, she decided to only take her spider spirit helper, since she was easily concealed and might be useful in freaking out the magician. As a back-up, she asked a raven she had befriended to guard the golden cross from

Yeshua for her, and loiter in the vicinity of the castle, so he could come to her aid and bring her the talisman if she required it. Lastly, she hid a small pistol in her boots. Thus equipped, she mounted a sturdy Mongolian horse and rode to the magician's castle.

The magician welcomed her with literally open arms, standing on the lowered drawbridge of his castle as Arnapak approached on her steed. However, he suddenly dropped them when Arnapak was within smelling distance; her methods of hygiene were unorthodox and disconcerting to those with sensitive olfactory powers. Instead she was given a swift but friendly handshake, and Florimonde – as he introduced himself – ushered his honoured guest into a set of rooms set aside for her use. He personally demonstrated to her the use of the cold and hot water faucets and how to run a bath, poured quantities of bubble bath into the tub, tried to get her interested in different types of soap but stopped when she tried to eat one of them that smelled of lemon, and in general did his level best to get her to clean herself up a bit. But Arnapak acted as though she had never seen a bathroom before, and behaved like the proverbial village idiot. When she finally tried to embrace her host in gratitude for taking such good care of her he fled, having told Arnapak that dinner would be in two hours.

Once alone, Arnapak proceeded to take bites out of all the soaps and spit them into the toilet, poured all of the bubble bath into the tub and stirred the water with the toilet brush until the bathroom was overflowing with bubbles, used the toothpaste to insulate a crack around one of the windows in her sitting room, and utilised all the toilet paper as extra padding under her shirt and pants. 'So far so good,' she thought. 'I bet the place is bugged, I better keep up the pretence.' Then she built a largish nest out of all the blankets, carpets, towels, curtains, and table cloths in her suite, burrowed down into its depths, and fell asleep.

Two hours later her host arrived to escort her personally to the dining hall, and was badly shaken by the appearance of the suite. However, he controlled his temper, and managed to rouse her by shouting repeatedly at the top of his voice. Eventually she emerged from the nest, pulled aside an expensive lace curtain that covered her face like a veil, and threw her host an amorous glance.

'Have you ever slept in a nest like this before? Why don't you join me in here? I am an old woman, you know, and have had plenty of time to learn all the arts of love. Now, that I am nearly eighty, there is little left for me to learn, but much I have to teach! I promise you an experience you will never forget!'

The magician retreated cautiously; he was all for orgies and erotic experiments, but ancient crones who smelled of rancid yak butter and only changed their clothes once a year were beyond the bounds of what even he was prepared to do. He told his guest he had unfortunately taken a vow of chastity and was therefore unable to take up her kind offer; however, if she saw anyone at the banquet tonight who struck her fancy he would gladly arrange a rendezvous. 'Ah well,' Arnapak said philosophically as she climbed out of the nest and joined her host, 'I suppose you are a little too dainty for me anyway.'

The dining hall was huge, draughty, and cold despite the large fireplace, and furnished with tapestries and nomadic rugs, heavy oak furniture, and numerous cast iron candleholders with dozens of lit candles. The general appearance was European medieval; indeed the whole castle gave that impression, and seemed strangely out of place in central Mongolia. The magician noticed her interest in his dining hall, and told her that the entire building was erected by magical means. 'My ancestors had some dealings with the crusaders, and I thought it amusing to re-create one of their fortresses in central Asia. It will cause a great deal of confusion amongst future archaeologists, don't you think?'

Arnapak pretended to have no knowledge of crusaders, and gently pumped her host on the subject during dinner. He told her a great many things he would have kept to himself had he known that she was not the ignorant simpleton he took her for.

'This building contains all the features of a medieval castle, even dungeons and torture chambers,' he bragged, 'and has all the amenities necessary to an adept, including an extensive library, laboratory, and receptacle of …..' he stopped abruptly.

Arnapak did not press him to complete his sentence, but changed the subject instead. 'Got you,' she thought – a good thing the magician could not read her cloaked mind!

After dinner they lingered over the port, and it was obvious that the magician was trying to intoxicate the shaman. Luckily the Buddhist monk who taught Arnapak how to cloak her mind also showed her how to isolate alcohol inside her body, such that it had no effect on her and went straight through, so by the end of the evening she was still sober while her host was getting increasingly inebriated. His conversation became more rambling, and ranged across many ages and lands, and he told her more than he thought wise the following day. But then he did not really intend her to leave his castle with her knowledge; as soon as he learned all she had to teach, he planned to incarcerate her in one of the dungeons. So he took less care with his confidences than was his wont.

They were about to retire to their rooms for the night, when a large spider darted across the floor, stopped short before the magician, and waved its front legs about, as though trying to communicate with him. The magician sat stock still, and barely seemed to breathe, while the spider appeared to get ever more agitated, and finally walked off in what seemed like a huff. The magician made a supreme effort to compose himself, and said casually to Arnapak,

'Do you understand the language of spiders? I have not yet mastered it.'

'I know a little of spider language, though not much. All I could make out is that this spider seems to think she knows you, and is unhappy about something you have done.'

Upon these words the magician grew very pale, and entreated her to act as interpreter between himself and the spider. To this she agreed with alacrity, but meanwhile the spider had disappeared, and as it was getting late they decided to sit up and wait for the spider the following evening, and hope she would show herself again. With this they went to bed, the magician courteously escorting Arnapak to her rooms before he went to his own. He slept badly that night, and his dreams were much disturbed. The shaman slept well, having thanked her spider spirit for her help with the Cosmocrator.

But the spider spirit did not sleep, and spent the night exploring the castle instead. At last Shefaka had met Selim again, and she was appalled at what he had become! After her exploration of the castle she wakened Arnapak, and together they hatched a plot.

43   The Potency of Elderberry Wine

The following morning the magician showed Arnapak around the castle, which was really most impressive. She evinced little interest in the torture chamber, lingered in the library, and noted in passing that there were two inhabitants of the dungeons. But when the magician asked her over lunch whether she had ever seen a habitation more perfectly suited to an adherent of the magic arts, she replied a little petulantly that it was hard to tell, since he had omitted to show her his laboratory and the Essential Receptacle, which were after all the most important features of a magician's dwelling. The magician was most astonished that she even knew of the Essential Receptacle, since this was a very recondite and secret part of an adept's life. 'However, if you indeed know what this is all about, you will understand that I cannot show you where I maintain it,' he told her.

But Arnapak, who had been filled in on the secrets of the castle by Shefaka, just laughed, and proceeded to describe to the magician in detail where his Essential Receptacle was, and what it contained.

'It is hidden deep beneath the castle, accessible only by a trapdoor which is concealed beneath the earth closet that is connected to all the toilets in the castle and turns all 'night-soil' into compost. No one except a powerful magician can access it without considerable soiling. A passage leads from a little cellar beneath the earth closet several hundred feet into the earth, ending in a small chamber. In the centre of this chamber stands a pillar, and on top of the pillar rests a large bowl fashioned from green jade.'

The magician watched Arnapak with clenched fists as she told her tale. 'How can you possibly know this,' he hissed through gritted teeth.

'The spiders told me,' she replied. 'But that is another story, let me finish this one first. The bowl contains a liquid in which all your vital organs float. They are perfectly preserved in the liquid, and thus cannot be injured while you are abroad in your body. While your organs are safe, you cannot die,' Arnapak finished her narrative.

The magician was furious that she knew his secret, and decided to kill her without delay as soon as he had learned all her secrets in the torture chamber. No more Mr Nice-Guy, he thought grimly, as he prepared to throw a magical restraining rope around her.

But Arnapak had still more revelations. 'According to the lore of my ancient Siberian ancestors, there is only one way of killing your organs, and that is through contact with the fruits of the elder. I don't suppose you are aware that one of your kitchen skivvies is addicted to elderberry wine, and always keeps a bottle or two in his cupboard? Well, earlier this morning I took the liberty of stealing one of the bottles. I decanted some of the wine into a tiny bladder and several of the spiders took it down into your Holy of Holies. There are spiders all around us, and others are stationed along the way between here and the chamber; as soon as I give the word, the elderberry wine will be tipped into the bowl that contains your vital organs, and you will die a painful long drawn-out death. So if I were you I would be a little careful about trying any tricks on me.'

The magician almost choked with anger; this uncivilised imbecilic old hag had actually gotten the better of him! It was insupportable, it was an outrage, such a thing had not happened since his friend Aleman Bey died. He controlled himself with a great effort, and asked Arnapak why she had gone to all this trouble to find out his secrets. Surely they could remain friends, and resolve this silly little tiff amicably?

Arnapak quite agreed. 'All I want is the soul of my great-granddaughter, and then I'll disappear and never trouble you again.'

'Great-granddaughter?' The magician appeared to be puzzled, so Arnapak gave him a few details.

'Remember, around eighteen years ago, in the Rockies you tried to sacrifice a Greenland girl called Elisabee? Her husband was my grandson. Somehow you managed to cause his death as well. Anyway, Elisabee gave birth to a child during the sacrifice, and this girl is suffering because she is missing one of her souls. Naturally I assumed that you held it in your care.'

Suddenly the magician began to understand a great many things, and realised how badly he had underestimated the shaman. All the same, he was unable to help her; although it was true that he had managed to entrap one of Nuliajuq's souls, it had escaped several year's later during the move to the Altais. He had no idea what had become of it.

Arnapak was dreadfully disappointed, but sensed that the magician was telling the truth. Moreover, Shafaka had searched the entire castle, and quizzed the spiders who inhabited it, and discovered no trace of an imprisoned soul. Arnapak had spent eighteen years hunting down the magician, and was no closer to finding Nuliajuq's soul than when she had started out. It was really most discouraging!

'Well, frightfully sorry I could not help, and all that, but I expect you will want to be on your way again immediately, and continue your search elsewhere,' the magician said to Arnapak and got up from his seat.

But Shefaka had other plans. She approached the magician at the head of an army of spiders, and spoke to him in the voice she had when still a human being, so many years ago. 'Sit down, Selim,' she said quietly, and he fell back into his chair, frightened and awed.

'So you have come back to me last,' he said, 'and still in spider form.'

'Yes, I am still a spider, still atoning for your crime. For seven centuries I have dragged out my lives, living as a spider, dieing as a spider, each time refusing to be reborn as anything but a spider, because I wished to atone for your transgression by living in the form of a lowly, despised creature. Each time I died I rejected the grace offered me by the Incarnation Tribunal to either enter Heaven or be re-born as a human being; each time I renewed my commitment to you and your memory. And what is my reward? You have sunk deeper and deeper into evil. I had fondly imagined that you only transgressed out of love for me, but now I understand this was a foolish notion. I shall not bid you farewell, for I have grown to loathe you, Selim. I shall wait for you no more, but petition the Incarnation Tribunal to let me be re-born immediately, as a human being. I shall start another line of lives, and forget what you were to me. Shefaka is no more.' She then turned to Arnapak, and asked to be released from service as her spirit helper. Arnapak just nodded sadly, and Shafaka's form grew transparent, and vanished, and was never seen again.

Shocked to the core, the magician jumped up from his seat, and ran towards the mass of spiders who had accompanied Shefaka. He went down on his hands and knees, and looked at the spiders one by one searchingly, as though he thought Shefaka might be hiding amongst them. But the spiders retreated from him, and hurried from the room. He turned to Arnapak, and said, grief-stricken, 'Did you hear what Shefaka said to me? She said she loathed me!'

'Does this surprise you? Of course she loathes you, everyone does! The tribes in the valleys speak of you with horror in their voices, and the beasts that roamed these lands abandoned them when you came. No birds sing in your castle, and no cricket lives in your hearth. The very gnats and spiders flee your presence.' She observed his look of pained surprise, and added, 'Come now, you knew all this.'

Although this was true on some level, the magician – like so many people – had an unlimited store of self deception to draw upon, and was thus able to display surprise without complete hypocrisy. He had not been aware of the impression he made on others, because he did not care to know; it had simply not been important to him. But strangely, now it was. 'Even the spiders flee from me,' he murmured, 'though I never harmed any of them.'

'Evil radiates from you as heat from a fire,' said Arnapak. 'Spiders are very sensitive creatures.'

Dear Reader! Human nature has strong roots in the old primitive brain we share with birds and reptiles. Here simple ancient emotions still hold sway, and need and fear, lust and hatred, love and pride, jostle for primacy deep below the conscious awareness of the mind they seek to dominate. Lucky indeed are those who manage to hold these basic urges in successful balance, and lead a life of tranquil equanimity! But the Cosmocrator, whose inner world grew ever more complicated and twisted as his life spanned the centuries, had never made any attempt to delve into the secrets of his subconscious mind and gain some understanding of his emotions. He was so preoccupied with his quest for knowledge of the outside world, that he completely neglected the world within himself. For hundreds of years he had suppressed his need for love and approbation, without even being aware that it existed.

When suddenly confronted with Shefaka, all his pent-up desire for love and true friendship erupted into his consciousness and demanded to be acknowledged. Her words to him rekindled all his love for her, and a deep desire to be with her again. He once more remembered the perfect happiness he had enjoyed in her company, and realized that she had been the only person who had ever truly loved him. And now he had lost her because she was repelled by the evil in his heart! He thought of her gentleness, and piety, and simple trusting nature, and heard again her cry, 'I loathe you Selim!' Shocked and dismayed, he relaxed for the first time in his long life the tight grip on his emotions, and thus became overwhelmed with unwelcome insights. Unable to refute the accusations levied against him from the depth of his own soul, he was at last forced to see himself as others looked upon him.

Filled with shame and disgust at the recollection of his evil deeds, he turned to Arnapak and cried: 'Tell then your spider friends to pour the elderberry wine onto my vital organs, for verily I desire to live no more!'

Although Arnapak was unable to talk to the spiders any more since Shafaka had left, and therefore could not comply with the magician's request, the spiders, worried about the disappearance of Shefaka, had meanwhile decided to take matters into their own hands, and tipped the elderberry wine into the bowl. At that the liquid in the bowl began to froth and boil over. Green bubbles formed and detached themselves from the liquid, and a stench like rotten eggs permeated the chamber. The organs in the bowl, which had been sustained for so long by the green liquid, slowly started to dissolve.

Above in the castle the magician jumped from his chair, clutched his belly, and allowed himself one piercing shriek of agony, before he controlled himself, and said to Arnapak:

'May Allah bless you, for having come to this castle with Shefaka and brought me to my senses! I am Selim once more, and will bear this pain without complaint, and accept it as just punishment for my evil deeds. I will not forget Shefaka, but treasure her in my heart, and hope to meet her once again many years hence when I have become worthy of her.' Then he sat down and bore his pain stoically, until at last his organs were completely dissolved. He grimaced slightly, and with his last strength asked Arnapak to liberate the two prisoners he held in his dungeons; then death took possession of him. At this the spiders returned to the hall, and rushed about in frantic merriment, and evinced signs of great joy, because the magician had not been popular amongst them, and also because they were rather proud of having achieved such a great victory over the Cosmocrator.

But Arnapak sat quietly and watched the dead magician, and saw his body turn grey and brittle and crumble slowly into dust, while his souls left one by one, and entered into the smallest, most timid, of the celebrating spiders[44]. This possessed spider became very calm, and walked towards Arnapak, stopping a few feet before her. Should she step on him, and take her revenge? Surely he would simply pass into another spider, and hide from her? After a few seconds of reflection, she opened one of her coat pockets, and said, 'Hop in little one, you will be safe in my pocket.' She had an inkling that an accomplished adept like Selim would not take long to work his way out of the spider's body into another human being, and thought it wise to keep an eye on him. Moreover, despite all he had done to her family she could not bear to destroy a being with so much

---

[44]   When Adepts die they usually refuse to submit to the judgement of the Incarnation Tribunal, preferring instead to take their chances and reincarnate without receiving any help by entering the body of some living being and ejecting its resident soul. However, since all creatures are at their weakest upon death, adepts usually only manage to take over a very small being like a mouse or spider. Selim was a true Adept, and chose to pass into the spider, despite having just expressed a desire for death, rather than submit to a judgement.

learning and determination. And who knows, perhaps he really had turned over a new leaf, and would improve his soul, and meet up with Shefaka at long last! The old shaman was nothing if not sentimental.

Arnapak went back to her room to pack and made ready to depart when she remembered the prisoners in the dungeons of the castle. The castle was deserted; all the magician's servants and hanger-ons had disappeared when they heard his terrible scream. 'They probably think that I am even worse than he was, seeing as I bested him,' Arnapak thought as she descended into the dungeons. There were no guards of any kind, and no one hindered her when she took a bundle of keys from what looked like the guards' room and used them to open the doors of the two prisoners' cells. 'Thank you very much indeed, noble lady,' said Sadek as he stepped from his cell. 'And about time, what took you so long?' yelled Gisela when her cell door opened.

44   Sadek and Gisela inflict themselves upon their relatives

Arnapak had every right to be proud of herself. She had finally tracked down and defeated the Cosmocrator, and thus rid the world of a dangerous menace, and freed two innocent human beings from his dungeons into the bargain. Yet she suddenly felt distraught, overcome by fatigue and world-weariness. For almost twenty years she had sought after the lost soul of Nuliajuq, and yet again she had drawn a blank. She was eighty years old, and had already lived many more years than was usual for her people; how much longer would she be able to go on? And if she could not find Nuliajuq's lost soul, who would?

Yet it was not in her nature to be despondent for long, and besides she had more immediate problems on her hands. Gisela and Sadek, the ex-prisoners of the Cosmocrator, were agitating for them to leave the Altai region and rejoin humanity. Unfortunately they did not agree upon a destination. Gisela longed for the life of a roaming nomad, and for freedom from all housework and earthly cares, while Sadek wanted to settle down in some quaint, civilised little country, far from all relatives, and devote the rest of his life to painting miniatures. He had been introduced to this art by exiled Byzantium monks before Gisela discovered him a few years ago. He was still cross with her for having taken him away from them, and tied him to the stirrups of her horse after he tried to escape one night, and dragged him half way across Asia, until they fell into the hands of the Cosmocrator.

'If you had not annoyed him so, but accepted his offer of joining his satanic sect, he would have set me free and I could have returned to the monks. But no, you had to reject his advances and spit in his face, until he imprisoned us both in his dankest dungeon!'

'You are the only man I ever gave myself to, and I shall never want another,' Gisela replied virtuously.

Arnapak suggested that they first visit their family in Arabia, and attend to their duties to their kin. That's what she herself was going to do. 'I can't take you anyway,' she told the two ex-prisoners. 'There is only enough room on my sledge for myself, so I suggest you make your way to Ulaanbaatar and catch a flight home.' Gisela and Sadek grumbled about this; their family did not feature greatly in their plans, and they had no desire to assume responsibility for them again. All the same they agreed they had better face the music, and after several weeks of arduous travel climbed aboard a plane to Arabia with gritted teeth and artificial smiles.

This is not the place to describe the complicated emotions that were aroused by the return of Gisela and Sadek to the bosom of their family. Obviously everyone was overjoyed to know they were alive and well, and Hadji Kurt for some time nursed the hope that Sadek would take over the leadership of the clan again. On the other hand Sadek had become very cranky, and his detailed discussions of the intricacies of miniature painting soon bored even the most devoted of his relatives. Gisela, too, proved a mixed blessing. Of course every one was most grateful to her for having saved and returned the head of the family, but she had become even more stridently opinionated during her long travels, and her feminist diatribes soon aroused the suspicion and attention of the religious police, who preferred their females silent and obedient.

Consequently barely a month after they had returned to Arabia, Sadek and Gisela were summoned before the family council and told firmly that they would have to leave again. The dismay this announcement caused them was evident upon their features, and did them great credit with everyone on the family council. Nevertheless the council stood firm. They were granted a generous allowance, of course, and would be permitted to return to the family home twice a year for one week at a time.

'I am really very sorry to have to ask you to make this sacrifice,' Hajji Kurt apologised to his parents, guilt-ridden to the core. 'But you can see how it is; it would be impossible to keep you here and preserve the peace.'

Sadek was outraged to be thus ejected from the warm embrace of his ancestral home. 'Accursed I am, who dreamt for many a long year of an affectionate welcome by his delighted relatives, only to be rejected upon arrival' he wailed and refused to be consoled.

But as usual, Gisela was more reasonable. 'Love of my life,' she addressed her wailing husband, 'Can't you see the family, rightly or wrongly, have decided that our continued presence within their midst would provoke discord and enmity and result in untold dire consequences? When you and I are nought but dust, the family will still endure; so let us bow our necks under the yoke of tradition and leave as we are bid. Power to the clan I say, and may the family prosper!'

Everyone who heard this was moved to shed bitter tears, and they all assured her that if it were up to them they would keep them both here until they died, but alas unfortunately ..... Gisela nodded bravely, as tearful as her husband, and thanked them for their kind words. The following morning she was ready and packed, and, with a mournful Sadek following reluctantly behind, mounted a camel and headed for the nearest airport.

Once settled comfortably in her seat next to Sadek, Gisela turned to the man of her dreams and said, 'now that wasn't all that difficult, was it?' And Sadek, as so many times before, knew why Gisela was the only woman he had ever loved, and was most grateful to his wily spouse. 'I even forgive you for having tied me to your stirrups,' he whispered into her ear and kissed it.

After some deliberation Sadek and Gisela bought a little house in Liechtenstein, where Sadek lived in joyful isolation and in due course acquired quite a reputation as a gifted artist and painter of miniatures, and Gisela sometimes visited him for a few weeks. But soon the travel bug would bite her again, and she would be off once more to have daring adventures in distant lands. Relations with the clan remained excellent, and Sadek and Gisela never failed to visit their adoring family twice a year for a week at a time. Thus they were rewarded for their manifold trials with a happy old age, each in their own way, and they are now out of the story.

45   Fleabrunckle hears of the demise of Florimonde, and Thérèse vows vengeance

The news of the demise of the fabled Cosmocrator reached Fleabrunckle soon after the event, and after an initial period of shock and worry about his own future he breathed a sigh of relief at being free at last of the unloved and overbearing Florimonde. He felt confident he was clever and resourceful enough to carry out their plans without the aid of his erstwhile master. Florimonde's last e-mail had advised him of an impending discovery in Tannu Tuva, and Fleabrunckle looked forward to implementing their scheme, and to reaping rewards he would not have to share.

He still saw Thérèse frequently for lunch or dinner, and when they next met up enquired about the state of her share & derivative portfolios.

'Do you think that it will warrant a sizable Christmas bonus?'

Thérèse doubted it. 'Dealing guidelines are much stricter at Bank of Libraria than they were at The Bog, and since I am not allowed to take risks how can I make large profits?'

Fleabrunckle sympathised. 'What you need is a windfall, a dead certain tip-off that will net you millions. Luckily I am in a position to give you such a tip! Only yesterday I overheard two high executives of the Prime Plastics Corporation discuss the current oversupply of the plastics market, which has been depressing prices for some time now. One of them said prices were certain to increase once PPC had taken over their rival, the Cheapo Plastics Corporation, and restricted supplies. So here's your tip. Go long in plastics and shares of PPC and sit tight for a week or two until the take-over hits the newspapers, and prices increase. Then sell at the new prices, make a huge profit, and see your bonus hit the roof! I am going to cash in on this myself, and have already bought several hundred thousand shares in PPC with my nest egg.'

Thérèse was most terribly grateful to Fleabrunckle, and so overwhelmed by this good fortune, that she failed to remember the strict laws on insider trading[45] that had been imposed on the financial community. She could hardly wait to get back to her trading

---

[45]   Insider trading means that market participants buy and sell on the basis of information that is not available to other people, thus gaining an unfair advantage; it is illegal and may be punished by large fines and a lengthy prison term.

desk, and left so quickly that she took no notice of the wolfish grin that suffused Fleabrunckle's features as she left the table. But she remembered it in months to come!

At first all went well. She built up huge positions in plastics and shares of PPC, at suitably low prices, and was initially gratified to see their prices increase slightly. But as the days passed by, and there was no announcement whatsoever about a takeover of CPC by PPC, she grew increasingly worried. She telephoned Fleabrunckle several times to ask for news, but all he could do was counsel her to be patient. But she could ill afford to be patient; she had overextended herself too much to wait long. In fact she had considerably exceeded her limits, and if she did not sell soon she would have to liquidate her positions and be in worse shape than before - she had tied up so much of her limits in plastics that she had no money left for trading other commodities to make a profit. And at the end of the month her portfolio would be audited!

Worse was to come. The following morning Thérèse heard the awful news before she had even arrived at her desk – a huge new plastics mine[46] had been discovered in Tannu Tuva, a tiny country near Mongolia, and the cash strapped government was entering the plastics market. Judging by her experience of similar developments in the energy market, Thérèse knew that Tannu Tuva would flood the plastics market, and as a result the price of plastic would fall until it hit the rock bottom, and her position would make a huge loss. She frantically tried to unload at least some of her shares in PPC, but prices were already so low that she would only be able to do so at huge costs. What on earth was she going to do? She telephoned Fleabrunckle.

'Oh dear, what a shame,' said her supposed friend when she sobbed out her story to him. 'Luckily I managed to off-load my shares yesterday, before the Tannu Tuva news hit the screens. Tell you what, I'll buy your entire position at current prices, that way at least you minimise your losses.'

Thérèse stopped crying and considered this offer. It would still leave her with a huge loss, and she would certainly lose her job for having overextended herself. It would moreover almost certainly ruin Bank of Libraria, who were in no position to cover her losses. She asked Fleabrunckle whether he would be able to get her another job?

But he just laughed when she suggested this. 'Really honey, you mustn't expect miracles from me! I'd be most surprised if you ever worked as a dealer again, either here or in any other financial market! Now just do as I say, and then as a final favour I will pay off your personal debts, so you can start a new life without any financial obligations. And by the way, you had better be careful about what you tell your boss, because you have engaged in insider trading, and that carries a jail sentence, remember! We wouldn't want you subjected to the conditions of the average British penal institution for a few years, would we?' With that he put down the telephone.

Thérèse was livid! Now she remembered Fleabrunckle's grin after he had told her of the supposed take-over of PSC by PPC, and his insincere crocodile tears when his team was disbanded by Sir Wilbur. She also remembered the many ways in which he had encouraged her to spend her money with abandon, and caused her to go ever deeper

---

[46]   Although nowadays most plastic is manufactured, it used to be obtained by surface mining. Natural plastic is usually found near oil and gas reserves, or under peat bogs, or even land-fill sites.

into debt. He obviously thought she was dead broke and had no option but to take up his offer. 'I bet he has an ulterior motive in offering to buy my plastics position and shares,' she thought. 'I bet there is something in it for him, something he planned with a long hand. If only I knew what it was! What is his long term game? That little copperhead! I'll show him! And if I go to jail I'll take him with me!' She went straight to Governor Pinchback at The Institution.

46   Governor Pinchback exerts himself, but the Maisonettes disappoint

Pinchback listened to Therèse' story attentively, and assured her he would do his utmost to bring the scoundrel Fleabrunckle to book; Therèse was not the only one who had been hoodwinked and cheated by him! He was uncertain whether he could protect her from the prison sentence Fleabrunckle had prophesied, but suggested as a 'super grass' her punishment would be lenient. At any rate, he hoped the matter could be dealt with without having to drag everyone through the courts. 'I'll talk to John de Bourg before you are audited,' he assured her as he escorted her out of his office, 'in the meantime you had better return to your desk and act as though nothing has happened. And don't liquidate your positions in plastics, until you hear from me!'

With Therèse was gone, Pinchback returned to his much greater problem of how to protect the financial community from the fall-out that was inevitable if Greenlandia disappeared into Hell. He had approached his usual contacts and cautiously enquired about their involvement with the project, and all reported that they had invested heavily, both their own and their clients' money, and were confident of a considerable return on their investments. They had simply laughed at his suggestion that Greenlandia was a risky investment and that they ought to reduce their share-holdings in the venture. 'Don't be ridiculous, we'll be making millions!' Only a handful of banks had stirred clear of Greenlandia, mainly because they were still broke from having risked their money in the North Sea bubble that had burst a few years ago and shook the City to its foundations. What a bunch of gullible fools his fellow bankers were! Governor Pinchback was getting quite exasperated.

He rang for Arthur Peterson.

'Peterson, I need your opinion.' 'Yes Sir, very good Sir. On any particular subject, Sir?'

'Is there anyone in The Institution with influence in the banking community who will believe me if I tell them an unbelievable story, and help me sort out an unholy mess?'

'Is it a true story, Sir?'

'Of course! Why would I want to tell an unbelievable lie? If I have to invent lies I invent believable ones!'

'Yes Sir, of course, Sir. May I hear the story first, Sir?'

Governor Pinchback obliged, and even Peterson barely managed to control his astonishment. 'I need to think about this, Sir,' he said when Pinchback had finished. Pinchback nodded, waved him into the other arm-chair beside the fireplace, and poured him a stiff whiskey. It was not the first time that Peterson had saved his bacon when all his heads of department had miserably failed[47].

Slowly sipping his whiskey, Peterson considered the possibilities. There was Stephen Grousst, Head of Policy and thoroughly dependable in every way. He was moreover devoted to the Governor, who had promoted him rapidly above the heads of several longer serving officials. But he was still young, and very very ambitious. Would he be prepared to get involved in what was sure to be a risky and probably unrewarding exercise, that might damage his future reputation and career, just to please a governor who was due to retire in a year or two and could be of little further use to him then? Peterson doubted it. Then there was Speedwell Klimpft, Head of Fraud Division and an obvious choice, given the nature of the problem. However, Klimpft was a prosaic pedantic sort of man, and more likely to have the Governor committed to a mental institution than to believe his story. Since his mysterious disappearance and re-appearance, and his unorthodox choice of location for the gold reserves, Governor Pinchback's credit rating had fallen dramatically in some circles, and many people were more than prepared to believe that he had become senile. No, Klimpft could not be entrusted with the Governor's tale. 'What about Izabella Kaputnik,' he said suddenly.

The Governor considered this. Ms Kapunik was Head of the Economics Division, and certainly had influence in the City. She was possibly the only employee of The Institution with any hands-on experience of dealing with unholy messes, and her common sense and can-do attitude were legendary throughout the financial community. She was definitely prepared to listen to unbelievable stories – had not she herself once come with an almost ludicrous one to the Governor, all those years ago when she was still a cleaner?

Izabella Kaputnik had been in charge of dusting and scrubbing the sub-vaults, which included the banknote-storage area. The country was in the grip of high inflation, and as a result The Institution held very few banknotes in storage - the demand for banknotes was so great that they were shipped out as soon as they arrived. This should have pleased Ms Kaputnik because it meant less dusting. But Ms Kaputnik was a cleaning lady who was interested in economics, and deeply concerned about the high level of inflation. She noticed that fewer banknotes seemed to leave the sub-vaults than arrived, which could obviously not be the result of theft, since no one ever stole from The Institution. So she kept her eyes open, until her patience was rewarded and she discovered that scourge of modern banking, the dreaded banknote aphid, feeding upon the banknotes she was attempting to dust. She had immediately gone to the Governor, and explained her find.

---

[47]   This was not really surprising, since Peterson was a retired Philosophy professor who had wormed his way into The Institution to study human behaviour in extreme situations, and was therefore not subject to the same intellectual and emotional constraints as the financial analysts and whiz kids who usually advised the Governor.

'Do you know what these are?' she had asked Pinchback excitedly when she showed him her find. 'These are banknote aphids, and I bet they are the cause of the high inflation we have been battling with these last few years.' Although Pinchback readily agreed that banknote-munching aphids were undesirable and needed to be discouraged at all costs, he failed to see the connection with inflation. That's when Izabella Kaputnik had explained her revolutionary theory to him, a theory that netted her the Nobel Prize for Economics and the position as Head of the Economics Department of The Institution.

In a nutshell, her theory ran as follows. Several decades ago a new strain of aphids began to emerge, a strain of aphids that subsisted entirely on banknotes. Since no one expects to find aphids on banknotes, they had gone entirely undetected, and were able to increase exponentially in number. 'Do you know that aphids are born already pregnant,' she asked Governor Pinchback. 'Can you imagine quite how fast they multiply?' Within a decade the aphids had become so numerous that they were destroying banknotes by their millions, and ever greater numbers of banknotes had to be printed to keep the economy going. Then suddenly, a few years ago, the banknote aphids were overcome by disaster. Changes in human personal hygiene meant the aphids came increasingly into contact with chemicals like soap and hand lotions which were apparently lethal to them, and soon their numbers fell dramatically. However, since no one knew of their existence, this phenomenal reduction in their number went entirely unnoticed for quite some time, and banknote printers all over the world saw no reason to reduce their production of banknotes. As a result they had flooded the market with an excessive number of banknotes, and the inevitable result had been galloping inflation. 'Yes,' reflected Governor Pinchback, 'Izabella Kaputnik was the perfect audience for an unbelievable story.'

Ms Kaputnik evinced no great astonishment at the Governor's tale of demonic plots and inevitable financial disaster. She had been suspicious of the Greenlandia Project from the beginning, as had her friends from the Maisonettes, the feminist masonic lodge of the City. As early as three years ago the Madam Maisonette (the titular head of the lodge) had received an anonymous warning not to become involved in the project, a warning that contained so much specific information, and was delivered with such authority, that the lodge had taken it seriously[48]. Several months later they received another warning, this time from one of their founder members, The Old Lady, and became sufficiently concerned to pass the message on to all its members. As a result very few lodge members had become involved with the project, although some of them suffered a down-turn in their careers as a result.

'What do you suggest we do to protect the City from its folly?' Governor Pinchback eagerly asked Ms Kaputnik after he finished his story. However, that lady was less helpful than he had anticipated. Instead of proposing some plan or other of how the financial community might be saved, she opined that they should be made to pay for their stupidity – didn't Pinchback always say that the market was the best arbiter in financial matters? But Governor Pinchback was not in the mood for sophistries, and insisted Ms Kaputnik applied herself to this thorny problem.

---

[48]   Although no one ever found out who had sent that message, I am pleased to be able to inform the reader that it came from Agrat herself, who as usual was loath to damage her fellow females by her schemes.

'What about those lady friends of yours, the Maisonettes? Can't they do something?'

Ms Kaputnik didn't think so, but agreed to ask them to hold an extraordinary general meeting on the matter that same evening. She rejected the Governor's plea to be allowed to attend it so he could put his case. 'No men allowed, as you well know. You will have to leave it to me to fill them in.'

Oh well, at least he would get an early night for once; Governor Pinchback was badly in need of rest.

The general assembly was duly called, and Ms Kaputnik explained the tricky situation the financial community faced if Greenlandia would indeed be transmogrified to Hell. Dozens, if not hundreds, of institutions could go bankrupt, and the City would change immeasurably. Was there anything her colleagues could suggest to avert this catastrophe? After the excited murmurs which followed her speech died down, various half-hearted proposals were put forward, and immediately rejected by Ms Kaputnik and the assembly.

Finally Ms Kazeem, an investment banker from the Middle East, dared to voice what practically everyone else in the assembly was thinking: 'Why on earth *should* we help to avert the impending 'catastrophe'? The City is dominated by men who have never given us an equal chance, but on the contrary, hindered and obstructed us at every possible occasion; now that they have to pay the price of their ill-considered avarice, I for one see no reason to come to their aid. Besides, I see many women here who suffered ridicule and abuse for their refusal to invest in the Greenlandia project, and had their warnings ignored, and even lost their jobs because they refused to get involved! No, I propose that we do not lift a finger to aid those banks who foolishly followed their greedy instincts which have brought them to this! I propose that we sit tight, watch what happens, and make sure we are in a good position to mop up the damage afterwards and get the credit and profits that go with it!'

Loud cheers followed Ms Kazeem's speech, and most lodge members agreed she was right. Even Izabella Kaputnik did not have the heart to argue against Ms Kazeem, since she largely agreed with her. Still, she did think the assembly was just a little heartless in their refusal to render any help at all to the hapless financial community; surely they could show a bit more compassion for their fellow bankers? But the assembly disagreed. Hadn't they already done their bit by warning their colleagues, male as well as female, off the project these last three years? And hadn't they suffered for it? Besides, what where they supposed to do anyway, did Izabella have any concrete suggestions? Ms Kaputnik had none, unfortunately, and the assembly soon broke up without having achieved anything that could comfort Governor Pinchback, who was livid when Ms Kaputnik reported back to him.

'Ha, let no one ever tell me again that women are better people than men,' he growled when he heard what Ms Kazeem had said. 'Such self-righteousness, such egotism, such greedy lust for power!' 'Well, what did you expect, they all work in the City!' retorted Ms Kaputnik.

Meanwhile Arnapak had at last finished her long tale, and told Walgren that although she had achieved much it was not what she set out to do. She felt quite disheartened again, and said she really didn't know what to do next. But Walgren was most impressed with her story, and congratulated her upon her great success in destroying the Cosmocrator.

'You have avenged the death of Niels and Elisabee, is that nothing? I am certain you will also succeed in finding Nuliajuq's soul. Why, you may even find help in the new temple that has recently been built in the town; people say the god who lives there, one Mithras, is powerful and grants many prayers.'

The old shaman was not about to change her religion in her old age, especially not after she had received so many favours from the Takanakapsaluk, but still, it seemed an interesting bit of news. She asked her son-in-law to elaborate, and tell her about any other developments in Greenland as well.

Walgren had much news, and most of it good, he thought. 'One of the men connected with the Greenlandia project, Cesare, has become Nuliajuq's frequent companion and completely turned her life around. She now goes to parties and restaurants and walks about in public in broad daylight, and people have gradually accepted her despite her looks, which have actually improved a little. Greenlandia itself is growing apace, and due to open within the next few months. Half-way through the project there were some delays, because the environmental faction of the Landsting insisted on imposing a large array of measures designed to minimise the impact of the project on the environment, but that is all to the good and as it should be. There have also been some problems with the pillar hermits, but when it proved impossible to move them, Cesare incorporated the hermits and their pillars into the design of Greenlandia, and now they form the core of the meditation dome. Of course they stink something fierce, but I am sure people will get used to that.'

Aranapak nodded, and asked, 'what is this I hear about a plant psychologist having come to Greenland?'

Walgren enlightened her. 'You are referring to Mithradates Devadorje, who is the High Priest of Mithras as well as a dab hand with all vegetation. I think he will completely transform the economy of Greenland, even more than Greenlandia. He is teaching the people to grow tomatoes and asparagus and grapes, and quinces and bananas and plums!' Mr Walgren grew positively lyrical as he expanded on the theme of the gifted priest. 'The people flock to his temple, and worship Mithras, because they believe if the priest can cause such miracles as growing grapes in Nuuk, then the god must be mightier still. And I tell you they are right! This new god has performed all sorts of miracles, he heals the sick, enriches the poor, and helps those who are unhappy in love!'

'So why have you not taken Nuliajuq to him and have her cured,' asked the astonished Angakkoq.

Walgren hung his head. 'I have considered it often,' he replied, 'but somehow it did not seem right. After all, she bears the name of the Mother of the Seals.'

'You have done right, my son-in-law,' said the old shaman. 'But I had better visit my old friend Ragna, and find out more about this.'

Ragna, too, had much news to tell and was full of praise for Devadorje. 'My tree farm has really taken off since I follow his advice, and I am looking forward to planting my first wood. But I agree, Nuliajuq should not ask Mithras to help her find her lost soul. This is Inuit business, and the preserve of Angakkut. Nevertheless, I think you should have a long chat with the young man, though not before you have paid your respect to the Takanakapsaluk, of course. Perhaps she has even heard of Devadorje - please do ask what she thinks about Greenlandia – ought we oppose it, or welcome it, as Devadorje suggests?'

As soon as Arnapak had rested and felt strong enough for the spirit journey, she went to visit the Takanakapsaluk.

The Takanakapsaluk had changed much since the old Angakkoq's first visit all those years ago. Her hair was shiny and untangled, she wore a handsome smock which looked quite clean, and her house and its surrounding area were tidy and comfortable. Moreover, she was in a much better mood, and welcomed Arnapak with open arms. She listened to the shaman's story with great interest, and was very pleased with the good use to which Arnapak had put her many gifts.

'What a pity you did not find Nuliajuq's soul! After all your troubles surely you deserved this piece of luck. But not to worry, I have a feeling you will find it soon. Now, show me the spider that the Cosmocrator has turned into!' Arnapak opened the pocket where her old adversary resided, and he emerged cautiously. The Takanakapsaluk looked at him silently for a long while. 'So much knowledge in such a fragile vessel! I probably would have stepped on him to rid the world of him and all his knowledge, but I can see why you chose a different course. Hide him well, and don't mention him to others, for he has many enemies who would fain slay him.'

Then she returned to the subject of Nuliajuq's soul, and suggested that Arnapak discuss the matter with the plant psychologist Mithradates Devadorje.

'He is under the protection of Yeshua and very powerful, and I believe he has the makings of a great shaman. I want you to talk to him to find out whether you might train him, so he can take over your role when your time has come.'

Arnapak was astonished and appalled. 'Do you not know that Devadorje serves the god Mithras?

The Takanakapsaluk brushed this aside. 'If he is what I think he is, he will not be content to be a mere priest, the slave of a god. He will wish to be a shaman, who bends the gods to his purpose!' She winked at Arnapak.

'Will you tell me your opinion of the Greenlandia project before I go, Mother of the Seals? My friends want to know whether we ought to oppose it, or whether it is a good thing for Greenland in the long run. Devadorje seems to be in favour of it, but then he is not Inuit.'

'I agree with Devadorje. Do not discount his opinions because he comes from abroad. Listen to his arguments and decide for yourself – apply the knowledge you have acquired on your travels.'

Arnapak and Ragna went to see Devadorje in his temple as soon as the Angakkoq returned from her spirit journey. He was surrounded by apprentice priests and followers, who implored him to intercede with Mithras for some favour or other they felt in need of. When he saw Ragna and the shaman, he freed himself from the crowd and led them into his conservatory, where he grew all the food for the temple. Ragna introduced her friend as 'the greatest living shaman of Greenland, if not the world', and at that Devadorje pricked up his ears and listened attentively to all Arnapak said. She told him of her long search for the lost soul of Nuliajuq, and how she found and defeated the Cosmocrator. When Devadorje asked to see the spider, and Arnapak opened her pocket, the spider came out with alacrity, and wholly without fear climbed onto the hand of the young priest. They spent some time communing, and Devadorje asked Arnapak if she minded if the spider stayed with him for a while? 'We have need for one another,' he told his visitors.

Arnapak agreed to let him have the spider, and asked whether he would be interested in becoming a shaman – did he know what this entailed? Devadorje did not, but he felt strangely drawn to the old woman and her story, and vaguely felt that he should take up her offer of training him in the ways of the shaman. So they entered into an agreement, and Arnapak accepted the young man as an apprentice. She vowed to teach him all she knew, and he in turned vowed obedience to her in all things until her death. This greatly astonished him, and as he listened to himself pronouncing his vow he wondered why he was doing this. Had he not found perfect happiness in his work as High-priest of Mithras, and did not his god smile upon him and grant him every favour? What need had he of ancient shaman lore? He had no answers to these questions, but knew in his heart he was doing the right thing.

'The Takanakapsaluk calls out for you,' said the old Angakkoq, 'and she will not be gainsaid.'

48   Devadorje experiences his first trance and discovers he is a shaman

Devadorje did not have to wait long for the start of his shamanic training, which was to start with a vision-quest and attempt to acquire a spirit helper. At the advice of Arnapak he told his priests and followers that he would be away for a while, and went towards the central part of Greenland, towards the ice and everlasting snow.

After several days of wandering, when he was getting exhausted with cold and hunger, he found a small cave in the mountains where he settled down to think. He rubbed two stones together in the ancient way Arnapak taught him, and thought about his previous life, of his experiences in Greenland, and what he hoped his future life would be. He carefully considered each thought one at a time and then laid it aside, until at last his mind was quite empty and ready to receive new thoughts.

Thus it occurred that he was worshipping a different god,

a god who naked hung upon a tree

and bled from many wounds and suffered greatly.

For a long while he watched this god, until

at last he raised his head and said,

'I am Tornarsuk, waiting for the Mother,

deep in the fir-tree forests of the utmost North.

Behold my face and knoweth I am He.'

But the god seemed to lack one eye and was

possessed of a great pain-encumbered wisdom.

Devadorje awoke from this vision, and wrote it down immediately, wondering about the god he had seen. The lack of one eye worried him and he thought it significant that this god came to him in his very first shamanic trance. Finally he composed himself again, and cleansed his mind of thoughts, to prepare for his next vision.

Soon he was riding on a giant eagle,

towards the moon and further to the stars.

He saw the huts and gardens of strange creatures,

who ghostly in the moonlight hoed their fields.

He wondered what strange plants these creatures tended,

in their strange gardens under such an eyrie light,

but forward forward sped his spectral dreambird,

and took him far away into the night.

Again he emerged from his vision, and wrote it down in verse, even as it occurred to him, although he had never before written poetry. Was this the flight to the moon the old Angakkoq had mentioned, when she prepared him for his first vision-quest? Was he just dreaming of something he would later experience in the flesh? Already he found it difficult to distinguish between his visions and reality. Once again he recovered his composure, and cleansed his mind, and allowed wisdom to pour into his soul.

He saw himself lie naked on a slab of stone

Quite dead and cold beneath the winter moon.

Bears came and tore and chewed his cherished body

And ants and beetles joined the feast at noon.

Picked clean he saw his gleaming naked skeleton

Get up from the cold stony bed at last

He saw it dance and whirl around quite madly

As if to celebrate what had now come to pass.

Devadorje awoke, and realised that he was now quite dead, and had been dead many times before and would be dead many times again, before he was finished with life. He understood that life resided in his bones, which would return to many wombs and re-emerge again and again covered in flesh. He saw his clothes flying towards him who was but a flesh-covered skeleton, and he was whole again. He recognised the power of his bones!

Although he did not understand any of this, he wrote it all down exactly as it came to him. He was getting very weak, and it became increasingly easy for new thoughts to enter the stage of his mind. But whereas his first visions had come in ordered sequence and been like stories, now they rushed upon him in a chaotic deluge, and he was overwhelmed by them. But there were two he remembered clearly and wrote down.

He saw a vessel filled with liquid laughter

Bubbling in the morning sun in spring.

He saw the playful butterfly a child ran after

He hugged a tree and saw it dance and sing.

From this vision he emerged light hearted and full of joy, quite certain that he could dance upon the tips of a picket fence if he chose to, because he felt light as a leaf in the wind. He quickly fell into another trance.

Cold, icy cold, river before me

Deathly white fog over the heath.

Starless black night freezing my marrow

Lone crying geese, hopeless I wait.

Emptiness calls deep in the river

Darkness demands death from my soul

Cold, icy cold, water surrounds me

Deathly white fog hovers above.

Half in trance he saw himself walking into the deep cold water and called out to himself not to go, but slowly, inexorably, he went ever deeper into the water, until the waves closed over his head and he was swallowed up by the cold and the dark. Of all his visions this one seemed most real, and haunted him most, and he could not bear to think about it, nor could he face another vision. Completely exhausted he curled up into a ball for warmth, and fell into a deep sleep.

The following morning he woke up barely refreshed, haunted by his visions and weak with cold and hunger. But he was determined to continue with his vision-quest until he had received a sign, and acquired a spirit helper. So once again he composed himself, and rubbed his two stones together, and, much faster than the day before, fell into a deep trance.

He saw before him a gigantic organ

Played by a madman with a fearsome tune.

And as he played the world sank into darkness

And all who lived felt an impending doom.

But then he saw another mighty organ

Well carved of ice and snow, glittering white

And he himself was playing on the keyboard

A melody of strength and secret might.

He saw these organs wage a rousing battle

He heard their music powerful and loud.

He saw the organ players test their mettle

Before a frightened, praying, deafened crowd.

At first the music clashed like duelling fighters

But then they hit like steel hits firestone

Until at last a high-pitched piercing screeching -

And then the ice-organ played on alone.

When Devadorje recovered from this vision he was well pleased, because he understood it foretold how he would prevent the transmogrification of Greenlandia to Hell. He knew it would take a great deal of time to carve the ice organ, and to write the melody that he would play upon it, and was therefore keen to return to Nuuk. However, he still had received neither sign nor spirit helper, and was unsure of what to do. After some deliberation he decided to have one more vision quest before he returned home. Again he rubbed his stones, again he fell into trance with frightening ease. But this time he heard no poetry and had no visions.

Instead he felt within himself a light, like a small candle. Although small, he could see by its power things that were hidden from ordinary humans. He looked deep into the hearts of all living things, and saw their souls both within and without. Then, suddenly, he realised there was no need for him to undergo any further shamanic rituals, and that he was trying to learn the hard way things he had known all his life, indeed had used all his life – he realised that he was in fact a born shaman who had no need of rules and rituals. Upon this realisation his trance fell from him like a discarded cloak, and he stood up, stretched his limbs, and prepared for his homeward journey. But just as he was leaving the cave, a small puppy dog entered his cave, bowed low, and offered his services. 'Are you then a spirit helper, come to aid me in my shaman endeavours,' Devadorje asked the puppy. 'I am indeed, and proud to,' said the puppy. 'Inoutliak at your service.'

Since Devadorje was exhausted from his long fast and the cold, it was a slow and painful return journey. Luckily Arnapak had received news of his successful quest – news travels fast along the astral plane – and came to greet him when he was half way home. 'Thanks be to the Mother of the Seals,' she greeted him when she saw that he was alive and well and filled with the Light, 'thanks be to the Takanakapsaluk who knew you for a shaman!' She embraced the young man, bundled him onto her magic sledge, and took him swiftly to Ragna's tree farm, so he could tell of his visions in secluded privacy, unencumbered by priests and followers.

49   <u>Arnapak interprets Devadorje's visions, and Devadorje builds the Ice Organ</u>

Once they arrived at Ragna's farm, Devadorje showed Arnapak his notes, and ate only a light meal to restore his strength without overloading his stomach. He refused to take a nap, and insisted he was well enough to discuss his visions with the old shaman. He requested Ragna to be present, because he wanted her help in recruiting carvers for the ice organ, and knew that Arnapak would leave as soon as she had heard his news about Tornarsuk.

The Angakkoq was indeed most interested in his first vision, and jumped up excitedly when she heard he had seen and heard Tornarsuk, who was hanging on a tree in the far north in a fir-tree forest. She knew the forest quite well, having visited it on countless spirit-journeys while she was still a young shaman learning her trade, and resolved to go again as soon as possible, to ask Tornarsuk for his help in finding the lost soul of Nuliajuq. But first she had to help Devadorje interpret his visions. She told him that it was quite common for aspiring shamans to meet Tornarsuk, who was a god much interested in mysteries and always ready to aid shamans in their quests.

The second vision had been interpreted quite correctly by Devadorje as a spirit journey to the moon, and the strange beings he had seen were the dead people who lived there. The third vision, too, was a fairly standard shaman dream, and again Devadorje had interpreted it nearly correctly. If he wanted to be a shaman he would first have to die as a person, and see himself reduced to bones. A shaman had to endure great feats of mental and physical torment, and seeing oneself die was an important part of the training.

The fourth and fifth vision Arnapak was not able to explain; they were certainly not standard visions of a shaman apprentice. However, since Devadorje was older than shaman trainees usually were, and had experienced much that fell outside of the range of an average Inuit, Arnapak thought that these visions were personal to him and would become clearer as time passed on. Perhaps they even related to a previous existence.

The vision of the Ice Organ was wholly mysterious to her, but Devadorje, who had been informed by Sophia of the plan to transmogrify Greenlandia by musically atomising it, explained to Arnapak that the vision had shown him at long last how he could prevent the transmogrification. Ragna, who listened silently to Devadorje and Arnapak until now, nodded and said that she knew exactly what was required, who could help him cave the ice organ, and where they could best carve it. But she had no help to offer regarding the music that would be required to stop Agrat's organ, and neither could Arnapak. The old shaman suggested that Devadorje use his inner light, which had made itself manifest in his last vision. 'All your life you have bend you mind towards understanding the minds of living creatures,' she said, 'now use your soul to sense the nature of ice and sound.' She assured him that his conviction to have always been a shaman, with all attendant powers, was very likely true. However, he would still need a modicum of instruction, and she promised to see to it once she returned from her journey to the northern fir-tree forest.

Having acquitted herself of her duty towards her apprentice, Arnapak went to Nuuk to visit Nuliajuq and her son-in-law, assured them of her continued affection, and commended her great-granddaughter to the protection of the Takanakapsaluk. Then she readied the sledge that was a gift from the Mother of the Seals, called on her 23 spirit helpers, loaded the sledge with all that she might need upon her journey, and left for the northern fir-tree forest.

But Devadorje, having slept his fill, returned to his temple and thought about the ice organ he needed to carve, and the melody he needed to play. He knew that the structure of the icy pipes of the organ and the melody he would play upon it needed to be constructed to exactly produce the sound which could not only overpower, but even shatter, the music played by Agrat's transmogrification instrument.

He soon found that thinking, or even musing, was of no help whatsoever in composing the melody, and eventually he contacted Sophia to see whether she had any suggestions. He told her of Arnapak's advice to listen to his inner light and focus on the nature of ice – how might he do this? Sophia considered this, and then recommended that he go to the spot where he was planning to carve the ice organ, and select the ice and snow he meant to carve it from. He should lay himself upon that ice or snow, and direct his inner light onto it. 'Visualise the structure of each individual molecule, and listen to the harmonics that exist between them,' she advised him. Accordingly he went to the site Ragna had suggested, and followed the advice of his demonic lover. Slowly, over long weeks of patient listening, the structure and quality of the ice became clear to him. As it become clear to him, a melody formed in his mind, which he tested and contrasted and amended against the musical score that Agrat's organ player was supposedly going to use.

When he was satisfied that he knew exactly both the melody and the form and structure of the organ pipes that were to shape it, he returned to Ragna and asked whether she could supply him with the necessary skilled ice carvers the project needed. This she was able to do, and they made good progress. Exactly one week before the great opening of Greenlandia the Ice Organ was completed, and Devadorje was fairly certain it would be able to stop the transmogrification. He would have loved to try it out, but since the organ was located on a mountain opposite Greenlandia, the noise might easily be noticed and their plan uncovered.

When The Old Lady heard of this great success she was not impressed, nor was Governor Pinchback. 'Fairly certain?' she screeched when Sophia reported what Devadorje had told her, 'fairly certain? That is not good enough, dear girl, he must do better!' Sophia was in no kind of mood to humour the old bag a minute longer. In another week her apprenticeship would be complete, and then she could return home and take up her duties as a fully fledged journeywoman demon. Although she was still most concerned about the City, she had enough of The Old Lady, who was forever griping and complaining and asking everyone else to do the impossible, while she herself took things easy and rested in her armchair.

'Well, maybe you should get off your backside and lend a hand,' she therefore retorted hotly. 'I curse the day I came here to talk to you and enlist your help. What help have you ever given to the cause, except high-minded words and a few pulled strings? We could have done better without you senile old hag! So shut up already, and be grateful to Devadorje who left his home and friends to brave the cold of Greenland, despite the fact that this isn't even his fight, and he despises the City and its financial convolutions!' The assertiveness training course The Institution had sent Sophia on had richly paid off, and turned an essentially polite teenage demon into a self-confident, slightly abrasive demonic woman.

After this outburst the Governor didn't have the bottle to add his complaints to those of The Old Lady, and only asked whether there was anything they might do to help Devadorje, or whether they could perhaps devise some sort of back-up plan? Sophia glared at him until he wished he was still in the Exalted Heavenly Dream-Stone, but when the Mouser rubbed against Sophia's legs and purringly counselled patience with the older generation, she relented and said curtly if Pinchback had any ideas she was prepared to listen to them.

Unfortunately he didn't have any. Ever since he joined the Foilers he had done his best to stop the City's financial community from getting even deeper involved in Greenlandia than they already were, and to give him credit, had managed to prevent several smallish banks from extending additional credit lines to the Consortium. But it was a drop in the ocean, and he knew it. He had little faith in Devadorje and his ice organ, and been living on tea and tranquillisers ever since the full extent of the tragedy that was to hit the City had become clear to him. 'I should have stayed in the Exalted Heavenly Dream-Stone,' he thought for the umpteenth time as he went home on the underground.

50   Trishy visits The Institution, and Fleabrunckle's future is decided

Governor Pinchback was sitting in his office nursing his grievances, when Arthur Peterson announced the arrival of a young lady who insisted that she had to see him on a most important matter. Reluctantly he agreed to give her 'ten minutes at most!' – after all, he could not remain inactively brooding in his office until he finally retired the following year. He was fed-up to the back teeth with his life right now. The week he had spent in the Exalted Heavenly Dream-Stone in peaceful daytime horticultural pursuits, and long evening discussions of obscure passages of ancient Chinese novels, had somehow ruined him for the rough and tumble of City life. He had a perfect horror of the coming week, when Greenlandia would officially open and almost certainly be transmogrified to Hell, leaving its financiers facing ignoble ruin. There was nothing, absolutely nothing, he could do, except hope that Devadorje's ice organ would do its job. A priest of Mithras playing an organ carved of ice! Demons who were defrauding the City! Gold bars publicly displayed as a backdrop for Dream-Stones! It was all getting too much for him. Old age was looking him squarely in the face, and he shrunk from it and shuddered. 'Think pension boy,' he thought, 'just one more year and then I can retire!'

The woman who entered looked quite ordinary, and introduced herself as Patricia Highgrove[49].

'The reason why I am here, Sir Governor Lord Pinchback' –

Pinchback interrupted her and said that 'Governor' or 'Mr Pinchback' would do, and Trishy wondered secretly whether she could whittle him down to Pinchy eventually.

'I am here to tell you a tale of horror and loathing, and of evil financial machinations, involving one Gingrich Fleabrunckle.'

Here the Governor pricked up his ears. Horror and loathing he was used to, and also to evil financial machinations, but the name Fleabrunckle rang an entire cathedral worth of bells! 'Fleabrunckle? Did you say Fleabrunckle? Is it the crook who works for Bog Bank, or some other gentleman?'

Trishy observed him pityingly. 'You really think there could be two men on earth called Gingrich Fleabrunckle?'

'Quite so, quite so', the Governor agreed, 'but I had to make sure. Now, I want you to wait here while I make a few phone-calls. Only a few days ago another young lady sat in that chair to complain about Fleabrunckle, and I want her and a few other people to hear what you have to say, if you are agreeable.'

Trishy assured him that she was happy to tell her tale to all and sundry, 'the more the merrier! That scumbag needs to be exposed and discredited!'

Governor Pinchback called Thérèse at Bank of Libraria, who at his advice had said nothing to her superiors about her exposed position so far, and asked her to come to his office immediately, and to bring John de Bourg with her. He also called and invited Sir Wilbur, and The Institution's Head of Fraud, Speedwell Klimpft. While waiting for his guests to arrive he offered tea and biscuits to Trishy, and chatted about this and that, but mainly about her daughter Cassy. They had barely started on Trishy's second handbag-sized album of Cassy's baby pictures when the others arrived.

Governor Pinchback placed them all around his conference table, and cleared his throat. 'My dear young ladies and gentlemen! I am pleased to have you gathered round this table in my office .....' He went on for a considerable length of time, saying nothing in particular, but very happy to be at the centre of a major financial fraud crisis, the sort of thing he knew how to deal with, rather than that dreadful Greenlandia business. He was especially gratified that everyone had come to *him* to sort out this particular mess, not to that up-start Gubernator Smithers from the Fraud Busters down in the Boon-Docklands, who had usurped some of the responsibilities and privileges of The Institution. Of course eventually Smithers might have to be involved, but so far everyone had come to Pinchback who consequently was in the know, while Smithers remained ignorant! Governor Pinchback revelled in his power.

---

[49]   Trish Trash decided to revert to her original name after her daughter Cassandra was born. She also adjusted her appearance, after a sweet little old lady, a neighbour in the village, anxiously enquired after her mental health when she first spotted her make-up and glad rags. Trishy wanted to be a responsible mother, and fit into village life to make things easy for her daughter.

When Pinchback finally finished his Dominant-Male-in-Power display, he asked Trishy to tell her story to the assembled company, which she proceeded to do, slightly amended to preserve credulity and protect the innocent. She gave them a short cleansed version of her travails in the Altai, and her rescue by a generous Italian gentleman.

She did not tell them that same kind gentleman had visited her earlier that week, and asked her to go to the Governor with her information about Fleabrunckle's financial infidelities. Casanova had heard on the grapevine that Fleabrunckle was about to bankrupt Bank of Libraria and ruin Bog Bank, and he was too fond of Sir Wilbur Wellbeloved to allow this to happen, even if it meant that Fleabrunckle would just be sent to jail, rather than suffer the horrific fate Agrat had devised for him.

Instead Trishy explained that she had always thought no one would believe her story, seeing how important and well-respected Fleabrunckle was, and therefore kept quiet. But last night she went to confession again for the first time in many years[50], and the priest counselled her to go to the great Governor Pinchback and entrust him with her knowledge. 'The Governor is an honourable man and will do right by you,' Father Timothy had said, 'Go and see him tomorrow, my child, and set your heart at rest.' Pinchback was most gratified when he heard this, and reflected that his career had not been entirely insignificant if even a humble countryside priest, and a simple working girl, knew his name and put their trust in him.

But Trishy had not finished; the best part of her story – from Pinchback's point of view – was still to come. While she was living with the Flea he had let slip all sorts of secrets, thinking her too stupid to understand what he was talking about and that she would be dead within a few months anyway. Therefore Trishy was in the happy position to inform her listeners that Fleabrunckle had made up his mind long ago to ruin Bank of Libraria, and use them to build his fortune. 'Trashy,' he told her a hundred times, 'just wait 'til I'm the majority shareholder of Bog Bank and have discredited Old Wilbur, and we'll be in Breadsville!' She didn't know exactly how he was going to bring this about, but apparently he had a scheme whereby he would corrupt a dealer, insert him into Bank of Libraria - 'Johnny's a gullible old fool, he'll do anything I say' – entice him to exceed his limits, and then offer to buy his position, leaving Bank of Libraria to carry the can. He would then wait until his cheaply bought shares increased in value – 'they will, you know, I just have to make sure I pick the right ones' – and 'buy up Bog Bank when their shares are low; I've got a great plan to depress them'.

At last Trishy stopped and looked at Pinchback expectantly. 'Does any of this make sense to you?'

Governor Pinchback fairly beamed at her. 'You have just provided the missing pieces of the puzzle! I think we have enough information now to bring Fleabrunckle to justice – would you be prepared to repeat all this in front of a judge?'

'Of course I am! That's why I am here!'

'And so will I', Thérèse joined in. 'You poor thing, he has been even more rotten to you than to me, the Skunk! the Wretch! the Creep! the filthy Weasel!' –

---

[50]   A lie if ever there was one, for Trishy was no catholic, nor indeed any kind of Christian.

Here Pinchback gently held up his hand and pleaded for restraint, and asked Thérèse to repeat what she had told him yesterday.

When she was finished everyone was appalled. Sacrificing an innocent young woman during a satanic mass was one thing, but trying to bankrupt an honest well-regarded financial institution and discredit a decent old financier like Sir Wilbur – why it was unheard off, it was an outrage, it was simply insupportable!

After stiff whiskies all around they considered what might be done to save the Bank of Libraria.

'I suggest you hang on to your plastics shares and wait for them to rise in value,' said the Governor. 'If this results in any cash flow problems, I am happy to ask several large financial players who owe me favours to extend a 'Lifeline' to Libraria until the shares are sold.' Pinchback knew that the Greenlandia troubles would probably finish off any number of banks in the City, and he was keen not to add to their number. Besides, he had always had a soft spot for Bank of Libraria, such a respectable, responsible, conservative bank!

'This is excellent advice, Governor, thank you very much for offering your help; I shall certainly do what you suggest,' replied John de Bourg. 'I think I shall continue to employ Thérèse in her current position – without her we might never have discovered Fleabrunckle's iniquity.'

Everyone agreed that far from having been duped by Fleabrunckle, Thérèse had known from the very beginning what he was up to, and only played along to entrap him and put an end to his dangerous financial shenanigans.

'Well, if we are all agreed,' said Governor Pinchback, 'I guess it is time to call Smithers in the Boon-Docklands.'

'I supposed you must, really,' Sir Wilbur said reluctantly. 'Is there no way to keep things quiet and deal with Fleabrunckle in some other way? Smithers and his agency have this annoying habit of complicating matters, and dragging them out into the public. If we involve them they will cause any amount of trouble for everyone.'

Pinchback privately agreed; the last thing the financial community needed now was another scandal. The recent collapse of the Little Green Moose Bank, and disgrace and imprisonment of it chief executive Habakkuk Huckleberry, was still fresh in everyone's mind. Exposing Fleabrunckle would only give fresh ammunition to the City's detractors. 'I suppose if Fleabrunckle disappeared, and never surfaced again, we would not have to involve Smithers at all,' he said. 'I know a young lady who specialises in disappearances, and I guarantee that Fleabrunckle would be more than adequately punished while in her care – would you like me to talk to her about it?'

Trishy looked a little suspicious – a young lady who made people disappear? – but since everyone else seemed to trust the Governor and agreed with his proposal, she, too, was happy to go along with it.

'I promise that man will be history before the end of the week,' Pinchback said when he escorted his guests to the marble lobby of The Institution. 'And thank you all very much for coming.'

Then he went to the Museum, looked stealthily around to make sure he was unobserved, slipped into the cage, entered the Great Exalted Heavenly Dream-Stone, and paid a visit to his friend the Emerald Maiden. 'I wonder whether you could do with a new servant,' he began.

51   Arnapak finds the Great Mother

While Devadorje was carving his ice organ, Arnapak had tracked down Tornarsuk. She found him in a mountainous region, well-wooded with a deep dark aboriginal forest. In the thickest part of the forest, which she was only able to reach with the help of her spirits, she finally found the god she had so long searched for. He hung from a top branch of a giant ash, tied up cruelly, and covered with dried blood from numerous wounds. When she asked him who had done this to him, and how she might release him, he replied thus in verse:

'I ween that I hung on this windy tree

Hung here for years full nine

With the spear I wounded, and offered myself

To the Mother, for the sake of mankind.'

'That is all very well,' said Arnapak, 'but I am just a humble Greenland Angakkoq, and not used to skaldic verse. Would you mind speaking in plain language henceforth, please? I am on an important errand, and would not risk misunderstanding your counsel.'

Tornarsuk sighed. 'Oh for a decent warrior-skald, where have they all gone to? What would I not give to encounter again the likes of Egil Skallagrimson! Instead I have to parley with an unkempt female wannabe shaman! Alas and alack, woe upon me!'

Arnapak was not impressed. 'Look here Tornarsuk, it may be true that I am not exactly top-drawer according to your standards, but I am one of the last few real shamans left, and I have an important job to do. I must find the stolen soul of my great-granddaughter, and you are my last hope. For twenty years almost I have searched high and low for it, and if you refuse to help me I shall have no option but to petition the Great Mother herself.'

Tornarsuk smiled disparagingly, and asked her how she proposed to find the Mother. 'My apprentice shaman Devadorje saw you in a dream, where you indicated that the Mother was not far from here,' Arnapak replied. Now, are you going to help me or not?'

But Tornarsuk ignored her and said: 'I am hanging here by my own free will, you know. My spirits have tied me up and hung me in the tree, after I slashed myself with my spear. I am hanging here as a sacrifice to the Great Mother - I am hoping to persuade her to come forth and take pity on her children who are in dire need and beyond my own efforts. For she has retreated into her holy of holies a long time ago, and refuses to have anything to do with the world anymore. But without her all her children will truly perish'

'What is it with our female gods that they have all withdrawn from humankind,' Arnapak asked, 'when the male gods are sticking around?'

'It is not for me to say,' Tornarsuk replied. 'However, although I hate to criticise my fellow male gods, it seems we were a little too eager to reduce the status and esteem in which the female gods were held, and as a result the ladies withdrew themselves. I for one now realise their importance, and especially that of the Great Mother. From her comes All, and without her is Nothing – only we did not realise this, in our desire for domination! That is why I am hanging here, hoping she will forgive our folly and rescue mankind, which I have come to love.'

'Well,' said Arnapak, 'you still have much to learn! How about calling us humankind, and not mankind?'

'Old habits die hard, 'replied Tornarsuk. 'I will try to be more careful in future.'

'I wish you luck with your self-improvement,' said Arnapak, 'but you still have not told me how to find Nuliajuq's soul.'

'Don't bother me about your great-granddaughter soul, can't you see I am suffering!' Tornarsuk cried. 'Did I not tell you that the very end of humanity is at hand, and you go blabbering on about some lost soul or other? Be gone, idiot Inuit!'

But Arnapak showed no inclination to go. Instead she collected dry branches, and started a fire to roast a squirrel she had shot earlier that day. The tree-bound god was getting annoyed and anxious. 'Didn't I tell you to leave,' he said to the persistent Angakkoq, who was blowing on the flames of her little fire. But Arnapak said that she had spent twenty years searching for Nuliajuq's lost soul, and would not budge until Tornarsuk had either told her where the soul was or given her directions to the dwelling place of the Great Mother.

'I've got plenty of time,' she told the angry god, 'and many potent spells to cajole gods like you; eventually you will simply have to help me.' After she had roasted the squirrel, she built up the fire with many resinous twigs and branches, and kept it going throughout the night.

The following morning Tornarsuk, his resistance weakened from hanging on the tree for all those years, and chocked by the smoke from Arnapak's fire, was so anxious to be rid of her that he gave the persistent Angakkoq detailed instructions of the way to the Great Mother.

Leaving Tornarsuk hanging in the tree, Arnapak set forth, and followed a barely discernable path from the Great Ash through thick undergrowth, until she reached a small glen, with a sheer cliff wall at one end. The foot of the cliff was completely overgrown with brambles, which Arnapak would never have attempted to penetrate without her instructions from Tornarsuk, who told her there was an opening in the middle of the thicket. Despite her tough fur clothing, she was considerably scratched by the bramble thorns when she finally discovered the opening, which was less than two feet in diameter. 'Another blood-letting in honour of the Great Mother,' she murmured to herself as she crawled through the long narrow tunnel that lead deep into the bowels of the mountain.

After twenty minutes or so of progressing snake-fashion through the tunnel, and getting increasingly claustrophobic, it widened into a smallish cave. The cave contained a stone bench, and a simple oil lamp, together with flints and some dry moss for making fire, presumably left behind by previous visitors. Another tunnel, large enough for Arnapak to walk upright, led from this cave. This tunnel was much longer than the first one. It went deeper and deeper into the mountain, and occasionally opened out into small or large caves, many of which were decorated with beautiful paintings of animals of the Great Hunt. In the light of her soapstone lamp, her gift from the Takanakapsaluk, she saw mammoths, horses, deer, bears, and even a shaman engaged in hunting magic. But one cave looked very different from the rest; it contained nothing but what looked like smears of brown paint, and several human skeletons in twisted positions on the floor.

After following this tunnel for almost an hour, Arnapak encountered the last and largest cave. As far as she could see by the light of her soapstone lamp, it was truly enormous. At the far end of the cave loomed a huge figure, surrounded by the kneeling skeletons of dozens of cave bears. In front of the figure was a large low altar, and on the altar were dozens of oil lamps. Arnapak lit all the lamps, and in their light was able to make out the details of the figure. It was the huge sculpture of a naked woman, with huge breasts, buttocks, and stomach. But the head had no face, and the woman had no feet. The statue completely dwarfed Arnapak; overcome with awe, she fell onto her knees and prayed.

Being a shaman, Arnapak knew of the Great Mother, and how she used to be depicted by artists in ancient times. The giant mother-image had not been given a face because the carvers of the past believed that the Great Mother was present in all things and at all times – she had too many faces to depict. Worshippers were not supposed to worship one sacred being in one place who was the Great Mother, but rather worship a sacred being who was present in every mother they encountered. The old artists had carved the Mother with such huge thighs and stomach and buttocks, because they thought that's how a human mother appeared to a tiny infant – ample, generous, huge, both frightening and protective. The Mother was depicted without feet, because unlike the other, later gods, she was of the Earth and belonged to the Earth completely; she had not come from somewhere else before the Earth came into being, and she would not go elsewhere when the Earth had ceased to exist. Indeed, some shamans held that she was simply a personification of Earth, rather than an individual who could be found and petitioned. But Arnapak did not believe this. She felt certain that the Great Mother was present in this cave; she felt her presence keenly, more than anywhere ever before.

Arnapak prayed to the Great Mother in many ways. She prayed to her as she might pray to Tornarsuk, but there was no response. Then she prayed using her spirits and amulets and talismans, but again to no avail. In desperation she used the little cross she had received from Yeshua, but still there was only silence. She even tried the painful rites she had always despised and rejected, and flogged herself with a thick knotted rope until she was covered in blood and unable to stand up any more, but still she received no answer, no indication that the Great Mother was taking any notice. Yet all through her days in the cave Arnapak felt a powerful presence shut up in the cave.

Eventually she broke down, and forgetting all her learning and training, with tears streaming down her face, she addressed the Great Mother in a completely unorthodox manner, defying all convention. 'Great Mother! I call upon you, not as shaman or worshipper, but as one mother upon another! I call upon you by right of the pain I suffered when giving birth, and by right of the pain I felt when my children died one after the other. Eighteen children I bore, and none are alive today. Only one great-grandchild remains to remind me of all those who have died, and she has lost one of her souls. Help me, fellow mother, to restore her soul to Nuliajuq.' Then she sat down, and waited patiently.

Finally, after a long while, she felt another's presence vaguely in her mind, whose thoughts seemed as though slowly stirred from long deep sleep, and focussing again on wakefulness after an eternity of dreams and dark oblivion. At long last, the presence in her mind became distinct and stronger, and Arnapak could clearly hear the voice of the Great Mother, and they spoke, one with the other, mind with mind.

'Eighteen children you bore.'

'Twelve girls and six boys.'

'Did you kill the girls, in the manner of some of your people?'

'None I killed – how could I, as a woman, kill my own kind?'

'What happened to them?'

'Seven girls and three boys died in infancy, of diseases. Two boys died while hunting whales – they were too young, but their father had died, and they felt they should provide for me and their sisters. One boy died in shaman trance – I had warned him that he had no horns in his stomach and could not be a shaman, but he took no heed. Since there were no boys left, I went out to hunt myself, taking the girls with me, and one died during a seal hunt. Another girl died in childbirth, refusing my help in a white man's hospital. One girl went abroad, and rode in a car which crashed and killed her. One girl against my counsel married a bad man, who killed her one day when he was drunk. The last girl died of grief, after her only son left home to become a shaman in America. This son's wife birthed my great-granddaughter Nuliajuq. None of my other children has surviving offspring.'

'You suffered much grief. The lot of women has not improved, since men and their gods began their rule.'

'Great Mother, will you help me save my great-granddaughter?'

But the Great Mother did not seem to hear Arnapak. She was lost in reminiscences. 'Such a long time ago, it seems, that the women came to me, with meat and fruit offerings, to thank me for their bounty. I often met them outside the cave, and even met the men. They loved me then, and carved my likeness in this cave, and little statues, too. Every family had one of those little figurines, and they prayed through them to me, when they were too far away to visit the temple cave. For many millennia there was peace and plenty. But then strange new gods arose. I think they came from beyond the stars, and were eager for worshippers. They knew that the women were faithful to me, so they came to the men in dreams, and whispered to them to rebel against the Great Mother, and be free of the rule of women. They told the men that they were physically stronger, and should overwhelm the women before and after birthing, when they were weakened by their children. Can you imagine such wickedness? Most men refused to listen to the new gods, but some did listen, and they were the strong ruthless evil ones, who longed to dominate both their fellow men and their women. They would never have succeeded, because my power is much greater than that of the new gods, had not the women themselves aided them. Yes, strangely, the women themselves seemed to long for male domination. They hold the key to the future, they risk their life and health to bring forth the next generation, they toil ceaselessly to succour and support their children, without them there is no one and without them no future, yet they renounced their natural right to rule so that the males might dominate them. Every generation does this anew, and I still cannot understand it. Thus I became alienated from the women, and retreated to my cave, and left them to their fate. Although I mainly sleep now, much comes to me in dreams, and I know well that the new gods and their worshippers have brought great ruin upon the Earth in the last ten-thousand years. Plants and animals are dying, rivers are drying up and deserts are expanding, and the life-giving force that maintains humankind is destroyed ever more rapidly. As for women, their ceding of power to the males has only added to their burdens. In most tribes the males steal the fruit of women's labour, and rape and otherwise ill-treat them to ensure they don't rebel and throw off the yoke of male domination. Yet still the men continue to rule, and the women bow down to the male gods. Even in those tribes where women have some power and independence, they are ready, even proud, to relinquish it to any male who desires it. Latest when they are with child, they accept male rule. They do not even keep their own names, but insist on being called Chattel of Male Z, rather than Female A. Mrs John Smith indeed! I don't know who I abhor most, the alien gods who misled the men, the men who lord it over the women, or the women who are so eager to enslave themselves to men. I have abandoned them a long time ago – why did you have to stir up the kettle of my bitterness after all these years?'

Arnapak listened to this outburst astonished, and with increasing worry. 'Great Mother, not all women are as you describe them. My friend, Ragna Sturlusdottir, has talked to me many a times about the importance of women keeping their own power, and showing solidarity to other women, rather than to men. It seems to me that more women than ever listen to voices such as hers, and try to maintain their independence from men. The men, too, have grown less keen to subjugate their women, and many are decent and kind. So perhaps the world is changing for the better, at least in this respect?' But then she reflected again on the words of the Mother, and remembered what the Takanakapsaluk and Tornarsuk had told her about the impending crisis that faced the world, and she asked, deeply troubled: 'What will become of you if the Earth dies, Mother of All?' There was no answer.

'Great Mother, is there nought that can be done? Humankind richly deserve the fate that we have wrought in ignorance and greed, but why should you suffer because of the foolishness of your children?'

The Great Mother sighed. 'Fellow mother, never has anyone worried about me, and I thank you for your concern. But know this, I am the Mother of all that lives, not just of humankind. The Earth will not die for many billions of years – it is humanity that is on the edge of extinction, not Earth, not even life on Earth. Still, it comforts me that there are some such as you still among humankind, and perhaps I shall stir myself in time to make a refuge for those who are in need and worthy of it. But as for now, you asked me for the soul of Nuliajuq, and I will help you. Walk behind the statue, and behold the Hall of Lost Souls.'

Arnapak walked behind the statue, and saw a long narrow cave, which was lined with shelves. On the shelves were small lidded jars of every material and shape, and each bore a little sign with a name.

'See the jar in green soapstone, on the bottom shelf near the entrance,' Arnapak heard the voice of the Great Mother. 'It holds the soul of Nuliajuq. Take the jar, and when you see your great-granddaughter again, explain to her that the jar contains her lost soul, which fled to the Hall of Lost Souls in search of refuge. Ask her if she is ready to be reunited with her soul. If she is, pray over her, and with her, according to the manner of your people. Then let her drink the contents of the jar, and she will be reunited with her soul. And take this comfort with you: Because Nuliajuq's soul has resided so long behind my statue, it has learned much wisdom; your great-granddaughter will survive, and be mighty among your people, and birth children who will carry on your heritage and honour your name. Bow down now before my statue, so that I may bestow my blessing upon you.'

Then Arnapak stood before the statue, and a great yellow and green light descended from it, and enveloped her, and hallowed her. 'Go forth now, my dear friend, and before you depart from these regions untie that fool Tornarsuk and tell him to come inside – I wish to converse with him!' Arnapak bowed deep three times, and thanked the Great Mother, and did as she was bidden.

52   Nuliajuq is reunited with her lost soul

Arnapak arrived in Nuuk just a few days before the great opening of Greenlandia. The town was overrun with tourists and all sorts of enterprising folk who hoped to cash-in on the new Greenland attraction. The newly established Zeppelin lines brought them in several hundred at a time, and every hotel in Nuuk and the surrounding area was fully booked. The town elders had ordered the erection of giant igloos on the outskirts of Nuuk, to accommodate late arrival who could not be housed in hotels or with private householders. The atmosphere was festive and expectant.

Her son-in-law Walgren, too, was most excited and looked forward with much anticipation to the great opening. Although he was as friendly and welcoming to the Angakkoq as always, she saw his mind was not on Nuliajuq and her missing soul just now, and it was with difficulty that she persuaded him attend the ceremony which would restore his granddaughter to her inherited natural looks.

'It is just three days before the opening,' he bleated ineffectually as Arnapak outlined her plans for the ceremony.

'I have spent twenty years on finding Nuliajuq's soul, and faced untold hardships for this; can you really look me in the eye and tell me you have better things to do?'

Walgren was no match for his steely mother-in-law, and nor was Devadorje, who also had his mind on other things, and tried to refuse Arnapak's summons. The old Angakkoq wanted all her family and friends to witness Nuliajuq drinking of her soul and the miraculous restoration of her face which was, the shaman was convinced, its inevitable outcome, and no one was allowed to refuse her invitation.

At last all Arnapak's friends and relations, and many other Inuit who still believed in the old faith, were gathered in the large igloo they helped her built in the morning. It had many windows of freshwater ice, and a wooden platform at its centre. Arnapak bade Nuliajuq kneel down on the platform, and asked everyone to join her in praying to the gods who helped her in her labours. They prayed to the Takanakapsaluk at length, and to Yeshua (although Arnapak wasn't quite sure whether he was a god, but he had helped and that was the main thing), and they prayed to Tornarsuk (who had been useful, albeit reluctantly), and after that for a very long while to the Great Mother. Then Arnapak thanked all her other helpers, and listed them, name by name, and thanked them, deed for deed. All this took a long time. Finally she took out the container that held Nuliajuq's soul, and asked her great-granddaughter to compose herself and put her mind into a solemn and receptive mode, and then Nuliajuq drank her soul. Behold, a green and yellow light began to shine upon the girl's distorted features, and hovered there and slowly smoothed them over, until a somewhat plain but wholly joyful countenance remained. Then the light flickered a little and vanished.

Everyone came to look at Nuliajuq, and praised her great-grandmother, and the Great Mother, and the Takanakapsaluk, and indeed everyone who had been involved in this great endeavour of restoring her face and joy to the girl. No one was happier than Cesare Borgia, who had sneaked away from Greenlandia against strictest orders and stood near the entrance of the igloo, crying his first ever selfless tears. But when Nuliajuq wanted to thank him for having been so kind to her when everyone else found her repellent, he had gone.

The news of the restoration of Nuliajuq's soul spread like a wildfire throughout Greenland, and was considered a good omen for the future of the island. 'Surely it cannot be an accident that this happened so close to the great opening of Greenlandia,' people said to each other, and firmly believed that a new exciting chapter in the history of Greenland was about to start. In time the story of the adventures of Arnapak the ancient Angakkoq, the great shaman of her people, became legendary and a great favourite of storytellers and their audience. Some people were so inspired that they decided to restore the old religion, and the Takanakapsaluk to the position she had held of old. But that was after the world had been remade, and all things changed, even the Takanakapsaluk.

53   Gingrich Fleabrunckle encounters his doom

The Emerald Maiden was more than pleased to help the Governor disappear The Flea. She was in dire need of an able bodied subject who could take over the vegetable garden, and The Flea struck her as just the right sort. Therefore she summoned

Adamantina, who after much explanation had been restored to her good graces, and discussed with her how best to entrap the evil banker.

Adamantina suggested an appeal to his greed for wealth and lust for domination. She would lure Fleabrunckle into the Exalted Heavenly Dream-Stone by intimating that is was the secret receptacle of untold riches (this was actually true), which she desired to possess in place of her current mistress. She would tell The Flea that she had chosen him as her champion, because she had long harboured a great passion for him on account of his handsome appearance, ruthless business practices, and leadership potential. After he had done away with the Emerald Maiden, they would rule the Exalted Heavenly Dream-Stone world forever in cruel harmony.

The Emerald Maiden did not like this plan. Indeed, she was rather taken aback that her Dream-Stone Guardian had come up with it at all! It was a little too realistic in her opinion, and she wondered whether she could still trust Adamantina – did she by any chance have a devoted lover, determined to usurp her position in the Exalted Heavenly Dream-Stone? Had perchance that demon Azazel turned the head of the once so haughty Guardian? The Emerald Maiden resolved to be on her guard, and to further increase the spiritual traps that protected her realm. To Adamantina she replied that she was tired of their worn-out old schemes and wanted to try a different approach on The Flea.

'Remember what that girl Trish told the Governor about him and his Saturday afternoon ritual of arranging flowers before a picture that depicts a scene similar to the Exalted Heavenly Dream-Stone? I want Azazel to go to his flat immediately and find out how similar that picture is.' Azazel, of course, was able to enter the flat easily by using his demonic powers, without the law-breaking Adamantina would have had to engage in, and was back in no time to report that the painting in Fleabrunckle's flat seemed to be an exact copy of the Exalted Heavenly Dream-Stone.

'What an amazing coincidence,' exclaimed Adamantina, but the Emerald Maiden disagreed. Many years ago she had painted a dozen pictures of the Exalted Heavenly Dream-Stone, for the express purpose of luring their owners into her realm. She had imbued the paintings with a fatal attraction for individuals whose character was easily seduced and dominated by her, and this aided her immeasurably over the years in keeping control over the Dream-Stone-World. Gingrich Fleabrunckle was just such an individual. His overwhelming need to succeed had led him to repress all finer feelings, which were pent up inside and could erupt into irrational behaviour if handled carefully. The Emerald Maiden was well skilled in causing such eruptions!

The following Saturday afternoon, when Fleabrunckle had completed his Ikebana arrangement and bowed before the alcove, he saw a tiny figure inside the painting motion him. Instead of dismissing this as a visual illusions, he knelt down in front of it to get a closer look, and noticed to his astonishment that the picture seemed to have turned into a three dimensional object, in fact a solid rock. Crouching as near as possible before the stone, he took off his glasses to examine the figure inside at close range. It was an exquisitely dressed, fragile Chinese beauty, with sophisticated arrogant features. Again she motioned him to come and join her, and as he bend down even further towards the stone he received a gentle push, toppled headfirst into the stone, and landed at her feet.

'Why, Liu Ming, how kind of you to pay me a visit,' said the Emerald Maiden to the new arrival. 'Your vegetable garden awaits your earnest attentions. But first you must tell me everything that has happened to you since you left the Exalted Heavenly Dream-Stone.'

Fleabrunckle quaked when he saw her cruel smile, and his feeble protests that he was Gingrich Fleabrunckle and not Liu Ming dismissed by his new mistress.

'In time you will remember, Liu Ming. Pain is a great aid to memory. And as you know, I am the mistress of excruciating pain, exquisitely inflicted. Don't you remember, Liu?'

Then he did remember, both the pain and why he had escaped from the Exalted Heavenly Dream-Stone all those years ago, and he shuddered.

54   Waiting for the storm

At last the great day had dawned upon Greenland. The guests of honour arrived in the last Zeppelin flight of the day, and Nuuk was now positively crawling with foreigners eager to attend the opening and grab a piece of the action. The train from Nuuk to Greenlandia was due to set off for the first time at noon, and then repeat the journey until all invited guests had arrived. Every hall and dome of Greenlandia would be opened to the public, and there would be guides and hosts to explain the purpose of each structure. There would be stalls of food that featured the newly home-grown foods pioneered by Devadorje, and modern bands would play both soothing and uplifting tunes. In the evening there was to be a banquet for the one-thousand most important guests, at which the Queen of Denmark would hold the opening speech. Afterwards there would be giant fantastic fireworks, the likes of which had never been seen before in Greenland, and they would be accompanied by the famous musician Acid Icepick playing a specially commissioned symphony on a gigantic organ designed and purpose-built for the event. Afterwards a dozen different bands would perform in the dozen largest domes, and everyone would dance and merry-make until sunrise. It would be a monumental show! Indeed, there was a rumour going around that there was an even bigger event planned, a huge surprise staged especially by the consortium who had built Greenlandia; but no one knew anything more definite about that.

Governor Pinchback had of course been invited to the opening, and only decided at the last possible moment to attend. He was by now just a bundle of nerves, and convinced the worst would happen. Neither Ragna's reassurances nor Sophia's veiled threats had the least effects on his mood, and in the last hours before the opening he was seen in the Magick-Market of Nuuk, purchasing ancient Inuit protective amulets by the dozen, and loitering in the vicinity of the Mithras temple, aching to enter and abase himself before the bronze idol enthroned inside. But as the last train left for Greenlandia he pulled himself together and put on his official jovial Governor's face; it just wouldn't do to let down the side. He took his seat amongst a group of financiers from the City, and smiled and laughed and joked with them, and was more scared than he had ever been in all his life. When he went to the bathroom shortly before the banquet, before he relieved himself, he knelt down inside the cubicle and prayed. So he was an atheist, so he hadn't prayed since infant school, so he knew that no god existed or would help him even if he did – it mattered none. He just couldn't handle the strain anymore. 'To whoever is in charge up there,' he began.

Sophia on the other hand was doing swell. Her apprenticeship was over, and she was now a fully certified journeywoman-demon, and allowed to roam all over Hell and The World as and when she pleased (she had had the freedom of Heaven ever since she became God's goddaughter). Of course she, too, was just the tiniest bit concerned that Devadorje's Ice Organ would fail to stop the transmogrification process, but she was still young and irresponsible and a demon to boot, and looked forward to the mayhem that was certain to follow, whether the transmogrification worked or not. She did not believe for a moment that Agrat and her lot would just meekly leave and be good losers when they found out that their great plan had been sabotaged. No, there would be much greater fireworks than the ones on the official programme, she was certain of that.

Mr Walgren, Arnapak, and Nuliajuq were also among the invited guests, and in the best possible mood. Although Arnapak had heard of the transmogrification from her friends Ragna and Devadorje, she did not concern herself much with it. What mattered to her was that Nuliajuq had regained her soul and looked like a good Inuit girl again. Nuliajuq of course was still ecstatic, not just because of her face but also because she had met the love of her life and planned to tell him so as soon as she could locate him.

Agrat still had no idea of the sabotage her niece Sophia and assorted allies had plotted. She was looking forward to the completion of the project, and the honours and rewards Lucifer was certain to shower upon her when he returned from his holidays. Beelzebub had done a good job too on his end, and the refurbished Hell would be a stunning place to get back to. Until then she planned to rest on her laurels, and enjoy the praise and admiration that were her due from her fellow demons. All that trouble she had gone through would be rewarded! When she remembered some of those disgusting humans she had to deal with, Judas and Gilligan and Fleabrunckle – yeech! But it had all been worth it. She changed into her stunning blood red evening gown, put on her black diamonds, and joined the revellers.

Judas Monkfish III was sitting next to Ragna, trying to pump her for information. Had she been able to do anything at all to stop the evil hellish plot to defraud the City? Over the last few years Ragna had told him very little, because she still did not trust him, which he was honest enough not to resent. All the same, he was on tenterhooks and needed reassurance. But Ragna just told him to be patient, and to consider his current suspense to be good training for when he went to Hell after he died. 'Very funny,' he grumbled – and stopped in mid track. Would he go to Hell? Now that he knew there was one, refurbished or not, it was no longer a joking matter. 'Oh Ragna,' he wailed, 'what do I have to do to go to Heaven?' Ragna eyed him without mercy, and changed the subject. 'Have I told you about the recent progress with my arctic hybrid tree project?' she said.

Hadjji Kurt, for his part, was cheerful and expansive. He had invited his great friend Hammad Emin, the translator of arctic travel stories into Arabic, to attend the opening of Greenlandia with him, and insisted on showing him every special feature of the complex. 'See this Sleeper-Dome?' he asked his friend. 'Total silence, total darkness, constant low temperatures, in fact no sensory inputs whatsoever! Ah such bliss, such joy!' The Hajji had had a rocky time since Agrat alerted him to the business practices of the erstwhile manager of his business empire, Abdullah, and although he managed to sort everything out with the help of the gifted accountant Mifleh, whom Agrat lent him for a while, it had been a sour piece of work, and he was thoroughly exhausted. That little interlude of his parents' return had further strained his nerves. If any man deserved a month or so of sensory deprivation in the arctic north it was Hajji Kurt! His was the first reservation of the Sleeper-Dome.

Cesare and Casanova, too, were happy and content with the result of their labours. Everything was ready and complete, now all they had to do was walk around and enjoy themselves and be nice to the guests. They had both been promised elevation to demonic status upon completion of the transmogrification, and looked forward to a long fruitful career in Hell, and many enjoyable visits to The World. Moreover, Casanova was pleased because Trishy was doing so well and Fleabrunckle had apparently been severely punished (Trishy had mentioned no details on the telephone but seemed quite certain that The Flea was history), and Cesare was overjoyed because Nuliajuq had been reunited with her soul and original looks, and radiated happiness.

Sir Wilbur Wellbeloved travelled to Greenland with his entire family, including grandchildren, and enjoyed himself enormously. He was overjoyed to have shed the annoying Fleabrunckle, who mysteriously disappeared recently, and was determined to love every new experience that came his way while there was still time. Florimonde's death had suddenly cut off his supply of Aqua Benedetta, and he felt his age catching up with him. He knew Greenlandia had been his last great venture, and after his return to London he would hand the banking business over to his youngest son Robert. Not entirely, of course. He would reserve the right to interfere whenever he felt it necessary, which was only fair and proper. Yes, as soon as he returned to London he would enjoy life to the full, and let Robert do the suffering! But he had not told Robert yet, so as not to spoil his holiday.

Devadorje was up on a mountain with his Ice Organ, polishing the pipes and oiling up the keys. Just a few more hours and he would know whether the organ would work and the melody was right! But he was not as nervous as one might have expected. He had fallen in love a few days ago, and when he confessed this to Sophia she had been most magnanimous. 'Well honey, my apprenticeship is over now anyway, and I have to move on, so don't you fret about me. Of course we will have to remain friends! I would never forgive you if you forgot me over this new love of yours.' Devadorje had most faithfully promised this, and unlike most men in such circumstances would keep his word. But then, how could anyone possibly forget Sophia?

Back in London, The Old Lady had, of course, stayed at home. 'It's all just nonsense and foolishness,' she muttered as she stirred her hot toddy and puffed her fifth cigar of the day. 'Mark my words Mr Mouser, it will all turn out to have been just a storm in a teacup, and we worried and worked needlessly.' The Mouser disagreed, but didn't bother to reply. He was dozing in front of the fire, thinking of Sophia, and her long fingernails, which had scratched him so deliciously, and he missed her. Would she ever return, he wondered? Perhaps he should pack in his job and retire. Like The Old Lady, he was getting too old and set in his ways for this job. Then he fell asleep.

Also in London Adamantina and Azazel were visiting the Emerald Maiden, who was full of praise for Governor Pinchback, who had not only restored her vegetable garden and thus ensured a steady supply of fresh produce to her table, but also arranged for a new servant to tend the crops. Although Goldlotus continued to have the general oversight, The Flea, as her new subject was generally known, did all the heavy work. At first he was a little truculent, but a few intimate sessions in the torture chamber had elicited his willing co-operation. At the insistence of the Governor Adamantina and Azazel had been put in charge of running Café Aladdin, which they did splendidly and to everyone's satisfaction.

Lastly in London, Miss Minnie Moochmerry was dusting the mahogany furniture in the drawing room, blissfully unaware of all the fuss over in Greenland. She was just a little worried about her good friends Tony and Rupert, who recently sent her a card from Timbuktu, where they had gone as foreign-aid workers to help educate the benighted natives, or so they had claimed. 'I do hope they took enough suntan lotion,' she worried as she dusted her aspidistra. Then she put on her second best hat and coat and went to have tea with Father Gottlieb in that exciting new café her young friend Adamantina had opened recently.

But Yeshua decided that the time had come for a chat with Jehovah, to fill him in on recent developments. He also alerted Mikāl to prepare himself for a mission in Greenland at very short notice, but Mikāl said that he didn't need notice to go to Greenland, or any of the other cold and snowy places of the world. 'Of course,' replied Yeshua, 'How silly of me[51].'

55   The battle of the organs

When the sumptuous dinner was finally over, the banqueting hall and every other dome of Greenlandia went dark, and a loud voice announced that the fireworks were about to begin. There was no need for the guests to leave their seats; the entire dome was constructed of glass and ice, and everyone would be able to see perfectly from where they were. Then a spotlight appeared, roved around a little, and fixed upon a mountain just behind the domes of Greenlandia. It revealed a giant organ, shimmering golden in the spotlight, and at the keyboard sat a wild-eyed player with black unkempt hair, a spindly skinny body, and long talon-like hands. He wore a black tailcoat with a red carnation in the lapel, and a black top hat. It was Acid Icepick, come back from the dead for his greatest gig, to perform his Cacophony of Deconstruction. Some of the guests stirred uneasily when they saw the organ player, 'wasn't that Acid Icepick who had died years ago?' But they were shushed by their neighbours, because Acid had begun to play, and the fireworks were being set off.

---

[51]   Like all archangels, Mikāl is made of snow.

So cunningly devised was Acid Icepick's music and so masterfully played, that every crash and bang and howl and whistle of the fireworks harmonised perfectly with his play. Ever more splendid were the fireworks, and Acid Icepick on the snowy mountain above Greenlandia played ever wilder and louder, and the pitch of his music climbed higher and higher, until it began to physically hurt the listening guests. Some of them shouted for the music to be turned down, but Acid Icepick laughed and changed to an even madder, higher pitch tune. The glasses on the tables began to tremble, and shattered one by one. A little later the glass of the domes themselves started to fracture, and by now panic had gripped the crowd. They tried to leave their seats and run for shelter, but that proved almost impossible, given the lack of light and general confusion.

Just when the music had become well-nigh unbearable, and people feared their eardrums would rupture, and all Greenlandia was mayhem and confusion, they saw the tables and chairs and even the domes themselves begin to turn translucent, and seemingly dissolving. And Acid Icepick laughed loudly and madly like a demon from hell, and behind him the huge figure of a beautiful woman with black hair and a red dress slowly took shape. She laughed even louder than Acid Icepick, triumphantly, victoriously, and some guests recognised her as Agrat.

But suddenly her laughter stopped, and she looked across Greenlandia to the mountain opposite her. People turned around and looked at that mountain, and in the light of the full moon and the multitude of stars they saw a second mighty organ. This organ seemed entirely made of ice and snow, and it glittered coldly and white. A young man, dressed in furs the Inuit way, bowed deeply to Agrat and Acid Icepick, sat down at the ice-organ and began to play. Such play had never before been heard upon earth, and at first it seemed just a jumble of high pitched screechy sounds. But then people listened more carefully, and realised that it had a meaning and a purpose, and that it clashed with Acid Icepick's cacophony. Acid Icepick had only briefly interrupted his playing, and recognised before anyone else the purpose of the music which came from the ice organ. 'You dare to fight me then, you miserable fool?' he cried as he pulled all registers of his organ. 'Very well, I accept your challenge! I hope you know that this will be a duel unto death!'

But Devadorje just nodded and smiled, and played on. As he played he remembered dimly a life he had lived before, the life of a musician, gifted but driven and mad, rather like Acid Icepick. He concentrated upon the light that he had recently discovered burning within him, and closed his eyes. Deeper and deeper he delved into the secret depths of his soul, and found there skills he had acquired in a previous existence. He held suspended in his mind all he had learned about the structure and harmonics of the ice-molecules that made up his organ, and what he knew about their interaction with high-pitched sounds. Louder and louder he played, and higher and higher went his pitch, until he matched Acid Icepick's perfectly. When Acid Icepick noticed this, and saw that Greenlandia, which had been in the early stages of disintegration, was solidifying again, he increased his efforts and played even wilder and louder, as though he wanted to annihilate the other organ with the sheer power of his music. But Devadorje would not be outdone, and called for help from all the spirits and gods of Greenland, and asked Mithras himself to intervene. They all came to his aid, and although he was growing exhausted he managed to hold his own against Acid Icepick; all the same it was clear to him that he could not defeat the other. This was only to be expected, for Acid Icepick had behind his play all the combined power and subtlety of Hell and its demons, who were long experienced in domination and ruthless in its execution. All the combined powers of Greenland's gods and spirits, even with Mithras joining in, could not overwhelm the powers of Hell.

Like two mighty animals engaged in a battle unto death, the two organs and their players battled beneath the star-lit sky, and luck went sometimes to one and then to the other, but no one was able to secure a final victory. Devadorje was growing tired very fast, and knew he could not last much longer. He needed still more help, but who else could he ask?

As if in answer to his question Selim, the little spider and erstwhile Cosmocrator, crawled out of Devadorje's pocket and up to his ear, and sang a melody that seemed both new and wonderful to Devadorje. Enchanted and seduced, he took it up to incorporate into his theme, although he knew that it fitted ill into the sound-scape he had woven to stop the transmogrification. And behold, the pipes of the ice-organ seemed to grow skywards as they vibrated with this new melody. While his earlier theme had been designed to confront and batter down Acid Icepick's cacophony, the Cosmocrator's melody wound itself suggestively around the other organ, and fascinated and beguiled Acid Icepick, who fell in love with it.

Acid Icepick was a great musician and composer, an artist with a true understanding of the deepest roots of his work. When he heard this new melody played by his opponent, he clearly recognised it for what it was, whereas everyone else, including Devadorje, just dimly felt its overwhelming force. It was the Music of the Celestial Spheres, which is composed of all the sounds and noises ever made, and harmonises them in an eternal all-enfolding symphony which permeates the universe. The first dominant notes were played by titan heat and gas explosions and electric storms, which raged across a starless swirling void, subtly tempered by the endless interplay of primordial particles which danced like motes in sunshine until the universe of stars emerged. Each universe and star created a new theme as it materialised, which grew and changed together with its agent, and formed another strand in the great cosmic theme. Each form of life, down to the smallest creature, brought into being yet another tune for the great melody. Onto this day the music continues to grow ever richer and stronger. Every falling drop of water, every word spoken, every leaf that rustles in the wind, adds its voice to the Great Symphony of the Universe. The Cosmocrator had spent many decades searching for it, and hunted for its echoes far and wide, at a great cost to himself, in riches and in pain, until he finally acquired enough sound-scraps and echoes to piece together the main theme. He had never thought it would be of any use, but sought it purely because it existed and was hidden from him, because that is the nature of adepts.[52]

---

[52]   Why he shared this dearly bought knowledge with Devadorje is unclear; some say that Selim was a reformed character and therefore felt compelled to aid the forces of righteousness, others that his friendship with the young shaman motivated him. However, I believe that he simply wanted to find out what its effect would be, for his curiosity was no less in spider form than when he inhabited a human body.

But when Acid Icepick heard the music he recognised it for the greatest theme that ever was, the master theme of the universe, and his artistic nature could not bear to fight against it. Instead he hit the keys with renewed gusto and, abandoning his own composition, fell into line with Devadorje, until they played in perfect harmony together. Gradually all the domes of Greenlandia were made whole again, and all the shattered glasses were restored, and all the blasted eardrums healed, so that people could hear better than ever before. As the great melody finally wound down to a tranquil finale, the guests awoke from the enchantment that had held them spellbound, and clapped their hands and cheered, thinking the whole performance had been planned for their entertainment. Then they heard an enormous screech of anger. Agrat's patience with Acid Icepick had finally run out.

56   The return of Lucifer

Lucifer's holiday had been a complete success. He was well rested in body and mind, and peaceably inclined towards all creatures great and small, and looking forward to confer with Jehovah about the great restructuring of Heaven and Hell he had been promised just before he went on his vacation. But first he went home to greet his bride and children, and make sure all was well in Hell.

However, Hell was strangely empty when he arrived. Most of the more important demons were nowhere to be seen, and those that greeted him seemed secretive and cagey in their replies; it was obvious they were hiding something from him, apparently some sort of celebration in honour of his return. When asked where everyone was they just smiled mysteriously and told him he would have to wait for a few more hours, and then he would 'receive the greatest surprise of his life!' How very kind, he thought. His fellow demons really were capital fellows. He felt quite guilty for having been so grumpy these last few hundred years.

Since he was clearly in the way in Hell just now, and didn't want to spoil their surprise, he decided to make a courtesy call on Jehovah and Yeshua. Who knows what news they might have to impart to him! Three years were a long time, and much might have happened in his absence.

Jehovah was of course overjoyed to see him again, and gratified to observe that his faithful old friend seemed to have fully recovered his good humour and positive outlook on life.

'Now you must tell me how you spent your holiday,' he said to Lucifer after the tea things had arrived and they were comfortably settled. 'Did you stay in Alpha Centauri, or did you go to the Zebulon Nebula instead?' While they were still chatting they heard several unusual noises in Heaven and Hell and on Earth, but were so absorbed in their conversation that they paid them no heed, and missed Mikāl sharpening his sword, Beelzebub evacuating Hell in preparation for the great reconstruction, and even the infernal fireworks and organ music down in Greenland.

Several times during their conversation Yeshua had tried to attract their attention, but they took no notice until at last he cleared his throat so loudly that they both looked up. 'Very sorry to interrupt,' said Yeshua, 'but' – and then he gave them a quick synopsis of what had been happening in Greenland. Three years' worth of vacationing just dropped off Lucifer, and he almost choked with rage when he heard what 'surprise' his underlings had prepared for him.

'So much for going on a holiday,' he roared as he attempted to snatch Mikāl's sword from the archangel's hand and prepared to stomp off to Greenland. 'First time in five-thousand years I take a little break, and all Hell breaks loose!' Observing Mikāl's grin, he snapped, 'Well you know what I mean! Now, are you coming or what?'

'You had better go along,' said Jehova to Yeshua and Mikāl, 'we don't want any scenes witnessed by mortals!'

Mikāl was the first to arrive, and just in time to prevent Agrat from throwing one of her famous fits. He unsheathed his sword, which burst into flame, and threatened Agrat with the combined anger of Heaven and Hell unless she calmed down and spared those hapless mortals. 'Really Agrat,' he said as he sheathed his sword, 'I am surprised a demon of your beauty and intelligence stoops to avenge herself on such insignificant mortals!' Agrat tried hard not to look flattered, but after all, this was Mikāl speaking. Before she had quite abandoned her vengeful impulses, she saw Lucifer appear behind Yeshua, and cried, 'Oh no! You're home early! You have quite ruined our surprise!' 'And how,' muttered Lucifer as he helped Yeshua and Mikāl round-up his errand demons and their human helpers for a swift return to Hell. 'Just wait 'til we are home!'

'Does this mean we aren't going to achieve demonic status?' asked Casanova just before he was bundled off by Mikāl.

'Shouldn't have thought so,' replied the archangel.

After Lucifer returned his miscreant flock to Hell, and assured Yeshua that he didn't need any help in dealing with them, thank you very much, he abandoned all pretence of being a kindly father-figure like Jehova, and laid into his subdued subordinates. Beelzebub was first in line for the wrath of the Head of Hell.

'Of all the moronic, imbecilic, idiotic schemes ever implemented by a fallen angel this one takes the biscuit! Whatever were you trying to do? Drive me completely over the edge of insanity, so you can take over Hell?' He paused to give Beelzebub a chance to reply, but his second in command was so hurt by Lucifer's insinuation that he failed to defend himself.

'This is so typical!' Lucifer shouted. 'You are always the first to condemn others and push them down the Pit of Pain or into the Cauldron of Corrosion, but when it comes to confronting the boss and defending yourself you're just five inches tall including horns!' But Beelzebub remained silent. Instead two large tears, one in each eye, slowly formed and obscured his vision.

'Bless him and stress him, a demon who cries! Aren't you ashamed of yourself?' Lucifer could barely conceal his disgust, and turned his attention to Agrat.

'And how about you, mighty Agrat, who is forever throwing tantrums when the rest of us have to control our tempers? Trusting that I would not punish my sister-in-law, were you? Hell and damnation, I don't know how I managed to be so patient with you all these centuries! But from now on there will be a different regime, I will rule with a fist of iron and make your lives a misery! I'll teach you to break every rule in the book and ignore the CAM! I'll stretch you on my procrustean bed until – '   But he could not finish his sentence, because Agrat lost her patience.

'Oh do shut up, all this shouting and blustering when you don't even know all the facts! The decision to refurbish Hell was taken by the Assembly, so stop picking on Beelzebub and me!'

Lucifer's ranting had attracted the attention of every demon in the vicinity, and they had formed a semicircle around Beelzebub and Agrat, and murmured 'Hear Hear' when Agrat finished. Thus emboldened, she continued.

'The whole idea was born out of concern for you. We were so worried about your deteriorating health that we decided to create a light pleasant restful retreat in place of the old dark dank nasty Hell.'

Shouts of 'That's right!' and 'You tell him, Agrat!' were heard from the crowd.

'So great was our concern, so overwhelming our affection for our beloved leader, that we braved the wrath of Jehovah to bring some joy into your life,' Agrat continued.

'Now wait a minute,' Lucifer retorted, 'the wrath of Jehovah – 'but Agrat was playing to the gallery and quite unstoppable.

'Yes, we braved the awful wrath of Jehovah, and terrible retribution from Yeshua,' Agrat continued, winking at her audience while barely suppressing a giggle.

'Terrible retribution from Yeshua?' Lucifer repeated incredulously. 'You are having me on!'

'Absolutely,' said Agrat, and burst out laughing, to the laud applause of the assembled demons, who knew that they had won. For Agrat's laughter was like a force of nature, like a mad-keen whirlwind that swept everyone off their feet, as overwhelming and irresistible as her anger. She grew in stature until she completely dominated the assembly. Her whole body convulsed and shook with merriment, and a thousand tiny flames flickered in her eyes. The strands of her hair rose up and writhed in the delight of her laughter, and her arms and legs began to twitch and move until at last she broke into an abandoned joyful dance.

'This is all most irregular,' Lucifer protested feebly, 'I really must insist that you are all properly punished for once.'

'But not just now,' said Lilith who had sidled up to him. 'Come on, let's leave them to it and go home. You have been away a long time.'

Lucifer looked at Agrat, who was laughing and dancing all over Hell, followed by a crowd of joyous demons who were equally abandoned and probably heading for an orgy of epic proportions.

'Quite a sister you've got,' he said to Lilith.

'Would you rather stay here and celebrate with them?' Lilith asked.

'Nah, I am too old for orgies!'

'That's what you think,' replied Agrat's sister and laughed, and a thousand little flames danced in her eyes as she took his hand and led him home.

Postscript – Many happy endings

Although this was the end of the great refurbishment of Hell, the damage done by the ambitious scheme was decidedly limited. Greenlandia became a huge success, and before too long most Greenlanders benefited from it in one way or another. The City of London profited even more, since most of the major shareholders of the scheme resided there. Thanks to Devadorje's revolutionary horticultural practices, Greenland became independent of imported agricultural products, and since more and more houses were build along the carbon-neutral lines the Mithras temple had pioneered, the environment actually benefited from the presence of Greenlandia.

Beelzebub and Agrat got off scot-free at Yeshua's instigation. Yeshua did not believe in punishment, especially of those who acted in good faith and from pure motives. He used the report that had been commissioned by the General Assembly of Hell, 'The Effect of Imprisonment on Human Subjects & The General Uselessness of Punishment to Improve Character', to demonstrate that Agrat and Beelzebub, far from being renegade demons, were simply ahead of their time. Besides, the demons involved in the Greenlandia fiasco were in the main the most enterprising and intelligent, and he needed them for the Great Restructuring of the Universe. 'It is punishment enough for them to know that they were defeated by a mere apprentice-demon and a mad plant psychologist,' he said to Lucifer when he pleaded their cause. Of course he knew that they had really been defeated by Selim the adept spider and Acid Icepick's artistic integrity, but Yeshua did not think it wise to remind them of that.

Acid Icepick had a few very nasty months, because everyone one in Hell blamed him for having ruined a brilliant scheme and the lovely surprise for the boss. They simply did not care about his musical integrity and emotional affinity with celestial spheres, the philistines! However, Acid Icepick had a habit of ignoring the people around him, and paid little attention to their attempts to torture him surreptitiously, when they thought Lucifer wasn't looking. 'They'll stop eventually,' he told Sophia when she dropped by one day to check he was alright. 'Could I have my organ back though, do you think? I want to write a piece based on the music the Ice-Organ played that night above Greenlandia!' Acid Icepick duly had the organ restored to him, and after the Great Restructuring he teamed up with some of the angels who had been involved with the original score of the music of the celestial sphere, and together they composed the rousing new anthem for the Integrated Universe.

Mithradates Devadorje handed his priestly responsibilities over to the humblest of his apprentice priests, and devoted his time to becoming the greatest shaman of all time. In due course he married the love of his life, Nuliajuq, who became an important politician and governed Greenland for many years to everyone's satisfaction. But Arnapak, the old Angakkoq, had spent too much time travelling the world to be content to stay at home for long. She continued to visit her friend the Takanakapsaluk and ran many errands for her.

Devadorje's first love, the demon Sophia, was greatly praised by Lucifer and Jehovah for her labours in protecting humankind from her fellow demons, and was offered an Angelship by her godfather, which she politely refused, much to the relief of Lucifer. 'I am what I am and proud of it,' she said, 'and no one can make me what I am not, even Jehovah.' But in due course all this became quite irrelevant, because the great restructuring of the universe would abolish all ranks, and soon there would be no great difference between angels and demons anymore. Sophia never forgot her first human lover, whom she continued to visit and aid whenever possible. Nor did she forget Mr Mouser, who was granted special status by Yeshua for his services, and became Sophia's closest friend. He accompanied her on all of her journeys, slept on her bed whenever she rested, and was much sought after in his own right as an authority on rodents.

The Institution continued to prosper, albeit under new leadership after Governor Pinchback retired. The government offered him an earldom upon his retirement to reward him for his forty years of service to the nation, but he rejected this and asked instead for a small farm near London, which they refused on grounds of cost. His colleagues in the City were so incensed by this that they took up a collection, and gave him a farm as a leaving present, with warmest wishes from the entire financial community. The farm was barely an hour's train journey from the City, where he continued to visit his friend the Emerald Maiden at regular intervals, and met his old colleagues for long lunches in Café Aladdin.

The Emerald Maiden's life continued much as it always had, except for a greatly improved diet. The extra vitamins and roughage did much to improve her health and temper, and her subjects' feet were all allowed to heal. The one exception was of course The Flea, who continued to be birched once a fortnight, so that the official birchers didn't forget their skills. Adamantina lost much of her haughtiness, partly due to Azazel's unfortunate influence. Agrat appeared to have forgotten all about him, and never questioned his decision to stay on at The Institution in Café Aladdin.

Gilligan Wang finally finished all his chores after six years of heavy labour (the ash seed planting took longer than expected). His chores left him plenty of time for reflection, and after he had finally completed his chores he was in every way a morally improved and better person. Henceforth he spent each weekend with his aging mother, and devoted the resources of his business empire, which had thrived while he was away, to the perfection and production of prosthetic limbs, which he distributed free of charge to victims of cluster bombs and mining disasters. In recognition of his services to the ash tree community he was voted Human of the Year by the Club of Scandinavian Gods & Demons shortly after he completed his ash seed planting.

Judas Monkfish II was completely changed by his experience with Agrat, and had not so much turned over a new leaf as purchased a whole new book. Although he was as keen as ever to make money, he henceforth made it squarely, and used all the proceeds for charitable causes, beginning with Ragna's project of reforesting Greenland. In time he turned into a veritable Gaius Bonus, and when he died penniless but happy a decade later, he was judged to have undone all the evil he had wrought, and was allowed to join his great love Laura in Heaven.

Ragna succeeded in her endeavours to reforest Greenland, and expanded her operation to Siberia and Canada, aided as ever by her faithful friend and helper Fridthjof Thorsteinson, whenever he could spare the time from his work with the Bonsai Liberation Front.

Casanova and Cesare Borgia, despite Mikāl's dire prediction, were granted their demonships after all by Lucifer on the instigation of his bride Lilith, on account of their chivalrous behaviour towards Trish Trash and Nuliajuq. Yeshua had offered to fast track them to Heaven, but like Sophia they knew what they were and proud of it. 'Better a good demon than a bad harp-plucker,' commented Lilith.

Trishy still lives with Varus in her little cottage. She recently opened a village shop / post office / bank/ citizens advice bureau / coffee shop / kindergarten, and her daughter Cassandra is thriving despite her paternal genes. Casanova still visits her occasionally, and helped her set up her village shop / post office / bank/ citizens advice bureau / coffee shop / kindergarten.

Flossy Pembrokeshire and Stanley Hunzucker finally did manage to meet up. They arranged a rendezvous in the walk-in cold store of the Feederia, and for the first time in their decade-long courtship were not interrupted. Unfortunately the extreme low temperature had a malign effect on Stanley, who proved unable to consummate their union. However, he had as always words of comfort for Flossy, 'Don't worry love, tomorrow is another day. I'll think of something else.'

Selim, the adept in spider form, disappeared one day while travelling with Devadorje to London, and eluded all efforts to trace his whereabouts.

Here, gentle Reader, ends my tapestry of tales - I'm looking forward to tremendous sales.

DB Lenck

Penned in the Nostalgia Studio, at the Knick-knackertory, Oxford.

Printed in Great Britain
by Amazon